The Boy With the Blue Cap
Van Gogh in Arles

A novel by

Norman Beaupré

*For Roger and Louette, may
you enjoy this work as much as
I we enjoyed writing it
Best wishes
Norman R Beaupré*

Llumina
Press

ISBN: 978-1-60594-153-0 (PB)
      978-1-60594-154-7 (HC)
      978-1-60594-155-4 (ebook)

Printed in the United States of America by Llumina Press

Library of Congress Control Number: 2008907195

From the same author:

L'Enclume et le couteau, the Life and Works of Adelard Coté, Folk Artist, NMDC, Manchester, N.H., 1982. Reprint by Llumina Press, Coral Springs, FL, 2007.

Le Petit Mangeur de Fleurs, Éd. JCL, Chicoutimi, Québec, 1999.

Lumineau, Éd. JCL, Chicoutimi, Québec, 2002.

Marginal Enemies, Llumina Press, Coral Springs, FL, 2004.

Deux Femmes, Deux Rêves, Llumina Press, Coral Springs, FL, 2005.

La Souillonne, Monologue sur scène, Llumina Press, Coral Springs, FL, 2006.

Before All Dignity Is Lost, Llumina Press, Coral Springs, FL, 2006.

Trails Within: Meditations on the walking trails at the Ghost Ranch in Abiquiu, New Mexico, Llumina Press, Coral Springs, FL, 2007.

La Souillonne, deusse, Llumina Press, Coral Springs, FL, 2008.

For Jim Doherty, c.s.c. who enjoys and appreciates fine arts and literature, my good friend, with joy and affection

*THANK YOU, Josh Groban. Your rendition of **Vincent** [Starry, Starry night] by Don McLean inspired me to write this novel.*

"Cet après-midi, j'ai eu un public choisi...de 4 ou 5 maqueraux et une douzaine de gamins, qui trouvaient surtout intéressant de voir la couleur sortir des tubes."

(This afternoon, I had a select group of onlookers, 4 or 5 pimps and a dozen or so street urchins who found the colors coming out of the tubes quite interesting.[Undated letter from Vincent to Théo].

Contents

Light and Color

C olor! Color! Color! Color! Everything is color! *Tout est couleur*! Without light there is no color. And here in Arles the light is dazzling. *Éblouissan*te! Like a bubble bursting with the splendor of light.

"That's your sun here in Provence. Pure light, pure color. A huge bubble of yellow. A thick daub of chrome yellow in the sky's blue dome. I just love it!" Vincent used to say this to me over and over again in his moments of creative ecstasy as he stood before a bare canvas, about to posit his first streak of pure color.

My name is Camille. Camille Roulin. I used to live at 10, rue de la Montagne des Cordes in Arles. I wasn't born in Arles. I was born in Lambesc, some sixty kilometers east of Arles, where my father and mother were born. I love Provence and when I die I want to be buried in my beloved land, *mon pays du Félibrige*, our poets and writers. I once lived in Marseille with my family, but I returned to Arles when my father died. My father's name is Joseph Roulin, postman for many years in Arles. He was really a *brigadier-chargeur,* in charge of unloading the postbags at the train station in Arles, but many people know him as a *facteur.* As far as I could tell he did not have much of a formal education but he was a smart man. He could read. However, he avoided writing. He only did it when he had to. He would have my mother or one of us two boys write for him. My mother was called Augustine. I have one brother, Armand, and one sister, Marcelle. But I don't really want to talk about them now. I want to talk about Monsieur Vincent. At first, I always called him Monsieur because my father wanted me to call him so out of respect for the man and the artist he was. I called him Monsieur Van Gogh at the very beginning, but then I started calling him Monsieur Vincent when I realized that he signed his paintings *VINCENT.* He thought that his last name on canvas would be an impediment to his selling any of his works. People here always had a difficult time pronouncing the hard letters of his family name. Besides, it seemed to me he wanted to distance himself from his last name and his Dutch family far up north. Except for his dear, dear brother, Théo. Poor Monsieur Vincent, he had such a hard time belonging. Anywhere. Especially belonging to someone here in Arles and making friends. Of course, there would be his new friend, Monsieur Gauguin, but I'll talk about that later. Yes, too many people around Arles didn't like my friend the painter. As a matter of fact, many thought him to be mad. But, I never thought he was mad. Bizarre in his ways of doing things, but not mad. He was first and foremost *un homme de couleurs*. Colors! That was his life. He thought in colors, heard colors, smelled colors and even tasted colors, I believe. I loved Monsieur Vincent. I learned so much from him. He was *différent des autres* but not mad. I was somewhat like him, *différent*, and that's why I could identify with him.

Let me tell you something about Monsieur Vincent. Later on, I'll tell you how I met him. You see, I was born a loser. I was not born under a favorable star as some people would put it. You know how some people believe in the arrangement and patterns of stars at the right time or wrong sequences of time? Well, I don't much believe in that design of fate, *la fatalité des étoiles,* as they call it. I don't believe in fate designing my life. Things happen, that's all. I know I could not choose any of the circumstances surrounding my birth and my growing up. I could only react to them, face up to them and choose from among the things I could control, such as following Monsieur around Arles. I'm glad I chose to do that early on in my life.

I was a loser because my father thought so and said so at times. Not that he was cruel, my father, but he said that I was destined for *le petit pain*, small things in life. I was not, in his mind, material for great things. He didn't mind that I was made that way and he thought that I might eventually amount to something, but he couldn't see my future as being very bright. Lusterless. I wasn't going to be another Mistral, a Daudet or even a doctor or lawyer because I did not show great promise as an exemplary student at school. My grades were not very high and I had very little interest in school. I went because I had to. It was compulsory as *l'État,* the state, put it. I had to realize that I was not meant for brighter situations in life, my father said. I knew it and I accepted it. My mother thought that way too except she never said it. She was more encouraging. She knew that I would grow up like any other child in Provence and possibly follow in my father's footsteps and become *un facteur* perhaps. I didn't want to disappoint her but I did not have it in me to be a mailman. It was a good and steady job but I did not want that for my future. I was a simple child of ten going on eleven and I had a lot of learning to do. I knew that. I loved reading adventure stories, I loved words, I loved being by myself and exploring things, I loved writing down notes in my notebook. About anything and everything, but I did not like schoolwork. I liked Monsieur Tallant, our teacher, since he wasn't too severe with me but he was boring. Dull. His monotonous voice was enough to make you fall asleep in class. He was not at all inspiring. The only thing I liked about him was when he would make us look up words and give us new words to work with. I loved words. I was fascinated with them even as a very young boy. I loved the way they explained things, defined things or simply described things or people. I loved adding to my vocabulary. The others hated it. But I loved it. I knew I could fill my notebook with new words as much as I wanted. It was like finding new coins and adding them to your *tirelire*, the piggy bank. I knew that I would not become famous in life. I could feel it in my bones that I was not destined for greatness. Sometimes I would feel sad, not sad because I was poor but sad about winding up as a nothing in life. At times, I felt like breaking away from this nothingness and try very hard to become someone my parents would be proud of. But I had a hard time believing in myself, so I retreated to my solitary self and my notebook. But then I would say, who cares about being a somebody except those who come from families with money. We were poor. Not poor like those in misery, but we were common people and had no luxuries in life. I never aspired for luxuries as long as I had a family who loved me and cared for me. Later on, I had Monsieur Vincent to follow on his painting and drawing trips. Then I was satisfied. I was happy to be who I was. You see, Monsieur Vincent gave me something special, the gift of believing in myself.

He told me one day when I was feeling like a sad puppy, "Camille, look at me and tell me that you are a loser."

"I'm a loser," I replied.

"No, tell it to me from your heart."

"I can't because I don't want to believe that I'm a loser."

"There, you see, you're not really a loser. I'll tell you why. You have talent. *Le mystère du talent.* Yes, real talent is a mystery. You can't fathom it, you can't wish for it, even feel it, it's there or it's not. You, my boy, have it."

"How?" I replied.

"You already have the talent of words. You have *la fascination des mots*. And that's very important. You love words, you play with words, and you have a hunger for words. You're a poet."

I looked at him and I started to blush and began to get excited all over. "I'm a poet?" I said.

"Yes, Camille, you're a poet because you have talent and your talent is already starting to come out in expressing the way you see things and the way you put them into words. You don't only see the blue sky with clouds, you see the limpidity of the blue color and the brightness and image-making design of the clouds. You try to express what you see in colorful words. What I do with colors, you can and will do with words. And, you know what? It will get better. Someday, you'll be able to blossom into a well-known poet that people will recognize."

"Really? I didn't know that playing with words and accumulating them was talent."

"Yes, really. It is. You not only play with words but you have a way of putting them together so as to transform them into phrases and sentences that show me you have the talent of a poet. You see things and express things differently than others do and that's talent. Losers do not have much talent."

"Really?" I said with some amazement.

And so I grew up knowing that what Monsieur had told me on that day would fill my life and make it more abundant with the colors of a bright promise. I might have been a loser in the eyes of my father, but not in the eyes of Monsieur Vincent.

Well, you see my father thought that I was losing my time daydreaming and playing with words. I mean, putting words together, spelling new words, searching for words in a dictionary even making up words and new sounds so that I could have a whole battery of words at my disposal. Words. And they were all free. My father kept saying that our language, *le Provençal*, had already enough words in it. Only Monsieur Mistral and his group of poets dealt with our dialect. They were out there in their gardens wasting their time writing Provençal poems. What good will that bring them? Besides, I already knew two languages, Provençal and French, he said. Why would I want to look for and collect new words?

"Learn the ones that you need in order to be successful in life. Apply yourself," he would say. "They teach you kids standard French in school so that you'll be able to succeed at a trade or a profession. Why would you want to bother that much with our dialect? That's of the past. That's good at home but not out there where not everyone understands le Provençal. You cannot take a civil service exam in it. So, be a studious boy like the others and learn a trade that will bring you money. You need money to live. You could even grow up to be like me *un bri-gardier-chargeur* or even a *facteur*."

But, I didn't want to be a postman, a deliverer of letters, parcels, and small talk like some people in town. Jabber mouths. No, I wanted to become someone *spécial*. Like Monsieur Vincent. I didn't mean special like being higher placed and more important than others. No, special in the way that you can see things differently than others do. Oh, it's nice to be special and live in your own little world. But, it can be lonely at times. That's when Monsieur came into my life and filled it with the vibrancy of colors and creative imagination. He told me that I already had those things and all I needed was to develop them to my full potential. He was going to show me how because he said I was pre-cocious and talented. At that time I did not know what precocious meant. So, I asked him. He told me that it meant ahead of my time, *très avancé pour mon âge*. I could understand things that other children could not and I had the capacity to absorb things faster than most had, even older people like my father and my brother. Not that they were stupid, but I had that very special capacity. The capacity to learn and to retain things almost like an older person who was mature and had gone to school a long time. He said that I didn't have a lot of school learning but I had the brain of a near genius. *Un génie*, he told me. But I wasn't a genius, I told him. Far from it. My father sometime called me *un gé-nie manqué*. I was bright but not too sharp with things, he said. I just couldn't learn how to do things the right way, I guess. He meant that I had very little talent to become a carpenter, a baker, a blacksmith, a whatever with a trade. Not that I couldn't do it, I would have told him, but it was because I didn't like doing those things. I did not want to be-come just a *métier,* a trade. I wanted deep in my heart to become a writer, a forger of words like Monsieur Vincent had become a forger of light and colors on canvas. Besides, he was also very good at drawing. A real draftsman. He did so many drawings in his life. He showed me some of them. He was exceptional, I thought. He tried to show me how to draw, but I just could not get the hang of it. It takes a special talent to draw, I'll have you know. You need to be born with it. Monsieur Vin-cent was born with it and how he had talent! Lots of it. Some people in Arles didn't appreciate his talent. They couldn't see straight when it came to observing a painter's talents. I saw it day in and day out when I spent so much time trailing him wherever he went to paint. That's if my father let me go.

But my mother would tell me once my father was gone, "*Vas-y*," go.

My mother understood me and my talent of following Monsieur Vincent around. It was truly a God-given talent that I did not fully understand then. But I knew deep in my heart that I would find my own way with him at my side. I didn't always stay at his side because I didn't want to be in his way, but he let me stand near him a little to his left and sometimes ask him questions. But not interrupt him in his painting. No, I didn't do that. It was after a long while when he stood up to relax his back would he start talking to me and I would then open up with all kinds of questions. He liked that.

He would even ask me some questions like "Did you see what I just did?" or "Do you know why I used this particular color?" or "Do you see how the light of the sun helps to liven up things?" or even "Do you understand now why the brilliant light of Arles makes me paint what I paint and why I came to here to Provence?"

And he would go on and on until I would simply say, "Yes, I do."

"Every true colorist must admit that there exists another coloration than that of the North. When Gauguin comes here he's going to like this *pays*, I'm sure."

"Who's Monsieur Gauguin?"

"He's an artist friend of mine who lives in Pont-Aven in Brittany. We both think alike as far as painting is concerned, especially colors. You'll meet him when he comes to Arles. I consider him to be one of my masters."

"Does he like light as you do?"

"Of course, he thinks of light as I do and he's going to be surprised when he sees for himself the intensity of light here. The intensity of light allows my inner eye to be that much more attentive to the shades of every color. This leads me to be that much more creative with the vividness and hues of colors. Light for me is a catalyst for the intensity of coloration. Light in Provence can be glaring and might dissipate colors but I can sift through it with my mind's eye and come up with the colors that are very intense and real. Light doesn't change as fast here as it does up north so that I am able to better capture the luminosity of what I see and render it with the intensity of colors that my creative eye sees. It's like having two sets of eyes, one outside and one inside. The inside one is the creative one. Do you understand what I'm telling you?"

I simply muttered a low "Yes," but I didn't get everything he was trying to explain to me. I was still very much ignorant of colors and light.

"I wish I could better explain it to you but the paintings themselves render concretely my creation of colors, you'll see."

"I know I don't see colors the way you see them but I'm better able to understand what you see when I look at your paintings, at least what I've seen so far. That I know."

"Stick with me, Camille, and I'll show you how to really see," he said with an honest pride in his voice.

"What does catalyst mean?" I asked him.

"A catalyst is a helping hand, an agent that helps to transmit things like a spark that lights up a fire."

Ah, a new word that I can put in my notebook, I told myself.

Then he would explain more things to me and I just stood there enthralled. He had a way of explaining things so that they became clearer and clearer and I would just take it in and store it away in my small mind. It stayed there though. Stayed there for a very long time to a point where I could go and retrieve it almost word for word. Especially when things were related in a concrete way to a painting or drawing.

Oh, Monsieur Vincent had a way with words. He wrote so often to his brother, Monsieur Théo, up north, to his sister, his close friend Monsieur Bernard, and his other friend Monsieur Gauguin, and some others too. He just loved to write letters. He would sometimes give me his letters so that I could give them to my father to post them. He even let me read some of his brother's letters sometimes just to show me how his brother cared, really cared for him. Quite often a one hundred franc note would fall from the letter as he opened it. He told me that was to buy canvas and tubes of colors. He would only keep a bit for his food and drink now and then, but most of the money was for his paintings. I think he would have gone without food if it meant he could paint more. He drank coffee a lot when he didn't have enough money to buy food. Sometimes I would sneak in some food from home for him. My mother knew that, but she just looked the other way. I used to put bread and some jam in a little jar in my large pockets and scurry along to meet him just so he would have something in his stomach that day. Poor man, he was so very much dedicated to his art. He would have died for it, I think. As a matter of fact, later on when I learned that he had died in Auvers, I knew that he had died for his art. And, died for his brother too since he didn't want to remain a burden on him. Well, Monsieur Théo had a wife and a child to support and things did not always prove to be successful for him. Anyway, I kept in my head and my heart all of the things that I learned from and about Monsieur Vincent until I was ready to write about them. I knew that someday it just had to come out. It just had to. I owed it to Monsieur Vincent and his talent. *Cet énorme talent* ! As big as a mountain. An enormous magical mountain. I liked telling him that I knew deep down that someday he would reach the very top of that mountain. People would come to appreciate his art and pay him loads of money for it.

And he would say to me in a sort of despondent way, "*Pas dans ma vie, Camille, pas dans ma vie.*"

And he was right, of course. Not in his lifetime.

He told me, one day, that he was born for the little stars not the big ones. But, each little star can help to form a huge mass of stars when it clung to other little stars like the milky way. The heavens are full of stars each with its own light and space. We humans can't begin to understand the stars and their capacity to brighten our human domain here on earth. We need to gaze at the stars at night when they come out in their full glory as scintillating lights. Nighttime is a magical moment for us human beings, he would say, because we are then given the privilege of not only of gazing at the stars but seeing and feeling the very movement of the stars.

You see he was born in the Netherlands, the land beneath the water level. The land of darkness below and above. The land where stars are so very important to a young boy who has to cope with a harsh and lonely life. It's then that the boy can rise above the harshness of life with his imagination and seek answers to his quest. The quest for understanding the world and himself. Especially understanding a father who was so very immersed in his strict Calvinistic interpretation of the Bible and disciplined ways of doing things as a staunch and austere minister of the Lord. Everything had to be done his way. His God was a God of power and might. A God of vengeance and repentance. An Old Testament God who commanded and expected his people to stay the course. His unrelenting course. Just like Monsieur Vincent's father's course. Unfortunately, Monsieur Vincent's mother wasn't too sympathetic either. She was a good woman and took good care of her family but she was made of salvation and damnation by the grace of God, black and white Calvinistic beliefs, just like the husband was. Those were her fundamental beliefs. She sided with her husband all the time and thought that her son was too lazy and too much of a dreamer. He did not conform enough. He realized, he said, that he wasn't always nice with his parents nor was he too kind to them. He rebelled a lot especially deep within himself. That's because he felt like they weren't listening to him and his need to express his full sentiments. Later on, he did take good care of his mother when she had seriously injured her hip and both his mother and father had truly appreciated his kindness then. However, he felt all along that he had been a disappointment to his mother. I guess she wasn't at all like my mother, kind and understanding. In any case, when Monsieur Vincent was in the mood, he liked to tell me about his young days growing up in Groot Zundert and his burdensome quest to conform like his parents and the elders wanted him to.

His childhood, he said, was gloomy, cold and sterile. He felt all along the heavy and overpowering burden of the words of the Bible, the sacred and revealed words of God that the Old Testament prophets kept announcing to the wearied and fallen away people of the covenant. He especially heard the forceful words of Isaiah like the tolling of a bell falling upon his heart and listless mind. When these words were read aloud by his own father, well they sounded just like the prophet himself come to life and wailing the fate of the people of God. He had wanted to emulate his father and serve in the ministry but they all wanted him to learn everything they said he had to learn before being accepted as a lay minister, and that had not worked out well. He tried. Oh, did he try with all of his heart and weary soul. He even went down into the coal-mines to minister to the poor and the needy but it practically ruined his health and his life.

Vincent was born on a gray blustery day in March. He grew up although not close to his father and mother, albeit close to his brother Théo and close enough to his youngest sister, Wilhelmina. He often felt solitary and had no meaningful conversation with anyone except the stars at night. Then he would open up about his dreams and his desires to do something with his emerging talent of drawing. He gave his father a simple drawing of some kind of a shed on his birthday. He was eleven.

His father took it and showed it to his wife who said, "Oh, that's nice."

Nice, it was more than nice. It was something an eleven-year old rarely did. He had drawn others, one when he was nine years old of a tone bridge and one of a duckling when he was but seven. But, no one thought he had talent. At least, no one told him so. Vincent loved to go out in the countryside just to gaze at nature in all its vibrant and stimulating life-giving inspiration. He stored in his mind all of these scenes that lingered on long after he had set eyes on them. However, he often found much of those scenes covered with grayness and soaked in the dull dreary light of a country not much given to bright sunshine.

He found within himself a fondness for reading, a liking that would eventually develop into a passion. He loved black and white drawings, he cherished colors too and he adored words. It seemed that everything in him was welled up deep down in his very guts, went through his veins and sinews and then up to his head and down through his receptive hands. An artist's hands. And his eyes. Those deep fiery eyes of his. They seemed grave and light-filled at the same time. His eyes lighted up when he spotted something he just had to paint. At least that's how I saw them when he was in Arles and I imagine that they were that way ever since he was a boy either drawing or thinking of painting.

His education was cut short at fifteen because his father ran out of money. His life was austere and at times monotonous. He was a very dutiful young man and was obedient to authority wherever he found himself either at home or at work. He read a lot and went to museums to learn how the masters did it. How they put on canvas the scenes or the people they painted. The gentle strokes, the fine daubs, and especially the way the design or drawing had been done before putting on the paint. And the paint, how beautiful the colors blended in one another to make the whole of the painting vibrant, precise and pleasing to the eye. He liked preciseness but at times he would have liked to see a little more vibrancy of colors. He especially enjoyed looking at Rembrandt's <u>The Jewish Bride</u> when he happened to find himself at the museum in Amsterdam. Monsieur Vincent so cherished the vibrancy of the yellow-gold coloring of the bridegroom's sleeve, that sun-soaked, golden-filled, thick daubs of rich paint replicating the richness of the weaver's art and pride. Some day, he would learn to paint like that and told me much more while talking about his youth. Yes, Rembrandt Harmensz Van Rijn, the master. Not to forget Jan Steen and his painting, <u>The Morning Toilet</u>. Monsieur Vincent must have seen it. I saw it some time ago and oh! that red stocking and the puppy asleep on the pillow. Little things, but important to the light in the painting. What craft! Monsieur Vincent told himself if Rembrandt and Jan Steen could do it, he could do it too. Someday. But first, he had to learn some more, not necessarily in an art school but out there where artists like Rembrandt learned their craft. Yes, painting was an art but it was also a craft that one had to learn step by step. Surely, some had it in their blood but they still had to learn in order to perfect their skill. By working very hard at it. By doing it over and over and over again. The masters showed the way but Monsieur Vincent also had to find his own way. His calling. Yes, he told me, drawing and painting was a gift, a call within the soul that had to be honed like a fine tool. A gem that had to be cut and crafted fully and artistically faceted in order to get out of it the light that was hidden. What the hands and fingers did in conjunction with the mind and in coordination with all of the nerves of the body were letting out the light in the artist's soul, he said.

"Mettre à jour sa propre lumière," he called it.

So many people put a snuffer on their inner light even before it starts to get out.

When both Monsieur Vincent and Monsieur Théo left home, the letter writing between the two brothers began in earnest. Without Monsieur Théo's letters, Monsieur Vincent would have felt lost and abandoned, he said. Long letters revealing his innermost feelings and thoughts to his dear brother. Letters were also a means of discussing Monsieur Vincent's views on art in general and in particular. It was a vehicle for sharing his theories of art and his experimentation with subject matter as well as with colors. No one else would have understood him and his strong urge to draw and paint. No one. Especially not his parents, he told me.

2

Witnessing the Master

$\mathcal{M}$onsieur Vincent didn't want me to call him Monsieur Van Gogh because he said I could not pronounce his last name well. Van Gokkkk. Nobody in Arles could. That's why he decided to sign his paintings, VINCENT. On one hand, it was true we could not pronounce his name right, but on the other hand, he could not speak our *Provenç*al. So there! With time, he did learn some words like « fada», «estello», « esquino», and « escoubo». That's how we say crazy, star, back and broom. I liked Monsieur Vincent. Right from the start. I did not taunt him nor did I stare at him as if he were a freak like some people did. They thought the idea of a redheaded, pale-skinned, evil-eye-looking painter from up north was kind of weird. Yes, evil eye just like the gypsies, they said. People in Provence were not used to strangers living among us, *les étrangiés*, they called them. Most people ignored him or wanted him gone as soon as he began poking around and especially when he started asking people to model for him. They just didn't want others to laugh at them. What, posing for that weird painter? My father was one of the first to sit for him and he was proud of it. I got my picture painted by him, twice, cap and all. I was somewhat shy about it then, but now I'm really proud of those two paintings. But, that's another story.

I met Monsieur Vincent when I was wandering in la rue Voltaire not far from where I lived. We lived close to Monsieur Vincent. He lived on rue de la Cavalerie then and I used to see him quite often in the neighborhood. He would come out with his backpack, as I called it, and start wandering about. He looked poor and so out of step with the rest of the Arles population. I started feeling sorry for him because he seemed to be a loner, a person with no friends. He just didn't look too happy. I told myself, he needs a friend, a companion. Someone to talk to, someone to listen. Who was going to do that in Arles with a complete stranger?

I was playing with some of my friends when one of them cried out, "There's the weird guy, the one from up north who roams around trying to paint things. He even asked Monsieur Leclerc to sit for him so that he could paint his picture. Imagine that!"

"What did Monsieur Leclerc reply?" asked Gabonet.

"Nothing. He just walked away and left the weird man standing there." And then they all laughed.

I didn't think it was too kind of them to laugh at a man they didn't even know. Sure he looked a bit strange, the way he dressed and the way he walked with brisk steps, but that was no reason to mock him. Fine friends they were. I decided then and there to find out more about him. I told my father about this man. My father knew just about everybody who lived in Arles especially in the local neighborhood. He told me that he knew little of this artist who had recently arrived in town but he would try to get to know him better since people in Arles are plain stubborn when it comes to accepting new neighbors especially if they come from far away and they're not *des Provençaux.*

"They're just as bad as the gypsies of Saintes-Maries-de-la-Mer, *un peu farouches,"* a bit untamed, he said.

Saintes-Maries-de-la-Mer? I had never been there. "Where is that?" I asked.

He said that it was further south next to the Mediterranean at the tip of La Camargue and that the town attracted many gypsies especially on the feast day of « Sainte Sarah, la noire.»

Well, I was really intrigued by that. I told my father that I would like to go there some day.

He replied, "Not for a very long time, *mon cher Camille*, only when you grow up and can make decisions on your own."

I was ten going on eleven then and although I wasn't too intelligent(the teacher had told my parents that I was a mediocre student), I had a very good memory and could remember things from way back. I could read and absorb things easily. Besides, Monsieur Vincent told me later when I got to know him that I would bloom, *m'épanouir,* he said. I loved to write and I collected scrap paper and kept it in an old folder that my father had given me along with my notebook. On Sundays, I wrote things down: what I remembered from the previous week and even the previous month, some tales my father had told the family and friends, and some writings of my own. I imagined things like a small bird landing on my windowsill and telling me about the other birds who flew away to other parts of the country. I had never been outside of Arles except for Nîmes where my father had taken me to buy some reed baskets that my mother wanted. We also bought some little *Croquants Villaret* that my father loved. They were little hard candies. I liked to be

with my father. He was a good man, a happy man who talked to everybody and never denied anyone his kind words. My father had a long
bushy beard and curly hair when you could see them without his cap
on. Oh! He was a handsome man when he wore his uniform, all blue
and gold. My mother told him so. Monsieur Vincent would eventually
do several paintings of my father and portraits of all of the other members of the family including my baby sister.

I didn't really "meet" him. I sneaked up on him and watched him
paint part of the Trinquetaille bridge. I wanted to know how he did his
paintings. Then some kids, I didn't know, started to mill around him as
did a few peculiar-looking men. They were all surprised when the colors were squeezed out of tubes. I wasn't because I had seen them
before when I looked at him paint in the town garden. He didn't see
me, but I saw him. It was really amazing to see yellows, reds, greens,
and blues coming out like that. He put dabs of them on a small board
with a hole for the thumb. The boys just giggled and fooled around after that. He then asked one of the men to sit for him. He wanted to paint
his face but the man just didn't want to. He looked somewhat disdainful
at Monsieur Vincent and walked away. The others did too. Even the
boys left. No one wanted to pose for him. I stayed behind and he asked
me my name.

I said, "Camille."

"You're the boy I saw slithering around like a snake in the public
garden watching me paint the other day."

"How did you know? I made sure I was far enough from you not to
see me."

"But I know everything. I have eyes behind my head. Small and
deep set in my reddish hair."

"No, you don't have eyes behind your head."

"Yes, I do. I'm like God."

I just smiled.

"I like your smile," he told me. "It's welcoming, more than most
people here are willing to do."

"Many grown-ups here are a bit bashful with strangers," I tried to
explain.

"It's more than bashfulness. It's downright meanness and I don't
need their consent to live in Arles. I live here because I chose to."

"I'm sorry," I said.

"Don't be. It's not your fault. Do you like paintings?" he asked.

"I think so."

"You think so?"

"You see, I don't know much about art."

"Would you like to learn more about it?"

"Oh, yes, sir."

"Would you like to pose for me? I mean sitting for a portrait." he asked.

I just stood there in amazement that he would even consider me for a portrait.

"I just may do a portrait of you someday. Do you have any brothers and sisters?" he asked.

"Just one brother, but you could do my father's and my mother's pictures. I think they'd like that," I said.

"I'll have to get to know your family and then we'll see."

I was filled with joy, pure, unadulterated joy, a joy that lights up your eyes and fills you with tiny bubbles like champagne does.

From that time on, I resolved that this artist would be my best friend. Of course, I had close friends like Milou, Calendau, Anfos and Blàsi but they weren't at all like him. He was different because he was an artist just like the *felibres de Provence*, our poets were different. I wanted to get close to this artist I had just met so that I might become an artist myself just like the *felibres*. Messieurs Aubanel, Brunet, Mathieu, Roumanille, Tavan and Giéra were our poets of Provence. Fine people but they weren't friendly like this artist was with me. And Monsieur Mistral, well, he was their leader, too highly considered by all to bother with a boy like me. I wasn't anybody. But that didn't matter to this artist. He bothered to talk to me. He told me later that being a somebody means what other people think of you and consider you as a somebody while being a nobody, you don't have to worry about what people think. Just the people who matter in your life. I'll always remember that.

So, I sat down on the bank close to the bridge and he made a drawing of my head. Then he gave it to me. He signed it, VINCENT. I ran home to show it to my mother and later on I showed it to my father when he came home from work. I told my parents that it was Vincent who had done the drawing and that he was my friend.

Papa corrected me and said, "Monsieur Vincent to you."

"What's his last name?" asked my mother.

"I don't know. I didn't ask him," I said.

My father then said, "Vincent Van Gogh. I know the *facteur* who delivers mail to him. He gets mail from a Monsieur Gauguin and a Monsieur Théo Van Gogh. This Théo must be his brother or a close relative. I have yet to meet this Vincent Van Gogh but I plan to introduce myself to him soon. *Je ne veux pas qu'il pense que les Arlésiens sont des sauvages,*" that people in Arles are some kind of unsociable people.

"Are we, father?"

"Are we what?"

"Not sociable people."

"No, but some of us are rather *sauvages*, a bit wild like animals and some of us don't want strangers in pour midst."

"Like Monsieur Belaval and Madame Granouche who would not give a smile to anybody not even Frederi Mistral our great poet?"

"Now, don't you go making up things. Be nice," said my father.

"Van Gogh. That's not a name from around here," said my mother.

"No, I think he comes from the northern countries," was my father's reply.

"Well it sounds Dutch or German to me," said my mother. "We don't often get people from that far up north. Not in Arles."

So, that's how I got to meet Monsieur Vincent at the Trinquetaille bridge. I will never forget that and the drawing he made of me. I still have it; it's in my folder with my writings. It was my secret portfolio for years until it became all ragged and I had to throw some papers away and get myself a new and larger folder for things I collected. But, I always kept my drawing. It was precious to me. It still is. Why? Because it was the first time anyone had given me something as precious as that. My face on paper drawn by an artist. I didn't show it to Armand because he would have laughed at it or else he would have said that it wasn't very important. I did show it to Calendou, one of my friends, but he simply smiled and told me that it was nice but that my head was a bit crooked. I told him that it wasn't crooked. It was the way Monsieur Vincent had drawn it and he knew what he was doing, I insisted.

That was many years ago and I still remember my first encounter with Vincent. It's still etched on my mind. Vincent had told me that I was precocious and I believed him. That's why I remembered things so well. Vincent had said that I had a special gift as young as I was. "Ordinary people forget things. You remember everything. You're special, you see," he told me.

Wow! Special. No one had told me that before. I always thought I was just plain and ordinary like the other kids. Not too intelligent either. I had told him how I remembered things from far back and that I kept them in my mind locked up so that I could recall them whenever I wished to. Even small things like the color of my first cap and the little toy dog my grandmother had given me when I was four years old. She lived in Fontvielle and we went to visit her once in a while then. She was my father's mother. She lived next to a windmill. She died when I was eight.

"I tell you, you have a gift, Camille. Yes, you have a gift, *un don de Dieu*," Monsieur Vincent said. "You were born with it."

I was all excited about my gift. I would use it someday to create something truly worthwhile. My memories and my writing. And that's what I'm doing now, writing about Vincent the artist in Arles as I knew him. Writing about Vincent also means that I have to write about the colors he used and how he explained them to me and the reason he used each and every one of them. I have to write about the light in Provence that he so loved, and I have to write about the many places he went to paint, and so many other things. Now, eighteen years have passed since I first met Vincent. From the vantage point of my maturity, I am able to recollect with a very good sense of accuracy all that I have seen with him and all that he has told me about painting, as well as all the conversations we had together. I have the words; I have the sharp memories. That's my special gift as Vincent was the very special gift to my childhood. I realize that it will take me several years to complete my account of Vincent's life and paintings in Arles since I want to check everything in my notebooks and make sure I'm using the proper words too. That's alright, I have the time. I just want to make everything I write as accurate as possible. After all, as I've told myself before, I want to be faithful to Vincent's creative spirit.

Monsieur Vincent told me that he had come to Arles to catch the brightness of the sun. Light! And he said it with a gleam in his eyes.

"You see there can be no colors without light. The brighter the light, the better and more vibrant the colors are for me. Oh, how I want to capture the light of Provence! Here in Provence light comes through your eyes right down to your very soul. It stirs all the colors up in one big cauldron in your belly and it shoots them back bright, vibrant, and dazzling through your mind's eye and right down to your fingers. Then you're ready to paint. But you have to capture that light when it's at its brightest and when things in nature dance in the light of the sun. Unfortunately, the light changes so you have to keep up with it. This is all too much for your little head, Camille, but someday, perhaps you'll understand."

"But I understand now," I replied.

"Good for you. You are my friend then, my disciple, and I will teach you all that I know about color. Not really everything because I'm still learning. You and I will get to know the language of nature from the perspective of light and color at different times of the day. You see, there is color even at night. Vibrating colors. You'll see."

I got very excited. I wanted to hug him then and there but I didn't think he would have wanted me to.

"Now, let's talk about colors," he told me one day.

"Chrome yellow. Jaune! Yellow! Yellow! Yellow! It's the sun dripping its color and brightness that is congealed in the bright yellow paint the artist uses. It oozes out of the tube like yellow blood that gives life to a canvas," Monsieur Vincent would shout.

"That's why sometimes I just put big globs of yellow on my canvas, rich and thick like pudding so that its texture can be not only seen but felt with the fingers and the heart that longs for vibrancy. You can almost taste it too. All your senses need to be at work."

Then he went on to tell me that, "Some artists only paint after they have drawn the shapes beforehand; others draw-paint at the same time. I often just like to put colors on my canvas as I see color out there and let the colors guide me, my eyes and my fingers. That's when color becomes inspiration."

A bit later on he told me, "I capture light as a cicada captures it and stores it away for when comes time to let it out in the form of its unique sound that makes the outdoors vibrate and scream with soundlight."

That's what he called it, *lumièreson*. That's why he had come all the way from Paris to Provence. To paint light. Bright and glorious light. Light that opens up new dimensions on painting just like others had done before Monsieur Vincent.

Oh, the brightness of light and color on the canvases that Monsieur Delacroix did in Africa. That's what Monsieur Vincent wanted to capture. I didn't know the artist Delacroix before my friend mentioned him to me, but I got to like his paintings once he showed me some. Like The Lion Hunt. What a grandiose painting of an adventurous combat with seven bold men struggling with two fierce-looking lions. What colors!

Here in Provence the bright light is somewhat yellowish, but in Africa it's blaring white. That's what Monsieur Vincent told me. To think that before the Impressionist painters, artists stayed indoors in a workshop to paint. That's what Monsieur called them, Impressionists. These artists didn't stay indoors because they wanted to paint outdoors in full daylight. The others called them stupid for doing that. Other artists only worked with filtered light, light through windows or other sources such as lamps. Never direct sunlight or under a cloudy sky. That might be alright for the painting of portraits but not for nature. Nature needs the natural outdoors. Natural light. Even if it means painting in the rain. Rainy weather has its own light. I learned all of that and much more from Monsieur Vincent. I also learned that in order to become a good painter, the artist has to learn from other painters. Monsieur wrote about his "starry sky" concept to his close artist friend, Émile Bernard. He told him that he liked his rendition of the shared self-portraits. He also told me that some of his masters were Millet the peasant-painter, Corot for his delicate nature scenes, Courbet for his keen sense of realism, Gustave Doré for his excellent drawings and Signac, the artist who painted with dots and short strokes of complementary colors. Of course, his own countryman, Rembrandt.

"I know you haven't traveled yet, but someday go to the museum in Amsterdam and take a look at his large painting of The Jewish Bride. There, you will not only see the flaming red of the bride's dress and the position of the hands that most people look at, but look at the right sleeve of the groom. Oh, the lush golden yellow of the sleeve and the texture, what a texture with brush strokes upon brush strokes of paint, layers upon layers of glittering colors. Golden luminous threads of paint. What an artist Rembrandt was. What skill. He loved color and he reveled in texture. Some people don't see that, but I do and I take him as my master," he said with the bursting joy of an artist.

Monsieur Vincent really liked this painting.

One of the first paintings Monsieur Vincent did in February when he first arrived in Arles was a painting with snow. He was expecting bright sun and warmth but when he saw the snow on the ground, he was baffled. He had come all the way down south just to get away from the snow and the cold.

"I was thoroughly disappointed at first," he told me when I got to know him. However, he made the best of it and he painted the snow on the ground in a field somewhere in Arles. It's one of the very few paint-

ings that he did with snow. He did another one of a snowy landscape
with Arles in the background. He wrote to his brother Monsieur Théo
about seeing snow on the ground in the countryside and he told him
that he was contemplating that Japanese look when he saw the snow in
Arles. In spite of the cold, it was very much like Japan, he noticed. He
often quoted to me passages from some of the letters he wrote Monsieur Théo. In this one he wrote: "The scenery in the snow with its
white summits against a sky as luminous as the snow is very much like
the winter scenes that the Japanese made."

Landscape with Snow shows a day in February in a harvested
field covered with snow. There's a man in a black hat with his dog at
his side while some of the bare spots on the ground are painted many
different colors such as, red, brown, blue, green and black to show
the natural winter variance of the color of the soil left bare with the
melting of the snow. In the background toward the left, one sees the
white houses with some blue brush strokes and at near center we can
spot a small shed painted yellow with a red roof. There are some
touches of yellow in the painting especially the short row of what
looks like wheat stalks leading upward in the middle. The snow
seems to be already melting in the sun and that's why there are so
many bare patches here and there. But there's a hazy-like sun and
the sky is overcast. Monsieur Vincent chose to paint the sky a bluish-green color to reflect the restrained luminosity of the day. The
overall ambience is that of cold and chilly weather that the artist
managed to capture on that late February day after he had just gotten
in from Paris. You see, it sometimes snows in Arles. Not very often,
but it does. However, the sun does warm us up and with time we recover the usual warmth of Provence. That's what Monsieur Vincent
did and that's why he came to Arles. He recovered the warmth and
brightness and learned to capture the light of the sun here in Arles.
And he painted his heart out.

He also painted other things such as, *la charcuterie*, the pork-
butcher shop, as seen from a window. He painted an old woman of Arles. I don't know the woman. In March, he painted the avenue of plane
trees near the Arles station, then a basket with oranges, an almond
branch in a glass, he loved the almond tree in bloom, a pair of wooden
clogs and some potatoes in a yellow dish. He loved potatoes unlike
most people in Provence. He painted all of these works before I met
him and found out who he was. When he showed me these paintings I

was stunned at the number of works he had done in the short period of time he had been in Arles. He told me that he had done many more while up north but, here in Arles, he planned to do hundreds of paintings now that he had the brightness of the light of the sun at his creative disposal.

That was just the beginning before he started to paint the many orchards in bloom. There were at least a dozen of those paintings as far as I could tell. He went at it with a passion since he said that he had finally found the Japan of the south of France. How he loved to paint the orchards in the bright light that rendered them luminous and oriental in the way the Japanese saw things, felt things and understood things all within the spirit of nature, he said. For Monsieur Vincent, the orchards in bloom became a magical moment of inspiration as if Arles and its surroundings were a blossom festival. His paintings of the orchards are all light. It's as if the very meaning behind his fruit trees is luminosity. Even where the shadows are suggested, the darker areas are like shadows cast by the blossoms themselves. There are no dark shadows in Monsieur Vincent's rendition of the orchards in bloom. It's all light. I got to realize this when I witnessed his painting of the white orchard in the fullness of springtime.

3

Fathers and Mothers

Old uncle Cent got Monsieur Vincent a job at the Hague branch of an art gallery whose headquarters was located in Paris, **Goupil and Company**. Then he was sent to London, a city he loved for its museums and art galleries. From London he got transferred to the main office in Paris where he delighted in the adventure of the discovery of artists and their works. However, he was let go the following April of 1876. He immediately left France to return to the London area where he taught for a while until he decided to go back home to Etten. Depression set in and he thought about his life and his sense of direction. He was haunted by the notion of God and the attraction to mysticism. He told me that he really thought that religion was his true calling at first. Like his father. But unlike him, Monsieur Vincent did not want to become a minister preacher in words only.

"Father had very little compassion for his flock. He preached to them, no, he preached at them. He commanded them to seek the stern God of the Old Testament and heed the words of the prophets. He was anything but a true pastor in my view of things. He was inflexible, hard-faced, cool-hearted and unwavering in his interpretation of the Bible. Just like Calvin himself," Vincent said of his father.

He didn't speak too much about him except when he talked about the stern, vengeful and damning God of his father. He said that he told himself that he would find his own God, not his father's God. Like the Christ-God in agony proving to us that God can be like us human beings. If the Christ of the gospels was poor in material things, compassionate, forgiving, welcoming and could talk about a loving father *"qui accueille,"* a father who embraces a prodigal son, then Monsieur Vincent could easily accept this God, this Lamb of God. To be Christ-like was his goal in life. Christ the Son and his loving relationship with the Father was what he yearned for. An approachable father. He said he had seen Rembrandt's painting of The Prodigal Son and he had loved it both in content and in the muted colors that the artist had so masterfully done. The fallen-away son and his father who extends his forgiveness with open arms. Later on, he told me that he always struggled with the figure of God. That's why he liked to depict him or his power in the form of movement or in the brilliant colors that he gave his flowers, especially the sunflowers. Color is god-like, he used to say.

Monsieur Vincent then decided to go the evangelical college in Laeken near Brussels. He took the final exam but failed it. Too dumb, they said. Not well versed in Reformed Calvinism and other matters. Unsuited for lay ministry, they told him. But he was truly and sincerely a man of God and he was a missionary at heart, he told them. He wanted to show them what he could do in God's ministry. The only post they thought suitable for him was Le Borinage in Belgium. So they sent him to Belgium. He was going to be at the service of the poorest of the poor, the indigent coal miners. He got down into the mines with them, got dirty with soot and coal dust, ate sparse meals with them, and prayed with them, and talked about the gospel. These people were so poor and needy that they could not even pay attention to what he had to say about the Bible. They were desperate for food that could sustain them physically not food that was meant for their soul, Monsieur Vincent said. It is then that he realized that he could not help them in their needs. He tried so hard, so very hard to become a good gospel missionary, but even at that he seemed to fail. Why, he even gave them everything he owned but he could not be one of them as hard as he tried. He could not fully understand them and they did not understand him and his determination to save their souls. They all loved him for his kindness and compassion and the way he tried so valiantly to help them in their misery. However, in the end, he was still haunted by his true calling. What was it? Why was he haunted so much by his thoughts? Why couldn't he be happy with what he had and where he was? He had nothing. He owned absolutely nothing. He was content with paper and ink so that he could write to his brother, Théo. At times, he would sketch things and even turn out some drawings. Now, drawing fulfilled him. He told Monsieur Théo that he often drew late at night just to recollect some memories that the had stored in his head. Was that his calling? he wondered. Was that what haunted him deep inside his soul? Drawing, making things and people come to life.

After le Borinage, Monsieur Vincent went to Brussels to study anatomical and perspective drawing at the Academy. He decided to become an artist and drawing would be crucial to his art, he thought. No more evangelical studies, no more fighting his true calling as an artist, he said. Then he moved to the Hague to be closer to his artist friend, Monsieur Anton Mauve. How highly he always spoke of Monsieur Mauve. It was precisely he who got Monsieur Vincent going. He gave him a box of colors, some brushes and a palette as well as lending him money. Monsieur Vincent also told me that it was Monsieur Mauve who urged him to get rid of his old mended and stained shirts and pants and get himself some decent clothes. After all, he shouldn't be seen as a bum when introduced to someone important to his budding career, he told him. Monsieur Vincent appreciated his advice. It was Monsieur Mauve also who urged him to do watercolors and to explore oil painting and colors.

After a while Monsieur Vincent got tired of drifting around and feeling lonely so he went to Neunen where his parents were then living. Pa and Moe as the family called them. He felt like a shaggy dog with wet paws that one allows to enter into their home, he said. He felt misplaced and misunderstood. At least, that's what he thought. Also, an intruder in the house of plenty. Then, he told me that he missed companionship, friends with whom he could talk and discuss things especially art. He so enjoyed the infrequent visits of his brother. They were really of the same cut, the same feelings, the same enjoyment of art and the same soul.

"You don't know, Camille, how much the soul reaches for it's mate or other people in tune with everything that makes one harmonize feelings, joys, even frustrations and failures. The greatest joy in life is to find someone with whom I can share the very soul of self."

Then I asked him, "Do you find your soul in me?"

"I'm beginning to," he replied, "I'm beginning but it takes time. You, my young friend, need to mature and cultivate your own soul and find your true self, your calling. What makes you who you are or going to be."

"But I know what I want to become, a writer."

"Then, work at it. Work very hard and don't let people keep you off track. Keep at it no matter what."

"Is that what you did, Monsieur Vincent?"

"I was lost for a long time. I moved to Paris to be closer to my brother and at the same time take lessons at the *atelier Cormon* where I met Émile Bernard for the first time. It's in Paris that I met Paul Gauguin and we seemed to appreciate the same things in art and the rendition of vivid colors. I thought then that I could work with someone like Paul Gauguin someday and we could create some kind of a workshop together.

Things didn't work out for me at the *atelier*. I met a lot of artists but they didn't impress me with their works and their way of seeing things. I was seeking something else, something different. Oh, I tried it their way but I wasn't pleased with the results. Not enough light, pure light that the north could not provide, I thought. I soon became depressed and listless. I couldn't find myself. I knew what I wanted but others refused to listen to me, really listen. I think, no, I know deep inside they all laughed at me, especially the artists in Paris. I wanted to belong to a colony of painters who understood my vision and my inner thrust. Most of all, I wanted to find light, pure light that would open up for me the true character of painting. After all, there is no painting without light of some kind, no colors without some form of light, and the best light in France was here in Provence. That's why I decided to come here. I took the train and came as far south as my money allowed me to. Then I got off and came to a town Toulouse-Lautrec, the artist, had mentioned to me in Paris, Arles."

I just smiled when he said Arles. That was my home and fate had sent him to me just so I could learn from him and find myself as a writer. I know I told you that I didn't believe in fate but this time it was fate. *Mon destin et le destin de l'artiste Vincent Van Gogh.* I'm telling you all of this, I mean Monsieur Vincent's background and all, not to bore you, readers, but because all of this has an impact on the way Monsieur painted. Don't think that he just arrived here in Arles, plucked himself down and started to paint and everything just poured out of him. No. All of the years he had worked hard at refining his painting and drawing did not come easy. He had to learn his trade, that of an artist. *Un artiste accompli.* Well, in order to become accomplished, one has to work very hard and endure every hardship in life that comes his way. And believe me, Monsieur Vincent had a lot of them. But, that's what made him what he was and what he became at the very summit of his painting career in Arles. He came to Arles alone and most probably very lonely, but he eventually made friends with the family Roulin.

My father loved his job as far as I could see. He didn't make a lot of money but he provided well for his family. We never lacked for anything, as far as I know. Of course, my mother knew how to stretch every franc she put her hand on. My father loved meeting people and talking to them. He loved Monsieur Vincent. They got along so very well. Most of the people around here did not like Monsieur Vincent. I don't know why. Perhaps because he was from the north. He was not a Provençal, you see. He seemed strange, so strange, to many people who would not open up to him. They were all rooted in the soil of their ancestors and they could not budge an inch to get out of the clay that pulled down their very soul, my father said. They're stubborn, my people. They're set in their ways and they will not allow themselves to see things differently. But, they're generous people, proud people and they love life and food. You need to get to know them and accept them as they are. You see Monsieur looked strange, he talked strangely, he did strange things and he managed to rub people the wrong way. He became a solitary man. People left him alone with his coffee, his absinthe, his demand for potatoes (of all things, potatoes, that's not us, potatoes) and his constant wanderings in and out of his house to find a place to paint. And his paintings, how strange they all seemed to my people. They did not like the colors or how much paint he used to apply and arrange his colors. They looked like bird spatters, they said, or in hushed tones, they would say *des vomissures*, vomit. But, I liked his paintings and I told him so.

Well, getting back to my father, he was not like the others. He accepted Monsieur Vincent as he was and that's why Monsieur liked him so much. Monsieur Vincent liked the way we were family. He cherished my mother. She had somewhat of a soft spot for him. She called him, "*Mon enfant perdu*," my lost child. And he delighted in my baby sister, Marcelle. She was a fat baby with fat cheeks. We all loved her. Years later, I would read some of my notes to her since I could not have done that with my brother, Armand. He was much older than me and he didn't want to listen to a child's gibberish, he told me. He wouldn't even give me a chance to explain to him what I did was going to be important someday.

"*Tu t'en fais*," he told me. You're full of it.

So, I read to my little sister even though she had no idea what I was reading. At least, I had a listener. Sometimes my mother would sit down and listen to me but she was so busy with the house chores and the baby that she didn't have much time to be idle. At least, she didn't tell me that I was wasting my time as some people did.

My father's name was Joseph Étienne Roulin, a solid name and a solid *citoyen* was he. He was *un républicain* and it took me some time to understand this term. Monsieur Vincent told me that it meant someone who is a strong partisan of the Republic. We're a republic. No more kings, emperors, and other high-minded men who want to control all. We are all in it together, my father said. Let the past be the past. We must move on to modern times. We must respect the rights of all citizens who form the republic. Yes, my father was *un vrai républicain.*He admired Eugène Pelletan and Rochefort and, later, was attracted to Général Boulanger. These people found *la République* more trustworthy than the Empire for they were dissatisfied with the government of the scandal-prone bourgeoisie. My father sometimes quoted Jean-Jacques Rousseau but I didn't know this man. He told me he was a great writer and wrote about the rights of people.

"Oh, a writer," I said.

I asked my teacher about him and he said that we were not at that period in history yet, so he did not give me any explanations on Jean-Jacques Rousseau. Monsieur Vincent did but he told me not to get too much involved with idealists and philosophers like Rousseau.

"They only muddy the waters," he said. "High-minded words and high-minded theories but little substance for those of us who have to work hard and eke out an existence when one tries to be the artist he is called to be. Monsieur Jean-Jacques would have probably banished artists from his society since we are non-productive people and we serve the republic meagerly. Although I love his ideas about nature and human nature."

That was a bit much for me so I decided to read some other writers like Alphonse Daudet and George Sand.

Monsieur Vincent painted my father in his postal uniform several times. My father looked so very proud and republican sitting there in his chair just the way Monsieur Vincent had set him up. My father had long fingers and long arms with a face that looked bushy due to his beard and mustaches. His eyes were liquid blue and when he would stare at you to talk or give you *sa façon de penser*, his chiding, his eyes would water and he had to wipe them with his big handkerchief that he would fold neatly and place in the left front pocket of his pants. I just loved his blue uniform with the gold buttons and gold trim on the lower part of his sleeves. It formed swoops and swirls so that it made him look official just like his cap with the word *"POSTES"* on the front band. He did say that he was an official of the governmental system of mail and delivery. He was very proud of being a civil servant. I was proud of him. My father just loved to wear that uniform whenever he could and that's why he posed with it on for Monsieur Vincent. I think that he would have slept in it if he could. On Sundays, well he dressed up like a family man did. He was no dandy, my father, nor was he an intellectual. He liked to tell people the way it was and had no patience for abstract talk when no one had the chance to cut into the conversation. His eyes would light up and his hands, like elegant birds, made constant gestures as he talked. He loved us, his family, and above all, he loved his country, *la République*. Sometimes Monsieur Vincent would tease him about this but he never went too far so as not to make my father feel stupid or defensive. Monsieur Vincent loved my father and I think he loved me. I know he did or otherwise why would he tolerate me around him all day long at times. My father, there was no one like him.

As for my mother, Augustine Roulin, well, she was an important part of the couple Roulin. She sewed, she baked, she cooked, she ironed, she ran errands, she cleaned, she took care of us and she worried sometimes about things such as having enough bread on the table or sufficient meat in her stews. Worried also about how much she would have liked us to have a better education, a trouble-free future, a secure job and a good wife for me and my brother. She wasn't worried about Marcelle. Women manage to do well, she would often say. She was especially relieved about my father having a steady and secure position. She didn't call it job but a position. In the government scheme of things, all of its workers had positions, at least that's what people employed by the government tended to call it. So, my father had a good position, my mother was a housewife taking care of the home and we the children would grow up to be proud and successful citizens according to my honorable father, the republican. Above all, we were a family that Monsieur Vincent admired and so wished to be part of.

"How about your own family?" I asked Monsieur Vincent one day.

"Well, *mon petit ami*, besides my brother Théo, I have no family. I have parents and other siblings, but I really have no family as such. No central core of love and attachment. I have no illusions either that I will ever have one of my own. Who would marry an artist, a loner and a drifter who gets depressed easily and spends all of his time painting?"

And I would tease him saying, "Jeanne Calment and Mirette *la frippette* would."

Mirette Girardou was a fiery-tempered, red-haired woman who lived in Arles and who had a eye on Monsieur Vincent. Nobody understood why but everyone knew about her sweet inclination for the artist. At times, she would even do favors, as people called them, for Monsieur Vincent. But he would have very little to do with her, and she knew it. She was a bit jealous of the girls with whom he drank or danced at the local bar. She frequented the Café d'Alcazar in town and she would often have a drink with the people there. That's where she met Monsieur Vincent and began to talk to him about art. Some say she was part Arlesian and part gypsy on her mother's side. Her father had been a fisherman and had met his wife, Imerine, in Avignon. Imerine was as wild as the beautiful mares of la Camargue, some said. The couple settled in Arles where Mirette grew up. The girl had a tawny complexion and deep dark eyes that could capture your very soul, they said. Others said she was a sorceress like her mother. She could cast spells on you just by looking at you in the eye. That's why people avoided her glance. Look out if she stared at you. I always looked down when I saw her, even from far away. Sometimes I would bump into things or stumble over a rock or a piece of wood left lying on the road. She frightened me and I think Monsieur Vincent was a bit afraid of her, but he liked her. He liked the fiery way about her.

"She's like fire," he would say, "she can devour your soul with her burning within."

So, I would always wait to see if fire would come out of her mouth. It never did and I told myself that Monsieur Vincent was using words just to make me feel conscious about my taking things literally. I was just a boy then and I did not know enough to be wise and knowledgeable about things especially about women.

Monsieur Vincent never talked about Mirette to me but I knew that she really had a soft spot for him and would cast an eager eye on him every time she saw him. I could tell. I was young and naïve, but I could tell. Sometimes, Monsieur Vincent would get mad at Mirette and swear that he would never see her again, but he always returned to the Café d'Alcazar on Friday and Saturday nights and she was always there for him. People started talking about the two of them. My mother warned him about the gypsies and how they can easily charm you into their power, but Monsieur Vincent just smiled at her and told her that he was, after all, *"un enfant perdu."*

Somehow Monsieur Vincent had a deep curiosity about the gypsies. He loved to go to Les Saintes-Maries-de-la-mer and strike up a conversation with one of them. He would go to their little church and talk to their saint, Sara, the black saint who drifted ashore with the two Marys. Monsieur Vincent would tell her to pray for him even if he didn't believe in saints and the Church. He wanted to have her intercession with God so that he would find himself and his art. He took me there a couple of times, but I'll tell you all about it later.

4

The Romantic Artist and the Peasant Painter

*M*onsieur Vincent's palette had among its colors, *ocre jaune, jaune de Naples...* yellow, the golden soul of colors. The bright sun of colors like the sunflower that faces the sun and glows with the brilliance of petals made of pure color.

"C'est une couleur accueillante tout comme l'amour pour un autre," Monsieur Vincent told me one day. A welcoming color just like the love given to another person.

"It's a symbolic Japanese color, a symbol of welcome," he informed me.

That's why he loved it so much and used it so very often, I suppose.

"It brightens everything by capturing and blending the sun into your paintings," he said. "How can I explain it to you or convince you of it except to tell you to feel the sun as much as you can. Feel the sun on your body and let it exhilarate you in all of its glorious intensity of color bright. It's like touching a piece of God himself," he insisted.

"I'm trying, I'm trying," I said. "I'm trying but the sun gets in my eyes."

"Then just let the feel of it rest upon your soul deep inside of you. Close your eyes and you can see the redness of the sun's rays on the inside of your eyelids just like being inside a glowing coal. *La rougeur sanglante du soleil sous les paupières*," the blood-redness of the sun inside your eyelids.

From yellow ochre early on to cadmium yellow on to chrome yellow, Monsieur Vincent transformed the light in his landscapes into pure color.

He told me that he had lost his youth early on and that he came to Arles to recover it. So, by the use of a rich bright yellow he was able to capture light as he saw it down South and revive his inner feeling of youth recaptured. Of course, he used the range of other colors too but yellow was his very favorite.

"Ma jeunesse qui s'était enfuie est retournée enfin." My lost youth finally returned, he said. "I may be the lost child to your mother, but my youth was my lost child until I found it here in the splendor of the Provençal landscape."

I took everything in just as he told it to me.

His paintings of the sunflowers are perhaps the very epitome of his love, no his passion, for yellow. Besides, he insisted that sunflowers that turn their faces to the sun are symbolic of creatures like us who perpetually try to face our Creator and look at him in the eye and tell him that we appreciate his glowing radiance, but that we can't always sustain his omnipresent rigor of abandonment. He had even abandoned his own son at the Garden of Gethsemane and at Golgotha.

"Do you know that?" Monsieur Vincent asked me one day.

"I don't know much about the Bible," I replied.

"Well, I know it's true, even Christ felt that way. He said so himself. *Comme le Christ, je suis un délaissé, un perdu.*" Like Christ, I'm an abandoned and lost child.

Sometimes he had tears in his eyes, but he tried not to show it. I just turned my head around for I think I would have done the same thing myself if I had not bit my lip.

First of all, let me tell you about sunflowers. For years, it was a project of mine to learn as much as I could about these huge flowers that are so profuse in my countryside, la Provence. I saw them everywhere. People loved them. Even today, they pick them up in their gardens or in the fields or they buy bunches of them in order to decorate their houses. They live with them because they fill up their senses. Sunflowers have become the perpetuation of the sunshine of their lives. I knew this lady who used to talk to her sunflowers.

She called them, "*Mes grosses faces d'or*," my big golden faces.

She would tell them all of her worries, her frustrations and her troubles with her husband when he wouldn't do what she wanted him to do. She was especially frustrated when he would not dress for the annual festival and stayed home brooding over glasses of pastis. I saw her once talking to her sunflowers when I was delivering some eggs from old man Grosvert, the farmer. He used to pay me four centimes to deliver eggs in the neighborhood.

She took me by the arm and led me to her sunflowers and said, "Talk to them. They listen, you know."

I got out of there as fast as my legs could take me. Me, talk to flowers in a vase? No way. I'm not that stupid. I like sunflowers but there's a limit to what I'll do for flowers. Besides, she was a strange sort of a woman, this Madame Vanireau, I thought, until I got to know her better. Monsieur Vincent liked her though. I don't know why. She got dressed up for him so he could paint her. Not too many people would do that for him. I don't know what happened to that painting of the lady with the white lace cap, Madame Vanireau. The lady who talked to sunflowers.

The Arlesians found him not only strange but gruff-looking, not at all someone they could approach. They called him the gruff and grubby man with paint on his shirt and pants. Always that *voyou* look, they would say. Just like a bum. Arlesians are stuck in their ways. They only like those who fit in, not those whose manners are considered odd and weird. As I already told you, they especially do not like artists who go wandering around and pry into people's lives just to paint their faces. Besides, an artist like Monsieur Vincent did not paint reasonable pictures like the masters did, they said. He put large daubs of paint on his canvases and did not do justice to those he painted. His paintings? Well, they just looked undone. That's it, not finished like the *barbouillage d'un enfant* , they said. Like a child's smearing. I thought his paintings were different from those in books, bright in color and they said something to me. They came alive. I liked the people's faces in some of his paintings, but I especially loved the flowers he painted like the sunflowers. That was really part of me and my Provence. I thought he captured us so marvelously well. Our hearts, our ways of being and doing things and particularly our lives, and the very being of our landscape, *la présence unique de notre paysage.*

Monsieur Vincent once told me that he looked at sunflowers pretty much as stained glass windows looked in a church where the light filters in and gives the faithful the feeling of intense sacredness. Colors filtered through light with a sacred touch unparalleled. Sacredness, *le sacré,* there's a another word for my notebook, I told myself.

"You know what sacred means, Camille?"

"No."

"Well, it means being closer to God, like one's soul being able to touch directly his presence."

"Sunflowers do that?" I asked.

"Yes, *mon petit ami,* they do that. At least for me. I almost feel like bending down before them and uttering a prayer before painting them. You know, I always ask their permission to paint them and they never refuse me."

"You pray?"

"Yes, with the heart and through my eyes. *La prière n'est pas une parole, mais plutôt un geste tréfonds.*" It's not words but a gesture out of the depth of the heart.

I learned so much from him and about him.

He did many paintings using yellow as a primary color. Take the sunflower paintings. Oh, I love them all. They say something to me. The language of sunflowers. Something special because they are so Provençal in character and essence. They always did. As Monsieur Vincent said to me a long time ago about the sacredness of the sunflowers, sunflowers are the Creator's presence among us. I also stand in awe of them. I marvel at them. I cherish them deep down in my very being of recognizing what is sacred and profoundly touching. If sunflowers were all green or blue or even purple, for instance, they wouldn't be the same. But God made them yellow, insisted Monsieur Vincent. Yellow because it's his color. God's favorite. Oh, sure he created all of the other colors, but the yellow is his. Artists try to reproduce yellow and the other colors by mixing paint and coming up with shades of various colors, but yellow has to be pure, bright, unmixed to be God's color, he said. And great big daubs of it like the sun itself. That's why Monsieur Vincent loved to paint a huge yellow sun made of big thick un-stretched daubs of paint. Why? Texture. You must feel the texture of a painting, he said. A painting is not a photograph, flat, even, like a reproduction. No, a painting is a work of artistry in color and texture. You must feel it with all of your senses. Some artists do not want the viewers to touch their painting once they're done. I say, go ahead and touch them, feel them with your nose, eyes, ears, and sense of touch. FEEL them! he would emphasize with his eyes and in his voice. At first, I did not dare do it, but later I learned how to take in Monsieur Vincent's painting with my senses. You do it gently, lovingly, sensually, without too much intellectualization. That's how you connect with the artist and his work. *Le contact et la participation des sens.* How the artist makes you see things, sense things, is the real measure of his art, he would say. Really see things. Of course, you have to let the paintings dry first. Sometimes, he said things so fast and with such passion that I had a hard time to follow him and write things down.

Then I would plead with him to slow down and repeat things and he would smile at me and say, "You know what I mean. You've already soaked in the important things of what I've said."

I had. In reality, I truly had. When I got home to redo my notes I could so easily remember things and even add things as if they were there fresh in my mind. I learned to take better notes and try not to write everything down word for word. Only the important ideas and meaningful words, and yes, new words. I learned how to listen and at the same time see what he was doing. Oh, Monsieur Vincent was a master teacher. If only people in Arles had listened to him and really seen what he did rather than measure the man and artist as *un voyou*. I know he didn't dress well and he looked shabby most of the time, but he didn't care what people called him or thought of him. He did try to conform to their likings at first but it didn't work. He just could not play games with his true feelings. He could not put on a mask of respectability as they wanted him to. All he wanted to do was paint. And did he paint, day and night sometimes. There are things at night that one needs to paint, he would say. How can one paint the stars during the daytime? How can one feel the lushness of nighttime when the sun is out? How about *la nuit étoilée et sa splendeur*, he would ask. Yes, starry night in its glory. Besides, there's a quietness at night when you can feel the hushed softness in your bones and at the same time smell the tangy stillness of the night. Nighttime has a movement at its very core and it's reflected not only in the myriads of stars but in the very essence of the whirling planet that is earth. Creation never stands still, he insisted. When I told my brother, Armand, about that, he simply replied that I was listening to the silly rambling of a dreamer and, besides, I had my nose in books too much. I should be out there playing with the other kids in the street. I needed to get my head screwed on right, he said. What did he know about being an artist and about the real world of writing? All he cared about was girls and nice clothes. He also teased me about flowers. If I played around with gardens and flowers too much I would become a sissy, not a real man. Real men didn't go around following a painter of flowers smelling them and wasting their time with such unmanly stuff, he told me.

"Monsieur Rolvaux plays with flowers," I responded. "He even owns a flower shop."

"But that's his trade. He has to earn a living."

"I don't care, I love flowers and I'll follow Monsieur Vincent when I want to," I told him flatly.

What did he know about flowers anyway? Armand was learning to be a blacksmith, not a flower man. I don't even know if he liked them.

Monsieur Vincent painted all kinds of flowers. He loved flowers and he loved walking through the fields to find them. He also loved gardens where they grew. He often asked permission of the gardener to go in and admire the flowers. The gardener was pleased that someone admired his garden and he would show the garden himself to Monsieur Vincent. Of course, I would follow him. He painted roses, irises, oleander, lavender, poppies, but his very favorite was the sunflower. Why? Because it was the flower of Provence in all of its yellow glory. And there were some huge ones as big as my head. Did you ever see an entire field of sunflowers? It's like a field of wheat, all yellow, except they stand up with their heads inclined so heavy and so full of sunlight. It's an ocean of color in the bright hot sun *de notre pays*. Only in our countryside can we find such hot colors. Not in the north, Monsieur Vincent would say. The shades of yellow dazzle your eye. They simply get into them like liquid sunshine being poured right out from the fiery furnace of the sun. If you stand too long gazing at the hot fields you can get dizzy and your head will begin to feel heavy. Then you start feeling drowsy and your eyelids close slowly without your wanting to. That's when you get to be in a warm daze while your whole body feels the effect of the sun slowly oozing up and down your blood vessels. And when the cicadas are in full swing, then your head wants to spin round and round so loud is the buzzing that surrounds you. Like the buzzing out of a nightmare. When Monsieur Vincent first heard this sound he wanted to shut everything down, his eyes, his ears, his mouth, his nose and his entire body. He said that his head was spinning and spinning and spinning like a giant top. I laughed and told him wait until you hear the sound of the mistral. With time, he grew accustomed to both and even drew several cicadas. Huge ones. He loved the cicada. It was part of us where we lived and where we called *notre Provence*. His heart was still up north but his soul was down south. That's where his art was transformed. *Par l'envoûtement de la Provence à travers la clarté du jour et la sérénité de la nuit*, the spell of Provence through the light of day and the serenity of night. He said very often he felt that this luminosity, so unique and so very necessary for colors to be painted creatively bright, was indeed a gift to the artist. I just listened to him and my heart was glad. I was glad I was part of his world of colors and brightness. After all, I lived here in Provence. I was born here. A gift indeed.

Monsieur Vincent did not speak too often about the other painters with whom he had associated in Paris, the Impressionists. He did not like the word Impressionist. He did not like their style of painting nor the lack of genuine luster and vibrancy in their paintings. The light seemed somewhat subdued, not bright enough for him. He did not want to be called an Impressionist either. Besides, the way they all painted was not what he wanted. Not his way. He wanted more. Where would he find it? He did like some of them. Claude Monet for instance. No, he didn't like the man, only some of his paintings. He didn't like him because he was a fat pompous ass, he said. He pontificated too much. He talked about light but his paintings lacked true light, brilliant light. Maybe someday he would find it. He did like Camille Pissarro because he was a man of the people and of simple things. He wasn't at all puffed up. He helped other painters and people seem to gravitate toward him. The Old Man, they called him. Manet, well he was a dandy, a man of Paris. A city person. He produced some excellent paintings, though, according to Monsieur Vincent. As for Gustave Caillebotte, he had met him only once. This man had talent and showed promise, he said. He truly liked his painting, <u>Les Raboteurs de Parquet</u>. It had the richness of art and the simplicity of a workman's task. The Salon of 1876 rejected his depiction of laborers preparing a wooden floor. Vulgar, they said. Monsieur just could not understand critics. And, the idea of a salon was simply elitist, he said. Snobbish intellectuals in their misappreciation of art, *foutus dans leur méconnaissance d'art*, that's what they were, he said.

Renoir was a good decorator, he thought. Monsieur Vincent did like the misty luminosity in his paintings, *cette luminosité brumeuse,* he called it, and he admired his treatment of young girls with their rosy cheeks, reddish hair and round figures, but this was not for him. As for the others, well, he just had not wanted to hang around with them in Paris. He did not like the Lapin Agile crowd, he called it. Sitting around and jabbering away about art. He did not want to idly discuss art, he wanted to be serious about it, he said. He wanted to form a fraternity of artists where they would join forces and really be innovative. They all seemed to think he was out of his mind with this fraternity. They, the Impressionists, wanted to be independent. Free from all dependence on others especially the classical ones. Those who wanted to draw and return to the past. Paris and its Salons. Salons for the elite and their selected artists of the *grands boulevards,* Monsieur Vincent would say. Paris was too old fashioned for him. Too much clinging to the old rules of the past. If you wanted to succeed in Paris you had to play the game, the game of being recognized and being part of the chosen ones, the established order. He had not wanted any part of it. That's why he decided to leave and find his own way, his own rules, and they certainly would not be rules of a political and social game, he insisted, but rules of painting and light. LIGHT !

Two painters he greatly admired were Delacroix and Millet. At times, he could not stop talking about them and the way they painted. As for Delacroix, well, he had found the brilliance of light in Africa. Deep down south across the Mediterranean where the sun has a very special radiance on things. One characteristic among many he liked of Delacroix was his vigor in the choice of colors. Sure, he was called a romantic for his choice of subject matter and his style of painting and simply because he had put feeling into his art, but Monsieur Vincent did not like tags on people. He didn't like schools or categories of painters such as the Barbizon School in which Millet was classified or the group called realists such as the tag they put on Courbet. A tag. Simply a tag in order to neatly categorize artists. He would have none of that. Not Vincent Van Gogh, the very different artist from Holland who recognized great art. Genuine art and unique talent.

Take some of the Delacroix's paintings and the use of vermilion. Ah! What a red. How the artist cleverly used this color to enrich his paintings: <u>The Combat of the Giaour and the Pasha</u>, the red slipper of the *giaour* and the red baggy pants (I didn't know what they were called)of the pasha matching the other red touches; <u>The Moroccan Caid Visiting His Tribe</u>, the red pouch and strings against the white of the Caid's kaftan(I think this is what it's called)and the red bonnet of the goatherd, what delights; <u>The Women of Algiers</u>, the deeply rich wine-colored inner of the slipper just lying there to attract our attention before we look up at the women. Delacroix! Delacroix! Monsieur Vincent would exclaim, how I would have loved to be in your fraternity of colors! The African sun, what a spellbinder for an artist.

As for Millet's work take <u>The Gleaners</u> and <u>The Shepherdess and her Sheep</u> as examples of the harshness and even the wretchedness of rural life. But the serenity of forms and colors lead us to believe that the artist was portraying a way of life he gently admired. Simple life, simple people, people of the earth. That's what Monsieur Vincent admired. *Pays-ans*, people of the land. Moreover, Millet's <u>Spring </u>and <u>Starry Night</u> truly inspired Monsieur Vincent. The rainbow and the eerie light that covers the landscape in one matches the starry light in the sky of the other that Monsieur Vincent so loved. In another painting, the artist plays with light, a burst of bright light at nighttime as if an apparition in <u>Les Dénicheurs d'oiseaux</u>, the spoilers of birds's nests. Monsieur Vincent called the torch light in the darkness of night when *de-nesters* come to seize the unsuspecting birds the, "hellish light." Yes, Millet's touch is magic and he is a giant among artists that Monsieur Vincent really loved. Light and color capture the very essence of painting if well harmonized and rendered with exuberance and fidelity, according to Monsieur Vincent. Then style comes in. I asked Monsieur Vincent once if he had a style of his own. He told me that he did not think so but that he had a way of knowing if he was on the right track when he set his brush to canvas. He didn't think about it, he didn't mull over it at length. He simply applied himself to his art that was set in motion by what he considered to be his inspiration and his craft. He simply knew. He knew what he saw before his eye and what he put down on canvas was what he wanted to paint. Rich, big fat daubs of color, bigger and thicker at times and that was what he called his style, if he had one. True colors, pure colors, undiluted colors were best for him. Sure, he had to blend in some tones at times and even stretch the vibrancy of paint on canvas, but he never failed his eye as an artist. That was his fidelity to color. Style, what is style? he asked. It's but a way of categorizing an artist or a craftsman. I don't want any of that, he insisted. Give me light and color. COLOR ! COLOR ! COLOR !

5

Sunflowers and Cicadas

$\mathcal{A}$s I have said, the color yellow was a favorite of Monsieur Vincent. He reveled in it. He said it was the color of the sun. That's why he loved sunflowers and painted so many of them. It was a bright color, a welcoming color, an exuberant color, a color of life itself, a color of love, and a color that brought you happiness. Monsieur Vincent had so very little happiness in his life. The only happiness he had was in his painting. He found it in nature, of course, but it was in painting nature in its pure light and its vigorousness of colors that he found himself happy. And he wanted so much to share that with other painters that he was willing to give everything he owned, everything he felt and loved, absolutely everything so that he could share his passion with other painters like himself who had the same vision of things. He did have his brother, Monsieur Théo, with whom he shared all of his ideas and feelings, and that was a marvelous thing for him. Every letter that Monsieur Théo sent was instantly opened and read several times. He even kissed some of them when his heart ached for companionship and a sharing of the things he so ardently believed in. Of course, he also liked the francs that his brother sent him. That was survival money for Monsieur Vincent. How could he paint without canvas and tubes of color? Monsieur Théo furnished him with letters of tenderness and encouragement as well as a genuine brotherly understanding while allowing him to paint by providing him with money and the possibility of selling some of his paintings, which did not happen very often.

Provence provided him with subject matter, light and the opportunity to wander around and even meet some people like Madame Ginoux, La Mousmé, Patience Escalier and the gypsies of Saintes-Maries-de-la-mer. I provided him with companionship. I wasn't always able to console him and help him the way he needed to be helped, but I did my best to be there. That's what he wanted and expected of me. I was like his puppy, the faithful dog at his side neither judging him nor asking too much of him except to be himself. I was the puppy with the dry paws. I was a Roulin, part of the family he kind of adopted. The only family he had away from his own. My father liked him, my mother liked him and I loved him. Even my baby sister, Marcelle, loved him in her own child's way. My brother Armand, well, he was of a different kind. He did not dislike Monsieur Vincent, but he wasn't close to him. He wouldn't allow himself to be. Armand liked what he liked, mostly girls. Monsieur Vincent liked to paint all of us Roulins . We were willing models for him. Many people in town didn't want to sit for him. They didn't have the patience nor the loving kindness for Monsieur Vincent. They simply shrugged him off like an old shoe. Besides, they were afraid of him as an artist. They lived with the superstition that many an Arlesian believed in, that having your likeness taken would attract the evil eye. Superstitious people they are. I know that he wasn't always likeable, but you had to understand him. He had his good side and his not so good side. His sickness sometimes got the best of him. It was a mysterious malady that no one understood, not even he could fathom it. It's a good thing Doctor Rey was able to take care of Monsieur Vincent and try to help him when he ended up at the hospital in late December of the first year he was in Arles. Monsieur Vincent really liked Doctor Rey. His mother did not like Monsieur Vincent. She couldn't even smell him. She hated his paintings. She even took the painting he did of her son, Doctor Rey, and stuck it in her attic. Can you imagine that? I think she wanted to keep her son's likeness as a photograph, not a Van Gogh portrait. That's the measure of the lack of esteem that some people around here had for Monsieur Vincent the man and artist. I can't imagine how much people frowned on him and his art. Unbelievable. That's why I stayed away from many of them and either played with my own friends or followed Monsieur Vincent when he allowed me to do so. Even some of the children did not respect Monsieur Vincent. They laughed at him, ridiculed him and were even spiteful in their treatment of him. How could I call them friends even if I knew them from school. I didn't. Monsieur Vincent was my friend and I cherished that friendship, even if it meant that I lost the esteem of my so-called friends in the process. I did remain faithful to four of my real friends. That's because they never laughed at Monsieur Vincent.

My mother and my father understood my fondness for Monsieur Vincent. They even allowed me to be with him after hours sometimes. They knew where I was and with whom. They trusted Monsieur Vincent. They understood his need for companionship. Sometimes, Monsieur Vincent did not want me around, but that was alright. I knew he had to be by himself at times or be with someone else like that girl, Rachel, at the dance hall, or the arena, or the Night Café in the Place Lamartine. Or even the brothel at Bout d'Arles. I knew that such a place existed but I wasn't too clear about what it was about. Besides, my father told me repeatedly to stay clear of the brothel, and I did. Sometimes, Monsieur Vincent would tell me all about his night outings except the brothel. That he kept to himself. Why would I want to know about something I knew nothing about and cared even less? What I really cared about was Monsieur Vincent's paintings and his words. He used words like a man who goes to a well for water and drinks tall drafts to slake his thirst. He wrote letters and read a lot. Words were as important to him as colors. Well, almost as much. Words defined thoughts. Words explained things. Words communicated expressions of artistry. Words were tools just like tubes of color and paintbrushes. The colors of literature are words turned into stories and human exploits. It's about people and their way of being human. Sometimes, it's about our relationship with nature and higher powers, but it's always about the deep down expression of the human story. Human beings are at their very core storytellers. I learned that over the years of reading and writing. That's why I loved Monsieur Vincent and hung around him as much as I did. Monsieur was a storyteller with colors. After all, I wanted desperately to become a writer. He wasn't like Monsieur Zola or some other writer of course, but he appreciated them and could appreciate their works as an artist himself. Would that I could write like them and be published someday. Would I ever become famous like them, I wondered. It didn't matter as long as I could write to my heart's content and to my very own ability.

"You have God-given talent, Camille," he would keep repeating to me, "don't say you're stupid or you can't do it. Work at it. Everything takes work and especially determination. I've told you that many times. The Creator did not waste his time on you or me. He doesn't make junk. He made us and then he threw us out there in the universe to make something of what he endowed us with. Sometimes, we don't always use it right but we learn by our mistakes. There is no perfection on earth. I only wish I could avoid the mistakes and the anguish that they cause me and others, but I can't give up. I can't. There wouldn't be any paintings. And paintings are my salvation. Do you understand that, Camille?"

I didn't always understand everything but I understood enough to know what he was saying . Later on, I would get to understand much more about Monsieur Vincent and his very own spirituality and feelings toward life, and living. As an eleven year-old, I just could not fathom it then. There were many dimensions to Monsieur Vincent. He was like a rainbow or a star filled with energy and filled with light from within.

I have much more to tell you about Monsieur Vincent, but I need to tell you about some of the paintings I witnessed here in Arles that he painted. I was there and I was a silent witness to it. I say silent because when he painted I kept quiet so as not to disturb him. That was our informal understanding. I only talked when he talked to me. Only after he had finished his work or took a pause was I able to ask him questions. Sometimes on our way home, if we happened to be out there in the fields or in a garden somewhere, I was able to ask the questions I wanted to ask. While he painted I took notes, copious notes. I never ran out of words to express what I had swimming in my head. That's why I read many books and even dictionaries. Words. If I found a new word and really fell in love with it, why, I kept repeating and repeating it until I knew I had it, and it would be mine forever. Oh, the freshness of words, the great joy of discovering them and using them. They tinkle like crystal, they shimmer jewel-like, their smooth roundness of polished stones hop and skip on the tongue, and they sometimes suck juices from your mouth. I have learned that words can be tools of affection or tools of disaffection for describing anything. It depends of your disposition towards objectivity or subjectivity. I learned them, I stored them, I used them and I loved them. Even today. Just like the colors Monsieur Vincent used for his paintings. He learned every day about their qualities as colors, he stored their vibrancy in his mind and in his heart, he used them to shape coloration and he loved them as friends of his artistry. Words are like colors. They're tools of the trade of shaping beauty. I learned that over the years. It takes time to master both.

Monsieur Vincent liked to paint and draw almost anything, moths, birds's nests, dead fish, and old shoes, grass, even cicadas. I know they didn't have cicadas in Paris or up north in Holland, so they fascinated him although he couldn't stand their loud sounds when they were chirring en masse. It can be a god-awful sound for the ears if you're not used to it. I can't begin to describe it to you. Some call it a song but I call it an ear-sizzling sound. Cicadas are huge insects with large eyes wide apart. They have transparent wings with veins that look like little windows when you see them sitting on top of lavender, for instance.

You can see the lavender color right through them. It's really nice. Some boys collect them and put pins through their crackly bodies, but I wouldn't do that. It must hurt. I once saw Pignoulet do it. I just walked away. They're hard to catch too just like fireflies. Cicadas are very popular here in Provence as popular as La Fontaine's fable that we learn in school. It's called, *"La Cigale et la Fourmi."* It's about a cicada and an ant. The cicada has been idle all summer eating all of its food not storing any for later and then finds itself without food when the cold weather comes. The cicada begs the ant to please borrow some food, but the ant refuses telling it "you wanted to sing all summer long, well, now dance." I always like that fable. Monsieur Vincent and I used to recite parts of it while out there in the fields. I learned the fable by heart when I was seven. The teacher found that I had a good memory and I could learn things fast if I wanted to. Some things I didn't care to learn by heart like grammar rules.

Unlike the cicada in the story though, Monsieur Vincent was never idle. He was always finding things to paint like the cicada and the moth. Why, he used to stop whenever he saw a cicada sitting somewhere, especially on lavender, and ever so gently touch the back of it and the cicada wouldn't even move, Can you imagine that! Then he would let the cicada climb on his sleeve and stay there as if it were stuck. It just wouldn't move. Monsieur Vincent would stare at it for a long time until the cicada decided to fly away. It was just mind-boggling. I never understood Monsieur Vincent's ability to attract cicadas to himself. Was it because he loved animals, especially insects that they responded to him so obligingly? Then Monsieur Vincent would take his large pad and start drawing the cicada from various perspectives either from memory or from up close. Fine, realistic drawings. I learned not to be afraid of cicadas with Monsieur Vincent. They're the jewels of Provence, I learned.

"Look at them with the sunlight on their transparent wings," he would say. "Veritable jewels. I like to compare them to the humming-birds, *les colibris, ces petits joyaux,*" he said. "Have you ever seen one, Camille?"

"No, never, but I'd like to," I replied. Hmm, *colibri*, a new word. "I'll have to find it in a book of birds. I think I'll go to the library to-morrow," I muttered.

Now, let me begin by describing as best I can the sunflower paintings of Monsieur Vincent as I saw them develop. First, he would prop himself before some sunflowers, adjust his hat if he had one on, he needed one by noontime, he would get his palette ready by vigorously oozing paint from the tubes onto it in the proper spot and then select his brushes. He would take one, look intently at his subject before scooping up some paint fresh from the tube onto his palette without mixing it with other colors. He very seldom mixed colors. If and when he needed to mix colors, he would deftly do it without too much hesitancy and with the full knowledge of what he was doing. He had such a canny ability of knowing just how to mix and how not to mix. And he told me that, at times, he had to do it fast because the light would change on him. He so wanted to capture just the right light, the right vibrancy of color onto his canvas.

"That's why I paint outdoors, *mon jeune ami*, to capture the genuine light of day. Even the light of day changes from hour to hour sometimes from minute to minute because the sun moves, you know. If the clouds get in the way, well wait until they move or else come back another day. I can't change the light or its motion. I can only try to capture it when it grants me its full range."

"Do you depend that much on light?"

"What do you think?"

"I guess so," I would mumble.

"You guess so? I know so."

Then he would plunge in a total immersion of self into his painting. I would then back away a little and look at what he was doing without even a whisper on my part. I didn't even dare to write too loud in my notebook fearing I would disturb his concentration. Pencils can have scratchy sounds on paper if they're not sharpened enough or have reached a stage where the lead is almost gone and you have to write with a scratchy piece of wood. That's why I carried three or four of them with me. Mother would often scold me for taking so many pencils from the sideboard drawer. "My tools," I would tell her running off making sure I would not miss Monsieur Vincent.

The first one I'll describe to you from memory, and it's deep inside my mind's remembrances, it's the **Three Sunflowers in a Vase**. I know he painted others, three with fourteen and, later on, some more, but I really like this one. I like it because it's simple in its presentation while at the same time filled with the very presence of the sunflower. They're three big sunflowers with two of them huge. I like the one in front. The one that looks like a huge yellow pompom. The one on top looks like an ordinary sunflower with its petals and seed core. The other to the left has a very big seed core with petals that look like disheveled hair. What draws my attention are the six short lighter yellow brush strokes on the bottom that heighten the texture and, at the same time, invigorates the colors. Oh, Monsieur Vincent knew his colors, especially the ones that were faithful to the exact shades and tones. Orangey and deep yellow with lighter yellows. But, the one I really love, as I told you, is the very large ball of a sunflower that just sits there being fat and round. There are so many different kinds of sunflowers. They're all wonderful and show the splendor of creation, as Monsieur Vincent used to say. "Just look at one flower, any flower," he told me, "and dissect it with your eye, you'll see not only the marvelous richness of texture but also the luxuriance of color. That's just with the eye. Then there's the perfume for the nose, for those flowers that have a perfume to smell. But, the sunflower, yes, the queen of all flowers, *le joyau du vitrail des champs*, the jewel of the stained glass window of the fields, that's the pride of Provence and the one that's an honor for me to paint. Yes, an honor because I bow down and venerate it. It is so magnificent and sacred to me like any icon that merits veneration," he would say with his eyes riveted to mine.

This particular sunflower is painted in rich yellows with touches of red. I especially like the big red blotch on the right of the seed core. It's a small seed core for this sunflower. It's different from the other two. Of course, I need to mention the big floppy leaves placed just right to accentuate the three sunflowers. They're made of different greens so as to heighten the effect of the light they catch. And the vase, yes, the vase, bright green on top with lighter shades at the bottom as if to either reflect light or water, but it has just the right effect on the eye. My eye, at least. The bluish-green tones of the background and the earth colors of the table on which sits the vase of sunflowers are perfect complements to the yellows, browns, orange and red of the flowers, I think. In my somewhat awkward way of dissecting the parts of this painting, I realize that I'm certainly no expert on Monsieur Vincent's art, but I try as best I can to bring the life I saw in the artistry of my friend to whoever will read these descriptions taken from my many notes. *J'y resterai toujours fidèle*, I will always be faithful to it.

The second painting I want to talk about is **Harvest at La Crau, with Montmajour in the Background**. It was painted in June, four months after Monsieur Vincent arrived in Arles. I know I'm skipping some months here but I'll get back to the sequence of months later. After all, this is not strictly an historical account but basically an esthetic aperçu of Vincent's life in Arles. I so enjoyed this painting that I wanted to put it in the context of the bright yellows such as the sunflowers.

I remember well. It was a very nice, warm, sunny day and I had brought a lunch in small basket my mother had packed with enough food for myself and Monsieur Vincent. My mother had told me to bring some for him. Monsieur Vincent didn't eat very much. He drank a lot of coffee and smoked a lot of cigarettes. I was glad to spend the day with him at La Crau. School was out and I wanted to be outdoors. We started early in the morning a little after the sun was up and we walked a fast pace and sometimes my legs would get tired. It was only a few kilometers away from the center of Arles, but it got very warm as we walked and the morning progressed. We stopped now and then but Monsieur Vincent urged me on because he did not want to miss any moment of the pure light of day, he said. My father had remarked that morning before he left to sort mail that he thought the walk to La Crau was a bit much for me, and that I should probably think it over.

"Remember the heat of June, *la chaleur*, Camille," he said.

However, he did not prevent me from going. He trusted Monsieur Vincent to take care of me. I was so glad. Besides, I was energetic and fearless and I could walk in the sun if I wanted to. I know I wasn't a big boy then and sometimes some of my friends would laugh at me and my flat arm muscles, but what I lacked in muscular prowess I gained in determination. Just like Monsieur Vincent.

"Just be careful," were my mother's last words to me as I left the house.

La Crau is a vast plain where they grow wheat and other crops. Some farmers live there and the neighbors are few and far between. They live there because there's a lot of land, huge fields that are golden when the harvest time comes. As far as the eye can see. It's the yellowish golden color that Monsieur Vincent liked so much. It's the color of the sun come to life and giving life through the growing of wheat, he said. We were lucky that the mistral was not blowing too strong that day. Sometimes, it was so strong that Monsieur Vincent could not keep his easel up and the wind would blow away his straw hat. When that happened, he would just pack up and leave the area to come back another day. Or else, he would clamp down his easel and buttress it against the wind, he told me. The wind and the mosquitoes. What a curse on a painter who wants to paint in the stillness of the day. Then, there was the shrilling sound of the cicadas. What a sound that was. Enough to drive one mad when he's trying to concentrate.

When we reached the spot where Monsieur Vincent wanted to paint, he unloaded his backpack, his easel and his canvas as well as his paints. He carried all of it in such a way that he managed quite well. The porcupine, he called himself. I sat quietly in the soft grass next to him, not too close to hamper his movements and not too far so as to be able to witness what he was doing. That was my calling in Arles, to be a witness to Monsieur Vincent the artist, not just an onlooker. I put the little basket of food behind me and took out *mon carnet*, my faithful notebook. That was my real food. I nourished myself by partaking of the inspiration from my friend who could transfigure what he saw before him into the brilliant array of colors on his canvas and make it appear as a miniature of the natural scene he was painting. A whole vast scenery onto one piece of canvas. And he worked fast too. He didn't want to lose any of the light that guided his every brush stroke. He looked at the wheat field as the farmers were harvesting and he dipped vigorously his paintbrushes into his paints and applied them as the artistic instinct guided him. He did it with the gusto of a Marseillais relishing every deep spoonful of his bouillabaisse. What a wonder to see the colors unfolding onto a scene right before your very eyes! And he knew exactly what color to use and when. How thick the daub needed to be or how thin the color needed to slide on his canvas. Monsieur Vincent relished texture by applying layer upon layers of paint just enough to make it look luxuriantly dazzling.

He could turn an ordinary vase of flowers into a bright and shining glass container with highlights of gold and shimmering yellows. I saw him do it. And the flowers, well, I've already talked about the sunflowers and how he transformed them into lasting blossoms that will never die. He liked color so much that he set out to paint every flower he met in whatever garden or whatever field. He especially loved entire fields of them, gardens filled with almost every Provençal blossom. Reds, whites, pinks, yellows, purples, lavender, orange, iridescent colors, silken colors, petals upon petals of color and the bearded irises that he so loved, he painted. He told me that he wasn't a photographer. He didn't want the exactitude of photography. What he wanted was color, splashes of color, and mounds of color, a dizzying of colors.

"J'ai le vertige de la couleur," he would tell me. Color vertigo! "That's what I paint."

Once he saw exactly what he wanted in a painting, he went right to work. It didn't matter to him if he were comfortable or not sitting on his little folding stool. He painted until it was time to pause and then start over again. In his short pauses, he would glance at me and I would smile in approval. He didn't need it but it made his eyes sparkle a bit. He had greenish-blue eyes, beautiful eyes I thought. It's funny but they would change color when his mood would change. Just like the sky changes when a storm is in the offing. When he was moody, I would just back away and return to see him later when his mood had changed. He never growled or scolded me. I never saw him angry. He simply looked sad. He would stop talking and his face would change to one of darkness, the opposite of what he so loved, light. I always wondered what went on his mind when these sad moments took hold of him. As soon as he went back to his painting, his eyes would take on the intensity of their former glow and the somber veil would disappear from his eyes. He was back into the light again. Strange. Some people would not even come close to him. They were afraid of him. They thought he just did not act like one of them. More like a foreigner or a person with a grievous mental illness. Some even crossed the street when they saw him coming, like Madame Gravel. He tried so hard to fit in but they would not let him. After a while, he simply went his way and tried not to think about it, but I know it bothered him. *Dieu merci de sa peinture!* Thank God for his painting or else he would have gone mad. He was never mad. What happened to him later on was not madness. He was sick. When people think you're mad and they behave as if you're mad, well, then you begin to feel as if you're mad. *"Fada!"* They would say. That's off your rocker in our language. No, Monsieur Vincent was not *fada.* He was different from the others and he hurt inside. Deep hurt. I got to realize that later on.

Sitting there at La Crau and painting the harvesters at work, I could see Monsieur Vincent was enjoying every minute of it. You see, we have an early and late harvest here in Provence. This was an early one. He painted sections after sections and then he would look at them and pursue yet another section until the painting started to come alive with the fields and the people working in it. He knew what the lower front of the painting would look like, he told me in one of his pauses, and he started to delineate more and more the mountain behind the view and

Montmajour, the ruins to the left. Montmajour was a very old Benedic-
tine abbey, he said. Then he started to explain to me who the
Benedictines were and their monastic rule. He thought of himself being
a monk sometimes, not a Christian monk but a Japanese one. One day,
he would follow a strict life style like that of a monk and live in the fraternity of other painters who sacrifice human comforts for their art, he
said. That's how much he loved his art, loved it enough to sacrifice all
to it. Yes, he was a good teacher, Monsieur Vincent, a very good one
and I learned more from him than any of my teachers. All they did was
to scold pupils and rap their knuckles or beat their behind with the punishment stick. Discipline, they called it. How can you learn when
you're perpetually afraid that someone will hit you if you don't have a
right answer?

Well, Montmajour was built many years ago. I read that it was built
between the 10th and the 13th century on what was then an island. You
had to take a boat to reach the island from the Arles area. Prior to that,
the island had served as a sanctuary for local residents during the inva-
sions of the Saracens and the Normans. It's really an ancient area in our
parts here in Provence. Montmajour became a very important pilgrim-
age site during the Middle Ages. So, it's recognized as an important
site for us too and for people who are interested in such things. Besides,
its ruins remain a testimony of our heritage as Provençaux. The people
of Arles love as if by instinct, Montmajour. They're very proud of these
ruins because they're the vestiges of a grand monastery and a well-
known past. The people have a kind of deep respect and even love for
this giant of the 14th century. Furthermore, legend affirms that Saint
Trophimus used to come here to seek rest from the labors of his aposto-
late during the fifth century. He's the patron saint of the church in
Arles. I only went there once to peek inside and see what it was like
since the members of my family were not practicing Catholics. We
were republicans after all. That's what my father said. One significant
piece of history is that in 1348 the Black Plague decimated half of the
population of Provence. Can you imagine half of the population. I'm
glad I did not live in the Middle Ages especially during the Dark Ages
when there was no writing and no fine arts. Very, very little human esthetic communication. No Van Goghs to brighten the lives of people.
Imagine. Yes, Montmajour played an important role in our lives here in
Arles. And it's Prosper Mérimée, inspector of ancient monuments,
who, in 1840, put the Abbey on the first list of French historical

monuments to be preserved. So, Monsieur Vincent knew about the importance of Montmajour as a backdrop for his painting of the harvest at La Crau. He had a special affinity for the cloistered life and its monastic intent. He said that he favored such a life filled with the meditative and soul-reaching dimensions. He found in this way of living an artistic and creative venue that favored the expression of the transcendental because, he said, all of us need to reach out to the stars and deep within the cosmos in order to find our true selves as human beings in touch with the supreme presence that is there but ever silent in our lives. That's what he told me. I did not quite take in everything he told me then, but years later it did sink in. That's the impact of his words and ideas on me. Besides, he enjoyed so much the vista that stood before him in all of its majesty and serenity. That, he told me later, was the inexpressible testimony of the presence of the Creator. And the colors. Yes, the colors that shone bright and splendidly bursting with light. That was the amazing voice of *la nature vivante*, living nature, in its abundance of life and light.

Now for the painting itself and what I remember about it on the day that Monsieur Vincent painted it. I remember that he was happy and even smiling when he sat down to paint once he had set himself ready for the task of putting on canvas the scene before him. How can one capture such a scene was my first question to him before he actually started to put paint on his canvas.

"Well, I first get it in my mind's eye firmly and solidly as an artist can and from there I envision the colors that will go in what some people call the geometric design, that is the drawing that most artists make either on the canvas itself or in their mind. That's the shell of the painting. The contours and the guide that allow one to paint scenery. You see, I can't capture all and everything at once just like that. You need a direction and a compass of light and colors. That's what counts. *Des taches de couleurs qui viennent animer le circuit de la peinture,* blots of paint that animate the channels of the painting. I can paint without lines and contours but without color and light nothing would be possible for me as an artist. At least, nothing important to the eye. Perspective done through color with light as its imaging factor, that's the true means of putting on canvas what I see and feel deep inside. Do you understand?"

I simply muttered a low, "Yes," and then added "But what is perspective?"

"Perspective, my dear Camille, is, let me see how I could explain it to you. It's picturing objects or scenes in such a way as to show them as they appear to the eye. Perspective deals with depth and distance. How the artist makes the scene before him appear to be real at a distance in relation to the closer objects that he paints. Is that clear to you?"

"I think so."

"Well, you'll understand it better when I finish this painting. Now let me paint," he said.

I sat there mute as a humble field flower relishing every moment I was with him. I did not understand much of what he was explaining to me but I could sense it deep inside of me since I trusted what he was saying and I knew that, later on after I had grown up and all of his words had matured inside my head, I would get to know what he truly had said to me. Of course, by then I would have the remarkable strength and power of many of his paintings to help me understand. All would coalesce. But it would take years. So, I just took everything in like a child takes in all of the words of a story told to him by an adult and letting his imagination work at it until pictures are formed in his mind, and he realizes that words can be the magic instrument of letting loose pictures in the mind and in the heart. So, I let Monsieur Vincent's words sit there and stew like a fairy tale that brightens one's imaginings. After all, one never tires of fairy tales.

6

Plains, Bridges and Orchards

W ith what I learned from Monsieur Vincent, I am able to explain to you what I witnessed at La Crau. La Crau is a vast plain that was used traditionally for the winter pasturing of large flocks of sheep. The area was eventually transformed into olive groves, almond trees, vine-yards, and undulating grassland with some farms here and there. Monsieur Vincent's **The Harvest at La Crau** is a painting that sets the scenery in such a marvelous perspective that it feels real, as if one is contemplating the entire scene, but in miniature. The details are not photographic but many of them are there in bright color, especially when one looks at it from a certain distance. And that's the way one has to look at a painting. Not scrutinize it like a researcher who looks for the minutest of detail to see how it is painted. The beauty of paintings is in the effect on the eye of painted details. They are there but not mi-nutely so as in a photograph. The eye sees them through the prism of color and light. And it's the overall painting that makes it work if the artist is as good as Monsieur Vincent.

First of all, let me say that perspective in this painting is absolutely tremendous. Flawless in my estimation. You can see as far as the eye can see, so to speak. The view stretches out like in a vast panorama. How can one contemplate such a view so real and so without hin-drances in capturing the essence of the scene? It's because the artist has mastered perspective and he has given us the genuineness of scenery. As for the colors, well, we start with the golden yellows that gleam in the sunlight of midday. The captured freshness of harvest, the sharp hues of the plots of land as well as the texture of uncut wheat in the foreground with the stick fence and the highlights of reddish hues in the back along with the lemony tall grasses of the immediate foreground contrast ever so harmoniously with the rich color of wheat. I saw it all while I was there that day at La Crau and the way Monsieur Vincent captured it with his brush. All the rich colors and hues of that Provençal day, and I can revisit it anytime I want in his painting of that very spot. I was there! What Monsieur Vincent captured with his brush, I tried to do with my pad and pencil but words failed me then to accurately paint what I saw with my eyes. So, I just wrote down glimpses of what I saw like impressions of the scene before me so that, later on, I was able to reconstruct what I had seen and felt on that very day. Seeing is only half of what is important to the eye, Monsieur Vincent said, feeling is the other half. I can only begin to imagine what Monsieur Vincent felt then and there, but I can tell you what I felt. Joyous! There was a tingling in my heart, a joy of perceiving things through Monsieur Vincent's eyes and magical brush. Oh, how much I learned from Monsieur Vincent and I would tell my mother all about that day when I was sitting not too far from Monsieur Vincent and I was learning how to capture light and color the way he taught me. Sometimes, he would not say a single word. He didn't have to. I knew what he was saying with his brush. He let me follow him because I did not talk a lot and never pestered him with many questions. He knew and I knew the language of words not spoken.

For me, the highlights of this painting is the light green rectangular plot in the middle contrasting with the yellows of the other plots of land, the tiny cart being pulled by a white horse in the middle of the painting, and the blue cart standing there without a horse not far from the red wheels with shaft devoid of cart. Those red wheels simply tingle your eyes. We did see the wheels but they weren't that red. Monsieur Vincent made them that way, I suppose, to add a splendid contrast to the other colors. You see an artist can do things like that, just to add his touch of color that makes things just right.

The sky is of another color that contrasts and, at the same time, harmonizes with the other colors. The greenish blue enhances the tone of the painting. I think it sets off a balance with the mountain range that is seen on the horizon with the Montmajour ruins to the left marking a point of rock-bound stability and lasting heritage. Also, I simply like the Arlesian woman in the foreground with her white scarf standing there among the dark green shrubs. Her presence there makes the whole painting seem alive with the feminine touch, I think. I don't know what she was doing but harvest time is a busy time for the farmers. I sort of waved to her and she seemed to smile back at me, but I could not really see what she was doing. That's when Monsieur Vincent took a break from his painting. Besides, he was almost done; we had something to drink since it was getting hot and I was thirsty. When he had finished his painting, we went back home. I wasn't tired at all, I was too wound up to be tired.

Of course, I could not follow him all the time since I had to go to school and get my chores done. Mother sometimes excused me from them knowing full well that I so itched to be with Monsieur Vincent.

"Go ahead," she would tell me, "the chores can wait for you."

I thought she was so understanding, so kind in her way of seeing things. I knew that she liked Monsieur Vincent and trusted him for my other schooling, as she called it. I was learning colors, perspective, balance and harmony, the effect of one color on another color, and especially how to see things. Really see things from an artist's point of view. At the same time, I was honing my skills as a writer since, with the new words I learned every day, I was able to put them to use when I saw what I saw through the eyes of Monsieur Vincent. What a discovery one can make in adjusting the eye to simple objects that were never seen before with an artistic eye. The artist captures things that other people have not seen because of a failure to grasp the essence of things. That essence lies in capturing what the object is when imbued with the freshness of light. Without light we can see nothing. Without the creative impulse very little is seen the way an artist sees. Colors do not exist in the void of darkness. The intensity of light makes the object glow like Monsieur Vincent's yellows glow. That's why he paints like he does. He needs to capture the essence of things....in pure light!

Another painting that I like very much for its yellows and blues is **The Gleize Bridge over the Vigueirat Canal**. Now, I'm picking up the sequence of the months from the time Vincent arrived in February and painted the snow scenes, and when this painting was done in March. The Vigueirat Canal extends from the north at Pont-neuf through Arles down to the marshes at Fos next to the sea. It's a very long canal. The women of Arles like to wash in its waters because of it's cleanliness and proximity. It was mid-March when Monsieur Vincent decided to go over to the Gleize Bridge and paint the women washing their clothes on a bright Monday morning. I skipped school that day without my mother knowing it. I would take my tongue lashings from my father later on in the day. He had to do it because he was a father. I understood and I forgave him for it. Besides, I learned from the other kids in my class that Monsieur Tallant was especially boring that day.

The women have spread out their wash on top of the bushes to dry while they keep scrubbing at the water's edge. There is one woman standing on the bridge watching. What caught my eye while Monsieur

Vincent was painting was the red boat right next to the bridge separating one woman from the other three. That red color heightens the intensity of the yellows of the bridge and the beaten down grass as well as the blues of the sky and canal. When I looked at the small boat it did not appear to be as bright red as I saw it developing on Monsieur Vincent's canvas. Once again, he intensified the brightness of the red so as to give the whole painting a focal point that harmonized with the other reds in the painting. Furthermore, the red boat matches very well the red scarf worn by the lady on the bridge. And that large splash of white on the side of the bridge makes the entire bridge glow like morning gold.

The sky is cloudy with great puffy clouds of March starting at the horizon and mounting until we can see the ridge of the sparkling blue of the sky at the very top of the painting . When I looked up that morning, I could see much more blue in the sky above but Monsieur Vincent captured just enough of it to bring an intense blue light to his puffy clouds. And the blue of the canal is the reflection of the sky with undulating shimmers of light. The trees in the background reveal their skeletal branches of March barely budding with the spring leaves all enclosed in tiny brownish covered scales of buds at the very tips of each branch. Soon it would be spring. I loved spring since it announced the coming of summer when there was no school and I was entirely free to roam with my friend Monsieur Vincent. A little later, he painted the Langlois Bridge with women washing there too, but I wasn't able to be with him that day. I had to go to school. After all, I couldn't miss school too often. My father would have been really mad at me. I didn't want him to prevent me from following Monsieur Vincent. I had to be cautious in my desire to be out there and not in the classroom. Rules can be cruel at times. However, I was there when he painted the Langlois bridge again with the two cypresses on the left side. It was May and it was a Wednesday afternoon. He loved that drawbridge and the people and horse driven carts going over the bridge. He called it his view of the *petit monde*, the little people.

Monsieur Vincent had just moved his studio to new quarters on rue Lamartine where he found himself to be more at ease. Not so cramped, he told me. It was to be his yellow house since he had insisted on having the house painted yellow. He rented four rooms there. The house had a green door and green shutters for I remember those very well. There were red tiles on the floor (I'm sure Monsieur Vincent liked the color) and the rooms were bright and sunny. It was very cheerful there. All he had to start with was a mat, a mattress and a blanket. He couldn't afford a bed then. But, at least, he now had a bigger studio. The left wing of the building housed some type of grocery store. *Comestibles* was written on the sign. The Avenue Montmajour on the right side ran down to the two railway bridges. To the left of the house was a public park where we used to go quite often. He told me that he would soon fill the house with furniture and, most of all, he would get himself a good solid bed.

"When I get the money," he said.

However, that would take almost five months before he could do that and call the yellow house his home.

Monsieur Vincent loved orchards in the spring. Apricot trees, almond trees, peach trees, plum trees and pear trees all budding and sprouting puffs of white pinkish flowers that smelled so delicately fresh. It was nature's moods and phenomena that were reflected in the blossoming orchards. He knew that these blossoms would not last very long and so he applied himself with such a frenzy that, day after day, he would paint and paint and paint orchard blossoms. They were timeless in their beauty but transient in their ability to last. He so wanted to capture the timeless quality of light, and at the same time, he was aware of its transience as the day grew old. Even from hour to hour would the intensity of light change as it went through its movements. Yes, light could be fleeting so seize the light, he would say. Fortunately for him, the light in Provence was much more intense than up north and seemed to last much longer, he told me. I remember one morning in April when I had just gotten to know him and I was still very shy around him, he grabbed me by the hand and pulled me out into Mr. Panachaud's orchard, the one with all those plum trees.

"See these trees with puffs of pink blossoms, that's what I'm going to paint. Do you want to watch me?" he said.

I muttered some kind of a "*oui*."

All that month he painted orchards in blossom one after the other.

"I have to paint them before they all disappear on me," he said with a his eyes ablaze with determination.

He scared me, so intense was his gaze, but I got over it. And he so wanted to paint Monsieur Roumaine's orchard too, the one with the red roof of the distant factory (here's that touch of red again) before the blossoms fell. He also painted Madame Giera's orchard bordered with cypresses, Madame Aucassin's peach tree orchard with a stick fence separating her orchard with that of Monsieur Milogrand. Then there was *la fadade Titino'* s father's apricot orchard on the far side of town. He never seemed to stop. I couldn't follow him with all of his comings and goings.

The one I really like is the one he called the "white orchard." **The White Orchard** is a large painting filled with blossoms and the colors are just splendid. Not much white in this painting but that's the way Monsieur Vincent saw the blossoms, golden and pink. It's not the exact color that counts, he told me, but the way it appears in the light of day. That's what the artist's eye captures and that's what he paints. The painting is lavishly springtime looking. It feels as if spring is in the air so much are the colors filled with bright yet subdued light. Yellow and pink elongated clouds cover most of the sky with bright patches of greenish blue that open up here and there. The tone is subdued what with the mellowness of the green grass and the stark black and brown branches that shoot up like giant arms uplifted. At a distance even the trunks take on the color of the green grasses. To me, the colors of this painting are like the hushed dormant sound of early spring. Things are just starting in this orchard awaiting the dazzling whiteness of the blossoms in full bloom. Then the birds will sing, the cicadas will come out with a full panoply of chirring voices while the bees will hum all over the city and countryside joyful of the multitude of the fragrant blossoms with their tempting nectar. Spring! I love it.

7

Le Japonisme: A New Way of Seeing

With all of those paintings of orchards and his running around to capture as many blossoms as he could, I did not have as much contact with Monsieur Vincent as I would have liked because I just could not follow him everywhere he went. I realized that his frenzy stemmed from a pressing desire to paint like the Japanese artists did. Fast and furious, I suppose. Of course, I knew nothing of the Japanese except that Japan was a small country in the Far East. The teacher had shown us the map of Japan in one of his atlases but that's about all he showed us. He never talked about the people of Japan, their cultural traits and their art. I had no reason to get interested in the Far East. It just existed and it was very far away. But I'm sure the Japanese had orchards just like we had and their artists painted them with probably the same gusto that Monsieur Vincent did.

One Sunday afternoon in early May, Monsieur Vincent came over our house to share our Sunday luncheon, *tout en famille*, as we know it. Every family had a large luncheon on Sundays. Sometimes, relatives came and the afternoon was spent talking about family and all kinds of things while the men smoked and usually played *pétanque*, you know that game with metal balls with a small wooden target called the *cochonnet*, the little pig. In Provence, the name of the game comes from the words *pés tanqués* which means "feet stuck" because, in *pétanque,* your feet are often stuck together within the small circle where the game is played. That's how we say it here. I sometimes watched, but I didn't play. I much preferred reading, writing in my notebook, or listening to conversations if they proved to be interesting. That afternoon with Monsieur Vincent at our table enjoying a meal of bouillabaisse that my mother had prepared because my father so enjoyed it and since his cousin from Marseille had given him the necessary ingredients of the day's catch, I preferred to stay at table. Everyone was enjoying the glass of wine they were sipping when my father's friends came to get him for a game of *pétanque*. He was reluctant to leave the table since Monsieur Vincent was there but he told him to go and enjoy his Sunday afternoon. He wasn't going to be staying long after his glass of wine, he said. Well, my father left with my cousin Fanfo and there sat my mother, my cousin Ninoun Tauvan from Tarascon, my aunt Simonou from Fontvieille and my brother Armand, who excused himself to be with his girlfriend, my baby sister, Marcelle and me. My mother, my aunt and my cousin were talking about the mild weather we were having and the fact that the blossom petals in the orchards were fast dropping to the ground making way for the fruit, and how delicious all of those fruits were going to be. They talked about fruit pies, jams, marmalades and compotes. I was getting a little weary of the conversation when Monsieur Vincent interrupted the conversation and started to talk about his adventure with the fruit orchards in Arles, and how he compared them to some of the Japanese paintings he had so much admired while in Paris. My mother and my cousin became fascinated with what he had to say about the Japanese and their art since neither one of them had heard about nor seen Japanese art. Neither had I, for that matter. My aunt did not say anything, she just listened.

First of all, Monsieur Vincent began to explain to us that Japanese art and culture turned out to be some kind of a phenomenon in Paris. They called it *le Japonisme* . Everything that was Japanese was considered innovational as a model, especially the Japanese prints. Printmakers such as Hiroshige, Utamaro and Hokusai were considered to be the most important ones, and that's why Monsieur Vincent had purchased some of their prints while in Paris. All of Paris was in awe of these prints. There was a craze over them and the Parisian avant-garde became obsessed with this *nouveauté de l'Orient*, this Far East novelty. Monsieur Vincent not only recognized the artistic worth of these prints but he began to experiment with the Japanese technique of cropping and focusing. There is some kind of spatial illusion in Japanese art, he said. Sometimes, the horizon is altogether left out and the edges are cropped in unexpected ways. The composition of things are shifted around. Instead of having a large focus in the middle ground, we have enlarged motifs in the foreground. It's a very different way of seeing things.

"You see, my friends, that's the measure of innovative thinking and seeing things. Shifting the emphasis on things. The Western way of painting was revolutionized by this new view of things. Old reality was toppled by a new reality. A delicacy of light and a boldness of things replaced the Western way of capturing objects. Here was the new in a resplendent fashion. Oh, it wasn't new for the Japanese since they had been doing it this way for centuries. Its graphic art was particularly striking for its quality and charm. You know what struck me the most? It's the way the Japanese artist draws rapidly, extremely rapid, almost like lightning, because his nerves are finer and his feelings simpler. You see this is perfect harmonization of style and deep feelings. My friends, if you study Japanese art, you see an unarguably wise, philosophical and intelligent man who spends his time......on what? Studying the distance between the earth and the moon? No. Certainly not studying Bismarck's politics. He studies a single blade of grass. You see, isn't that almost a true religion that we are taught by the Japanese who are so simple and live in nature as if they themselves were flowers. Their art makes us return to nature, despite our education and our work in a world full of conventions," he said with such enthusiasm that my mother and cousin sat there with some glimpse of rapture on their faces.

Monsieur Vincent even copied Hiroshige's print of a sudden shower and called his version, **Bridge in the rain**. "He painted rain," I muttered to myself. I didn't want to interrupt him but when our cousin asked him to show it to her, I added that I also wanted to see it.

"Later," he said as he resumed his explanation of Japanese art.

While I was taking notes as swiftly as I could, I tried not to miss a single word of his conversation. I couldn't spell the Japanese names but I wrote down the sounds I heard thinking that, later, I would ask Monsieur Vincent to spell the names for me.

We all felt enraptured by Monsieur Vincent's explanation of Japanese art since none of us knew anything about it, not even my mother. He went on to say that this craze prompted some writers to join in the vogue of *le Japonisme* like Edmond de Goncourt with his novel, "Chérie" and Pierre Loti and his work, "Madame Chrysanthème." Loti's novel is about a Westerner whose brief stay in Japan to explore the exotic and foreign world around him leads him to a marriage of convenience with a young Japanese woman that he soon leaves behind.

"I really like Loti's novel that I'm now reading. Did you know that the chrysanthemum is the flower of death in Japanese culture?" he said

"I'd like to read this novel if I can," responded Ninoun.

"I'll pass it on to you when I get it done."

"Oh, I want to read it too," I exclaimed.

"You're too young to read such literature," admonished my mother.

"But there is nothing perverse in it, Madame Roulin," replied Monsieur Vincent, "it will open the eyes of young Camille to a new and exciting world."

"We'll see," she added.

Monsieur Vincent then started explaining to us how Arles compared to the subject matter and the style of Japanese art. First of all, there is the bright light that dominates Provence. Nowhere in the north does light ever come close to that of Provence. And the orchards in bloom, how Japanese-like are they, so much intensity of light and color, he told us.

"That's why some artists came to Provence to paint. To capture that intensity of light," he added. "Arles is like a Japanese dream," he stated.

"Really?" said my cousin. "I never figured that there was anything special about Arles. It's just a sleepy Provençal town like so many other towns in the Midi."

"Ah, but my dear Mademoiselle Tauvan, Arles and it's surroundings are enchanting by their light and natural beauty. You may not have taken the time to really observe these qualities. Go out there and really look. Look not only with your eyes but with the heart of an artist."

My cousin blushed just then as he was calling her to explore her own surroundings. I felt a twitch of pain for not having the time to fully get in touch with Arles and its natural surroundings because I had chores to do and my schooling that waited for me every day of the week except Sundays. I was then fully determined to follow Monsieur Vincent as much as I could come time or place. I would really work at it and make my mother understand that this was important to me and my aim in life. My mother would understand and, as for my father, well, he was seldom around and whatever my mother said he would go along with it. I would not disobey them but I would certainly take full advantage of the unusual opportunities opened to me by *Monsieur l'artiste*. The other people in town might not appreciate him but I did, and every single day with him I grew more and more impatient to be with him in his artistic adventures in Arles.

It was getting late in the afternoon and just then my father walked in. "What! You're still at the table eating?" he said.

"Oh, but we're listening to Monsieur Vincent elaborating on Japanese art, cousin."

"Japanese art! What does Japanese art have to do with us here in Arles?"

Each one of us smiled just then without saying a word.

"*Mon ami*," said Monsieur Vincent to my father, "I just got done explaining the reason why I'm here in Arles. Someday, I'll also explain it to you. Ask your son, Camille, he's been taking notes all afternoon."

"He's always taking down something in his notebooks, Camille. *Ce sera notre grand écrivain, un jour, ne penses-tu pas ma mouié?*" our very own great writer, a writer of Provencal tales.

"He has a lot of growing up to do before he reaches that level," replied my mother with a twinkle in her eye as she turned her head to look at me.

I don't know about tales, I told myself, but as for writing, yes, I certainly would exert myself to follow my talents, and I would profit from my time spent with Monsieur Vincent to gather materials for my future work that I would someday be very proud of. In the meantime, I had to continue taking notes as much as I could and whenever I could. If only I didn't have to go to school.

Before Monsieur Vincent left, my mother thanked him for informing her about Japanese art and the similarities between Arles and Japan.

"I've learned a lot this afternoon," she said. "Thank you."

Then my aunt joined in the conversation for the first time and said, " You know, Monsieur Vincent, I thought that you were off your rocker because so many people in Arles said so, but now I know they were wrong. I think you're very smart and you know a lot about art. I've enjoyed everything you told us about Japan. It was simply fascinating."

Monsieur Vincent seemed thrilled by my mother's and my aunt's remarks since very few people liked to listen to him talking about art. I was so pleased that my mother liked what he had said that afternoon. I didn't know my mother was interested in art. I really didn't.

It would be later in August that Monsieur Vincent set about to do my father's portrait, one of many. Then in September, the Second Lieutenant Milliet's portrait followed. In November-December came the portrait of Armand as well as my portrait with the blue cap, and many other portraits that I witnessed. That was later in 1888. The one I really liked was the one of my mother as *une berceuse*, rocking the cradle, in January of the following year.

8

Gypsies and Tales

We were approaching the end of the school year when Monsieur Vincent told me to ask my father if it would be alright to go with him to Les Saintes-Maries-de-la-Mer in the Camargue region. He wanted to paint there. That was the region of the gypsies, he said, but there would be nothing to be afraid of since he would be there to watch over me. He had been there before, he said. I had never been that far away from home before. It was going to be a true adventure.

At first my mother said, "No."

My father said, "We'll see."

I said, "We'll see, we'll see, that's all you ever say."

"Now don't start getting on your high horse, my young man. I said we'll see."

I went to my room and wrote in my notebook that we would see. Well, I suppose my father and my mother talked it over and they finally said I could go if I stayed close to Monsieur Vincent and listened to him. They had had a talk with Monsieur Vincent about it, a long talk, but I wasn't there. I must say they were a bit leery about it, especially my mother, because I could see it in my mother's eyes, but they let me go anyway. It would take several hours by horse-driven cart to go there, some 30 kilometers away. There was no train. The very first train, *le petit train de Carmague* that linked Arles and Saintes-Maries, came only in operation four years later in 1892. So, we got ready for the ride. Monsieur Vincent knew this gentleman, a Monsieur Brèzet, who would take us as far as Albaron and then a gypsy friend of Brèzet would take us to Saintes-Maries. Of course, we would need to stay at least two nights at this village on the Mediterranean because Monsieur Vincent wanted to spend time painting there. He would have to further explore the area. He had already informed my parents about it and I told him that I did not mind spending that amount of time with him. It would definitely be an adventure what with sleeping under the stars, eating outdoor, following Monsieur Vincent around and meeting all kinds of people. I couldn't wait.

My mother had packed my belongings that I was to take with me and a huge bundle of food in case we got hungry along the way, enough to sustain us through the two days and nights.

"Take care of yourselves and be careful about night fires," said my mother as we left.

Poor mother, how she worked hard for us and she grew tired fast since she was expecting my baby sister soon. Monsieur Vincent thanked her and off we went to meet Monsieur Brèzet who was waiting for us in front of l'Hôtel Voltaire. Monsieur Vincent had all of his paraphernalia with him on his back that he took off as soon as we got on the cart. I said hello to Monsieur Brèzet and Monsieur Vincent told the old gentleman how much he appreciated the ride to Albaron.

"Don't you worry both of you, we're going to have a nice time of it. My horse, Danizetou, knows the way. He's been with me for years. I'm going to deliver some cheese to my sister in Albaron. I make it myself. Would you like some?"

"We wouldn't want to deprive you of it, Monsieur Brèzet," said Monsieur Vincent.

"Oh, not at all. You'll enjoy it. It's goat cheese. The best. Here take some for your journey."

"Thank you, sir," I said. "It's my first trip outside of Arles."

"Well now, a novice sojourner. You'll like la Camargue. It's vast and the air fills your lungs with fresh and invigorating air that comes from the sea. And you'll find that the people in Saintes-Maries are warm and welcoming, *boni con pan,"* good as warm bread."

"Yes, I can attest to that," said Monsieur Vincent.

I was sitting next to him with my hands in my vest pockets checking to see that my notebook was still there. I had verified dozens of times to make sure that I had brought along my notebook so important was it to me and my destiny in life. An artist who paints needs his paints, his brushes and his canvases. I needed my pencils and my notebook. They were my lifeline to where I was sailing through life. Vast and colorfully important was to be my journey like my dreams. I just knew it had to be, especially with Monsieur Vincent at my side. I felt the warmth of his body next to mine and I was satisfied. Life was good, the sky was blue and the trip to Saintes-Maries was going to fill my head with all kinds of notes that I would transcribe into my notebook. As I said farewell to Arles, I could feel the warmth of the sun touching my face, and the smell of the lavender was ever so delicious to my nostrils.

Monsieur Brèzet kept singing songs of old Provence all the way to Albaron. He would occasionally stop to swallow some water from an old jug but then he would start up again. Monsieur Vincent kept quiet and still. I just listened.

"Un jour de sa santo escrituro, Es mountra au cèu sus lis auturo. Auprès de l'Enfant Jèsu, soun fiéu tant precious/A trouva la Vierge assetado. En meme tèms l'a saludado/Elo i'a di: Sigués tou bènvengu, nebout! Bello coupagno, a di soun enfant, qu'avès vous? Ai soufert sèt doulour asmaro/Que vous li voie counta aro," sang Brèzet in a full tenor voice.

He was signing the legendary song of the Virgin Mary and her seven sorrows so ingrained in the hearts of the people of Provence. It owed its renewed popularity to the renaissance of our dialect through the efforts of Frédéric Mistral and his Trésor du Félibrige, which is the treasure of the Provençal language and celebrated by the seven Félibres de Font Ségugne.

"One day from his sacred scriptures he rose to the very height of heaven next to the Child Jesus, her very precious son, he found the Virgin seated and right away he greeted her. Welcome, nephew said the Virgin. Beautiful companion, said her child, what's wrong with you? I suffered seven bitter sorrows that I desire to relate to you."

The song goes on and on but he kept repeating the same stanza. I had heard the song at some family gathering some time ago and I always remembered the sweet sonorous voice that had strung the lyrics together. It belonged to my aunt Isabelle, Babello, as she was called. Such a sweet lady, so generous with her time and talents. She died a widow at the age of 93. She was the oldest in my father's family. She was a dyed-in-the-wool Arlésienne. Her beauty was such when she was young that she had countless young men who pursued her in the hopes of winning her love. But, she loved only one man, my uncle, Andriéu, who was able to bring her to the altar of God in marriage. Some people said that aunt Babello had broken many hearts but her love was ever true and single-minded. It was said that one man, Bertranoun, had attempted to kill himself over his love for her, but that was only said in hushed tones, never in front of the children. I overheard it once when I happened to cross the room where my cousins were chatting. Isn't love strange, I told myself. I still think it is, even at 29 years old.

When we arrived at Alabron, we got out of the cart and we waited for Monsieur Brèzet's friend to pick us up.

"You may have to wait a while," said Brèzet, "because gypsies are not always on time. They could care less about time. He'll be here for sure. He's a trustworthy man and when he gives his word he keeps it."

Then he left. Monsieur Vincent looked around and saw that the sun would soon reach its summit in the sky, brilliantly hot, and it's warmth was beginning to sear our necks. We hurried to sit under a nearby tree waiting for the gypsy man. I swallowed a few gulps of tepid water and settled back leaning against the tree trunk. Monsieur Vincent looked at me and smiled. I smiled back at him. Just that, no words, no small talk. Just the understanding of smiles. Later, the gypsy man with his small green caravan, two large wheels in the back and two small ones in the front, arrived. His skin was tawny, his teeth glowing white and his hair and eyes were as dark as midnight. He greeted us and told us that his name was Nicolae. Monsieur Vincent greeted him back and introduced himself and me to him.

"So you're going to Saintes-Maries," he said.

"Yes, we're going there to relax and I to paint," replied Monsieur Vincent.

"You'll love the area. Too bad you did not come last month during our celebration of Sara-la-kâli."

"Who is that?" I asked.

"I'll tell you all about it on our way."

We soon found out that his horse was called Kalyi jag, "black fire", he told us as he prompted it to get going. I felt a bit like a gypsy myself, a wanderer, finding myself out of place and traveling the roads not knowing where we were going to spend the night or where we were going to eat. The caravan looked like the ones I had seen in one of my books. I had read that the *gitans,* as they were called, lived a nomadic life and wandered here and there since they really had no home base. They wandered all over the place seeking their fortune wherever they could find it. They were all somewhat devious and even treacherous at times. They were known to cheat and were agile thieves. That's what one of the books said. Their women were fortune tellers and loved gold coins. As for their children, well, they did not go to school; they learned everything they needed to know from their families. On that score, I envied them. The men wore earrings and they sometimes wore bandannas wrapped around their heads. You had to be very careful around them since they had knives hidden up their sleeves. All of the gypsies were dirty and never washed since they hated water. The

French were very leery about meeting up with gypsies and they stayed away from them as much as they could. All of that and much more had I read in the few books that I had picked up about gypsies. I liked to read those books since they were filled with all kinds of adventures such as, gypsies kidnapping children and bringing them up as their own, men filled with wanderlust and sailing ships to faraway places just like pirates, gypsy women weaving tales about ill luck circumstances and doomed love affairs, and gypsies wearing red strings around their wrists and gold medals of the Virgin around their necks to protect them against mysterious wolves and eerie ghosts. All of that was alright in a book but actually being with gypsies somewhat gave me goose bumps as I rode along with this *gitan* called, Nicolae. Good thing I had Monsieur Vincent close to me.

All of a sudden Nicolae burst out into song. I thought, do all drivers on this long road sing as did Brèzet, and now this gypsy man? I knew gypsies were good musicians, especially playing the violin, but I had never heard one sing. Nicolae's voice was mellow and delicious as the taste of sweet Mediterranean lemons when he began singing, *Gelem, Gelem lungone dromenca, Maladilem chorore romenca. Gerlem, Gelem lungone dromenca, Maladilem baxtale romenca.*

"I learned this romani song from my grandfather who was Romanian," he said. "It's an old folk song that tells about an unfortunate rom traveling long roads where he meets other roms and he calls them fortunate and full of luck, *baxtale*, for having traveled the lucky roads and set up tents with large families. Do you believe in luck, Monsieur painter?"

Monsieur Vincent looked at him and smiling with his deep set eyes, replied, "I believe that one makes his own luck. Our luck may be in the stars, but we need to decipher it through our own energy and discernment. That's why I paint, to probe the movement of the stars and touch the vast aura of infinity."

"That's very deep," said Nicolae. "Are you a mystic of some kind?"

"No, but I believe in some kind of mysticism linking us to transcendence. There is movement that originates from what Aristotle called 'the unmoved mover.' The great force of the universe."

"I don't know about that because I'm not an educated man like you, but I do believe in some mind of mystical energy out there that touches our lives, we call it *Del.*"

I was taking all of this in while not totally understanding what they were saying, but I was ever so impressed with Monsieur Vincent and the knowledge he had about things. Not only could he paint with great talent but he also knew things, things about the stars and great thinkers. I envied him and I wanted to learn so much from him, all of the things he knew because I would have to learn as much if not more in order to become a great writer like our own Monsieur Mistral and Messieurs Zola and Daudet whose works Monsieur Vincent had read. He read all of the time. He had books all over his house. He and my father would often discuss the books that they both read. Oftentimes, my father was way behind Monsieur Vincent in reading. What an amazing mind he had that Monsieur Vincent.

As promised, Nicolae started to tell us about the celebration at Saintes-Maries, the one about Sara–la-Kâli, the black saint. First of all there were three saints with two Maries after whom the church had been named. They were Marie-Salomé and Marie-Jacobé and, of course, Sara the black saint.

"It is said," Nicolae explained, "that Marie-Salomé and Marie-Jacobé were at the foot of the cross with the Virgin Mary and that, after the death of the Christ, the Jews, according to legend, forced the Holy Women, Lazarus and his sisters, Martha and Mary, to get into a boat and sail at their own peril. I believe there's an old song cited by your very own Mistral that says, '*Vous périrez dans cette nef, Allez sans voile et sans cordage, Sans mât, sans ancre, sans timon, Sans aliment, sans aviron, Allez faire un triste naufrage!*' My mother used to sing this and we found out later on that your Monsieur Mistral had plucked it out of some old traditions that he had unearthed. So the song says that without sails, food and oars they were bound to be shipwrecked. It is said that they did not perish but landed miraculously in the lower parts of Provence in the proximity of where Saintes-Maries-de-la-Mer is today. Tradition has it that Sara, a gypsy herself who was living on the Provençal banks, rescued the two Maries from the sea. Many years after their death, a church was built to honor all three of them and their statues are in the crypt with a full length statue of Sara-la-Kâli who is all dressed up with robes and many colored ribbons. Each year, on May 24, the *gitans* assemble at this spot by the thousands and follow a solemn procession after the descent of the shrines of the saints from the crypt to the sea. Camargue gardians on horseback riding their strikingly beautiful horses accompany the statues into the sea. The women of Arles honor the escort too but it is the *gitans* who sing hymns loud and clear without ceasing and shout 'Vive Sainte Sara!' in the evenings at the chapel accompanied by guitars and violins. A large candle is placed in the middle of the nave and then lit amid the hundreds of other smaller candles that each person holds in their hands. People pray and earnestly recite invocations while many are at the feet of Sainte Sara begging for her intercession. It's very moving and I've been there many times. On the day following the celebrations, everyone has fun as on a holiday. We sing, we eat, we dance and we celebrate the Camargue and its bulls and stallions. It's great fun."

I was soaking all of this in trying to retain it in my restless mind in order to put all of this information in my notebook that night by fire-light. As we arrived at Saintes-Maries, we met several people assembled in the square selling food, baubles, ribbons and all kinds of wares. Monsieur Vincent pointed toward the sea with his right hand and said with spontaneous delight,

"Look, the Mediterranean, see how it gleams in the sunlight. Let's have our lunch on the shore."

We thanked Nicolae for the ride and his story and then proceeded to walk to the seashore. All was well, all was just the way I had hoped it would be with Monsieur Vincent at my side. I ran to the shore and took off my shoes to wade in the water. My feet were hot. My mother had made me wear my warm socks for the trip. You know how mothers are. The water felt cool and refreshing. I let the water gurgle by my legs and feet as if it was welcoming me with its sounds of delight. I had never been near the Mediterranean before. I had only seen it on an old world globe that our teacher had in the classroom. It was just a blue spot on the map.

"Put your cap back on, Camille, for you'll burn easily with the sun and the sea air," shouted Monsieur Vincent.

I went back to be with him and I listened to him as I had promised my parents and put back my cap on my head. I was hungry. We spread out the small blanket we had brought and we placed some of the food that we had in the basket. A large bird came swooping down next to us and Monsieur Vincent shooed him away.

"That's a Mediterranean gull, a voracious bird. I think it's called a *gabian* here in Provence. It could eat all of our food if we let him. We have to save some for later on."

We began eating some cheese and bread and then a little bit of sausage with a piece of fruit. Then we had some water since Monsieur Vincent wanted to save the wine for later. I just followed what he wanted us to do. He lit a cigarette and I went to fetch some pieces of driftwood that I saw from afar. He told me not to wander too far while he relaxed and thought about his next painting. He knew what he wanted to paint, he said, but was waiting for the right moment and the right objects or exact location that would stimulate his urge to paint the colors and light that were being produced here at Saintes-Maries.

When I returned with my trophies, he started to tell me about the deep blue of the sky and the changing colors of the sea. He told me what he saw in it.

"The Mediterranean has shades of color much like the mackerel. It keeps changing all the time from for one doesn't know if its green or violet, and we don't really know if it's blue either because as soon as the reflection hits the eye it seems to take on a pink or gray hue. I remember one night when I first came here walking alone on the deserted beach. It felt neither gay nor sad. It was simply.....beautiful. The night sky was deep blue spotted with clouds turning a deeper blue than the fundamental blue of an intense cobalt color while others were of a lighter blue like the bluish whiteness of the milky way. In the depth of the blue background, stars were shining bright, greenish, yellow, white, pink, and even brighter like diamonds with facets of gleam like home and even in Paris. One could say like opals, emeralds, lapis lazuli, rubies, and sapphires. It seemed to me that the sea took on the aspect of a very deep look of a faraway sea ------the beach, a purplish and pale reddish hue with bushes on the dune of a Prussian blue. Ah, the very mystery of it all engulfs me."

I just stood there thinking, wow! what beautiful words he uses to describe the scene he saw in the night, and how I wished I could do the same with my words. That's when I realized that I had so very much to learn and learn I must.

We slept on the beach that night and when I woke up at dawn I noticed that Monsieur Vincent was already up, and that he had thrown his blanket over me. He was not too far away where he stood gazing at the sun slowly rising over the swell of the sea. I stretched my arms and let out a deep yawn. I got up and ran over to Monsieur Vincent. He turned around and smiled, a smile that could only be of contentment.

"A new day has been given to us. Let's get going. I have a lot to do today. Are you hungry?"

I responded with a big smile. After breakfast of bread and butter with some apricot jam, we didn't have *café au lait* of course, we bundled up our belongings and stashed them under a tree whose trunk was bent almost horizontally towards the sea. We knew that we wouldn't be too far away so that we could watch over our belongings. Monsieur Vincent planned to paint some *bateaus* that would be coming in soon after the fishermen had returned and hauled in their catch in their nets that they dragged to shore. There were a few men on the shore talking. I heard some of them say they were going to bring in the fish because the summer weather allowed them to do so.

"What did they say?" asked Monsieur Vincent.

"I'm not quite sure. They call it *faire la mancado* but I don't understand exactly what they mean by it. I think it means hauling in the fish."

"Never mind, we'll wait until they're done. Let's watch."

Monsieur Vincent and I watched the fishermen hauling their nets filled with fish while the gulls hovered and shrieked overhead. They were all hungry and expected to fill their stomachs with whatever the fishermen would allow them to eat, if anything. Men attracted to fish for nourishment and beasts of the air naturally drawn to the same catch. The same ritual repeated itself every day, said Monsieur. The nets were thrown out into the sea and the fish swam into them getting caught by the cunning ways of men. The fishermen would then sell their catch at the market for women to check for freshness and weight so that the daily meals could repeat themselves the way it always had been done around the Mediterranean. Yes, the ritual of men, boats and nets all centered on the sea that had been feeding mouths for centuries. That's what Monsieur Vincent and I were witnessing that morning in mid-June.

The sun kept getting brighter and brighter as the fishermen took their catch to market while some cleaned their nets and rolled them into huge bundles ready for the next day. The *bateaus* stood there idle in the morning sun. That's when Monsieur Vincent got up, took his reed pen and ink and started to draw the idle boats. They were all colorful, red, blue, green and yellow. One of them was named AMITIÉ. That was exactly what existed between Monsieur Vincent and myself, friendship. He was my friend and I was his. We had bonded together the way two human beings who share the same thoughts and same feelings except mine were not as advanced and refined as Monsieur Vincent's. We never talked about it; we just knew. We felt it and that was enough. I was so glad that Monsieur Vincent held me in the cup of his friendship as he did with my father, brother, his brother Théo, and his artist friend, Paul Gauguin who was coming to live with him and form an artist colony, he said. Monsieur Vincent was excited about that. That's when he talked and talked about it with my father. You could see his eyes filling up with delight and anticipation then. I was so happy for him.

Looking back at this time in my life, I can see that with the exuberance of a child of eleven, I saw everything through the prism of my young years when things were simple, uncomplicated and serene. I imagined the world of the artist, such as Monsieur Vincent's, as being that way too. Never did I even suspect that within his heart and soul, a storm was brewing in his life and things would become complicated and troubled. I had no way of suspecting that since Monsieur Vincent was my rock, my teacher and my stalwart friend who could do no wrong. He was an artist, a very good one at that, and my young, impressionable mind was not in a state of measuring restless impulses, troubled heartbeats and artistic passion. I simply lived life as if it were going to be sunshine, rainbows and illuminating stars all the rest of my life. Now the sea added a new dimension to my life. I was beginning to see vastness and profound depths that came to fill the limited geography of my naive years. I was also beginning to understand that experiences come to fill the hollows left by education in school and book learning. Monsieur Vincent came at a time when I was open to those experiences that enriched my life and filled with a passion in the bud for words, colorful words and expressions that I could store in my head for years to come.

Since it was getting hot, I went up to the tree where our belongings were in order to get some shade and write all of the notes about our trip down to Saintes-Maries, the tales of Nicolae, the night before on the beach, the bright morning watching the fishermen, and now witnessing Monsieur Vincent drawing the four boats on the shore. Drawings were complicated for me what with perspective and the right touch of the pencil or pen on paper. He had such a sharp sense of knowing what to draw and how to draw it and it simply flowed out of his head through his hands. He told me that he had started doing some drawings when he was very young, even younger than me, and that his parents didn't encourage him much to continue his *penchant* for art.

"That's too bad," I told him, "since parents should encourage their children to grow and develop their talents, don't you think?"

"My father was a stern man, a man of the cloth, and he resisted impulses to be undisciplined, as he called it, and my mother, well, she just followed my father's ways of thinking and doing things although she was very talented, my mother. She loved to write letters to her friends and read art books. I was different, that's all, yes, I was bewilderingly different from other children my age," he replied with his eyes cast downward and his hands held tight as if in a knot.

As I was resting by myself under the tree, a young girl came close to me and asked what I was doing there. I replied that I was from Arles and that I had come to Saintes-Maries with my friend who was now doing a drawing of the four boats on the shore.

"Is he an artist, your friend?" she asked.

"Yes, and what an artist. He's the best in Provence."

"How come you're with him?"

"Because he's my friend and we do a lot of things together."

"Does he have any children?"

"No. He's alone. He comes from up north. He decided to come to Provence to paint the light and the bright colors that we have here in the south."

"How can you paint light? You can't paint light, it's not visible and no one can capture it," she said with assurance.

"Oh, but you can paint light in the sense that light brings everything out, it makes the colors more brilliant, it makes the sunflowers look like they were stained glass windows in a church, it makes the yellows buttery-rich and the blues deeper while the reds and greens become intense and brighter. That's what light does and if you're an artist, well, you can capture light through things and even people. That's what I learned from Monsieur Vincent."

"Is that his name?"

"Yes, Vincent Van Gogh, but since few people can pronounce the last name, he uses only his first name."

"Where is he from?"

"I told you, from up north. He came to Arles from Paris but he was born in Holland."

"Holland?"

"Yes, Holland. He's Dutch. Don't you know anything?"

"I'm a gypsy and we don't go to school. Everything we learn comes from the elders, especially the men. All we're expected to do is obey and get married when we reach fourteen or fifteen."

"Fourteen or fifteen?"

"Yes, that's our life. We travel a lot and we never stay at the same place."

"You're nomads." That was a word I had learned in class about Africans in the desert.

"What's that?"

"You know, going from place to place without staying in a single one. Always on the go."

"If you say so."

"What's your name?" I asked her.

"I'm not supposed to give out my name to a *gadjé*," she said.

"I'm not a gadget."

"Not a gadget, a *gadjé*, a stranger, a non-gypsy."

"Why?"

"Because that's the way it is. Don't you know anything about gypsies?"

"Very little except what Nicolae told me coming down here in his caravan," I replied.

"Nicolae Dragu, the teller of tales and the violin maker? I know him. He's part of our clan. What did he tell you?"

"He told us about Sara-la-Kâli and the celebration in May."

"Oh, that. Well, there's plenty more to know about us the gypsies, *les gitans et les gitanes*. I can't stay here with you any longer because I'm not supposed to talk to you."

"Why?"

"Because you're a *gadjé,* I told you."

And with that she started to walk away.

"Hey, what's your name?"

"I'm not supposed to tell you," and she whispered, "Mireille, just like the story."

"But that's not a gypsy story," I said.

"Oh, no? Who says?" and she flew away like a little black bird with hair as black as the night and as shiny as the feathers of a crow.

I resumed my writing and it covered some ten pages. I had a lot to write about. I just could not imagine how much I was absorbing in just a day. A good thing my mind was like a sponge and I retained almost everything that I was told and what I saw. What was it that Monsieur Vincent called me? Yes, precocious. I was precocious and I was happy to be advanced for my age. I know it was a gift from God, as Monsieur Vincent used to say about his art. Talents were gifts from God and I thanked him for them and for having met Monsieur Vincent, the bearer of so many talents who also uncovered them in others like me.

"Talents are meant to be opened up not hidden," he told me one day. "So, if you have them, open them up. They're not to be wasted."

"But, how do I know if I have them?" I asked.

"You'll know as soon as you use them. They're like young birds that learn how to fly by testing the air. Fly, Camille. Fly."

I've been flying ever since.

After Monsieur Vincent had finished his drawing, he came to sit down next to me and showed it to me. He had written in all the colors that he would later fill in when he did the painting of the boats on shore. It seemed that every object on the boats, every board, mast and even the jutting sticks, as I called them, had a color attached to it. He drew in black ink but thought also in color since he saw color. His mind was like that, especially since he had come to Provence to capture the burst of light on colors. *Rouge, bleu, bleu pale, jaune, jaune citron, orange, blanc*, all the colors he needed were written there in appropriate places on the boat drawing. The drawing, by itself, was superb but I knew that Vincent wanted color added to what he had seen on the beach. Later on, he would paint, **Fishing Boats on the Beach at Saintes-Maries,** and the same subject matter in watercolor. He put the drawing away in his backpack and then showed me another drawing, a kind of a sketch, a small one of a boy with a young girl under a tree. "That's me!" I said.

"Who was that girl with you?" he asked.

"Her name is Mireille, a gypsy girl."

"Did you know her?"

"No. She came over to talk to me."

"Well, you can have this. It will be a memento of your trip to Saintes-Maries."

I've always kept it and never showed it to anyone. My second drawing from Monsieur Vincent. I would put it with my other one back home in my folder.

Late that afternoon, while we were drinking some water and eating fruit by the jetty, a woman, tugging a little girl by the hand as if the youngster didn't want to go where the woman was taking her, headed in our direction. I recognized Mireille. The woman wore a long cotton printed dress with red faded ribbons pinned here and there at her hips and she seemed to be determined to talk to us. Her hair was tousled and half hid huge earrings that hung from her ears like small golden grapes, all jangling. Her eyes were lit with fire and her mouth pinched as if she were about to spit. The little girl had tears in her eyes.

"Here," said the woman, "here's your apricot," and she threw the fruit at Monsieur Vincent who was stunned for the moment.

"We're not thieves. My daughter dared to talk to this boy here and got chummy with him. She took his apricot while he wasn't looking. We may be poor but we're not thieves."

"Why, Mireille?" I asked.

She said nothing, half pouting.

"Because she was hungry, that's why." said the mother.

"When was the last time you ate a good meal?" asked Monsieur Vincent.

"We're poor, we're not thieves," insisted the woman.

"I know, I know," said Vincent, "But are you hungry?"

"Oh, sir we are indeed," said Mireille without hesitation.

"Shut up girl, we don't do business with *gadjés*."

"*Gadjés*?" repeated Vincent.

"That means strangers, non-gypsies," I explained.

"We may be strangers but we're not heartless," insisted Monsieur Vincent. "Do you want some food? I can't give you money because I don't have any."

"Sir, we beg for our food and we're not looking for your money. We just happen to be down in our luck."

"But, don't you belong to some clan? Don't you have a family?" asked Monsieur Vincent.

"That's a long story, sir, and I'm not about to tell you my life's story on an empty stomach. Besides, I have my pride, I'll have you know. I just don't tell private matters to perfect strangers," she said with a tone of faint disdain.

"Oh, I wouldn't want you to reveal what you don't want me to know. That's not my intent. I don't have to know anything about you and your story if you don't want to reveal it. All I'm asking is, are you hungry?"

"My child is."

"Well, we're willing to share some of our food with you, Camille and I."

"That's very kind of you, sir. Are you an artist? Mireille tells me that you draw."

"You could say I'm an artist. That's my passion. I came to Provence to paint in the splendid light of the south that is so captivating."

"I know," she said, replacing her disdain with a warm smile. "Colors are one of the essential things in our lives," she continued, "without colors our lives would be drab and meaningless. They're part of our soul. Gypsies know that."

"Are you an artist?" asked Vincent.

"No, but I'm good at sewing and making lovely things to sell to people who enjoy them. My hands are talented."

"There, you see you are an artist," said Vincent. "You do what I do, turn everyday things into joys for others to buy....when and if they buy," he said a bit despondently. "Why don't you make things and sell them so that you can have money to buy food?"

"It's not that simple when you have nothing to begin with. I have nothing, not even a place to sleep. I have no pots and pans, no clothes, no furniture, nothing I can call my own. All we have are each other, my daughter and me. But, I do have some talent. I was part of the clan of violin makers. I used to make wonderful bows. I made them out of boxwood or rosewood. I would have loved to put my hands on Brazilian wood but there was none available to me then. The frog was made of tortoise shell that I myself collected, and the hairs were horse hair. I didn't skimp. I used 150 hairs on each bow I made. You see, a bow needs to have good weight, flexibility and balance between the frog and the tip. Mine had all of that. That was my talent. My bows made the violin sing with zingara magic, a woman's fire."

"Let's not talk right now, let's have some food," said Monsieur Vincent.

And we enjoyed pieces of cheese, some bread that we broke up, some water and each a fruit. The woman and the little girl devoured what we gave them. I felt like giving them everything we had but I knew that we had to stretch things as long as we were in Saintes-Maries.

After we finished eating, the woman said, "Now that I have eaten your food with you, we are friends and I can talk about myself and the gypsies."

She told us how gypsies are fond of coming to this village.

"Saintes-Maries-de-la-Mer," she said, "is a sacred place for us. It's the shrine of Sara-la-Kâli and she is our patroness, our protector. She keeps us from all harm. That's why we wear her medal. It's very special."

And underneath all of her bangles around her neck, she took out her own medal of the black saint.

"Gypsies come from far and away to the saint's celebration in May since they know that Sara-la-Kâli and the two Marys will protect them from harm and evil spirits all year long. You see the good exists but evil also exists in the world, sometimes as powerful as the good. So, we must be on guard all the time. We have to wear our amulets and the red thread around our wrists. Saintes-Maries is our religious center here in Provence. Celebration day is also a time to greet one another and renew old friendships. Families renew ties with other families. One's family is the very core of its existence and without it we are lost like the wandering Jew. Once you break family ties you become isolated and you have to fend for yourself. Like me."

"What do you mean?" asked Vincent.

"Well, I was cursed when I was young, a curse thrown at me by an old aunt who hated my guts because she said that I had cast a spell on her youngest boy, the *mal ojo*, the evil eye, and that's why his face was troubled with ticks. It wasn't true but she believed I had done it. He was a runt of a boy with warts all over his hands and face. She was an old crone and her evil powers were stronger than my good spirits, so I succumbed to her spell. I was destined to fall in love with a *gadjé*, the worst of curses for a gypsy. We are not supposed to have any love or sexual relationships with strangers. It's the code. I fought and fought it but it was no use. I drank potions and fasted and prayed to the Virgin and to Saint Sara but in the end love overpowered me in the form of a man of the Camargue who was only half gypsy. A half-breed that is shunned by gypsies. Tainted, they said. Oh, he was as handsome as the stunning white horses of the Camargue. He stood tall and proud with hair as black as any gypsy but his skin was whiter than that of gypsies. His smile was enough to lure you into his web of passion. I resisted his charm but to no avail. I fell madly in love with him. The old aunt's spell had fully developed in me like an all consuming fire that rages in one's soul. Not only was my heart affected but my very soul. I was doomed to love, to be consumed by the passion of love. So, we made love and he carried me away to his lodging where I stayed with him for a year until he disappeared after I told him I was with child. Then, I was alone, completely alone with no family ties. I had forsaken my family and that meant that I had no more rights to be not only with my family but all clans. I was tainted. I was the woman of the half-breed. What could I do? I had been cursed. I had my child and did the best I could to raise her going from village to village. I named her Mireille because I loved the story and because it's also the story of the gypsies. It belongs to them too, to us. Except in the gypsy version, Mireille is named Myriam. You didn't know about that did you?"

"No," Monsieur Vincent replied. "I've never read the tale of Mireille."

"In our language, she is called *Mirèio*," I added.

"Well, Mireille, Myriam or *Mirèio*, it's all the same tale. Let me tell you about the legend, whatever one calls her, and her fated love. One of the fishermen, a good friend of mine, related to me the Provençal version. In that version, Mireille is the daughter of Maître Ramon, the owner of the domain. She's an only child and is revered by her father. She is destined to inherit, one day, the entire domain, she and her future husband to be hand picked by the father. He must be of equal or higher rank and must be lordly in his ways so as to merit the hand of the daughter of good fortune. She is pure, chaste and virtuous, all that a father could hope for. She is the young demoiselle of the domain, the gifted land passed on from generation to generation. That's the destiny of the young Mireille. Her demise is that fate has her meet a young man who is far below her stature in life. He is Vincent, the basket maker, a bohemian of sorts. He comes from Vallebrègues, a poor village of low repute where the basket makers live. These people became the itinerant workers of La Crau. In those days, every village had its social outcasts but the villagers accepted them and even gave them food, work and a resting place in their *mas*. They became the nomads of La Crau and the carriers of news as well as the tellers of tales and adventures.

The young Vincent is such an outcast, due to his low rank in society and his lot in life, that he is destined to live a miserable life and die poor. However, he not only has a tawny complexion, a fine waist and wears a red *bonnet*, a kind of a stocking hat, but he is endowed with the rich and lively talents of a poet, a weaver of tales. At the crossroads of the village, Mireille hears Vincent's fine voice retelling a tale of forlorn love. She is so taken with his voice that it remains as if grafted on her heart. That springtime evening she says repeatedly, 'Oh, how I would spend my nights and my life listening to him.' And then Vincent appears in person and tells her that there is a special place of worship and love that is the chapel of Saintes-Maries. He describes to her in great details the sanctuary of the two Marys. In the gypsy version, he begs her to go and see Sara-la-Kâli to plead with her to make all things right for them. He knows that their love is fated to wither and die. But, through her intercession they will somehow remain clean of heart and soul and salvage their true love. However, their cruel destiny is to die since the gypsy code has been broken. In the Provençal version Mireille goes to Saintes-Maries to find solace and encouragement for her love. She only finds the silence and cold comfort for a love that is beyond her reach. When she tries to return to the land of her domain, she dies from the blazing heat of the sun and Vincent, filled with deep sorrow, disappears to wander the rest of his life. That's the story and that's why I named my daughter, Mireille. She too is fated to remain out of the clan, isolated and deprived of the love of family and friends. I just hope someday she may find her love and be able to have a family of her own, but not with a gypsy. Both of us are tainted. I'm considered by the gypsy code to be in the state of *marimé*, a state of impurity brought on by my behavior disruptive to the Roma community. So you see, I'm an outcast. My daughter is an outcast on account of me. Both of us are wanderers like the poor and unfortunate Vincent of the legend."

"My friend's name is Vincent," I blurted out.

"Oh, what a coincidence," the gypsy woman said. "Vincent, I must tell your fortune someday."

"My mother is a *drabardi*, a fortune teller," added the young girl.

"Yes, I am, that's my other talent as a gypsy. I can read in the cards what other people cannot see."

"That's very interesting," said Monsieur Vincent. "I'll await the day when you come to me and tell me my fortune since mine is nebulous to say the least."

"A gypsy really knows how to delve into the mystery of the future," she said.

"But, why did you name your daughter, Mireille, and not Myriam?" I asked. "She's a gypsy."

"Because, young *gadjé*, she's not a gypsy to me. She's a half breed gypsy. The child born of a curse. I didn't want her to have a name that reminded her of it. That's why."

We spent another night at Saintes-Maries since Vincent wanted to paint the *mas*, the cottages in Saintes-Maries. I was having great fun at Saintes-Maries and I was getting a lot of things for my notebook. The gypsy woman had given me enough for almost a whole day. What a fascinating story that was, the story of her life, and the tale of Mireille and Vincent. I knew that Frédéric Mistral had written about them, but I had never read the full story before. I had heard about it, that's all. Possibly because my father had not encouraged me to read Monsieur Mistral's tale. As I said before, my father was modern, he didn't like old literature and tales of the past. He did read some of the classics but he much preferred politics and history. I was thus resolved to read all of it when I got home and read it in our very own dialect that some teachers were discouraging us from using. I knew of some boys who were punished for speaking Provençal at recess. Can you imagine?

After breakfast, Monsieur Vincent and I walked over to one of the streets where there was a whole row of *mas*. Bright colored cottages standing in the morning sun. He started to unload his canvases, his easel, his palette, his brushes and tubes of paint. I watched him as he sat down on his small stool and got everything in order for him to get started. He stared at the cottages and then at the sun overhead and said softly, "Perfect." I sat on the ground a little behind him where I would not intrude. He put fresh paint on his palette and took a brush from his collection of brushes. I always wondered how he chose one over another but he seemed to know instinctively which one to use first and which one to use next. How much paint to apply, thick or thin. I suppose if he wanted a good texture, he would use more paint, enough to reveal the brush strokes so that one could actually see and even feel the layers of paint as he did with the sunflowers.

I could see that he was using contrast to heighten the colors in his painting: red and green on the right, blue and orange to the left and yellow and violet in the center. The bright yellows of the sky achieved the impact of the contrasts, I noticed. I liked the perspective in the painting showing the bright colored cottages on the left side and the greenery on the right with one red roof of a cottage towards the very end. That bright red color again, redder than the actual roof that I saw. The bright red flowers in the foreground harmonize with the red roof to set a tone of light and contrasts. I sat on the ground for a long while sometimes getting up to stretch my legs. When he had finished, I walked over to him and told him that I really liked what he had just painted. "*C'est à ton goût, mon p'tit Camille?*"

"*Oui, tout à fait à mon goût* ," all according to my taste, I said. I truly liked the painting, **Street in Saintes-Maries**.

We both stood there looking at the painting and admiring the colors in the intense light of the sun that shone so bright that day. I think, that day, the sun took a particular stance to shine even brighter than usual. Just for him. That's what I think. He painted some other things that day but I sat under some awning in the center of town putting my thoughts down in my notebook and later on dozing in the warmth of the afternoon shade. When I woke up, my mouth felt dry so I went to the village fountain to drink some water. I looked around and saw that the square was deserted. It felt eerie until I saw from afar, at the edge of the sea, a huge crowd standing there. I took my belongings and rushed to see what was happening. Standing on the side of the crowd of people was Monsieur Vincent who was looking in the direction of the sea.

"What's happening?" I asked him.

"Somebody drowned and they're fishing the body out of the waters."

"I wonder who it is?" I replied.

"It's a woman. She left her clothing on shore. She must have been desperate."

"Do you think it's the gypsy lady, Mireille's mother?" I asked with apprehension.

"I don't think so because her daughter would be around, I suppose."

"What did she do? Walk right into the sea?"

"I don't know. I didn't see her drown. I only came when the crowd was gathering."

All of a sudden there was a tug at my left sleeve. It was Mireille.

"What's happening?" she asked.

"A woman just drowned," I said.

"Who is it?"

"I don't know. I was afraid it would be your mother."

"No. Not my mother. My mother wouldn't do something like that. She's had a rough spell, but time has strengthened her, toughened her up to any hardship in life. My mother never gives up. She's with some fishermen begging for food so that we can eat tonight. Sometimes, they give us some of their catch of the day."

Mireille's mother showed up at that moment with a bag of something under her arm.

"I got mussels," she said. "Now we can eat supper. Would you like to join us, you and the boy?" she asked Monsieur Vincent, as she turned to him.

"Do you like *moules*, Camille?" he asked.

"Yes, I really like them. My mother uses them in her bouillabaisse."

"Well, let's go and I'll cook some for you," said the gypsy woman.

"Do you know what the fishermen call me?" she asked.

"No," replied Monsieur Vincent.

"They call me *la gitane aux semelles de vent*. That's when I'm wearing shoes." The wandering beggar, the woman who follows the wind.

We went over to some part of the nearby woods where the gypsy woman and her daughter had spent the night. She built a fire and placed a big pot with water over the burning sticks.

"I found this," she said. "I cleaned it and it's just right for boiling mussels. Too bad I don't have any wine since it would go well with mussels."

"I have a small bottle of table wine with me," offered Monsieur Vincent.

"Great, that will do just fine. In the meantime, I'll tell your fortune. Give me your right hand."

Vincent tended his hand to her. It was a fine hand with long fingers and just a touch of paint on them.

"Does that matter?" he asked.

"No, after all, I'm doing an artist's hand," she replied half jokingly.

"You know that woman who drowned herself this afternoon, she was a gypsy friend of mine when I was growing up. Her name was Lilyaje. She also became tainted, broke a taboo. She dared to touch and serve the meat to her husband when she was having her periods. That's not acceptable in our culture. That was unclean. After that, her husband dismissed her and she was left alone fending for herself. No one helped her out. She even tried to kill her husband out of hatred and frustration. The dagger fell out of her hand while attempting to stab her husband. He wanted to strangle her but she ran away. She became a thief and a scrounger. No one wanted to associate with her and so she became a wanderer without a family. Just like me. Except, I did not let it get me down. I'm a fighter. She wasn't. Damn code, damn people who abide by it so strictly. Forgive me for saying words like that especially in front of the children. Forgive me. It's tough being a gypsy woman. Very hard indeed. That's why I want Mireille to get away from here as far as she can when she's grown up. As far away from the code as she can. I'm responsible for her and her destiny. She's carrying in her body my cross, my punishment for being with a *gadjé*. It's not her fault."

The three of us kept silent. Then she took Monsieur Vincent's hand in her palm and began to read it.

"You have very good lines in your palm. I cannot tell you if you'll have a long life since your line is broken, but you do have a warm heart, a hunger in your soul to create and your minor lines point to the stars."

Monsieur Vincent looked at her and smiled.

She seemed to be struggling with her words in letting out what was on her mind and about what she saw in Monsieur Vincent's palm. As if something was preventing her from revealing the truth in what she saw there.

Then she said, "I can't see much in palm reading but I'll tell your fortune in the cards. That's my real talent anyway. Unfortunately, I don't have my Tarots anymore but I'll use the deck I have. It's old but it will do."

"Tell me your name. We've been with you and shared meals together. You know mine. What's yours?" asked Monsieur Vincent.

"You don't need to know my name," she replied.

"But a friend without a name is not a friend."

"Alright then. My name is Sara. Sara the wandering *gitane*." She said that with a faraway look in her eyes.

Once the meal was over, the gypsy lady, Sara, insisted on telling Monsieur Vincent's fortune. She took out an old deck of cards that she had in her pocket and started to shuffle the cards. She then lay the deck on the ground and took the first card on top and continued to do so one by one. She plucked down the king of clubs and said that Vincent would receive company soon and that the man would be an important factor in his life. Then she revealed the jack of hearts and put it side by side with the king of clubs.

"This means," she said, "that you will have severe disagreements with this new person, a man from the north, who will become part of your life but that your heart will do everything necessary to preserve the joint efforts of whatever you two will do. He will be a brother to you but at the same time he will wrench your heart."

She then put down the ace of diamonds and told Vincent that this meant a serious effort to make financial gains on his part. The two of spades followed it. It meant that the results would be somewhat meager. Then she slowly looked at the following card and quickly hid it under the pack followed by another card that was placed on top of the deck. It was the queen of hearts and it meant that Monsieur Vincent would try to open a relationship with a woman but that this woman tended to be shy and distant.

"However," she said, "there is a woman in your life who has been constant with you and lives somewhere up in a distant northern country since the next card that is placed next to it is the five of hearts."

She said that she saw a pattern in the cards that came up and that what she saw was a pattern of physical difficulties and even mental erratic tensions. "Your artistic life will help you to cope with all of this since the ace of diamonds that I already picked is now followed by the ace of hearts. These two cards together means that you have someone in your life that is close to you and is like a rock. Rely on that rock. It will bring you comfort."

She then flipped the jack of hearts and the ace of clubs and told Monsieur Vincent that this meant that fame and fortune were in the future for him. He looked at her a bit astonished.

"How about the card you slipped under the deck?" asked Vincent.

"What card?"

"I saw you. The card under the deck. Show me the card."

"Alright if you insist, but it doesn't mean what it signifies. It's the ace of spades."

"*La mort*, death. I know I'm going to die someday," he said

"But," she added, "this card, in the pattern I see, means that death could be early in life. However, I could be wrong."

"How often are you wrong, Sara?"

There was no reply. The air was suddenly heavy and filled with the shrill sound of the cicadas.

"This is enough to make one go mad," said Monsieur Vincent and he stood up holding his ears.

We left the gypsy lady, Sara, and her daughter and thanked them for the meal of mussels and wine. It was still daylight and the sun was yet in the sky barely approaching dusk. There was a beautiful glow in the Mediterranean sky and the few clouds left up there were like pink rags stretched out with tattered ends of faint gold. We then walked toward the church and Monsieur Vincent started to draw this monument since he had no more canvases with him. He likes to draw anyway. Since it was late afternoon early evening, the sun was still warm and brought Vincent enough light to draw the tall building in front of us. He no sooner sat down before his easel when a rather tall gypsy lady came to touch him on the shoulder. I knew she was gypsy because of her dark complexion and her clothes with all of her gold chains around her neck and the many bracelets around both wrists. Her deep dark eyes could have drilled right into my eyes so intense was her glance. I looked away so as not to meet that glance. Monsieur Vincent looked at her quizzically.

"I realize that you don't know me but I belong to the clan of the horse tamers and I want to warn you about Sara the beggar, the woman you hang around with. She is of no good augury. She is tainted and will bring you harm. Stay away. You will need something to protect you in the meantime and I will give you a medal of Sara-la-Kâli, the protector. But you must heed me. Stay away from the beggar or else..... People are watching you. Our people know."

She held out a medal with a small red ribbon tied to it while holding out her left hand as if for an offering. Monsieur Vincent told her he had no money to give and her face changed from a smile to a frown. She tried to pin it on his chest when Monsieur Vincent backed off as if she had pinched him. She took her handkerchief and went inside his open shirt and dabbed the spot. The handkerchief revealed a drop of his blood. She spun around and disappeared into the crowd.

"Strange person," I said.

"Yes, she's a bit strange doing what she did. I don't like all of what is happening with our friend Sara the beggar and her daughter. It all seems so mysterious. I really don't want to get involved with this. I do feel sorry for Sara, now that we know her name, but I'm afraid we have stepped into a hornet's nest. That's it, we're leaving for sure tomorrow morning."

"Why did that woman prick you in the chest? I wonder if it was deliberate?" I asked.

"I don't know but all of this taboo and broken code as well as warnings don't sit well with me. Are you afraid, Camille?"

"No. I just think it's like a mystery novel. You never know much until all the pieces of the puzzle come together."

"Wise comment, my young friend. How did you get to be so smart?"

"I guess by listening and reading. Like you, I love to read."

"Ah, yes, reading opens up a whole universe. What are you reading now, Camille?"

"Well, in class, we finished reading a good story, *La Dernière classe* by Alphonse Daudet."

"Yes, a very patriotic tale. Every schoolboy reads it, I believe."

"Right now I started his 'Tartarin de Tarascon.' "

"Oh, that's a very interesting book. Loads of adventures, some wild ones in Africa. I really like that book. Daudet is a real artist. He knows how to create and put life into words. Very imaginative too," he said.

"What are you reading ?" I asked.

"I'm reading Balzac, 'César Birotteau.' I think I'd like to reread all of Balzac. He's such a gifted writer. Read him, you'll learn a lot about writing. His descriptions are beyond compare and his characters truly carved out of reality."

Monsieur Vincent picked up his drawing and we went to the fountain to get some water. It was a very nice drawing. It showed the front of the church with its tower from the perspective of a close-up, as if you were looking at it with your two eyes aimed at the sky. Just like a little boy looking up at a tall building from up close. We went to the butcher's and we bought some sausages with the money I had. I had brought a franc and some centimes that I had taken from my bank. I had been saving for a small train set that I had seen in Marchet's store, but I thought that our excursion down south might benefit from a bit of money in case we happened to run out of food or something. Monsieur Vincent was a bit embarrassed by this but I reassured him that the train set was not vital to me. I told him that I could get it later on when I had saved sufficient funds to buy it. It so happened that I never did buy that train set since my uncle, Marius, from Marseille bought me one for *les étrennes du Jour de l'An,* a New Year's gift, a couple of years later.

"Just the same, I'll make it up to you," reassured Monsieur Vincent.

Silently I told myself that he had already done so by allowing me to witness his paintings and drawings. That meant so much to me and the fact that I was going to fill notebook after notebook taking notes on my artistic adventures with the master.

We kept the left-over bread and the sausage that we bought at the butcher's for the following morning before we were scheduled to leave. No fruit since we had no more. We did find some little red berries at the edge of the woods and that night we devoured them by stuffing them into our mouths with our hands all the time laughing and having a great time. Then we rested. Monsieur Vincent looked at his paintings while I took my notebook and filled nine pages with notes from the day's events. I wrote about the strange gypsy woman and about my thoughts on Saintes-Maries now that we were close to leaving the village. It was getting dark what with dusk setting in. A kind of moment when the light is being extinguished slowly and the dying day lingers on with its rosy-purplish streaks of clouds in the sky fading away. One more night and we spent it on the shore of the Mediterranean since Monsieur Vincent so loved that place. I think he spent the better part of the night looking at the stars in the deep dark blue sky. They were really spectacular those stars for they seemed to throw off sparks of multicolored jets of light just so we could feel enraptured by the night. I didn't stay up too long because I soon fell asleep as soon as my head hit the sand beneath my blanket. I was lulled to sleep by the whispers of the water gently flowing in and out on shore. The last I saw of Monsieur Vincent, he was staring at the sky and smiling with his right hand in his tousled red hair. I fell asleep knowing that I was safe and secure with him.

As the first light of morning started to creep over the horizon, I heard some footsteps behind me. I dared not open my eyes. Besides, I was still half asleep. I then heard a whisper, a woman's voice.

"Sir, Monsieur Vincent, please wake up. I need to talk to you."

Monsieur Vincent stirred and woke up surprised for the moment.

"What's wrong?" he said.

"I have to talk to you."

It was Sara and her voice sounded somewhat desperate.

"What about?" he asked.

"An important matter. Let's talk while the boy is still sleeping," she suggested in a whisper.

I wasn't asleep but my eyes were closed and I dared not stir even one muscle for I knew that what she had to tell Monsieur Vincent was not meant for my ears. However, I could hear the exchange between her and Monsieur Vincent and I was able to hear everything she told him that morning on the beach.

"You must get away from Saintes-Maries quickly," she said. "There is grave danger awaiting you if you stay."

"Why?"

"Are you missing something, anything?" she asked.

"Come to think of it, as I just put my hand in my hair, I felt that a chunk of hair was missing as if it had been cut. But, how could that happen? I felt nothing while asleep."

"That's just it. They come in the night like smooth cats with felted paws and do their sinister work."

"Who? What work?"

"The renegade gypsies who are out to get you because you dare to associate with me. They want revenge on me and you."

"Come to think about it there was a gypsy woman who came to talk to me and give me a medal yesterday in front of the church. Not only that, but she pricked my chest while trying to pin it on me. She wiped the spot of blood with her handkerchief. I thought the whole thing was weird."

"That's it, she collected some of your blood for the hex."

"What hex?"

"A hex is something supposed to bring bad luck. It's some form of a curse. What did the woman look like?"

"I don't remember her too well except she had a big wart under her bottom lip."

"Mirnanoun! She's a member of my parent clan. She's an evil one that one. A vengeful one."

"She did tell me to stay away from you or else."

"Yes, she's out to get me as much as she can but she can't, so she tries to hinder any relationship I have by threatening those with whom I come into contact. Beware, she knows how to hurt people. Don't touch anything that seems suspicious like a dead bird or a mouse or even a withered flower that she might leave on your trail. That's why you need to get away as soon as possible."

"Yes, I will as soon as I can put my things together."

Then she put something around Vincent's wrist that I discovered later was a red thread.

"Don't take it off and don't tell the boy," she cautioned and then she left as surreptitiously as she had come.

I did not stir under my blanket and waited for the sun to warm my bones because I was a bit cold in the early hours of daybreak.

"Wake up, boy," Monsieur Vincent said as he was packing his things.

"What are we doing today?" I asked.

"We're leaving town."

"Already?"

"Yes, we need to leave now. We'll walk for a while until we come up to a cart that will give us a ride to Arles, but no gypsy caravan."

"Why not?" I asked but knowing full well why.

We left Saintes-Maries in a bit of a hurry, I thought, but, after all, this was the third day there. Now, the sun was slowly climbing in the sky and the day promised to be bright and full of scents and visions of the Camargue countryside.

"Shake the dust off your shoes and pants," said Monsieur Vincent "because we are leaving this village of mystery on one hand and of delight on the other hand. The land of tales and hexes."

We walked side by side in silence. Monsieur Vincent seemed pensive and distant. I asked him if there was anything wrong.

He replied, "Oh, I have a headache and it's my tooth, it hurts again. I often have this pain. My teeth are not what they should be."

I didn't know what to tell him, so I took his hand and squeezed it slightly. He smiled at me and I smiled back.

"You're a good companion, Camille. Thank you."

I knew that he needed space and time to think things over and resolve them in his own mind. He never again mentioned the incident with the gypsy lady who threatened him that morning. So, we walked in silence until we reached the crossroads at Glaude. As we stopped to catch our breath, we leaned on the large signpost and saw beneath it a dead bird. It was a blackbird with a large pin stuck in its head.

"What's a dead bird doing here?" I asked.

"Don't touch it because it's probably meant for me. Sara did warn me about not touching any dead animal in my path. Gypsies are wont to leave signs at crossroads either to guide or threaten their own or even *gadjés*. I hate these games. I won't have anything to do with them. I know, not all gypsies are vengeful and treacherous. There are some good ones. I've met some before but there are some that seem to be dangerous."

"Where?"

"In the surroundings of Arles. They were camping there in caravans."

"I've never met any until the last few days. I like Mireille and Sara. I think they're nice."

By then, we were very tired. Monsieur Vincent looked around to find a place to rest, and at a distance we saw a small farmhouse, *un mazet blanc*. We walked toward it and asked the tenants for some water. Both the husband and the wife were kind and offered us some food and drink. The man even offered us a ride to Arles if we didn't mind riding with him and his small pigs in the back of his cart. He told us he would be heading for Arles in late afternoon. We stayed there sitting on the grass under two large plane trees so that we could get some rest and savor the warmth of the day in the shade of the trees. It was a delicious day filled with the smell of new mown hay, lavender and the aroma of freshly baked bread. At a not too far distance from the cottage we could see an entire field filled with wild poppies and small yellow flowers. There was enough there to fill one's eye with color.

"Look," said Monsieur Vincent, "the colors of Provence in abundance, the reds of the poppy, the yellow of the buttercups and, further away, the burst of the lavender. Isn't this just amazing, exactly like a painter's palette but here it's real, it's natural and so brilliant in the light of day that it makes you feel that you want to spend your entire day just gazing at it."

"Oh, yes, it's truly beautiful. You know, I never really noticed the wild flowers and their glowing colors before I met you. I mean really see them. You're the one who makes me see these things in a special light," I said and started to take notes on it.

My faithful notebook, what would I do without you? I only wished then that I could have had, at my disposal, all the words I would have needed to paint this scene in my notebook as Monsieur Vincent could on canvas. When we got back to Arles, it was getting dark already.

9

Colors of the Fields

$\mathcal{T}$he next two weeks were very quiet and somewhat lonely for me since I hardly saw Monsieur Vincent. I didn't know if he was avoiding me or if he was too busy to bother with me. I began to worry. I thought we were friends, I asked myself. Since it was summertime and the heat of the afternoon was so intense that it virtually overcame anyone who tried to resist it, any outside activity rendered one sluggish and even limp. Most afternoons were spent inside either at home or under some roof where one could at least try to cool off and drink lots of water or fresh *limonade*. My mother kept herself busy but her movements were slower than usual since she was expecting very soon. That's why my father used to tell us then to take care of our mother and not make her work too hard. Armand was seldom home, so I did my best to help out my mother. I helped with the dishes, with the washing and with whatever she would allow me to do in the house. She would tell my father and me that having a child is not a sickness and that, after all, she already had had two.

"Je ne suis pas infirme," I'm not a cripple, "I'm fully capable of doing my work," she would insist.

But it was summer, late June going on July and the weather was hot at times, enough to make anyone feel sluggish and limp from sweating. But my mother didn't perspire. She simply went about doing what she had to do and wanted to do without ever complaining. Of course, my father was working hard at the train station unloading mailbags. I'm sure he was hot just doing his work, perhaps lifting and carrying those bags and sorting mail. Poor father, he was out in the sun sweating like most workers on the job. On occasions, he would wear his uniform of deep blue color with gold braid on his lower sleeves and brass buttons on the front of his jacket. Eight on the front with one each on his cuffs. That made it ten. I counted them one day. He looked so handsome in it. My mother always kept his uniform clean and pressed. With his long curling deep blond mustache and beard and his piercing blue eyes, he looked like any hero out of my books, a Charlemagne, a Vercingétorix, or even a Tartarin. I loved my father. He was an honest man, a good *citoyen de la République*. I did not know too much about politics and all that, but I knew enough to be able to distinguish between a royalist and a republican. A republican does not believe in privileges and inequality, in church affiliated aristocracy and high honors. He staunchly believes in the rights of man, in liberty, equality and fraternity. That, I knew because once my father started expounding on the subject, there was no way of stopping him. I will always remember the fight between my father and Monsieur Cachinet. It was not a fist fight but rather a fight of words over ideals. I had never seen my father get angry before, but when he got going with his rival, Monsieur Cachinet, it was a determined fight between a republican and a royalist. There was no violence, no name calling but a lot of table pounding. However, it always ended up as a draw with my father taking his old friend, Cachinet, out for a drink at the local bar. My mother said that it was just a lot of steam that had to come out so that the locomotive could start up again and run smoothly. I knew what she meant by the locomotive.

I met Monsieur Vincent for the first time after our trip to Saintes-Maries at the store around the corner where they sold fabrics, brushes, and some furniture. **Calment & Fils**, it was called. That's where I saw Jeanne Calment who was two years older than me although she claimed she was older than that. Her father owned the store. I had gone there to get some turpentine for my mother. I had seen her before strutting her young body like a bloated pigeon that makes cooing sounds in its throat. She was a pretty girl and everybody said so. She knew it and did her best to amplify her reputation as a desirable young woman by puffing up her chest to show her budding maturity. However, that did not seem to impress Monsieur Vincent at all that day. All he wanted was to talk about his brushes with the clerk. Jeanne seemed miffed by his disinterested attitude toward her. She gave me a cool hello and walked by me without so much as a smile. I stood there a bit baffled. Later on, she would tell people that Monsieur Vincent was a vulgar man. She said that he had made inappropriate comments to her while visiting her father's store. When Monsieur Vincent finished with the clerk, it was my turn, so I asked for the turpentine. When I paid for it, Monsieur Vincent turned to me and said, "I'll see you sometime this week since I'm going to do some drawings and you might be interested in coming along."

Would I? I didn't have time to answer when Monsieur Vincent turned around and left the store. Why wasn't he painting? Oh well, he was in his drawing mood, I suppose. I went home, gave my mother her turpentine and went to my room and finished reading "Tartarin de Tarascon." When I put it down, I started daydreaming about the hero Tartarin and his magical exploits: the lions, the camel that Tartarin finds, the Moorish lady in the Casbah, Prince Gregory from Montenegro, the marabout in his tent, the finely dressed Zouave, and the old battered diligence that had traveled a lot. Most of all, the part when he comes back home to Tarascon warmed my heart. All these things swam in my mind like fishes going in all directions. I told myself I'd like to travel to Africa someday and see all kinds of wild things and be part of some kind of grand adventure, but right now I felt more comfortable being home and just traveling in my mind. That's what reading was all about, wasn't it? It could transport you anywhere in the world or even beyond the stars like the visitor from Sirius in Voltaire's "Micromégas." That's what Monsieur Vincent had told me, that the mind was a wondrous thing. It could create all kinds of things. All you had to do was to imagine them and let yourself be transported by its powers. Just like Monsieur Vincent did with his paintings. He saw things and people but he transformed them with his own mind in his imagination and that's what made them different from other paintings other artists made. Imagine, yes imagine things all in color in the bright sun of Provence! Then I started imagining things in color, daydreaming in color, bright colors, red, green, blue, orange, yellow, all kinds of yellows, gold, golden wheat fields, huge brilliant golden suns with layers and layers and layers of dripping buttery yellow paint.... and before I knew it, I fell asleep on the soft pillows of my feathery bed.

Since it was still June and the summer vacation period was still fresh and new, I decided to wander in and around the park and the vicinity of the Trinquetaille bridge over Rue Montmajour where I would meet some of my friends under the bridge. It was cool there and we could throw the ball against the wall. Anfos, Blàsi, Calendau and Milou liked playing ball but they couldn't always be there since their mothers hounded them for extra chores. Not like my mother who was more understanding about my need to do things that I liked. I also loved sitting on a park bench to review my notes and to sit in the shade after I had done my daily chores. I also loved to look at the Rhône from the bridge and, at times, talk to Madame Flourènço about her cat, Girome. He was a big yellow cat with white streaks here and there like Madame Tavan's hair when she dyed them. Girome was a nice cat, not at all wild or grumpy. He would let me take him in my arms and I rubbed him under his neck so he could purr. He was so big for my arms that I had a hard time to hold him. That's when Madame Flourènço would take him and just smile at me. Nice lady, Madame Flourènço. Sometimes, she would give me a piece of taffy she had made. I liked her. Not like the old lady Matevoun who yelled at kids who played around her house. She didn't like kids.

She would shout at us, "*Fan de chichourlo* !" Damn it, go play elsewhere.

We knew we were not wanted there. Then, there was Monsieur Ginoux who was always joyful and full of tricks. He liked to play tricks on people and make them laugh. Some didn't like it but most of the time people smiled or laughed. As for his wife, Madame Ginoux, well, she was a bit snobbish. She had her nose in the air. Not that she didn't like people but they had to be her kind of people. She didn't always have time for us kids. She loved the Arlésienne stylish way of doing things and dressed the part when the occasion arrived. She and her husband made a handsome couple. People said so.

The following day, I met Monsieur Vincent early in the morning on his way to paint some field where there were haystacks, he told me.

"Want to come along?"

"Yes, oh, yes," I replied.

"Well, get your hat and tell your mother."

I hurried before he could change his mind, and returned with my battered straw hat on my head. We headed for Monsieur Sanouton's field. Farmers had been cutting the hay and putting it into haystacks here and there in their open fields. It was hard work. Tiring work in the day's sun, morning and afternoon, although some avoided the blazing afternoon sun. Too hot and it made you feel sleepy. That's why some workers took naps on the hay in mid-afternoon. When we got there, Monsieur Vincent unloaded his pack and settled in ready to paint haystacks. He chose two of them and the tall farmhouse with green shutters on the left. First, he tackled the haystacks. He only wanted to paint two since, he said, he wanted to include on his canvas the farmhouse and some kind of storage shed with a white roof and a small cottage with a red roof. Yes, that touch of bright red in Monsieur's paintings. There was also the presence of a woman with a pail in her right hand to the left of the haystacks. That might have been Madame Sanouton. I didn't know the lady. She didn't wave at us and simply continued her work. She didn't send us away either. She just did not mind our being there, I guess.

Haystacks, yellow, one brighter than the other since the back one is in the shade of the other. That's why Monsieur Vincent used a kind of russet tone highlighted by reddish licks of paint for that one. There are two ladders against this haystack, one taller than the other and there's a young worker on top of the haystack tying down or adjusting some kind of cloth. I suppose that was to protect the hay against the rain. There's a third haystack, mostly hidden by the one in the foreground, but I could see the side of it in the bright sunlight. As for the larger one, this one is full blown yellow with the visible texture of brush strokes. To the left, down below, is a patch of brighter color that highlights the yellows. The ground is covered with some mown hay except for some spots where the green grass shows and that contrasts with the brightness of the lighter yellow tones. I tried to put all of that in my notebook but, at times, I lacked the proper words. I left blank spaces to be filled in later. However, my memory worked very well to a point that I could recollect every tone of color that Monsieur Vincent had painted even years after a particular painting was done. One thing I like about this painting, besides the haystacks, is the sky. The color of the sky, because it reflects the changing sky of Provence, bright at one spot while it can be cloudy at another spot, like the sky in this particular painting. The right side is much brighter than the middle toward the left side where it seems that a storm may be on its way what with a deep grayish blue and even some strokes of green to heighten the intensity of the clouds. Yes, he captured that effect so well. Above all, the artist that was Monsieur Vincent painted yet another true reflection of Provençal life in Arles by painting, **Haystacks in Provence**. Lodged irrevocably in my head was the fact that Monsieur Vincent had come to Arles precisely to capture the sharp brightness of light and the intensity of color. After all, Monsieur Vincent kept insisting that color was everything. It was. Besides, with this painting, once again, he is beholden to the pioneering work of the artist Millet and how much he owed him as a master.

"An artist of the people, of nature and of simple life," he kept saying to me. "Take his own painting of haystacks that you haven't seen. It's a fine execution of the colors of autumn. That's what the painting is actually called, <u>Autumn, The Haystacks</u>. He was the artist of seasons. He taught me well through his paintings that I so admired. For instance, the fact that he had requested from the color merchant, Blanchet, that he prepare for him canvases with a deep lilac rose preparation. And that's what Millet used for his painting of the haystacks. If one looks closely at that painting, one can see the lilac pink ground in some spots. What a wondrous touch! The sheep are his signature of country life in the serene atmosphere of daytime light and shadows. And the haystacks themselves, they're so perfectly painted like soft colored cones ready to whirl skyward like three small tornadoes. Now the sky. What a tremendous artist he was in capturing the grim boldness of a giant cluster of darkening clouds overhead. His execution of haystacks, I must say, is far superior to mine."

I just sat there listening to him in awe of his use of words in his descriptions. Someday, I told myself, someday.

Once he was done doing the painting, we packed up and returned to town. Monsieur Vincent had something to show me, he said. I didn't often go to his house, but this time he insisted. He wanted to show me another painting of his, **Sower with the Setting Sun**. It was always a favorite of his on account of the brush stroke effect and especially the use of color and, of course, that marvelous sun right in the middle of it. A huge, round, lustrous yellow sun in a buttery sky from left to right of the top of the canvas. Yellow upon yellow, sitting on a bed of tall deeper colored reeds or stalks as a background to the variegated earth tones below.

"But these earth tones are not the actual color of dirt that you pick up in your hands. No, it's what the eye sees in that light," Monsieur Vincent explained to me. "The colors are real because the colors in one's eye are real. And what makes the colors like that? It's the light. Light, my boy, light. Here, you see the sower sowing on the upturned clods of earth that reflect that light. They're not at all brown. No, they're blues, reds, whites, browns, and many colors to reflect the beauty of the ground under a slowly fading light. I had to hurry to capture that light at the right moment because light changes ever so fast and I wanted to grasp that exact light at that exact moment in time. Not easy to do. What I really wanted was to get that serenity and harmony of man and his task of sowing. I know that you don't read the gospels but the parable of the sower was brought to mind when I painted this one. The sower goes out and begins to sow seeds. Some fall by the wayside and the birds come to eat them up while others fall on rocky ground and, because there is very little dirt there, the seeds sprout fast and, as soon as the sun rises, they're scorched. There are no roots there, and so they wither away. Others fall among thorns and the thorns grow and choke them, and so the seeds yield no fruit. Finally, other seeds fall upon good ground and grow well and healthy, enough to provide fruit."

That's what I remember from Vincent's words on the Bible.

"I hope that my paintings will yield fruit and my seeds will not have been sown in vain, for I am like the sower, I trust in the ground I walk on where I also sow. You have to trust in someone, in something, Camille."

"Yes, Monsieur Vincent."

"But you're too young to think about such things, gospel things, Bible truths. Someday perhaps, you will find your own way on your very own journey and then you will discover truths that will guide you along the way. Perhaps those very same gospels truths."

I did eventually find some of them, especially during times of crisis in my life, but that is another time, another place.

Next, came the Zouave paintings. Monsieur Vincent had hardly arrived in Arles when there was a murder of two Zouaves at the hands of two Italian men. The crime was committed at the door of one of the houses of ill-repute in Arles. It happened in the rue *des ricolettes,* as they say around here. These men were arrested and there was an inquiry into the crime. Monsieur Vincent went to the inquiry just to see what had happened. That's what he told my father. The men were being held in prison at city hall. Well, wouldn't you know there was almost a lynching by the crowd. What excitement in our usually quiet town. In the end, all Italians, men and women as well as the savoyard kids, were forced out of town. The Arlesians were angry for what was happening to their town. It had become a place of fights and debauchery, some said, all because of the garrison. The soldiers went to the bordellos and there were a lot of fights that led to violence. Scandalous! Black mark on our town! the good ladies like Madame Froitamain said. My mother had warned me repeatedly not to go near *des ricolettes* and stay away from the Zouaves.

She kept telling me, "Don't ever let me catch you around that place. Even if I don't go out much, I have eyes and ears out there to tell me what's happening all the time."

I believed her and I also believed she had eyes behind her head. Why, she could see everything, even when she wasn't looking.

Monsieur Vincent didn't like the violence and all this *chamallerie,* the quarrels, but he liked the liveliness of Arles, its streets and its people. He also liked the colorful uniform of the Zouaves. The Zouaves were Algerian-born French soldiers and their uniform was gaudy and very visible in town, so much so, that they reminded me of clowns. Monsieur Vincent thought they were amazingly colorful. He painted a young Zouave that he met when he first came to Arles. His name was Jean-Bernard, he told me. He painted him by juxtaposing the red, the green, the orange and the blue to emphasize the bold physical quality of the bull-necked young man. Monsieur Vincent repeated to me what he had recently written to his brother Théo: "Finally I have a model—a Zouave—a boy with a small face, a thick neck and eyes like a tiger. With his cat-like eyes under a reddish cap, I placed him against a green door and the orange bricks of a wall."

I think he painted him on account of the bold embroidery on his dark tunic as well as the bright red cap(Monsieur Vincent loved red but I've already told you that) that he wears on the right side of his head.

"I don't think he looks so young what with his black mustache," I told Monsieur Vincent.

"He may look old to you because you're so young, but he looks young to me."

Monsieur Vincent also painted another portrait of the young soldier that he called, **The Seated Zouave**. We can see his full uniform in this one what with his bright red baggy pants, his embroidered tunic and his red cap, this time, fully on his right ear with a dark blue tassel hanging down. I suppose that Monsieur Vincent wanted the soldier to spread his legs wide so that he was able to paint the fullness of his garment of shining red cloth. That's why the artist used yellow zigzags to simulate the light on his trousers. The wall is white and the floor is made up of a geometrical design of orange and brown tiles. And the wall's texture looks so much like plaster. What I like about this painting are the soft eyes and slender hands of the soldier. That does make him look young. I didn't know Jean-Bernard. I never met him and I never saw him around town afterward. He must have gone back to Algeria by he time Monsieur Vincent showed me the paintings. Anyway, my mother had warned me to stay away from the Zouaves and I deferentially obeyed her.

One Monday morning, Monsieur took me right outside of town to paint a wheat field. The painting is called, **Wheat Stacks with Reaper**. It was another day of bright light, intense sun and deep warmth. A day for yellows, I told myself while Monsieur Vincent was busy getting ready to paint. I counted at least fourteen stacks out in the hayfield. Stacks with little twists on top of them, and I wondered how they had gotten that way. The wheat looked like wavelets on the seas except these were golden yellow. The warm gentle morning breeze was just tilting the stalks enough so as to make them look that way. Ever since I had seen the sea at Saintes-Maries, I measured things by swells, lapping waves and breezes. They were engraved in my mind and those characteristics of the sea lent me not only images but the power of new words.

There was one solitary reaper with a sickle cutting the wheat. He had his straw hat on and didn't seem to mind the blazing sun overhead. I felt it and, at times, I sought refuge under a large bush nearby. Monsieur Vincent was in his glory painting outdoors under the sun with a dazzling light hovering over everything in nature.

"*La nature est tout à fait à elle-même ce matin, Camille, elle vibre de lumière naturellement,*" nature is totally herself and it vibrates with natural power.

The artist in him was singing a hymn to nature as he was painting the scenery before him.

"*Oui, maître, elle est suprême.*"

I liked using this word. My teacher used it all the time. He would say, "*Un repas suprême, Une phrase suprême, Un délice suprême.*" Everything was supreme with him, meal, sentence, delight, and so on.

Monsieur Vincent painted the field of wheat in the yellowiest of colors, the most intense, I thought, given the light of day. The stacks are of a deeper tone with his signature red flip on one of them. The city of Arles is in the background as a contrast with the natural beauty of the fields and the city colors being dimmer and paler. A bluish tone prevails. The sky is greenish blue with puffy clouds and on both, the sky and the clouds, he left the brush stroke effect as texture.

"It's a beautiful painting," I told him once he was done," but all your paintings are beautiful."

"Not all of them, some are not good, not good at all. I must work harder still to render that special quality to my paintings that will make them as natural as the light of day filtering through my brush strokes."

There is another wheat field that Monsieur Vincent painted and it's named, **Wheat Field**. The canvas shows the field, a tall house to the left and, of course, the red roof of a distant house in the right foreground. I say, of course, because it's ever so present this touch of red in Monsieur Vincent's paintings. But, what I admire the most about this one is the sky. It has touches of violet, violet pink at times, white, green and blue, a greening blue. The whole thing looks stupendous to me. It's imbued with a soft, serene light that seems to hover there like a magic lantern. How I love that sky. Then, there's another painting he did when I was with him and it's called, **Green Ears of Wheat.** It was done the same week that the other wheat fields were made. I remember so well the Friday morning we set out to find that spot. Monsieur Vincent had seen it before and had passed it by, but then he felt sorry that he had not painted it then, he told me.

"Do things when the spirit of creativity beckons you, Camille, otherwise the moment, that precious time where everything is just right for you to do it, passes by and you may or may not be able to recapture it. *Carpe diem*, the Latin phrase says, seize the day. Seize the day, the moment, the light and the inspiration when they come to you and run with it for it may be too late at a future time. There is a synchronization and harmony of things in nature with the light and color effect that need to be grasped immediately as soon as the whole thing hits you in the eye, for the eye is truly the mirror of the artistic capacity in you. It is for me."

Another gem for my notebook, I told myself. Another one of those keys to the wisdom of creativity. *Carpe diem,* seize the day in Latin, hmm, but what was synchronization?

"What's synchronization?"

"It means to move or come together at the same time."

I was indeed learning more and more all the time, and learning is what it was all about out there in the fields of wheat and flowers.

This painting was done with full gusto on Monsieur Vincent's part. I could sense it. Not that he didn't do the others that way but this one, he did it with the urge to create something special, flowers and wheat stalks. The flowers are poppies, red poppies all over the place. We don't see too many ears of green wheat since there are but two of them in the painting. There were more out there in the field but Monsieur Vincent chose to paint only two. The one in the very center is magnificent as its jutting in the air with its yellowish but not quite fully grown heads. This one appears to me as *un épouvantail*, a scarecrow, with its arms shooting in all directions. It's a testimony to the green boldness of the theme contrasting with the red color of the poppies and the muted light coming from the sky overhead while remaining in harmony with the whole. Monsieur Vincent captured everything just right that day and, fortunately for him, he was able to recapture the moment in time that had remained with him since he had first seen that scene.

The sky looks as if light is raining down on the field. Raining light like gentle soft rain does when the fields below thirst for it. Raining light so that my artist friend can paint the softness of a sky with the texture of blue, green and white. He painted a mood, I thought. I sat there feeling it and enjoying the scenery of my Provençal fields. Of course, Monsieur Vincent enjoyed painting this one, I think, because of the presence of the poppies. A lot of them. Poppies almost everywhere in this field. Red splotches, red daubs, red sprinkled everywhere to rejoice the eye. It gives the painting an effect of vitality. After he had finished his painting, I ran out into the field and reveled in the poppies. I plucked some, bent over some to gaze at them more closely, felt the tissue-like petals, (did you know that you can easily see sunlight through those petals?) and just absorbed them into my eyes so that they remained with me for a long, long time. I took a large poppy and carried it over to Monsieur Vincent who was preparing to leave. He looked at me with a look of tenderness and joy. He said nothing but I knew that he appreciated that gesture. Flowers have a language of their own, I know. By the way, I brought a poppy home to put it in my folder and one for my mother.

The following Monday, Monsieur Vincent and I set out to explore the edge of the city and he decided to paint the Roubine du roi canal where some women were washing their clothes. Monday was wash day, after all. It's called, **The « Roubine du roi» Canal with Washerwomen**. It's a very busy painting what with the bridge, the waters of the canal, the green banks, the small wharfs, the gasworks in the background with its tall black smokestack, the steeple of the Carmelite convent to the right in the background corner and, of course, the women, some washing, some walking about. (I'm told that the women from *les maisons de tolérance* would come and wash their clothes at la Roubine on account of its proximity with the rue Bout d'Arles).The colors are bold and sometimes harsh possibly to reflect the atmosphere of the city life. This is not the serene countryside of Arles. Monsieur Vincent did this one fast, I mean with fast strokes of the hand. He seemed to be in a hurry, but what he really wanted to do was to grasp the instantaneousness of the moment. He told me that the Japanese artists worked that way.

In this painting, we see washerwomen crouching down on the left side of the canal to wash their clothes with some of the clothes spread out onto the green bank. On the other side, other women are taking wa-

ter from the canal to do their washing and spreading their clothes on the
rise of the right bank. The bridge is a small walking bridge that looks
like sticks and planks in the painting. Passers-by are walking the length
of the road that winds its way on the left side. Two things that catch the
eye, first the water and then the vibrating sun. The waters of the canal
are moving and the movement is caught by the intensity of the bold
colors, the streak-like effect and the choice of colors, blue, white, yellow and green reflect the vibrancy of a bold yellow sun and its halo-like
vibrations in a somber green sky. All the elements are there for a canvas that whirls and hums with intense palpable boldness. Later on,
Gauguin would paint the same spot but from a very different angle
choosing not to paint the bridge and concentrate only on the washerwomen. His was done on burlap.

I met Madame Trèmonton at the canal while I was sitting on the
bank watching Monsieur Vincent paint. She happened to pass by and
stopped to tap me on the head.

"What are you doing here?" she said in a sharp tone of voice.

"I'm watching Monsieur Vincent paint," I replied.

"Don't hang around with that *voyou*," a bum, she said, "he's dangerous, you know."

"But he's a good man, he paints and doesn't bother anyone. I wish
people like you would leave him alone."

Well, she got mad at what I said to her.

"*Impertinent petit chien*," she said in a huff and walked away.

I wasn't a dog and I wasn't impolite. I simply told her what I
thought of her and people like her who do not treat Monsieur Vincent
right. They think that just because he's a stranger in our midst, he
doesn't fit in and he's no good. I should have told her then and there
that he was better than her. At least he didn't go around attacking people and ruining their reputation. Just because he was an artist didn't
mean that he was jobless and an idle tramp. She was a mean women
anyway. She was always meddling in people's business, always telling
people what to do. I'm sure she was going to tell my parents about me,
but I didn't care. I had to defend Monsieur Vincent. It was the right
thing to do. Besides, my parents knew her all too well, busybody that
she was. She was *une écornifleuse* as my father said, a parasite.

10

Ruins and Gardens

$\mathcal{T}$his is what I wrote in my note book. Today is July 10th and it's my birthday. I'm eleven years old.

I was so proud to add another year to my age. I wanted to grow up fast. Times have changed since then and I've stopped wishing to grow up fast and get ahead of myself. I wanted to grow up so that I would become a real companion to Mister Vincent. That was my thinking then. Funny how a child reasons.

I remember so well, my mother made a special supper for me with my favorite food of *saucissons et aubergines,* sausages and eggplants. My father gave me two shiny one franc pieces telling me not to spend it all.

"One franc from me and the other from your uncle, Marius," he said.

I thanked him and told him I would write to my uncle to thank him. I put one in my bank and the other piece, I only spent ten centimes for some licorice. The other centimes, I tied in the corner of my handkerchief so as not to lose them and I tucked it deep inside my pants pocket. My brother didn't give me anything.

He just told me, "Well, it's your birthday, what do you know?"

I told him he could enjoy some of my favorite food that mother had prepared but I didn't share my piece of pastry my mother bought at the *pâtisserie* for me, a chocolate éclair. I would have shared it with our new little baby but it was still in my mother's stomach.

I couldn't wait then to tell Monsieur Vincent about my becoming eleven but I only saw him the following day when he was buying coffee at the *épicerie.* Monsieur drank a lot of coffee. All day long. When I told him about my birthday, he wished me *un joyeux anniversaire* and asked me what I most wanted for my birthday. I told him that what I most wanted was a small drawing of a diligence just like the one in *Tartarin de Tarascon.*

"You know" he said, "I was going to paint a diligence but I decided to do it later on since I ran out of canvas. However, I will draw one for you. That I can do."

I would keep it forever, I told myself. And he did draw one for me. It's somewhat a miniature of the painting he did in October 1888 of the Tarascon Diligence. But, I got the first version, imagine that!

One morning, Monsieur Vincent received a huge package from his brother, Monsieur Théo. It came by train from Paris. He showed it to me and I helped him unfold the Kraft paper in which it came because Monsieur Vincent kept the paper.

"It can be very useful," he said opening up the contents.

Canvases, paints and other supplies were all there in front of us and I looked into Monsieur Vincent's eyes and could see that he was really glad.

"Now I can paint," he shouted.

Too bad he was so poor and had to rely on his brother for artistic survival, I told myself. But, thank God for his brother, Monsieur Théo, his dear beloved brother. I wish I could be that close to my brother, I thought fervently. Monsieur Vincent adored his brother and I'm sure his brother adored Monsieur Vincent. That was his only real family. The other members of his family, well, I didn't hear too much about them. He had some artist friends but very few came to visit him. He would have liked the *félibres* to visit him sometime but they avoided him and even scorned him, especially Monsieur Mistral. He was an outsider to them, *un étranger fada*, as some of the group said. So, he had no one except us the Roulins and very few others like Monsieur and Madame Ginoux. He had made a few friends at the Restaurant Carrel and the Night Café as well as the Dance Hall but they were just acquaintances with whom he drank, not real friends. He did talk about a Monsieur Gauguin from time to time, but I didn't know this Monsieur Gauguin. Little did I know then that I would get to know him very well when he would come to Arles to live with Monsieur Vincent.

The following day, I was feeling a little blue and I didn't know what to do with myself, so I went the Alyscamps, the old Roman ruins in Arles, and took my notebook along to look at my notes and to make sense of what I had written so far. I often did that just to clarify the notes and at the same time rewrite some passages that were not too clear. That's what happens when you write things in a hurry and don't have time to be precise and thus miss some of the things that complete the reporting. Besides, it offered me an opportunity to reminisce and think back as to what I had seen, heard, or wanted to say at that very moment in time. My notebook had grown a lot since I had met Monsieur Vincent. My mother used to tell my father who, at times worried about me, that it was better that I spent time with my notebook than wander about the streets in search of trouble. I would occasionally tell my mother what I had seen and what I had written in my notebook and she was very glad to hear me telling her about what I called *mes aventures de Tartarin.* She never said that what I was doing was foolish and that little boys didn't spend their time writing stupid things in a notebook as some of my buddies said about me and my adventures. No, my mother was a warm and understanding woman. I loved my mother and I was glad to have her as the trusting core of the family. My father, well, he was the rock steady part of the core. All of us relied on him to take care of us and to provide the things we needed. My father never worried about things and he liked to listen to people when they needed advice.

As I was sitting there on a big rock, I noticed, all of a sudden, Monsieur Vincent walking the long path lined with plane trees. He was alone. I questioned if I should interrupt him in his thoughts or go and talk to him. Well, the talking part got the best of me and I scurried over to be near him.

"Hi!" I said, "Would I interrupt you if I just walked with you and perhaps talk a bit?"

"No," he replied, "I was thinking about how I'm going to survive painting if I keep lacking what I need to paint and money to feed myself adequately. But, that's not your problem and you're too young to understand all of this."

"But I do understand....somewhat."

"You're very fortunate, Camille, for you have a good family and things are provided for you. I'm sure you never run out of things, you and your family. I have to struggle even to get the next meal and, at times, even another cup of coffee. But, I don't complain as long as I can paint. I don't need things, just a roof over my head and canvas and paint. I may be poor but I'm not indigent. I'm not scraping the bottom of the barrel yet. Camille, do you know what being poor is? Really poor?"

"I know some poor people," I said.

"But to be poor and without hope like the people at le Borinage where I was once."

"Where is that?" I asked.

"Let me tell you about my stay in a town where poverty was rampant and the plight of the people practically hopeless."

Then he began his story.

"Le Borinage is in Belgium. I was there for two years working among the poor people, the coal miners and their families. I lived in Petit-Wasmes, a tiny village where the coal mines were. I desperately tried to bring comfort to the people through the Gospels. Christ the great consoler and comforter who understands the life of misery and suffering. You see, in those days I thought that my calling was to become a preacher, one who carries the Lord's word to the people and I wanted to be like those poor people detached of ease and comfort. I wanted to become one of them. I even went down a coal mine. The *Marcasse* as it was called. I was there for six hours. It was so dark and gloomy down there. There were five levels where the workers spent their days mining and gathering coal so that big industry could run its plants. To my dismay, there were many boys and girls working down there. Their youth had been stolen from them. Snatched away forever. The village had a desolate, deadly air about it. That's because people's lives were concentrated on what lay below the ground not what was above it. Oh, it was a miserable life with the sick, the starving and the weakened. Here the sick took care of the sick and the poor took care of the poor. These people were slaves to the mines. I know you haven't read "Uncle Tom's Cabin," it's an American novel about slavery. You see, slavery exists everywhere in the world. You should read it someday. You should also read some of Charles Dickens' novels such as "Hard Times." It's the story about big industry ruling people's lives and destroying their dreams. There's little Sissy who loves the circus and this Mister Gradgrind who wants to destroy her imagination. It's also about a poor devil, Stephen Blackpool, who feels the crush of misery and the meanness of the wealthier class. Dickens is a true artist, a giant in the literary world. You would learn a lot from him. You need to read him, my boy."

Without stopping or even pausing, he continued his story. "Yes, le Borinage, the depth of inhumanity in a coal mine. I couldn't stay there, not only because I felt useless but because I had no encouragement from the Academy. Only defeat, that's what I felt. I was lost with my dreams and grimly alone. My only salvation out of the hole of restlessness, rejection and pain came from my drawings. That's where I stood as a destitute man without the hope and comfort that makes a human being feel wanted and understood. Not in the Bible or the ministry but in the solace and comfort of art. I decided, then and there, that my true calling was in art. I was good at it and it made me feel good about my-self. So, Camille, I may be poor in things but I'm rich in what talents God has given me to bear fruit. I never feel sorry for myself. I go through some pretty terrible times now and then but things work out for me as long as I can count on my art and the determination to keep on striving for more and better drawings and paintings. So never pity yourself in life, my little friend, count on your talents. *Fais les fructi-fier,* make them bear fruit like the almond tree that gives us both the blossoms and the almonds."

I never fully realized that Monsieur Vincent had such a hard time in life before he came to Arles, but now I knew and I admired him for it. For sticking it out and relying on his art. Now, I knew why his art was so very important to him. Now, I knew. If only the other people in town knew about it, they would most probably treat him better and with a greater sense of respect, I told myself. I wanted to shout, Monsieur Vincent is not *fada*. He's an intelligent man, a man who cares about people and likes living in Arles. But would they hear me?

July was a time of flowering gardens, bees and cicadas, lazy after-noons, celebrating Bastille Day, and the hot sun with its vibrating heat. For Monsieur Vincent, it was a time of blazing colors. He loved the or-chards in the spring and he reveled in the flower gardens during summertime. He related to me that he had told his sister he was not preoccupied with the individual flowers or their names since he left that to gardeners, but rather the colors that splashed the gardens. Splashes of red, yellow, blue, violet, green and white. It's what the eye sees in that most precious instance of visual delight that was important to him as an artist. He did not want to paint flowers but the colorful essence of flow-ers in the bright and lilting light. He didn't have time to "photograph", as he called it, the subject he was painting. He had to capture the light and shadows of that very moment given to him at that very time and space.

"Don't you see, Camille, that I have to go fast in grasping color with my brush?" he would say to me. "What I see and what you see may be the same subject but what I see is the artist's rendition of color and light."

I simply nodded in approval since what did I know about the play of light and color from an artist's point of view? I knew that he was try-ing to teach me how to see, really see things, and not just look at them with a casual glance.

That day, I saw Monsieur Vincent paint the garden of flowers that Monsieur Quenou had and it was spectacular. That's the only word for it. Flowers and flowers, colors and colors of blossoms, all in bloom.

"Camille, it's a feast of colors. Eat and enjoy as you would a meal, but eat with your eyes."

And, I did as he urged me to do. There were the velvety blues, the spicy reds, the sparkling whites, the burnt oranges, the feathery yellows and the cool greens. One could take all of this in one gulp of the eye like one takes down a delicious drink. It bubbled in the eye so effervescent that it was. Like drinking champagne on a holiday.

"So many people don't know how to use their senses to the full, Camille," he said painting away, "that they only enjoy the half of it. God gave us five senses so that we can fully enjoy all things of beauty like flowers. We must learn to smell them, see them, hear their soothing voice, touch them with the touch of a poet and taste them as you would a feast."

Right there before me was that glorious feast and Monsieur Vincent was busy doing brush stroke after brush stroke of textured colors.

During a pause, Monsieur Vincent emphasized to me that, "Nature doesn't have *des jardins à l'anglaise*, English gardens, all well trimmed, hedged, and very orderly, no, she puts things there in patches and great big blobs of color, at times. Not that she doesn't have symmetry in her disposition of things, but it's not organized as human beings like to organize things and that's what makes things like flowers, trees, and grasses look natural. It's all out there in natural modes ready for us to enjoy the splendor of color and texture as revealed in the light of day, especially in Provence where the light is dazzling. Gardens are fine examples of rich collections of flowers according to the taste and whims of gardeners. Some will over-organize things like putting each and every species in its own place and within its color harmony. Others have no sense of harmony and will put certain colors of flowers that, to the eye, seem to clash. The good gardener, in my estimation, is the one who tends to imitate nature and puts clusters and patches of flowers that will resonate with color. Five or six flowers here and there may look alright to some but dozens and dozens of flowers in clusters will highlight the principal color and make it gleam with ardor. Sometimes, you may want to concentrate on only one blossom and enjoy focusing on that specific flower, and that's fine. But, Oh! Those clusters and patches! How pleasant they are to the eye and all of the senses. What a marvelous feast for a painter who exalts in color. That's what I love to paint. Bursts of colors. Explosion of colors. Of course, with the sunflower that's somewhat of a different thing. Yes, I love fields and fields of them but I much appreciate, even more, the individual blossom or even a few of them together in a vase because they are so huge and eye filling with yellowness."

He went on without stopping. "Take this garden that I'm painting, it's natural, it's formed with clusters and blobs of rich color, and it's real. Up close, you'll see individual flowers in your limited eye space but further away, you can drink with your eye all of the fullness of color that each flower offers when it is clustered with others. Then you get an eyeful of colors: the reds, the blues, the yellows, the orange, the purple, the lavender and the whites all in patches. The gardener did well here by allowing for groups of flowers reflecting groups of colors all blended in a single garden."

I just smiled in perfect contentment simply sitting there in the grass and taking notes and enjoying the garden that Monsieur Vincent painted in his **Flowering Garden**.

Monsieur Vincent painted everything in the vast Provençal outdoors from orchards, gardens, green lawns, trees, bushes, wheat fields, ploughed fields, canals, skies, clouds, butterflies and cicadas to humble things such as, thistles, rocks and clumps of grass. Of course, he also painted the sun, the sea and the stars. No subject matter, be it large or small, humble or glorious, was excluded from his palette. Since he wanted to complete his scope as an artist, he sought models to paint, people that he thought were unique in their appearance or that he simply wanted to paint them for artistic exercise. His range of artistic endeavors was so great that he seemed to be continuously painting or drawing.

"I must keep my hands busy because my mind needs creative activity. I don't want to calcify like old bones left on the sand out to dry," he would say.

I think he was afraid of becoming useless to himself and to others. Especially to his brother, Monsieur Théo. I think that's why he painted himself as an artist on the road.

His painting, **The Painter on His Way to Work,** shows a man loaded with maulsticks, easel, canvases and other merchandise walking to his destination and leaving the city behind. The man and his shadow. That's what he painted. He's out there on the road with his faithful straw hat on his head to protect him from the searing glare of the sun. The road is speckled with short brush strokes of deeper and lighter yellow, some red-orange and some blue and behind him two fields juxtaposed, one of yellow wheat and one fallow in green. The artist is exactly in the center of the painting suggesting that he is at the core of creative activity in nature. He's on the move, on a quest. What quest? Perhaps searching for his own identity as a person who strives ever so hard to find himself. Had he found himself here in Arles, I wondered. Or, was Arles just a reprieve from his quest as an artist? At least, he had found a place where he could wander and paint as long as he had the strength and mental clarity to do so. And, of course, he still clung to his dream of *l'atelier du Midi*. That kept him truly alive and hopeful. But, hopes are dashed very easily and I only wish now that what happened to his hopes and dreams had not happened then. That he would have realized his dream of a workshop and that he would have gathered his artist friends together and set a model for all artists to come in the future. That would have been his creative legacy. But, that is wishful thinking. However, he did set a creative legacy. That was with his art and that will last for a very long time, if not forever. I predict that his art will keep growing and growing in appreciation over the years to come. I may be wrong, but I sense it in my bones and in my heart that this is a very good feeling because it's real and not just wishful thinking on my part. Anyway, I really liked "The Painter on his Way to Work" and I told Monsieur Vincent so. He smiled with that blue twinkle in his eyes appreciating my presence in his life. This painting, I feel, projects and conserves on canvas the eternal quest of the artist going off to paint as an everyday event in his life. Monsieur Vincent's life in Arles.

Later on, he showed me another work of his. It wasn't an oil painting but a watercolor. I didn't realize that he used that medium. He told me that watercolors were somewhat more difficult to do since they required another skill, another way of doing things. Watercolors were not oil paints, of course, and he tried to explain to me that he had to experiment with that medium first before he was able to master it and be satisfied with the product. His friend Mauve had initiated him to it. Watercolors run and they're fussy, he said. They can disintegrate in tone if you don't know how to use them. One color can easily run into another color thus ruining the effect and clarity the artist wants. Of course, with watercolors we don't see brush strokes. The lines and the colors are clear and even. The painting he showed me looked as if it were taken from a children's book or a magazine of some kind. It looked like an illustration. It had what I would call a dreamlike quality to it. I must say that it was different from the other works that he had made. He liked variety and challenges, Monsieur Vincent did.

The watercolor is of Monsieur Daudet's mill and it's entitled, **The Mill of Alphonse Daudet at Fontvieille.** Fontvieille is in the vicinity of Arles. It had to be the mill Daudet writes about in his collection of tales, *Lettres de mon moulin.* I like the story, *La légende de l'homme à la cervelle d'or,* while my teacher preferred, *Les trois messes basses.* As for Monsieur Vincent, he said that his favorites were, *Les étoiles* and *L'Arlésienne.* They're all good stories written by one of our own here in Provence. I like the one about the man with a golden brain because it's a tale of fantasy and delight, a man mining his own head for gold. What a crazy story but it's delightful as a tale.

Monsieur Vincent's painting has a vineyard in its foreground with a yellow windmill sitting on top of a small hill except the arms of the windmill are on the other side practically hidden. The sky is full of puffy white clouds, not storm clouds. The ambience we get is one of quietude and reverie and I think that's what the artist wanted to capture in this watercolor. When I think back on this watercolor and link it to Daudet's stories, I imagine that I'm flying in the wind that the windmill produces with its thrashing arms and I'm off to a distant land, a land of enchantment and colors.

11

Portraits and Models

$\mathcal{A}$délaïde Dandelou was a young girl of fourteen who was a close friend of Jeanne Calment. She had deep dark eyes and black hair. She was tall for her age and had *une taille de guêpe*, as people said, a very slim waist. She was smart in school and had a gentle disposition. People liked her. Unlike Jeanne, she wasn't at all talkative nor did she blow up her chest to attract attention from the boys. I got to know her when she used to come to my aunt Estello's house on the rue Voltaire. She liked to play cards with my cousin, Couleto, and sometimes the three girls, Adélaïde, Jeanne and Couleto would talk for hours about different things. You know, girl's things. Adélaïde's mother was a true Arlésienne with glowing dark eyes, jet-black hair and a lovely complexion. People said that in her youth, Crestino Bellaval was a real beauty desired by all the young suitors in town. But, she married the young and boldly charming Glaudi Dandelou whose father owned a fishing vessel and made runs to Marseille for the delivery of mussels, some fish, like *le loup* and *le rouget*, sometimes sea urchins. When his father died, Glaudi acquired more vessels until he had a well-established fleet of fishing vessels. The Dandelous were not rich but well off. They had many friends and Madame Dandelou could entertain with the best of them in town. She loved to attract attention to herself and to her daughter, her prized *objet de fierté*, her pride and joy. She lavished on her daughter choice food and choice articles of clothing because she wanted the finest *toilette* for her daughter. There was some jealousy between Madame Dandelou and Madame Calment as to which girl would have the finest dress and the finest ribbons in her hair. Madame Dandelou spared no expense for her daughter's *toilette*. She even traveled to Marseille to get merchandise not seen yet in Arles. Had she gotten her way (her husband had put a stop to her extravagance, they said) she would have taken the train to Paris to purchase the very best. Not that she was a spendthrift, but she loved nice things. Some people said that Adélaïde was getting spoiled and that she would grow up a snob. However, she remained untouched by her mother's attempts to spoil her. She was simply a nice young girl. Ironically, she later married a cabinet maker who, although well respected and liked, became a drunk on the sly and Adélaïde turned out to be the town's *femme dou-lour*, for she carried in her heart a painful burden all her married life. Her mother, not wanting to face her daughter and her son-in-law's decline in society, moved away and no one knew where. Completely dispirited. Her husband had died a few years before.

Well, Adélaïde became Monsieur Vincent's first model for the portrait of a Provençal girl. Adélaïde's mother was so very happy and proud that Monsieur Vincent had chosen her daughter for a portrait that she invited all her neighbors to her home for a celebration. My mother could not go because she was expecting her child soon and she wanted to stay at home. I remember so well the day Monsieur started the portrait. He had borrowed a cane chair from us and installed it in his yellow house, ready for the sitter. I wasn't there the first day but I managed to be invited for the fourth one when he was almost done with the portrait.

He was telling my parents how well the portrait was coming along when he said to me, "Why don't you drop in tomorrow and see what I've done so far." Adélaïde came into Monsieur Vincent's house dressed the same way she had done for three days and sat down the way Monsieur Vincent had positioned her.

"Do you mind if Camille watches?" he asked the young girl.

She said demurely, "No, Monsieur."

I was glad she didn't object since I wanted to be there to see a portrait in its final stages.

The portrait was completed the following day and Adélaïde left telling Monsieur Vincent that her mother desperately wanted to see the finished painting. He told her that she could come the day after next when he would have it ready for showing.

"Nice young girl, Adélaïde is. Her mother came with her the first day. She's a fidgety woman. Do you know Adelaïde well?" he asked me.

"No, I only know her like that. She's a friend of Jeanne Calment."

"Oh, that girl," he said with recognition. "That one wants to impress me every time I meet her. I don't know why. There's nothing remarkable about me. I don't think she likes me deep down because she tells people that I'm not at all sophisticated, even mean looking as well as grubby. I know what people say about me, you know. I didn't choose her for my model because I didn't think she was unsophisticated enough. I mean, she was too bold for me. I like boldness in a woman but not in a young girl. Besides, her features were not the ones I was seeking."

I didn't know what to say.

"Let me tell you about the portrait, Camille. You see the colors there, pointing to the girl's face. I used the ones I thought would highlight the young girl's features and personality. I call her a *mousmé* because, to me, she's like a Japanese girl, her age, and so I made her features a bit Oriental on account of that. Young Japanese girls are reserved and not whatsoever bold in their appearance and demeanor. I read about a *mousmé* in Pierre Loti's new novel, 'Madame Chrysanthème.' Remember, I told you about the story and your mother objected to your reading the novel? It's about Japanese life and the story tells of a love affair between a Japanese woman and a Westerner. I suppose you're too young to enjoy love stories. Maybe some day you'll want to read it. Anyway, the painting juxtaposes colors just as I have seen in Japanese prints. I wanted to imitate the masters, you see."

He went on to tell me about the other colors he used in this painting. He used the same description of color techniques he described later on to his brother: "The *mousmé's* costume is a royal blue skirt with large yellow-orange dots topped with a striped blood red and violet bodice. The flesh tones are yellowish-gray, her hair is touched with violet, and black brows and lashes frame her eyes, Prussian blue with orange in them. The background is white, heavily tinged with malachite green, and she holds a bunch of oleanders in her hands."

"Do you know why, Camille?"

"Because it represents the Midi?" I said.

"Yes, because it reminds me of the delicate side to the Midi," he replied.

The portrait is called, **Mousmé, Sitting in a Cane Chair, Half-Figure**. I told him that the portrait was truly different. Not at all like a photograph. He looked at me and he smiled. A wide smile. I liked the colors and how they brought out Adélaïde's fine features. And, of course, I did notice the bright red ribbon in Adélaïde's hair, Monsieur Vincent's signature. That's what I call it.

Adélaïde's features as a *mousmé* are well defined in this portrait, I think, because we can see her long and thin eyebrows, her elongated hand and fingers as well as her full pink mouth ever so lightly opened. She has become the demure Japanese young lady that Monsieur Vincent wanted to paint in this portrait. He was such a master with subject matter and colors. It seemed that every day, I was forever learning something different from him either about painting, or literature, or something else. I paid special attention that day making sure I was putting down the full description of colors in my notebook as given to me by the master. I learned later on that Madame Dandelou said that the portrait wasn't quite to her liking. The colors were too bold, she said, and her daughter's features were exaggerated. I don't think Madame Dandelou knew too much about art and painting.

Monsieur Vincent decided to shave off his beard in late July. He looked strange, so different from what I was accustomed to. His face looked bare. He didn't say why he had done it. Simply because he wanted to, I suppose. Maybe because it was getting too hot or that he wanted to look clean. In any case, it was done. I must say that he looked like a pale northerner. He even did a self-portrait without a beard and mustache. I really like his eyes in that one. Big expressive eyes with a small golden glint in the left eye. The lips are full and pink, the same shade as his left ear. He looks healthy and strong in this one, just the way I knew him until his illness. Of all the self-portraits he showed me, this one is arguably the best of the lot. Not that I didn't like him with a beard and mustache.

Right about that time, my mother had her baby, July 31st to be exact. It was a girl; my very first baby sister and my parents were going to call her, Marcelle. My father was ecstatic. The first girl in the family. We drank wine, not *un vin de table*, cheap wine, but a hardy Châteauneuf-du-Pape and celebrated the birth of my sister. Monsieur Vincent came over to join us in our celebration. He congratulated my mother and father on the new arrival and told them that he wished he had a family like ours. I could tell that he loved us, all of us and now the baby.

"I hope you'll paint the baby's portrait someday," said my father to Monsieur Vincent.

"Oh, not only the baby Marcelle but also the entire family," he responded.

I could see the gleam in my father's eyes and I had a gleam in my heart. The master was going to paint my portrait, imagine that! My mother sat in her wicker chair and said nothing. I think she was a bit apprehensive of going to Monsieur Vincent's house to have her portrait done, not that she didn't like him, "but going to his house, well..." she said later. My father used to tell her that she would get to know him better because he had invited Monsieur Vincent over the house for soup one of these days. Besides, he already had come over one Sunday afternoon to share our Sunday meal when he talked about the Japanese and their art, he said. My mother told my father to let her know when his friend was coming so she could prepare herself for his visit.

"It's just soup with bread and some wine, *sa mère*," he would say, and my mother replied, "I know, I know, but he's company."

Well, Monsieur Vincent did come for soup two weeks following the birth of Marcelle knowing that my mother had fully regained her strength. We had *la soupe de pistou* that I liked very much, and he liked it too.

"Soup warms the inside and the heart," he told my mother.

She smiled at him, a great big motherly smile. He liked to look at the baby and touch her little hands.

"A gift from God," he said, "a precious little human being that belongs to all of you Roulins."

My father put his arm around his shoulders and gave him a big proud smile and said, "Perhaps some day you'll have a little family of your own, *mon ami*."

"No, *Père Roulin*, not for me. It's not in the cards."

I loved going over to the walnut crib and gazing fondly at my baby sister. I even talked to her even though she could not talk yet. She seemed to grow every day. She had big fat cheeks, a double chin and huge eyes that stared at me when I began to talk to her. Even my brother Armand came once in a while to look at the baby. He would rock the cradle with the cord attached to it, and the cradle swayed a little.

My father did not like priests and so he refused to have my baby sister christened at Saint Trophime church as other families in Arles had done. It was traditional. No, he simply refused because he did not trust priests and their ceremonies. He was a disciple of Voltaire, he had told Monsieur Vincent. The entire family of the Roulins and the Pellicots, aunts, uncles and some of my cousins showed their displeasure and grumbled at not having a christening and especially the traditional feast following the baptism. No baptism, my father said.

"We will have a feast and I will do the naming myself," stated my father with authority and boldness.

He was emphatic about that. So, we had a feast and all of the family, even Monsieur Vincent was there. My aunt Berenguiero, my mother's sister, and her husband Roumié looked *endimanchés*, in their Sunday best, and were disappointed that they had not been asked to be godparents of the child, my sister. That is all they talked about at the feast. After all, the custom was that, if a girl, then the godparents would be chosen from the mother's side of the family. It was traditional and no one dared to break tradition among the Provençaux. I think it was true throughout France.

My aunt had her flowery hat on and my uncle wore a white shirt and a tie that seemed to strangle his reddening neck. My aunt Babello and my uncle Jaquet had Monsieur Vincent by both arms and they were talking up a storm. I suppose they got to like him or they were just trying to be nice to him. He had on a nice shirt and pants, a black velvet jacket with pearl buttons. He even had a scarf around his neck. A red one. I had never seen him dressed up that way since he was always with his painting clothes when I saw him. Sometimes, he looked somewhat *frippé*, wrinkled, my mother would say, but I never looked at his clothes, just the way he painted. Some people in town only looked at his appearance and judged him from that, nothing else. I know that he looked somewhat like a *clochard* at times, a street bum, but he was an amazing person, at least that's the way I saw things with him.

People at the feast ate, drank and had fun. There were little sachets of *dragées*, sugarcoated almonds that were handed out. I got two little bags, one whose content I ate and the other I stored away. People told stories and talked about old times. That's the way it always went when my family got together, things way back when, and people of olden times who formed the soul and history of our family.

I learned things about my family then, funny things, odd things, heart-warming things and things that usually grown-ups didn't want children to know, but came out in the open when grown-ups have a little too much wine to drink. For instance, I learned that my mother's grandfather had been one of the pioneers of Arles and had come to France from Italy to marry a French girl, and his family had disowned him. I also learned that my father's twin cousins, Ernestine and Alphonsine, who were born in Montpelier, had escaped to Alsace when they learned that their father had secretly made an agreement to marry them off to some tenant farmers, brothers who were as old as the hills, they said. They preferred to be in exile, as they said, rather than marry some old goats. Everybody knew that their father had left them out of his will. Interesting things like that. Finally, I got to talk to Monsieur

Vincent after he left a conversation between my father and my uncle Davioun. They were talking about the politics of General Boulanger. Monsieur Vincent came over to see me and told me that my father had agreed to pose for him and that he would do it soon. First, he would do a drawing, then, later a portrait. I was so glad, so glad that he was doing my father, the family man, the *brigadier-chargeur*, and a man who was truly Monsieur Vincent's friend.

My father was a man of principles. He lived by them and expected people to do the same. He liked Monsieur Vincent because he considered him a man of principles and strength of character. That's the way he saw him. He befriended him and he was loyal to him as a friend. Early on, when Monsieur Vincent came to Arles, he became his friend while many of the townspeople refused to even talk to the stranger artist. They all thought he was weird and they wanted nothing to do with him. They didn't harm him or anything like that but they were very cold and not at all friendly towards him. Why? He was considered to be crazy. Principally, he was not a Provençal and so he was considered completely out of it. First of all, he did not speak Provençal and that did not ingratiate him with the natives. He told me repeatedly that he wished he could speak and understand our language. I used to translate things for him, at times, when he asked me to. For instance, he would ask me what does this mean, what does that say, what's the meaning of this, and so on, such as: *félibre, pièi, estello, caminaire, parpaioun, calabrun* and *dina*. Poet, then, star, walker, butterfly, dusk and lunch, I would tell him. That was besides the names of people that he did not always get like, *Bertoun* for Albert, *Touneto* for Antoinette, *Ricou* for Henri and *Titino* for Christine. He smiled and shook his head.

My father was kind to Monsieur Vincent. He never refused him anything, especially a kind word or some piece of advice. He trusted him with me and he considered him like a son and I considered him like a brother. He became part of the family. That's how openhearted my father was. Of course, my father had his political views and strong republican tendencies but he was opened, as far as people's views and ideas. For instance, my father was not one for art but he respected the man that was Monsieur Vincent. I must say that, with time, my father began to appreciate the artist and his work and he would defend the skill and product of a man who worked terribly hard at producing works of art. Although my father was not too educated, he could read and understand things he read, enough to be able to discuss things intelligently. I believe Monsieur Vincent sympathized with my father because he himself had had a hard time with schooling when he was younger. School and book learning was not Monsieur Vincent's forté, just like me. However, he grew up to be a very intelligent man, one who could read voraciously, draw and paint marvelously well. Moreover, he was a man with a big heart. Too bad he didn't have a family because he would have been a very good father like my father was.

When Monsieur Vincent told my father that he wanted to do his portrait, my father beamed with delight. He told him that he was honored to be asked to sit for an artist who, some day, would become famous because he had something to offer the world, something different and done with genuine talent. Monsieur Vincent told him that he was not out to seek fame and glory, only a public and a market so that he could live better than he was doing now and continue to paint without worrying about where the next franc was coming and how he was going to be able to afford to buy canvas and paint. My father always encouraged him by telling him that a day would come when he would be able to afford all the things he needed. He never mentioned the fact that Monsieur Vincent had to rely constantly on his brother to survive. My father never ever talked about it, nor insinuated that Monsieur Vincent should get a real job and earn a living.

Well, on the day of the sitting, my father put on his uniform all cleaned and pressed by my mother, his cap on his head and he had even brushed his long curly beard. He looked truly presentable, as my mother told him that morning. I thought so too. We walked over to Monsieur Vincent's. He had my father sit in the cane chair, the same one that Adélaïde sat in for her portrait. He told my father that, first, he was going to do a drawing of his head and father shook his head in assent. My father wanted to take his cap off in deference to politeness being inside a house and respect for the artist. Monsieur Vincent told him to leave it on since he wanted him in full uniform. I sat on a straight chair in a corner of the room not wanting to hinder the artist at work and, perhaps, make my father feel ill at ease if I stood too close. I was simply happy being there and watching. Of course, I had my faithful notebook with me.

Monsieur Vincent started drawing with a reed pen, a quill pen and brown ink. He said that he wanted to draw my father first like he had drawn *Mousmé*'s half figure first, just to get the feel of the subject and to refine his drawing skills. He loved to draw, he said, and he was good at it. Reed pens, explained Monsieur Vincent, were used by the Egyptians for writing on papyrus. They're stiffer than quill pens and don't retain a sharp point for long but they make bold strokes that the artist sometimes needs to strengthen his drawing strokes. On the other hand, the quill pen made of a large bird's feather such as a goose, is just right for making fine lines, and between the reed and quill pens, Monsieur Vincent was able to make a drawing according to his own specifications. Sometimes, he used just the reed pen, he said. My father found that his friend, the artist, knew quite a lot about drawing and he was glad to sit for one so that he could tell his friends that he had posed for an artist's drawing.

Monsieur did the profile and then the rest of the head and shoulders down to my father's jacket where he used the reed pen for bolder strokes. I could see now why he used this kind of pen. He also used it for the cap with the word POSTES on the front just above the visor. As for the face and the background, it was the quill pen, much finer lines. What was amazing to me was seeing my father's resemblance coming through at every stroke and line. It was like an image emerging out of darkness and into the light of day. What talent, what skill and dexterity on the artist's part. I stood there wishing I could do that myself, but I had no talent for drawing. It takes special talent to be able to draw, that I knew, more so with this drawing.

The next day, Sunday, Monsieur Vincent started early on my father's portrait in oil. He said that he loved to have my father as a model since he was still and serene, hardly moving a muscle. There he was, straight as an picket sitting in the cane chair with his left arm leaning on the little table next to him. He was dressed proudly in his *brigadier-chargeur* double-breasted uniform with the eight shiny brass buttons on the front of his jacket and one on the cuff of each sleeve. Right above each cuff button was a swirl of gold braid that looked like two bows of tied shoelaces at the bottom swirling higher into a giant oval. The gold braid really made him look official, I thought. And on his postal cap with visor, there was written in gold letters, POSTES. We could see his white shirt underneath at the neck and chest, and his two hands with long fingers were resting one on the table and the other on the arm of the chair. They really looked like the hands of a refined gentleman, I thought. His beard was tinged with white as Monsieur Vincent painted it, and for the first time, I realized that my father was getting older, not old like an old man, but on in years. Of course, forty-seven was old for me. The beard, burnt gold and bristling like a magnetic field, looked just imperial. As a matter of fact, Monsieur Vincent thought that my father looked Russian. Like a czar, I suppose. I must say that my father was not your typical Provençal male. He was different, and I suppose that's why my mother had chosen him among many in Lambesc. What was most captivating about my father was his solid face full of soft strength and color, and his eyes, liquid and clear in their gaze. That's what the artist captured in his painting, **Portrait of the Postman Joseph Roulin**, and that's why the painting is so true.

The colors are bright, pure and eye-catching. Monsieur Vincent said later that he had used yellows, pinks, violets, greens, and reds for the broken tones in the face set against a blue-white background. The uniform is Prussian blue with yellow decorations. And these colors make the portrait of my father unusual and at the same time real. I thought it was perfect. Unfortunately for Monsieur Vincent who was a perfectionist if not an idealist, he wasn't altogether satisfied with the portrait, especially the face. He asked my father to sit another time for another portrait, this time only the upper part. This one has a light blue background, and I thought it wasn't as well *réussi* as the full portrait. My father looks somewhat stiff and a bit sad in the second one, I thought. I still do today, as I edit my notes.

Monsieur Vincent then asked a woman of the night, as they called them, to serve as model for him for he thought that she would make a fine model, but she refused saying that people would mock her seeing her face in a painting by the stranger artist. Besides, many people thought that his paintings were *pleins de peinture*, full of paint and messy, and they would not want to be seen in one of his works. What would people say, what would they think? That's all these people thought, only what others might say. That holy reputation of theirs is the only thing they thought of and it wasn't that holy most of the time, that's what my father said. He never talked about anybody, my father, but, at times, he just had to let it out so disenchanted was he with some people in Arles.

Monsieur Vincent did find himself another model. This time it was a peasant farmer called Patience Escalier. He had been, at one time, a *gardian* in the Camargue. He loved horses. He was now a sort of gardener in a *mas* at La Crau, a gardener and shepherd who reminded Monsieur Vincent of the peasant portrait sitters he had done in Nuenen. He had done several drawings of poor people there and he loved those subjects as an artist, he told me. Moreover, he saw a remarkable resemblance between the peasants of the Camargue countryside and those in Millet's paintings. Millet was, after all, according to Monsieur Vincent, the poet artist of peasant life. After his first encounter with Patience Escalier, Monsieur Vincent described him to his brother as the kind of figure found in Millet's well-known <u>The Man with a Hoe</u>. Monsieur Vincent told me that he had selected Escalier as model because he saw in him the essential man of the earth, a true peasant, *un pays-an,* a man of the land. He admired the hardiness and strength of character of these poor people who earned their living taking care of soil, beast and fields. They were rugged individuals and they survived the hardships of the seasons as well as the toil of everyday living. In their faces were engraved the years of struggles and pain that daily existence demanded of them. Theirs was a noble figure worthy of any artist's brush or pen, he said.

I first met Patience Escalier after Monsieur Vincent had already painted his portrait in the Camargue. It was the second time that I accompanied Monsieur Vincent to that region right before school started again in the fall. I found Escalier to be a simple man living meagerly on the *mas* doing some harvesting and taking care of a small flock of sheep that belonged to the tenant-farmer he worked for. He was a quiet man, a man of few words who allowed Monsieur Vincent to do his portrait because no one else had done him the honor of asking him to be the subject of a portrait. I could tell that he was a proud, *fier,* yet humble man. Proud of his labor and of his being a man of the plains, *un vrai Camarguais*, he told us. I don't know how old he was but he must have been as old as Monsieur Brèchamps, the old sheepherder that I knew. He was eighty years old. He had done a lot of sheep herding in his life and he still did some when someone asked him to help out. What a strong and willful man he was, Monsieur Brèchamps. When he set his mind to it, nothing would stop him. A dyed-in-the-wool Provençal, he was. We are people of *le Midi* and we are hardy people, people of the sun, wind, rain, and soil, and fields of wheat, of traditions, family bound and rich in how to do things on our own. We don't rely on the capital, Paris, and all of its politics and styles. We have our own way of doing things and practice our own politics. We are *têtus et un peu fadas parfois*, hardheaded and a bit crazy at times, yes, but we are sane in our way of living. And, we have our very own language, *le Provençal*, that Mistral put into prominence again after a disuse, because some people thought it was *passé* and quaint, not practical for the modern world. Well, he made us proud again, proud to be a Provençal. Later on, he even got the Nobel Prize for literature. Imagine that. My father would have been surprised. It showed that we were important, that our culture was important enough for the world to take notice. Paris, especially, because *Paris n'est pas le nombril du monde.* No, it's not the navel of the world. It's but a wrinkle, an important one, but not the entire center of importance.

I really like Patience Escalier's portrait, after all, what did I not like about Monsieur Vincent's work. This particular painting has a deep realness to it. It has the colors of harvest, the old gold, russet and orange of harvest time. It is we at the season of the fullness of the fruit and grain. It's all of us here of the *Midi* in the person of Patience Escalier, the gardener, sheepherder and gatherer of the fruits of the earth. The painting shows him in full ripening of color. The artist highlighted the fact that Escalier was tanned and air-swept, thus suggesting the outdoor life in the full sun and wind of the Midi. In this painting, he uses bold colors thus rendering the portrait forcefully alive. The old peasant is suffused by the vivid, hot colors of the harvest landscape and climate in which he labored daily for years. It all can be seen in the old man's face. *C'est un homme du territoire*, a man of the land we live in.

The ultramarine green, the white and blues of his jacket and the contrast of the bright yellow broad-rim hat make him look fresh and clean. His sad eyes and ruddy cheeks attest to his name of Patience, since the old gardener and sheep herder of La Camargue remains a creature of God who is tested by time, climate and labor. The background of this work is a swirling dark blue with some lighter highlights, all with thick brush strokes probably evoking the deep and weary struggles in the life of this old man. In any case, the figure and the background colors make a nice contrast and enhance Monsieur Vincent's attempt at painting the portrait of a typical, if not legendary, peasant among us. I thought that this work, **Portrait of Patience Escalier, Shepherd in Provence**, was a genuine success at painting man linked so closely to nature. Just his face says it all, features of the Provençal soil at harvest time. A time to bring in the profits of our labor and share them with others, just as the farmer does. Monsieur Vincent painted another portrait of Escalier, this time with a dark blue smock, a reddish yellow background and a red ribbon around the crown of his hat. It's the same old wizened face with the sad eyes. This time the peasant is leaning with both hands on the knob of his walking stick. I know that Monsieur Vincent liked this man and loved painting his portrait because he was following in the footsteps of one of his masters, Jean-François Millet.

The next time I saw Monsieur Vincent, he was painting a pair of old shoes. Just that, old shoes. A simple pair of worn shoes, on the floor. That's it. At first, I thought it would look odd or even too simple a subject to paint since I was accustomed to vast sceneries in nature, flower gardens that seized the eye or boats on the Mediterranean shore, and the portraits, yes, the exquisite portraits, not a pair of dirty old shoes. It was too banal, too ordinary for a painting, I thought, but Monsieur Vincent showed me, no, he taught me, that even an old pair of discarded shoes can become noble enough for a painting. How? By its very essence of shoeness, he said, and by the touch of the artist in bringing to a banal subject color, perspective, light and shadow. In other words, the subject matter doesn't really count, it could be anything, and it's the treatment given by the artist that counts. We must not be judgmental about what is being painted, he said, we must not place our own values on it, rather we should look with our creative eye and behold the plenitude of the object itself being painted by the artist.

"I paint anything," he stated, "I paint what I see with my mind's eye and I render those things that I see in a way that reflects the artist in me. That's what counts, not the object itself. The object is the conduit of inspiration. Too many people want nice and pleasant things painted in a nice and pleasant way, things that they want for their nice and pleasant walls, but I paint for the satisfaction of painting, in other words, being creative with an object, be it a shoe or a sunflower. The sunflower is a common, ordinary flower that grows anywhere here in Provence, but what treatment the Creator has given it. I just imitate that treatment in my paintings of the sunflowers because I'm imitating nature."

I never forgot those words. They're still in my notebook, underlined.

A Pair of Old Shoes is the name of this painting. A very common name for a common thing lying on the tile floor. The colors are subdued in tone, not vivid or loud. Browns, yellows and whites dominate the painting except for the blue and black brush strokes that seem to be vibrating as light would on the left side of the left shoe. Of course, there's the red effect on the one tile on the bottom right. Shoes, old shoes, how many kilometers have they walked, how many times have they been put on and then taken off, how much dust have they collected in the hot sun, and where will they land finally? How many years have they been subjected to? Those and many more questions could be asked. It's up to the one who contemplates this painting to ask them for the artist has simply posited his creative treatment of these shoes. Shoes are like old friends. They get worn and tired but you hate to throw them out since they've brought you comfort for a long time. So you keep them and wish you could find a pair just like them.

Then, Monsieur Vincent told me all about still life paintings. A still life, he said, *une nature morte*, is a painting with inanimate things typically commonplace objects. It could be fish, fruits, flowers, or even a cup, or a plate. According to Monsieur Vincent, the still life gives the artist the opportunity to arrange the design of things within a composition. Take Monsieur Vincent's painting, **Still Life: Vase with Oleanders and Books**. You have a table with flowers in a jar and two books, one on top of the other. The flowers are oleander blossoms, the jar a Majolica jar and the books, well, one is Zola's, "La joie de vivre." I asked Monsieur Vincent what the Zola book was all about and he told me that it was the story of a woman named, Pauline Quenu, who devotes her life to others.

"You should read it someday. It's part of Zola's long saga entitled, 'Les Rougon-Macquart.' It's called a *roman-fleuve.*"

As for the oleander, it has long been associated with Provence. It was one of Monsieur Vincent's favorites. He said it represented le Midi for him. The arrangement of the flowers looks like two arms spread out in both directions with three clusters of different height in the middle. The flowers themselves are red and cream-colored that the artist has captured so very well. Of course, he couldn't get the smell of those beautiful blossoms on canvas but if you use your creative sense of smell you can easily get that aroma tingling in your nose, the smell of oleanders being so sweet and powerful. I love the smell of oleanders and so does my mother. My uncle Roumié loved oleander so much that he planted lots of oleander bushes right outside his home.

With the oleanders are branches of green leaves like fingers sticking out here and there. Then, there's the jar with the handle. It's pottery with bright designs on it. We call it *faience*. The bottom of the jar is green and the top, black with a red flower design, just like the oleanders. The entire effect of jar and flowers is simply harmonious, and that's why the artist chose this element. The top of the table is made up of yellows, browns and reds with three green stripes on the right. The books, to the left, harmonize with the top of the table since one is yellow and the other russet brown. The wall is green with what looks like tinges of yellow on the left side. Then, there is the texture. The flowers have their own texture and it's not as heavy as that of the table and wall. The texture of the table is heavier with mixed strokes while that of the wall is done with short and bold vertical brush strokes. I came to appreciate still life paintings the more Monsieur Vincent painted them and explained them to me. Not the subject matter but the design and specifically the treatment. I had learned a new word, treatment, and I now knew what it meant in art. I was going to put it in my notebook.

"I don't know what happened to my notebook," I shouted in muted despair to my mother.

"What about your notebook?" my mother answered me. "I didn't take it. No one did. You always have it with you. Don't be alarmed. I know it's important to you."

"Important? Important?" I said in tones of incredulity. "It's my most important thing in life."

"Now, now, Camille, we'll find it. Just calm down."

"If I don't find it, I don't know what I'll do. I'll go mad. It's just about the worse thing that could have happened to me. All that I've collected from my learning about art from Monsieur Vincent is in there. It's precious to me. It's my whole life, *maman*," I said with an emphasis to my words.

"I know, I know. We'll look for it, but right now I have to feed Marcelle. Your notebook can wait for a while," she replied half scolding me.

"But, I don't know what I'll do if I don't find it. I have to go to the Carrel restaurant with Monsieur Vincent tomorrow."

"What are you going to do there? Certainly not to eat. We have food in the house."

"No, not to eat. Monsieur Vincent wants to paint the inside of the restaurant."

"Paint the walls?"

"No, he's an artist. He wants to do a painting of the restaurant's interior."

"Well, artists can paint walls too."

"I know, but he's not going to waste time painting walls."

"Sometimes, I think he would gain more by painting walls than painting things like fields and bugs, or like the cicadas he draws and the moths he paints."

"He doesn't need a job, *maman*, he's an artist."

"Artists need to work and earn a living too, *mon fils*, don't forget that."

"Some day, Monsieur Vincent will be famous and earn a lot of money with his art, you'll see."

"That day has a very long time coming. Has he sold any? Do you see how's he dressed and how he doesn't eat well? Some say he's practically a beggar."

"Who says that?"

"Some people. Not me, but some people who see him around town say that. He's a nice man but I'm not too comfortable around him."

"*Maman*, he's more than a nice man, he's a splendid artist and he's a man of good heart. Ask *papa*."

Anyway, the conversation went on for a while and I still had not found my notebook.

"Retrace your steps, Camille, you may have left it somewhere else, perhaps at Monsieur Vincent's place."

Well, I did and I realized that I could have left it on the small table in Monsieur Vincent's house. I rushed over there and found him cleaning his brushes.

"*Bonjour, Camille*," he said. "Did you know you forgot your notebook here yesterday? I know how you cherish it and how important it is to you. I was going to go over and bring it to you later."

"Oh, Monsieur Vincent, you don't know how much I was worried about losing it. Without my notebook, I'm lost."

"Now, now, it's not a matter of life and death, Camille, you could always reconstruct your notebook because you have a very good memory."

"With everything that I have in there? No, Monsieur Vincent, I could never recall everything."

"Well, you have it now. Take good care of it. Are you ready for tomorrow?"

"Yes, sir, I'm ready," and I held tight to my faithful notebook in my pants pocket as I went home to tell my mother.

The Restaurant Carrel was situated at 30 Rue Cavalerie. It was part hotel, part restaurant. I knew the address very well because I went by it almost every day. Monsieur Vincent used to stay at the hotel and he quite often took his meals at the restaurant. He left the hotel on account of some misunderstanding he had with the owners. He claimed that they didn't like him taking too much space with his paintings. Besides, they were charging him more money than other clients, he said, and he was giving them more money than the fly-by-nights, he insisted. He didn't like it there. Furthermore, he had a hard time going in and out of the place with his paraphernalia. Things did not work out for him there and that's why he rented the *atelier* space he later lived in. That's what my father had said.

The painting, **Interior of the Restaurant Carrel in Arles**, shows several long tables with chairs set up for guests who go and eat there. At first, Monsieur Vincent used to go there often but he stopped going after he moved and probably before that. He liked simple things such as potatoes, rice and macaroni but none of the cooks would make him some. They insisted on their own fares. He couldn't even get a good hot broth, he told my father. He had a sensitive stomach and his health wasn't always very good. I think that's why my father invited him sometimes to have soup with us. In this painting, we see several customers with a lady server dressed in a white apron and headdress with arms folded. The perspective that the artist took is rather distant since in the foreground we see many empty tables. The people sitting are in the back. That's the perspective he wanted, I suppose. The work has a soft and brownish tone to render the poor light quality of the room. I watched him as I sat on one of the chairs sipping a glass of juice. He was ardently at work impervious to others in the room. Years later, thinking about this painting, I thought that what he had painted was a mood, one of isolation and perhaps loneliness. This work is in complete contrast with his other works painted in the full, bright and lustrous sun. There are no vivid colors. No sparkle, no lush liveliness as in the still life with the oleanders. It's a quiet painting. One that hardly breathes. It's not my favorite.

Of course, it was August and the sunflowers were in full bloom. Monsieur Vincent painted many of them in vases or pots: one with twelve sunflowers, one with three, one with five and another with fourteen. All huge and bursting with yellow, burnt-orange and brownish colors. I've already talked about the sunflowers of Monsieur Vincent. All I can say is that they're stupendously Provençal and magnificently Vincent as is his signature on each one.

One day, I decided to walk about in the streets of Arles and went to the Forum area where the church of Saint Trophime stands in its Provençal Romanesque bearing. I stood in front of the portal and gazed at the sculpted stones. With my head raised upward, I saw, to my right, two very young children hanging down from the two arms of a man with his back turned to me. Strange posture, I thought. A little further up, the lady Virgin in bed with her baby Jesus lying there with the two oxen breathing on him. As I turned around, to my left there was an angel handing over a child, and to his left, two old men holding two children on their lap. Below that, I could see kings with their crowns and a knight on horseback. I didn't know then what to make of all this. I simply took it as some stories that were carved in stone for people to look at. It didn't make too much sense to me. Then, I recognized the voices of two of my friends, Blàsi and Calendau. They were with a boy older than me. A big boy with a ruffian look.

"Hi there," said Calendau, "we were looking for you."

"Yes," said Blàsi, "we thought you were with that artist friend of yours, that Monsieur Gokk."

"His name is not Gokk," I replied, "it's Monsieur Vincent. Vincent, that's how he signs his name."

"Well," said the other boy, "this Monsieur Vincent is quite a queer type. He runs around at night in the *rue des ricolettes,* the street where the women of the night hang out. My father calls them *putains.*"

"Don't say that word," retorted Blàsi, "it's not a nice word."

"Nice?" shouted out the other boy, "Nice? It's those women of the night that are not nice. They wander around and chase men for favors. You know." Turning to me he said, "And your artist friend is no better than the other men who go there. Tramps, my mother calls them. No better than *voyous.* Your man is *un voyou, un sacré voyou!*"

"Don't say that about him," I warned, "he's not a tramp. He's a good man. He's an artist."

I knew that Monsieur Vincent went to that area at times. For companionship, he said, since he felt lonely at times. But, he wasn't a tramp.

"I can say what I want about anyone," taunted the other boy. "What are you going to do about it?"

My two friends backed off since they didn't want to get involved.

"I'm calling you a tramp since you lie and are to no good. You're the one who's the tramp," I said mustering all the daring I could. "Tramp, tramp," I said to him right in his face.

I wasn't afraid of him. I felt I needed to defend my friend, Monsieur Vincent.

"Take that back," said the other boy, "or else."

"Or else what?" I replied taunting him, big bully, I thought.

"This," he said as he punched me in the eye and ran away.

I fell down.

My friends picked me up and said to me, "What did you want to do that for? You know he's a mean guy."

"I don't even know him. Why did you bring him here with you?"

"We didn't bring him here, he followed us. His name is Bronoué, an odd name. His parents let him go out at night and hang around."

"Well, he's certainly not my friend," I said. "He's just like the other people who hate Monsieur Vincent and don't even know him."

"We don't hate Monsieur Vincent," they said, "we know he's your friend. Why do you hang around him so often and not with us?"

"Because Monsieur Vincent teaches me things and I put them in my notebook."

"Your notebook, your notebook. Is that all you think about?"

"Not all the time, but most of the time, because it's my future in there. All my notes will serve me well when I become a writer."

"A writer?" they said astounded. "Is that what you want to become? You're not smart enough to become a writer. You want to become *un félibre*? You?" and they started laughing.

"Don't laugh. Some day you'll see, you'll see."

"Hey," said Calendau, "your eye has started swelling."

"What will my mother say?" I blurted out.

My mother? Well, she said what any mother would say.

"What happened? Where did you go? I told you not to play with ruffians. Who hit you? What for?"

"*Maman,* it wasn't my fault. I didn't play with him and I didn't provoke him. He's just a mean boy, that's all."

"I have a mind to tell his parents. Who are they?"

"You don't want to do that, *maman*, because they might insult you. I don't think they're good people."

"Never mind," she said, "I'll handle it my way. Now, let's see about your eye. You're going to have a black eye, don't you know?"

I did indeed have a black eye and I went about holding my hand to my eye not wanting people to stare at me and tell me that I had a black eye. I didn't feel like explaining things.

Two days after the incident that put the color purple on my face, I went to Monsieur Vincent's *atelier*. I didn't want to let my pride prevent me from seeing him and participating in his work as an artist. I hadn't done anything bad except my pride had been hurt and I now showed the badge of defending my friend from a good-for-nothing.

"What happened to you?" asked Monsieur Vincent.

"Oh, nothing serious." I replied, "I met up with a ruffian near Saint Trophime."

"Why did he punch you in the face? Did you do anything to him?"

"No, but he said things about you that I didn't like."

"You took a punch in the face for me?"

"Well, I had to defend you. You're my friend and I hate lies about you."

"What did he say about me?"

"He said that he had seen you at *rue des ricolettes* and that you were *un voyou*. I know you're not a tramp, so I took my lumps for standing up to that ruffian."

"Camille, you did that for me? You're a true and kind friend, but you didn't have to suffer for it. You know that I go to *rue des ricolettes* sometimes because I get lonely, really lonely at nighttime. I didn't want you to know all the details about my wandering in the night. You're too young to understand that and besides I know your parents would not approve of it, but I'm not a bad person, you know that, and I would never hurt anyone, especially not you."

"My father says that no one should judge another person."

"He's right, you know. Your father is a very tolerant man, understanding too. Some day when you're older you'll go to *rue des ricolettes* and you'll understand then why I go there like other men do."

"Oh, I understand more than you think I do," I replied smiling.

Monsieur's next painting was, **Coal Barges**. He painted two versions. The one I like is the one with the brighter sky and a barge with the French flag. We went there at sunset. A beautiful August sunset. The sky was still bright with yellows and tongues of red and that's the way Monsieur Vincent painted it. The river mirrors those colors and both sky and river seem to flow harmoniously into the artist's treatment of reflected color and light. The silhouettes of the barges and the workers are stark reminders of the day's end when the coal barges are unloaded and the men go home for the night. To the right we see the tricolor, red, white and blue, waving in the gentle breeze, a reminder that Arles is part of the nation. This work is another view of nature, the transition to night. Later on, Monsieur Vincent would venture into nighttime paintings and those would have their very own ambience. Just like this painting. I see a mood painted here, an ambience of color and light being extinguished slowly as night falls. It creates for me, and I'm sure it did for Monsieur Vincent, a mood that lingers on and on, even beyond the time we made our way back home.

I did not see Monsieur Vincent for several days after the painting of the barges. He told me later that he had gone away from Arles to paint and that he had come across gypsy caravans. He wanted to paint the scene of encampment, so he asked the people there for their permission to do so. To his astonishment, he saw young Mireille playing in the field, the young girl we had met at Saintes-Maries-de-la Mer. Sara's child. She ran to him and he picked her up in his arms. The people with her were surprised that she knew this *gadjé*. He started to explain how he had gotten to know her and one of the men told him to put the child down since he didn't think it appropriate for a stranger to do so. Monsieur Vincent felt a certain coldness between the gypsy and himself, he told me later. He backed off and they told him that he could paint their caravans if he stayed away from the child. Gypsies are not unfriendly, they told him. Besides, they saw that Monsieur Vincent was wearing a red string around his wrist, a mark of gypsy beliefs.

The painting, **Encampment of Gypsies with Caravans,** depicts two caravans, a loaded wagon and three women, a man and two children, a girl and a boy. Three horses are shown, a white horse in the center, a gray one on the left side and a brown one to the right of the caravans. One can see the side of some kind of a tent on the far right under the tree. They're wanderers, gypsies are, and they go where they can set up camp. It's a life filled with wanderlust that some people envy but there's very little stability in their lives, no permanent home for many of them. The colors of this painting are of varying hues from red, green, brown and a few touches of blue. The sky is totally green with a texture that is rich with some short, some long vertical and horizontal brush strokes. The ground is basically yellowish-beige with a similar texture as that of the sky. The two caravans occupy the center of this work. There is tranquility in this scene. Monsieur Vincent painted Mireille in her deep pink dress standing between the gray horse and the wagon. She's the little gypsy girl whose father was a *gadjé*. He told me that he thought that the little girl had been taken from her mother and that those gypsies had run away trying to hide the child. There was a feeling deep inside Monsieur Vincent that Mireille had been kidnapped.

"But why?" asked Monsieur Vincent.

There was something that didn't feel right about this, something suspicious, but of course the gypsies wouldn't tell. They were very secretive, especially about their own. Poor Sara, the only thing that meant anything to her in her life, taken away. She must be desperate right now, we both thought. Was she alright, we wondered. Perhaps murdered. No one knew about these things. The veil of silence had already been lowered and Mireille was part of the secret. What happened?

When September rolled around, I was fearing the beginning of school once again. Every year was the same thing. Book learning, which meant learning things by heart to repeat them word for word in front of the class. That was part of the master's discipline. The discipline of doing everything the master told us to do and doing it his way all the time without questioning. No interrupting the teacher in his long monologues. No way. Would it ever end? Of course, I didn't revolt knowing full well that I had to submit to this exercise of formal learning. My parents wanted me to. It was an unspoken but long established rule of bringing up children. That was very clear in people's minds. Even the state had stated its case for it. I had no recourse but to go to school. And so I did, reluctantly. However, I had reconciled in my mind the fact that I had to be in school while at the same time learning with my best of teachers, Monsieur Vincent. I had another factor that softened the blow of school learning, books. Yes, books and reading were a solace to me. This I had in common with Monsieur Vincent. Even with my father. My father didn't read much but he read occasionally, and we sometimes talked about books. He loved history and I loved adventure stories. My brother Armand liked science in school. He was good at it. I wasn't. I hated science, especially math. Too complicated. Science and mathematics are not conducive to daydreaming and the world of the imagination, I told myself. You had to be alert and fully rational to be able to calculate and deal with formulas. I could take grammar and *les dictées* but theorems and multiplication tables, no. I preferred words to numbers. Numbers never changed. They were stiff like old men. Words, well, you could color them, infuse them with some symbolic meaning, make them your own by choosing the right metaphor. Words, well, they're words. They become tools for constructing what the mind needs when it becomes the architect. Not that numbers are not important but words are so much more vital, I told my-self. Words and paintbrushes with paints, how important are they when one is being creative? Is poetry important? Extremely important to those who use words and to those of us who care.

12

Stars and Infinity

In late September early October, Arles begins to slip into fall and the colors slowly change to harvest hues. Even the sun is different. The light begins to be mellower and suffused. The air is different. It feels lighter and less heavy on your skin. It's a gradual change but it's there. The leaves in the trees change, the vineyards change and the sunflowers drop their heavy heads waiting for the birds to pluck at their large saucers of seeds. As their name indicates, they not only turn toward the sun but when the time comes they also turn toward the ground, *tourne--sols*.

The purple circle under my eye had turned yellow, a sign of healing, my mother said. Marcelle gurgled in her cradle and Armand was out working in the blacksmith shop helping Monsieur Matamore. My father, as usual, was at the train station unloading mailbags. I had never been on a train and I wished then that, some day, I would go far on a train or set sail on the seas. Whichever would carry me away from Arles. Not that I did not like Arles, but I wanted to see other cities, other countries or even, perhaps, Africa. Tartarin's adventure. But even Tartarin came back home to Tarascon. Was I destined never to set off for a distant land?

We were reading excerpts from Voltaire's "Candide" in class and I was beginning to like Madame Hugonet's class more and more. She was our new teacher. The adventures of Candide are interesting insofar as they're both entertaining and filled with perceptions of learning, or I should say, unlearning, for a young philosophy disciple like Candide. He didn't even know he was learning philosophy, the philosophy of the best of all possible worlds, our teacher started to explain. I read "Candide" all in one gulp at home and waited for the teacher to explain the chapters, paragraph by paragraph. We were doing *analyse de texte*, textual analysis. Not everybody likes it. Some students really get confused about analyzing words and ideas. I loved it. I was good at it. And I really wanted to know what was meant by the last line, "*Il faut cultiver son jardin.*" That one had me intrigued. I asked Monsieur Vincent what it meant in the story but he told me to wait until the teacher herself explained it to the class. I suppose that he didn't want me to miss out on the official explanation but I'm sure that Monsieur Vincent's explanation would have been just as good. He was in the middle of reading a book by the Russian, Tolstoy. He told me that the title was, "My Religion."

"It's about revolution and it's too heavy a reading for you at the present time. Stick to your Voltaire," he said.

The title was "My Religion" and it was about revolution? I wondered what that was all about. Even my father had not read that book. As a good republican, my father wasn't too interested in any religion.

"It was part responsible for our having a revolution in France," Monsieur Vincent told me. "You'll read about it later in school. It's part of your history, you know."

I guess that religion was indeed linked to revolution after all. But, I couldn't begin to fathom the meaning behind the two. I was still figuring out the last line of Voltaire's "Candide."

Monsieur Vincent started explaining to me something that was very close to his inner being.

"You know, Camille, I'm a believer. I believe in God, not so much the biblical God of my father's religion but in God the creator and redeemer. The Christ of the cross, the suffering and loving Christ. The God who taught us to love and forgive, and who was filled with compassion for the lowly and the poor. Real Christian values mean forgiving and giving your life for the poor and the less favored in life. That's why I went to Le Borinage. It didn't work out because they, the church and the congregation, wouldn't have me. Religion comes from the Latin and it means tying people together in a spiritual union, that's what I learned in those poor and wretched places like Le Borinage. Religion is not an institution, it's a binding process. It binds people together. It cannot be cold, rigid and static. It must be dynamic. To me, it really means changing the old ways within and without and helping the very poor. Helping the poor potato eaters in Nuenen, helping the tillers of the soil scraping for an existence in Drenthe, helping the poor and desperate woman who has to prostitute herself to put food on the table for herself and her children in the Hague. Otherwise, religion is hypocritical, needlessly hurtful. Do you understand, Camille? Do you believe what I'm telling you? I know that it's all beyond your grasp right now but I trust someday you'll discover the real truths about religion and the values that it must impart. Religion must be a sharing, a communion of souls or else it's not truly religion."

I just stood there completely awed by his words, I who knew so very little about religion. One thing I knew, he was a good man, a man who was sincerely trying to follow the right path of giving of oneself to others. If others would have him. Sometimes, his frustrations with himself and religion put him in a very awkward position of having to rebel and fight back the pressures of conformity. He didn't know why, but he had to and he tried to explain to me the reasons behind his plight. He just could not fit in since people rejected his ideas and values. He wasn't looking to be right or even wrong, he was simply trying to follow his deep intuition of what truth was. He was tired of any religion as a tag put on people.

"I'm a peg in the wrong hole," he would tell me.

On a lovely Wednesday afternoon, Monsieur Vincent and I went to the public garden. It was warm and the sun filtered through the branches of the trees. There were several people in the garden, women especially. They were all dressed up and carried parasols, even in the shade. Monsieur Vincent chose his position for painting away from the people, not too far so as to be able to see them but far enough not to be bothered by them. He didn't want to paint a portrait but a public scene in the garden. The garden was a restful place for people and a gift to themselves as townspeople. Every town needs a place of respite and relaxation. A piece of nature close by. Arles was surrounded by natural beauty and vast scenery but this garden was special in that it offered people a quiet place with trees, flowers and shade when the sun beat down right in the center of Arles.

Monsieur Vincent was seated near a lane in the garden where he could capture the huge evergreen in front of him and the other trees overhead as well as the people a little further away. Those branches overhead are the ones with flutes of yellow on the top right. But, everything else in this painting looks green, feels green and even smells green, it seems. That's because the artist has captured what I would call the green shade. If I were asked to name this painting that is called, *A Lane in the Public Garden in Arles*, I would call it "Green Serenity." Monsieur Vincent painted two more Public Park paintings, the one with the yellow sky, the tall grasses and the wild flowers, **Public Park with Weeping Willow: The Poet's Garden I,** and the one with a man reading a newspaper at the entrance and where people dressed in black are sitting on the park benches, **Entrance to the Public Park in Arles**. The Public Park was a favorite place of his and he often would go there to read a book, mediate and relax and, of course, paint.

"Just like a monk does," he would tell me. "Meditate and be part of nature and its quietude."

The Green Vineyard was painted on a day that was bright with birds singing and some cicadas still chirring. I wasn't able to accompany Monsieur Vincent because I was in school (see how school interferes with my art learning, I wrote in my notebook), but I saw the painting afterward. The sky is a September sky, from touches of green near the skyline to light blue, then to a darker blue. There are thick brush strokes of white that form a patch of sky on the left. Overall, the brush stroke effect looks like birds flying here and there. Grey willows line the horizon, and a wine press with a red roof appears in the far distance with the lilac silhouette of the town, he explained to me. There are six ladies and two men gathering grapes with their cart, three ladies with parasols that are painted red (the signature color, I kept insisting then). The predominant color of the vineyard is deep green with tinges of orange, from a lighter orange to a burnt orange with some brown to delineate the creeping vine branches. I only wish I had been there. It's a painting that captivates one, what with its harmony of colors and tone.

The next time I saw Monsieur Vincent, he was in his *atelier* preparing a canvas for a portrait, he said. He asked me to leave since he was expecting an artist friend who was living with an American artist in Fontvielle. His name was Eugène Boch and he was a native of Belgium.

"I wouldn't want him to be surprised by your being here watching. I hope you're not upset by my not asking you to stay. You know that I enjoy having you with me," Monsieur Vincent explained to me.

"I'm not upset. I was just wondering what you were doing. I was getting bored at home."

"I'll tell you what, I promise to show you the portrait and tell you all about it. Alright?"

"Yes, sir," I replied.

"Now you're calling me sir. You are upset."

"Not at all. My mother wants me to call you sir all the time."

"That's fine if that's what your mother wants you to do, but you can call me simply, Vincent, from now on."

I left feeling a bit upset not really wanting to show it, but I couldn't help it. I wanted to be with him that day and I could not. I felt down and out. My feelings were tossed about like a pinwheel in the wind. I went home sad. My mother was washing the baby's clothes and she asked me to look in on Marcelle. I went over to the bedroom and saw she was in her crib. She was almost two months old now and chubby. She smiled and I smiled back at her. She made me feel happy. I took her little hands into mine and kissed them. Her eyes looked into mine. They were huge and filled with light coming from the bedroom window. I was going to teach her my name, C-a-m-i-l-l-e, so she would be able to call me when she needed me. She gurgled some kind of sound at me and I played with her while *maman* was doing the washing.

A couple of days later, I ventured to see if I could drop in on Monsieur Vincent, I mean Vincent. He welcomed me and we had something to drink, he a cup of coffee and I some cool water.

"Come and see my portrait of Monsieur Boch," he said.

I leaned over and saw that he was heading for his bedroom. It was hanging there over his mat and mattress.

"I put it here for now until I get some furniture," he said.

"You're finally getting a bed and things?"

"Yes, I want to make this my home, not just a studio. Besides, I want my friend Gauguin to come and live with me. I want to set up a real artist workshop that I will call *l'atelier du Midi*. I hope he comes soon. My brother is arranging things for him to come."

"That will be nice. Then you'll have someone living and working with you all the time. Like family."

"Yes. Wouldn't that be great. Two artists working together and teaching each other techniques of texture, composition and light. I need that. I need companionship, Camille, creative companionship when artist friends can create together."

"I know and I'm really glad for you. Do you know when he's coming?"

"Not yet, not the exact date but I'm getting ready for him."

I was truly glad for him. He needed to be happy and it showed in his eyes.

"Well, take a good look at my painting," he said as I stared at his work. "Look at this, Camille. Look how I painted him, this poet, this artist friend from up north. That's what I call him, 'the poet.' He's really a poet since he writes poetry and paints. I call this painting, **Portrait of Eugène Boch. The Poet.**"

I was looking at the portrait and was a bit astonished by the background. It wasn't a wall nor was it a plain light color, but a very dark shade of color with things blinking here and there. The man looked serious and his face was very lean, almost gaunt. The brown eyes were deep with an intent look. Vincent had spent some time with the poet the summer before often discussing the artist Delacroix, the colorist, he said. They both liked him very much as an artist and a master painter.

Vincent said that he was drawn to his friend's Flemish features.

"I wrote to my brother last week telling him that I wanted to express my appreciation and affection for Boch in the picture I was going to paint. I told him that I intended to complete the picture as an arbitrary colorist, emphasizing Boch's fair hair, even to the point of using orange chromes, and pale citron-yellow. I will paint a vision of infinity, I told him, a plain background of the richest most intense blue I can contrive, and by placing his bright head against the deep background, I will give the effect of a star in the depth of an azure sky. I want to achieve with color the kind of eternal radiance that used to be symbolized by a halo. That's what I told him and that's what I did. Do you understand what I did, Camille?"

I told him that I didn't understand everything but that I knew that the artist understands his painting better than anyone else and explaining things, sometimes just complicates the real meaning of the work, and if one doesn't get it well, he doesn't get it at all.

"But it will sink in with time, Vincent, it will sink in," I told him.

"You're a wise little man, Camille, a wise little man, precocious as I've said before."

What I really didn't understand was the notion of infinity to which he often referred. "What is infinity?"

"Infinity," he told me, "is in a child's eyes, it's in the starry skies at night, it resides in deep dark regions of the mind where creativity bubbles and expands like yeast. It's in the mystery of a man's soul and it becomes a longing and a hounding for creating art that will dare to use colors and light and will surpass itself every time you paint a canvas that is infinitely and daringly bold in its perspective and coloration. That's part of the concept of infinity, not the total sum. It's part of the mystery of things, Camille."

Wow! I thought, this is deep. I'm too young to fully understand infinity but I know that it's a concept that hounds Vincent and he's trying to make it part of his work as an artist. I left him there contemplating Boch's portrait, without a word or the blink of an eye. Like he was meditating in front of an icon.

The day had finally arrived. It was September 18 and Vincent was then fully installed in his house. He called it his yellow house because he wanted everything yellow like the sunflower, the color of welcoming, as the Japanese see it. Yellow! Yellow! Yellow!

"Tout est jaune qui veut recevoir un ami," he told me, everything is yellow when you want to make a friend feel welcomed.

Of course the friend was Gauguin. He had talked so much about him, about his art, his coming to Arles and how he and Gauguin were going to build a community of artists in the south. I was so happy for him because he was happy and gay. I didn't often see him that way and it was good. Not only good but stupendously good. We danced and we sang in his new house. We were happy and we were filled with anticipation of the new tomorrow opening up today. That's how happy we were. Vincent finally had a new bed, a solid one made of *bois blanc*, whitewood, and another one, a walnut bed for a guest be it his brother, Gauguin, or someone else, he said. They were large beds, *du pays*, as he put it, so that it gave the rooms an aspect of solidity, duration and calm. He had invited his brother to come down south to Arles for a visit repeatedly. He would have loved to have his brother close to him to talk and exchange things like brothers did.

"Il faut que cela ait du caractère," it must have character, he said of the new beds.

He had also bought twelve chairs, a mirror and other things. Moreover, he wanted to put two oleanders in small barrels before the entrance door just so his friend Gauguin would see that he had made it look like he had a permanent home. It was a nice place for him and he loved it. I loved it too. On September 17, the eve before he was fully installed in his new house, and I remember well this date, Vincent spent his first night in his new bed in the sparsely furnished yellow house.

Two days later, Vincent decided to do a painting of his house, the yellow house. He had been planning to do this for weeks. He said he was going to call it *"La Maison et son entourage."* He told me that he wrote to his brother earlier about how he was going to do this, saying that the house and its setting were going to be under a sulphur sun and a pure cobalt sky. It's fantastic, he told him, to see these yellow houses in the sun and also the incomparable freshness of the blue. All the ground is yellow. He continued by saying that he also wanted to paint the restaurant where he ate every day. He even told him that his friend, the postman, (that's my father) lived at the end of the street on the left between the two bridges of the railroad.

Well, he did it. He showed it to me. What a painting! It's exactly the way he had told his brother he was going to do it. Yes, the yellow house with bright sunlight and the amazing blue. He finally had a furnished house and he wanted to do a painting of it just so he could prove to himself and others that he had a home. That's the way I saw it. Later he opted for a more meaningful title and called the painting, **La Rue,** but in the end it turned out to be, **Vincent's House (The Yellow House)**.

Vincent was all fired up to paint, even more so than he had been before. He was so enthused by the very fact of painting what he liked and what he felt. Now, he indulged himself by painting at nighttime. He had found a new inspiration, a new way of bringing color and mystery into provenance. Vincent now painted the stars outside and the lights inside. Outside at nighttime was more of a challenge since he didn't have the proper light to paint, but he found a way by propping lit candles onto the brim of his broad brim hat. Sometimes, he would also put lighted candles at his feet and around his canvas. It was far from being perfect but it gave him sufficient light for painting. He showed me how it was done. I pleaded with my parents to let me go and watch Vincent at work at the Café Terrace but they would not even hear of it. Not my mother.

"A child like you going out alone at night in la Place du Forum? Never on my life. Not while your living under my roof and under my care, " my mother fumed.

I had never seen her like that before.

"What will people say and besides, what business is it of yours to follow *un étrangié* at night in a café? *C'est un endroit malsain où les sans-abri rôdent.*" It's a dirty place where homeless people roam, she said.

"Now, now, *sa mère,*" replied my father, "it's not that bad and besides Monsieur Vincent is not a stranger to us."

My father, although opposed to the idea, tried to calm her down in her motherly anger.

He seemed to waiver a little until my mother said, "*Non, non, non, il n'ira pas s'exposer au danger comme ça.* It's too dangerous for him. Besides, what kind of a father would allow his young son to go out at night without family supervision?" she said.

That's it. That did it. My mother had hit upon the sensitive issue of family responsibility and my father was not going to challenge that, I knew that as sure as the sun rises and sets every day.

My mother started getting ready to go to bed when she told me, *"Vas te coucher,"* go to bed.

I wasn't sleepy and I desperately wanted to go watch Vincent at the café. My father lingered a while smoking his cigarette. He gave me a look of veiled sympathy couched in a conquered defense for his child. He had given it his best shot.

I went to bed overcome by authority and despair. I took off my shoes and lay on the bed fully clothed. Feelings of despondency and thoughts of rebellion stirred in me. Why? Why was I not permitted to follow my destiny as a writer? A writer needs a full range of experiences, I told myself. Daytime as well as nighttime. I had never disobeyed my parents before and now I was thinking of it. Not because I wanted to be a disobedient child but I just could not see how a small nighttime excursion with a good friend would, in any way, harm me. I was eleven. I was precocious. I was going to be a writer. I was, well, under the thumb of my mother. I loved my mother but sometimes she could be darn so obstinate. When she had her mind made up, you could not budge her. On the other hand, my father had often told us boys to take responsibility by the horns and act accordingly. A man needs to affirm himself, he had told my mother when she argued with him about letting my brother Armand go to Lambesc to work in a forge during the summer months. He went and he came back that much more a man, according to my father. He had taken on the full responsibility of a worker who earns a living. On that score, my mother saw the light.

Well, I wasn't going to shun responsibility. I would take responsibility for my actions come what may, I told myself, in my room, in the dark looking for my shoes. I waited until my parents fell asleep and I tiptoed through the kitchen since I was now sleeping downstairs. I didn't have to unlock the back door since my parents kept it unlocked all the time. Everyone trusted the neighbors, most of whom were friends anyhow. I then walked very carefully like a cat with hushed steps mindful of not making any noise whatsoever. I stumbled in the dark but I picked myself up and hurried on. I finally reached the Place du Forum and found Vincent near the café, painting.

"Well, you did come, I see," said Vincent somewhat surprised. "I didn't think your parents would let you come. Of course, I didn't want to create any problems for you with your parents, so I did not push the issue."

"No problem," I said. "My parents are very understanding when it comes to my learning," I said sheepishly.

"Are you alright, Camille?"

"Yes, perfectly alright."

"Are you sure your parents want you to be here tonight at the café with me?"

"Yes, yes," I replied trying to hide my consternation over what I felt was petty disobedience.

"Alright then, sit here and watch," as he pointed to a small metal chair next to him.

He was right. He could put small lit candles on the brim of his hat and paint with free hands. The night was still and balmy for a September eve. I could see the many stars in the dark sky above sparkling and giving off all kinds of colors.

"That's what I'm painting, infinity," Vincent said to me as he watched me looking at the sky.

There goes that word again, infinity, I thought to myself. He had already sketched out the preliminaries of the painting and was now applying colors.

"With this one, it's a matter of perspective," he said. "I want to be able to catch the starry sky up above and at the same time highlight the yellow brightness of the café with the depth of perspective. This is my intended treatment of this café terrace. You will see the lines of perspective come to a point of full convergence like a tunnel. But my tunnel, this alley in front of us, will have an open sky, a nighttime canopy of bright stars. Infinity!"

Then he began painting in earnest, yellows, blues, white, greens and some red. The bright-lit awning of yellows on the left with the yellow, orange and green wall of the restaurant with the deep orange doors harmonize with the brilliance of the awning. Being used to the bright open sky with blazing sun as light source, I could now see how Vincent was capturing light differently. The gaslight effect on the terrace and windows of the buildings to the right was his only recourse, except for the sparkling lights of the sky above. The painting, **Café Terrace at Night**, forces you to look up at the night sky, for the entire perspective is aimed at making viewers look up because that's what the artist wants. Café lights are not sufficient to inspire infinity. The stars in the cobalt blue sky do. Even the blue post with lintel of the store jutting out on the left along with the blue apartments with covered porch above the café leads you to the dark blueness of the sky. That's what the artist saw from his vantage point and that's what he projects in his painting, treatment. Treatment says it all.

Vincent wasn't done with his painting, and it had been several hours since I had been there when I saw my father appearing in the night on the cobblestone square. Now my act of disobedience came to me full force. How was I going to try to explain this to both Vincent and my father and later on to my mother? I felt pangs of discontent in my stomach and my head was getting sleepy. My eyes were seeing double.

"What are you doing here after we told you not to come?" roared my father.

He looked stern and somewhat unforgiving at that very moment. Vincent stopped painting and looked astonished at this abrupt pause in his painting. I mumbled something as my father grabbed me by the arm to lead me away. He apologized to Vincent for having interrupted him and said that this was way past my bedtime. Vincent simply nodded his head half apologetically. He didn't say one word.

"Why did you disobey us and sneak out of the house like a thief?" my father asked. "Didn't you know that you would get caught somehow? Your mother discovered your room empty after she checked on your baby sister. You were gone. '*Mon Dieu*!' she cried out and I woke up."

By then, his voice had taken on a more lenient tone. When we got home, my mother was waiting for me. I was in for the tongue lashing of my life. Perhaps a spanking from my father, although he very rarely did that. I knew it and I expected it even though my head was getting more and more foggy with sleep.

"Come now, let's go to bed and we'll talk about this tomorrow." That's all she said.

I was totally flabbergasted and sleepy. Very sleepy. The following morning, expecting my mother to have fully prepared her scolding, I waited for the onslaught of words. Harsh words.

However, she simply served me breakfast quietly and then sent me off to school saying, "Pay attention to the teacher, Camille, for you didn't have much sleep last night."

That's all she said. I walked to school confused and somewhat apprehensive of the lack of reproach awaiting, I was sure, for the time when she would indeed explode. Assuredly this afternoon or even tonight after dinner. All day long I was on edge and nervously waiting with each tic tock of the clock for the time when I would have to leave the classroom and wend my way home to punishment. I was sure that it would happen, this scolding and punishment justly deserved. I was ready for it. Let's get it done, I thought. I walked silently home taking every step as a cautionary step toward my destiny and that ominous moment after perpetration. My mother was doing housework and didn't seem too much set on scolding me. I waited, then I went to my room to take my notebook out and begin reading what I had written so far about last night's episode and Vincent's painting. I tried and I tried to concentrate but my mind would not cooperate with my motives of thinking and writing. I closed my notebook and started reading in my new book, "François le Champi." Nothing seemed to sink into my mind, just words. I was reading words but no thoughts came to synchronize these words. I closed the book. I walked over to the window and saw the clouds in the sky. Ominous looking and gray. It looked like a storm was coming and the mistral was whistling it's strong cry through the branches of the trees. A haunting sound. That's it, I was going to the kitchen and ask my mother to get it over with. I could not stand it anymore. It was hounding me to no end this waiting and waiting for punishment to fit the crime of my disobedience. Why wasn't she saying anything? Mothers are strange sometimes.

So I picked up my flagging courage and went to the kitchen and asked my mother, "*Maman*, why don't you say something?"

"About what?" she replied.

"About last night," I said.

"Oh, about that. Well, I think you've already had your punishment, don't you think?"

"My punishment?"

"Yes, the punishment of my silence. Didn't that carve out your insides and make you feel edgy and even repentant? What more are you expecting of me?" she asked with a touch of pleading in her voice.

I was floored. I had expected her to give me a good scolding and a punishment for disobeying her and my father. Then, it would have been over and done with. I had not expected this. I was thoroughly baffled and did not find words enough to express my sentiments to her. Should they be of regret, compunction, resolve or even gratitude? I was frozen in my feelings and my words.

"Of course," she said, "your real punishment is for you to refrain from seeing Monsieur Vincent for a while and to stay indoors for at least a week doing extra chores, except when you have to go to school."

It was said without harshness or self-satisfaction.

"Yes, *maman*," I said and walked slowly, head low toward my room.

I wasn't sad. I didn't even feel chastised. Just relieved. *Enfin!* Finally the punishment had been handed out. I wasn't too disappointed in it, not at all, since in my isolation at home I could enjoy the pleasure of my own company through reading and especially through my notebook. Mothers are indeed strange sometimes. Not only strange but also shrewd.

I found out after my punishment had been lifted that Vincent had been very busy at work with his painting of night life, *Le Café de la Nuit,* in the Place Lamartine that prostitutes frequented and where night prowlers with no money for lodging lingered during the night. It was not a place I knew very well. The painting sets a tone of gloom and torment of the soul, so to speak, what with the dark red of the wall and the bold green of the ceiling. The reverberating light of the gaslight lamps coming down from the ceiling gives the work an eerie feeling. Some of the people there are slouching on the tables while the others seem frozen in time. I don't think Vincent really liked this place, especially at nighttime, because his painting of the Café de l'Alcazar, the night café, where he sometimes went, reflects that. He told me later that man has a bright and a dark side to his soul and that sometimes he lowers himself into the dark side and sees things that make him shudder. It's enough to make one go mad. He was serious when he told me that. Very serious. I was somewhat afraid of what he told me because that was not the Vincent that I had gotten to know and wanted to know. I found this painting eerie-looking.

The other nighttime painting that I saw was, **The Starry Night**. It's a beautiful painting that I like a lot. Of course, I wasn't able to be there when he did it, not after the incident of the café terrace. I was now very careful in selecting what would be deemed an appropriate time for witnessing Vincent at work. Nighttime was not an appropriate time for me but I loved that time for how the stars made me feel by their sparkling presence in the depth of night. I sometimes stayed up in the dark in my room just to look at the stars through my window. It was so beautiful a sight that it made me imagine things such as, lands and continents beyond France, Tartarin and his adventures in Africa, the books I would write someday and things like that. Of course, Vincent saw infinity in them, but I was still trying to find out what that meant.

"The Starry Night" painting has a couple walking in the night along the river while the bright stars of heaven shine with utmost brilliance on them and the river. They don't just sparkle but appear to be lamps with a glow illuminating the night. The lights from the buildings on the bank reflected in the deep and dark waters seem to echo the lights in the sky so yellowish bright are they. Vincent explained the color composition to me.

"The town is blue and violet, the gaslight is yellow, and its reflections range from russet-gold down to greenish-bronze. The constellation of the Great Bear sparkles green and pink against the expanse of the blue-green sky," he told me. "Do you know what the Great Bear is and how to find it, Camille?"

"No," I replied.

"Well, the Great Bear is a group of stars called a constellation. It's supposed to look like a bear in the sky. See up there where the brightest stars are painted green and pink, that's the Great Bear. The Big Dipper is also part of that cluster of stars. It looks like a little pot with a handle. And the North Star is up on top of that cluster. It's the star that points to the north and guides navigators in their bearings at sea. So, stars are very important."

"Do you know all the names of the stars?" I asked him.

"No, Camille, there too many. Millions and millions of them, an infinite number all up there in the vast firmament. Stars are the pin pricks in the firmament so far are we from them. They're there all the time, you know, night and day, except we see them better at nighttime. At night, we can feel the deep and vast presence of infinity that's beyond us, beyond everything that's here on earth, everything physical and touchable. That's why the presence of the stars make me dream. I dream of being with the stars, creating my own universe where colors are dominant and the bright light of the sun becomes infused within my flesh and bones so that I become light itself with stars as my eyes. Then, I can paint endlessly dipping my brush into the colors of dawn or dusk or even nighttime as my fancy dictates. Sometimes, I even wonder if I'm going mad with all of these thoughts swirling in my mind."

He paused for a moment then he added, "You know, I've often wondered what exists beyond there, passed the firmament, passed the vastness of the universe, into the infinite. Some people call it the void, but I cannot be persuaded that nothing exists beyond the firmament of stars. Something's there, I know, I feel it in the marrow of my bones and in every creative fiber of my soul. That's the mystery of it all. Infinity. I so wish I could capture it on my canvases. I try, but I fail. I only come up with a faint *aperçu* of infinity as in this painting."

He wrote to his brother about stars and told him: "The sight of stars always makes me dream, they make me dream just like the dark spots representing towns and cities on a map do. If we take the train for Tarascon or for Rouen, we must take the train of death to go to one of the stars."

Stars are the vehicle to infinity, he reasoned. So, the stars say it all. That's the focus here and that's what Vincent wanted to paint. Vincent and his stars at the magical, mysterious and profound time of the day. Nighttime. Much later, after Vincent had passed away up north in Auvers-sur-Oise, I began to realize what he meant by infinity and I was still searching for it in my own life. I got to know that infinity is a concept that's untouchable with the hand or eye and can only be felt through the creative mind that I was ever attempting to develop within me. For Vincent, it was the surge of infinity and for me it's been the feeling of the sea and its call ever since I saw the Mediterranean at Saintes-Maries-de-la-Mer. The feeling of the swell of the sea reaching my inner thoughts and feelings like the stars were for Vincent. You see, Vincent is still teaching me beyond the grave. I know.

Vincent had been painting furiously sometimes almost all day long. That's all he would do paint, eat a little and sleep twelve hour stretches at a time, he told me. Day and night, he would paint. He was so taken up with his own creativity that he felt he was on a locomotive full speed ahead. By late September, Vincent returned to portrait painting and he chose a second lieutenant from the Zouaves, a young man of twenty-five. He introduced him to me and told me that he had been taking drawing lessons from Vincent and was doing quite well. Vincent was a master at drawing, so I'm sure the lieutenant could not have done better. His name was Milliet, *sous-lieutenant* Paul-Eugène Milliet of the third regiment of the Zouaves, the lieutenant told me. The regiment had just returned from Tonkin in Indochina. He was certain that he would leave for Algeria sometime soon. He also said that he and Vincent were good friends and both had gone to Montmajour and had explored the old garden and plucked and eaten some huge figs there. Vincent smiled as he stood there preparing his paints. The memory of that day must have been deliciously pleasant to him.

The *sous-lieutenant* appeared to be somewhat nervous after sitting straight on a chair for quite a while. He fidgeted with his hands and had a nervous motion of the leg. His head would, at times, bob left to right. Vincent didn't say much but I could see that he didn't like it. Not every portrait sitter was like my father, I thought. Steady, calm and still like a rock. I thought that my presence there could lead to further ill ease with the lieutenant, so I excused myself and went home knowing that Vincent would show me the portrait when it was done.

It was completed that very night. I only got to see the painting the day after next because I was busy with my homework and my chores, and my mother had insisted that I finished them both. The portrait shows Milliet in full uniform with his commemorative medal from his expedition to Tonkin, I was told. The background is a deep green of bold brush strokes and his face reflects the green tone of the background. The only flourish in the background is the crescent moon and star in the right hand corner, a symbol of the coat of arms for Milliet's Zouave regiment, as Vincent explained. He included this touch of military identity because he liked the soldiers associated with the Zouaves he had met, he said. The lieutenant's bearing is stiff and a bit rigid, I thought. His young face seems tense while his long brown mustache and whiskers give him an appearance of maturity. But his eyes, yes, his eyes are ever so sad, a look that appears lost. He seems to be staring into the void. What makes up for the lack of brightness though is the blood red military cap with gold braid. It matches the red of his lips. Vincent must have been glad to paint that red. He painted what he saw in the lieutenant's face and gave the portrait a mood that lent itself to the sitter's disposition. Strange that later in an interview with a man named Monsieur Weiller, lieutenant Milliet said that he thought that Vincent's paintings were not drawn enough.

"He let color take the place of drawing which is nonsense," he said. "Excessive, abnormal, inadmissible color. Tones too hot, violent, not restrained enough," he went on. "You see, my friend, a painter has to make a painting with love, not with passion...he raped it....Sometimes he was a veritable brute ----'hard-assed,' as they say."

Some friend and some connoisseur of the art of painting. Vincent revolutionized painting, didn't he realize that? 'Hard-assed'? He did not really know my Vincent the artist, the person. Had he truly known him, he would have found out the quality of the man and artist that he embodied. I know, I know, Vincent had his faults like everyone else and his were, at times, magnified by his sickness, his headaches and even his toothaches, but how many people could match his consummate skills as an artist? How many? And not to paint with passion? What does he mean? How can an artist not put all of himself into his work with passion, with boundless energy and enthusiasm? Passion is the necessary ingredient for utter commitment to one's art. A writer without passion is a scribbler of lines, a mechanical human being of sorts. A robot! Delacroix painted with passion, Zola wrote with passion, I'm sure, Vincent worked with passion and how many more poured out their souls for creativity and art? I only wish I had Vincent's passion for being creative. God, how I wish I had it, then I would fly like an eagle over the clouds and write, write like mad.

13

Diligences and Dragons

September went by and we fell into October with the thrust of the second blossoming of autumn. We are so fortunate here in Provence. We have the first blossoming in the spring and then, come fall, we get another one. Flowers for everyone's hunger and thirst for beauty. Besides the blooms in gardens and fields, we also get the changing of the color of leaves. From green to yellows, the leaves of the trees seem to change almost overnight, or is it because we haven't been following the transition closely enough. First, it starts with the top of the trees and gradually the color yellow takes over, and there you have it, the leaves of autumn. Of course, the evergreens like the pines don't change, they keep their green needles and make a dramatic contrast with the bright yellow of the other trees, just like the cypress trees.

The weeks slipped away and families slowly prepared for the changes of weather and the anticipated, sometimes spontaneous, *farandole*. I loved to watch the boys and girls dance while holding a handkerchief. Of course, there were also the coming celebrations of *les fêtes*, Christmastime, ending with *la Chandeleur* in early February. But, it was still October. Time for the little furry animals to gather for the winter months and for humans to continue their daily activities such as, cleaning house for mothers, going to school for kids, going to work for fathers and, for Vincent, preparing for the arrival of his artist friend, Paul Gauguin.

The much anticipated arrival of Gauguin was ever so delayed due to financial complications as well as postponements. In the meantime, Vincent continued to paint never wanting to put too great a hiatus on his performance of creativity. He went back to portrait painting and painted his mother's portrait from a photograph that he owned. He showed me the photograph and I thought that Madame Van Gogh was a good-looking woman for her age. She was sixty-nine at the time, he told me. He loved his mother despite their differences. Those differences were, in great part, his fault, he said, but he didn't want to elaborate. His mother's name was, Anna Cornelia Van Gogh. The family called her Moe. She was born in the Hague where her father was a bookbinder. Anna Cornelia had a lively spirit and managed to retain it, although she was stuck in the placid monotony of a small quiet village with her husband preacher. Vincent said that she had a deep love of nature and had a great facility in expressing her thoughts on paper. She loved letter writing. Sad that there was little correspondence between her and her son, Vincent. I think that Vincent missed that but he did not blame her but insisted that it was his fault, not hers. He also said that his mother was very protective of him as a child. He remembered once getting his ears boxed by his grandmother who lived with them, and that his mother had had harsh words with the old lady. As a child, he felt well protected and loved by his mother, he said. He was just sorry that he could not live up to her expectations.

I was only there part of the time when Vincent was painting **Portrait of the Artist's Mother**. I would stop in now and then to see how he was doing. It didn't take him too much time to finish it. Vincent was fast and skillful with his brushes and paint. The background is a bright and joyful citrus green to contrast with the more somber black of the clothing and hat. At least, that's how I saw it. He didn't say, and I didn't ask him. What strikes the viewer the most is the face of a kind, modest-looking and serene old woman who looks like she enjoys life. This can be seen in her photograph too. Not like the old stiff-looking, stern-faced photos of some couple we see in certain homes. Her demure smile is engaging while her soft blue eyes are wide opened to reveal an honesty and serenity that must have permeated her life. Vincent painted her with the eyes much more opened than the photograph shows. I suppose that he wanted it that way since she must have stayed in his mind open and joyful. Her dress is not completely black since there are touches of brown in it to relieve the blackness of her actual dress, I suppose. As for her hat or bonnet, the bottom part has small streaks of red while the upper part, consisting primarily of gray tulle ribbons, help to accentuate her white hair, here painted with a few green brush strokes to reflect the indoor light. It's a painting of fondness and nostalgic remembrances. I couldn't wait for Vincent to paint my mother's portrait. He said he was going to do it not too long from then.

Vincent admitted to me that he had not been eating right. Too busy painting, he said. He told me that he had taken some twenty-three cups of coffee during four days with just a bite of bread from a loaf that he still owed the baker. That was all. No real food. I told him that was not good for him and that he should come over to our house for some soup.

At least some soup, I pleaded. He replied that he would but not then, not until he had finished what he had planned to do while the inspiration was still with him.

"You see, I have to work, work hard, for if my mind loses it then I'll be lost," he told me.

"Lost?"

"Yes, lost to myself and to my art. You don't understand. I'm haunted by my art. It drives me to a point of madness practically. I'm not *fada* as the people around here call me. No, I'm mad like a man filled with the passion for creating art and time has neither importance nor food. I told you, I'm heading for a fast train and it's going to leave me behind if I don't climb aboard. At times, I'm really afraid of losing my mind so harsh are my hallucinations that come and go, especially after I've been drinking."

"Well, fast train or not, I think you should at least take time to eat a little," I replied.

I left him to his painting since I had to go home and eat lunch

The next time I saw Vincent it was Saturday afternoon. He was busy painting his bedroom. I don't mean painting the walls but doing a painting of his room. He told me that his eyes hurt and that he felt that his head was empty, *la caboche vide*, he said. He felt knocked out by work. Almost senseless. One night he had slept sixteen hours straight, he said.

"I'm not sick but I feel that I could be if I don't stop for a while. I really need some nourishment. I know it. I've been painting indoors because the mistral wind has been violent these past few days, raising clouds of dust that whiten the trees on the plain from top to bottom. I just had to rest my eyes."

"I know how bad it can get, this wind of the beast, as I call it. I've been reading in my room and haven't gone out much. My father says that you get used to the wind. I don't know about that. Anfos, Blàsi and Milou don't like it at all. They can't go outside and play."

"Those are your little friends?"

"Yes."

He put his brush down and looked at me.

"Let's get some food, Camille."

He ate something at Madame Ginoux's restaurant while I watched him gulp down his food. She told him that he should come in more often. He answered that he would if he had more money in his pockets.

She told him that the food at the Café de la Gare was always available for him and that she would neither overcharge him nor run after him for money.

"*On peut s'arranger,*" here we can work things out, she said.

He smiled awkwardly and continued eating. I was just glad he was getting some food in his stomach. I watched him while I drank something cold.

The following day, Vincent was at work again painting **Vincent's Bedroom**. He said while he was painting, "I just wrote to my brother and told him that it's just a bedroom, but here color will be everything----looking at the picture should put the mind or perhaps rather the imagination at ease and encourage sleep. You see, Camille, resting the imagination when it's been hard at work is beneficial to painting. I know I need rest but I don't always take time for it. Anyway, the walls are pale violet, I told Théo, the floor is made of red tiles, and the bed and chairs are yellow wood, the color of fresh butter. The sheets and pillows are light greenish-citron, the bed's coverlet is scarlet (why would it be any other color? I thought to myself), and the window is green. There is no white."

I could see that he had hung a self-portrait and a couple of Japanese prints over his bed. It was a simple room, a comfortable room similar to mine, except I didn't have a yellow bed. I thought that when I grow up, I'll paint my bed yellow too. I like yellow. My mother preferred the natural color of wood. Come to think of it, I never did get a yellow bed. I must get one some day.

Vincent wrote to his brother that the native land of Tartartin was an odd place, this Provence. It wasn't a sublime place but that he was content with it. I told him that was all I knew this land of Tartarin and that I also was content with it. He smiled and nodded his head.

"Listen, you've read 'Tartarin.' Do you remember that wonderful passage where we find the complaint about the Tarascon diligence? Well, I'm going to paint that old green and red vehicle in the courtyard at the inn now that the wind has died down," Vincent told me.

"Wow! That's great," I said. "Can I go with you?"

"Ask your father. If he says, yes, then your mother will not contradict him. Yes?"

"Yes."

And so on a bright holiday morning, Vincent and I got ready to walk to Tarascon. It was a nice sunny day when the sun warms your neck and your arms, and you don't have to worry about school. Vincent was loaded with his painting necessities and I had brought some food and water for the excursion.

"Just like another picnic," I said.

"Yes, just like a picnic. Isn't this fun, Camille?"

"Yes, more fun than playing in the streets with guys who don't know what to do on a free day."

"We know what to do, don't we?" said Vincent.

We got there around eight in the morning since we left early at five thirty and an old farmer gave us a ride in his cart half the way up since he was going to market in Tarascon. Altogether, it's about seventeen kilometers north of Arles. The old farmer said that he did not often meet a father and son walking this road. I replied that we were not father and son but that Vincent was like my father. I think that made Vincent smile a bit. He seemed happy. I liked to see him smile since he didn't do it often. He was too serious all the time. He needed a son to make him smile.

The air was warm but not hot. The smell of the road lingered in our nostrils, the perfume of oleander, of wild flowers and of pine needles. It was so good to be out in the open again, especially with Vincent. Just like the old days, I told myself. I felt a warm and joyful feeling inside me.

"We are going to create today," I said out loud. "You with your canvas and paint and I with my notebook. I haven't taken down notes on painting out in the open for quite some time."

"Yes, it's time you write notes on my creation again, Camille."

We both laughed. The old farmer dropped us off at the château du roi René, a really old castle. We saw the steeple of Saint Martha's church and I was reminded of how St. Martha of Bethany had saved the region from the Tarasque, the giant monster. It's one of my favorite stories. I read that the Tarasque was a huge "dragoness" that had emerged from the sea and had chosen the river Rhône as its new home. She was half land mammal and half fish, and that she outsized twelve elephants. It had a lion's head, horse's ears, and the face of a bitter old man, and a scaly tail that ended in a scorpion's sting. She was horrible. She scared everyone and terrorized the region. She breathed flames, destroyed houses, frightened animals, cows stopped giving milk, and she even destroyed bridges, so that no one could cross the river. It was Martha who had landed at Saintes-Maries-de-la-Mer with the two

Maries that saved the town of Tarascon. It was said that she eventually found herself in the region's Nerluc marketplace where everyone was talking about the dragon. Martha set out barefoot in her white dress with no other weapon than a big jar of holy water. She held up two sticks in the shape of a cross and stopped the dragon cold. She then sprinkled holy water on it and the dragon stopped spitting fire. She then led the defeated dragon to town where the people, who were still terribly afraid of the Tarasque, threw a shower of stones and killed the monster. The people built a new church in honor of Saint Martha and changed the name of the town from Nerluc to Tarascon in honor of the defeat of the Tarasque. It's a fascinating story; I like stories like that. We can see the mask of the Tarasque almost everywhere in and around Tarascon. I had one in my room in Arles, and I still have it. My uncle, Marius, had given it to me for my birthday two years before I turned ten. My mother didn't like it. I think she was afraid of it.

When we got to the inn, I got some water to drink and offered some to Vincent. I also took a pear and tried to give one to Vincent, but he refused it. I gave him an apricot and he put it in his pocket. He set up his easel and went right to work for he said he had a busy day ahead of him wanting to finish the painting during the daylight hours and reach home before dusk. I sat on a little stool behind him and watched him set up his canvas, prepare his paints for his palette and pick up the brushes he needed. Everything seemed easy for him, almost mechanical.

"Take a look at that monster will you," pointing to the diligence in the yard against the wall. "It's huge and it's Tartarin's vehicle for his adventures, remember?"

"Yes."

I didn't want to lengthen the conversation knowing that he was intent on painting that canvas today all in one big surge of creative energy. I kept quiet while he adjusted his straw hat and took a brush in his right hand. I noticed that he didn't have the red string around his wrist anymore. It must have broken off, I thought.

He began to paint and I could see the outline being done with colors, pink and yellow walls, two closed shutters, green, a white building to the side, a corner of blue sky with a foreground of gray sand color. Slowly, the painting was taking shape. By early afternoon, Vincent had started painting the diligences, one up front and the other in the back. Very colorful with green and red, the wheels white, yellow, black, blue and orange. Thickly laid paint. There's a brown ladder leaning against the side of the first diligence for passengers to climb to the top of the carriage. That's where I would have chosen to ride. High up on the monster on our way to Africa. From time to time, people came up to Vincent and looked. Some stayed a while, others left. A few children hovered around like chirping birds and I motioned them to go away. Monsieur was working and needed to be quiet. They laughed and made gestures with their hands. I looked at Vincent and he seemed impervious to all that. The children finally took off and I grew tired of sitting there taking notes. I got up and walked away for a while and then came back. He was still painting intently and fast. Layer upon layer, brush stroke after brush stroke. The painting came alive with color. I could see Tartarin getting on the boat for Africa, the dark continent where the lions live. Then once there, he takes the old diligence to make his way to the convent of lions. It's nighttime and the conductor lights his lanterns. The old rusty diligence jumps up and down, squeaking from her tired springs, and the horses galloping, and the bells tinkling, that's what I recollected. Tartarin was off to his adventures in the wild.

Vincent finished the painting, **Tarascon Diligence,** late that afternoon. He had not eaten anything except his apricot with some water. I had eaten all of my lunch.

"I could go for a cup of coffee right now," he said, as he started to pack up his things. "I had a good day, a very good day," he said with a sense of accomplishment.

I looked at the diligence in the yard and the one in the painting. I liked the painted one better. It seemed alive and bursting with color. That's what the artist wanted to do and he had done well. I put my notebook back into my pocket and felt content to have added to my notes again. My notebook was getting filled up and I would have to get another one soon. We left for Arles around five and walked for about two hours when a man from Tarascon, on his way to Aleron, picked us up. He was going to visit his son for a few days, he told us. I was glad we had a ride because my legs were getting tired and I was hungry.

I slept soundly that night and woke up in time to have breakfast and get ready for school. It was Thursday, a somewhat cloudy day with big puffy dark clouds in the sky. Some of them were deep gray, turning black as if something ominous was going to occur. A storm, maybe? Another violent gust of the mistral? I was hurrying to school when a gypsy lady, at least I thought she was a gypsy by her long brightly colored dress and kerchief, stopped me and asked me where Vincent lived.

I looked at her and said, "Do you know him? What do you want with him?"

"I have something very important to tell him," she said.

"I don't know if I should tell you where he lives. He doesn't like to be bothered by strangers."

I was trying to protect him from further contact with gypsies, for Vincent had told me that he didn't want to meet up with any of them for fear of being associated with taboos and hexes. He had had enough of that.

"Come, tell me if you know because I can get the information from someone else," she said with a glint of fire in her eyes.

Since I was dying to find out what this was all about and since school was not that important right then and there, I decided to lead her to Vincent's house myself.

"Come," I told her, "I'll bring you there."

"You're a good boy for a *gadjé*," she said.

Vincent was drinking coffee and seemed surprised to see me with a gypsy.

"This lady wants to talk to you," I said as I introduced myself into his kitchen.

"Aren't you going to school today?" he asked me.

"No. It's not necessary since I took my *dictée* last Tuesday and the teacher has to give it again to those who failed it."

It was true, but that did not exempt me from being at school. I was hedging and I sensed that Vincent knew that.

"It's true, I don't have to be there," I insisted.

He signaled for me to go upstairs while the gypsy was with him talking. I climbed the stairs and went into his bedroom being careful to keep the door ajar so I could listen to what was so important.

"Do you remember me?" she asked. "I'm Mirnanoun, Sara's friend. I met you at Saintes-Maries-de-la-Mer last June. I'm the one who warned you about associating with Sara since this could lead to an ugly affair. I gave you a medal of Sara-la-Kâli, remember?"

"Yes, yes, I remember now. But you're not really Sara's friend are you?" he said.

"I was once, a very close friend, until..."

"Until what?"

"It's a long story about a private matter, but I'll tell you about it since you deserve to know. You're not like the other *gadgés*," she said.

"It's about two gypsy clan families. Sara's and mine. Sara was once in love with my brother, Kevja. A mad, passionate, gypsy love. Only a gypsy knows how to love that much and that hard. A gypsy loves with passion and it oftentimes leads to the fate of death, *la muerte*, so powerful is its control over heart and soul. Like a curse. Kevja was a *razeteur*, a man who deftly removes the rosettes from the bull's horns while running swift and smooth in the ring. In all of the Camargue, he had no equal. Oh, he was a fine *razeteur* all dressed in white and as lithe and agile as any bull chaser can be. And the horses, how he loved them. He had been a *gardian* of the beautiful horses of Camargue and even paraded with a pole and banner at several festivals at Saintes-Maries. He was indeed a knight-*razeteur*. He loved those animals and he knew how to handle them. Kevja was a most handsome young man full of the vigor of gypsy manhood in its prime, tall, jet black hair that curled like no other, piercing eyes the color of the mystery of night and bronze skin. His lean face looked as if it had been chiseled out of Italian marble, the golden one, so daringly handsome was he. Strong as a bull too. There was nothing that frightened him, no danger, not even death."

Then somewhat hesitatingly she continued her story.

"Sara," and she paused, "Sara pursued him and made him fall in love with her. She was a very beautiful gypsy woman with eyes that had the effect of gold and onyx each time she gazed at you. She could bewitch any man and have him as a lover, so irresistible was her beauty and so strong was her charm. Well, she fell in love with Kevja, even though he had already vowed his love to another. She desired him with jealousy; she wanted him come what may. My brother could not resist her. He had her under his skin and could not shake her off. That was the beginning of the end for my brother. My family liked Sara but my mother didn't trust her. Such a powerful attraction leads to disastrous consequences, she maintained. She was right. The affair lasted but for a short while until Sara fell out of love with Kevja. However, my brother was still madly in love with Sara and could not shake her off. She played coy, she tossed him about like a ball never fully realizing that he was hurting. I warned her about playing with my brother's heart. A man's heart is easily shattered when he finds that his lover is not faithful to their love. A woman can smash it like pottery on tile. A million pieces. That's what she did with Kevja's heart. Shattered. He wasn't living anymore, he was just existing. He had the curse, the curse of ill-fated love. No one had put that curse on him but Sara's defiant and untrustworthy love had done it to him. He stopped riding the horses he so loved, he didn't want to train the young bulls anymore, and he even stopped eating. My father pleaded with him. He told my father that he wanted to die. I, in turn, pleaded with Sara to stop what she was doing and give my brother back his heart. She just laughed it off. I cursed her, I cursed her as only a gypsy can do. She didn't mind, she said, for her strength was stronger than any curse. I feared for her even more so than my brother for I knew in my gypsy soul that she was cursed to roam forever on this earth never finding a home or a place to put her head. That was the result of my curse on her and the result of her treacherous love. You see, I loved Sara as a sister. I was torn between her and my brother, but blood is thicker than anything. I had to find a way to protect my brother and at the same time give him back his life."

She paused a long time before she could resume her words.

"Death, my dear sir, death is the most powerful of black stars. You see there are white stars and then there are black ones. The black ones rule our destiny. One day, my brother went to the ring and decided that his black star was in its orbit. As accustomed as he was to bulls, he allowed himself to be gored by one of them. He bled to death with Sara's name on his lips. His friends told us about his tragic death. There was nothing we could have done about it, it was in the stars. Oh, I began to hate Sara. That's what happens when love is turned around, hate sets in. Moreover, we learned that Sara had befriended a *gadjé* and that she was in love with him. Six months later she had a daughter that she named Mireille. Mireille, you see is not the *gadjé*'s child, she's my brother's child. Everyone knows that."

"But she told me that it was the stranger's child," responded Vincent.

I was listening to all of what was being said by the gypsy, somewhat astounded by everything she said about Sara, about Mireille. I didn't dare move a muscle.

"She lied to you just to get your sympathy. She's a beggar and a thief. She'll tell you anything to get what she wants. Beware of her."

"What about Mireille? I saw her last month with a gypsy caravan that I was painting. It was she, I'm sure. She recognized me. Sara wasn't there though."

"The clan took the child that is theirs. They took her away from a tramp and a renegade gypsy woman."

"But that's kidnapping," objected Vincent.

"That's *gadjé* talk, not gypsy law," she replied.

"But where were they taking her? I'm sure that Sara will eventually find her."

"No. All of the clans have come together to protect one of their very own. The child is gypsy and she will remain that way, and not a gypsy with a hex on her head like her mother."

"But, she's part *gadjé*," said Vincent.

"No she's not. She's one hundred percent gypsy."

"How do you know?" asked Vincent.

"Look at her eyes and her complexion. My brother's eyes and my brother's complexion. Solid bronze, not that of a *gadjé*. Besides, Sara had told Kevja that she was with child before he killed himself."

"Why would she do that?"

"What?"

"Deny her own child her heritage as a gypsy."

"Oh, that's because she was cursed and wanted to keep the girl. She knew that the family was out to get the child, so she lied, cheated, hid herself from all of us and sought the *gadjé* law to protect her whenever she suspected that anyone of us was after her. She invented that story about her half-*gadjé* lover. She was a turncoat. No loyalty to her clan or to her birthright as a gypsy. She's doomed to die alone carrying with her the dregs of her misgiven life."

"I feel for her and her daughter, little Mireille." said Vincent.

"Don't. Besides, that's not the child's name anymore. Mireille is a *gadjé* name. Her name is Nadja. Don't lose your sympathy on Sara. She has to pay for what she did. Don't get involved anymore than you already have. Remember that I put a curse on you at Saintes-Maries after I had gotten some blood from you. That's because we didn't want you to get involved and we knew that you would anyway. You're a soft *gadjé* with the heart of a gazelle."

"It's just the human thing to do," he retorted.

"*Gadjé* talk."

I was somewhat embarrassed for Vincent. Here he was trying to explain things to her, how he felt as person and how he cared for the little girl.

"Just remember the black bird with a pin in its head that I put at the crossroads on your way back from Saintes-Maries."

"So, it was you who put it there."

"Yes, it was me."

"But I didn't touch it. I left it there as Sara had warned me."

"It doesn't matter, a curse is a curse."

Now I was trembling for Vincent.

"So that you be forever warned, the curse will work it's power and you will experience terrible headaches, your head will seem to spin, your eyes will seem as if they're coming out of your head and you will feel that you are going mad at times. The balance of your existence has been put on an ever winding and whirling path. Dare not to defy us. Furthermore, you will shed blood and you will die outside of Provence."

"Why do this to me. I haven't done anything wrong. All I want to do is paint and form an *atelier* where artists like me can create freely. If I can't create freely I shall die."

"You should have thought about that before you got involved with Sara the fallen gypsy. Besides, I know you had sexual encounters with her when you returned to Saintes-Maries after your trip with that boy. That's taboo."

"You're a spy, a woman of devious ways," Vincent told her. "Get out of my house. I don't want to have anything to do with you and your kind, nothing with curses, red strings and medals. Nothing of that hocus-pocus. Nothing."

He was angry. I had never heard him that mad before. I shuddered.

"Mind you, you cannot win over us. We are more powerful than you," and with that she left.

I didn't know what to say or do. For the first time, my being with Vincent was painful. I wanted to go home. I felt sorry for him while being apprehensive of what could happen to me by association with him. A child's mind can play so many twists and turns with what frightens him.

"Come down here, Camille," Vincent called.

I came down the stairs slowly and came face to face with Vincent. I could see he was troubled.

"I'm sorry you heard all of that. I should have sent you home. I didn't think it would be this way."

I didn't know what to say. He tried to reassure me that nothing, absolutely nothing, was going to happen to him and to me. Did I believe him then? I don't quite remember. Things were all jumbled in my head. He looked at me straight in the eye and I met his gaze where I was able to see sincerity and a tender fervor that was coaxing me to believe him.

Here was the man I knew, a warm, sincere person. An artist who believed in himself and in others. A master who had all along encouraged me to believe in myself and to follow my guiding star out there in the vast infinity. I was going to be a writer and I needed this push on my soul to fully develop my capacity to write and create. I needed Vincent, my friend.

"Come back tomorrow and we'll talk," he said.

I didn't go back. I waited for him to ease matters between Sara and Mireille within himself. I felt as if I had been an intruder in that bedroom listening to that woman's dangerous talk. Every time I thought about it, I had goose bumps. That woman had no right to say all of that. Was she right? Was that the whole story? What about Mireille? I liked her. Changing her name to Nadja, that's not the way to do things. Poor Mireille, lost out there without her mother. I didn't like people who put curses on others. I didn't like curses and I still don't. I prefer benevolent things happening to people. I wondered if she was right about black stars. No, couldn't be, I thought. If they were black, we couldn't ever see them. Vincent could never paint them either. No, black stars don't exist. Only white stars. Those that scintillate in the deep nighttime sky. But, what about the strange prophecy she told Vincent? Would that turn out to be true? I stayed home terribly confused and quite worried about all of this gypsy stuff.

I later learned that Vincent had gone to see the old shepherd, Patience Lescalier, since he was supposedly a *démascaire*, a shepherd who was considered to be a holder of supernatural powers, someone who held the secrets of nature. He was considered an enemy of sorcerers by his supposed powers. Since Vincent had been *emmasqué*, cursed, he was told to seek out the help of a shepherd. At first, he didn't want to do it. He didn't believe in it, he said. But, when his headaches began and his head pounded in pain, he decided to seek the help of his friend, the shepherd. Unfortunately, Lescalier was very sick and could not spend time with Vincent. The tenant farmer had taken Lescalier to another town for treatment and no one knew where he was. The farmer did not want to tell anyone. Therefore, Vincent had to live with his pain and his curse. He didn't call it that but it turned out that way, what with his strange illness that would put him in the asylum later on. People said that he had a rare disease, and Doctor Rey tried to explain it to my father and to Vincent's brother, Monsieur Théo, but no one could explain Vincent's malady. It just came and wrecked his life. Was it a curse or what? People will ever be trying to explain Vincent's illness but I don't think anyone will ever succeed. Perhaps, after I die, someone will, someone who can understand advanced science, but not in my lifetime. I don't think so.

Vincent's next painting was, **The Trinquetaille Bridge**. I was there when he did it. He was in a good mood ever expecting the arrival of his friend Paul Gauguin. He kept mentioning his name and the fact that he and Monsieur Gauguin were going to create *l'atelier du Midi*, this famous artists' workshop. I heard him mention that so many times. Vincent seemed serene, happier and much more content with himself, and even with others. He even went over to the Café de la Gare and told Madame Ginoux and her husband to expect great things for Arles as the cradle of the artists' domain in Provence. He and Monsieur Gauguin were going to revolutionize the way paintings would henceforth be made and sold. No more of the Paris effete cliques, he said. No more dealers taking advantage of artists who were poor and could hardly afford to eke out an existence. No more Salons where only the works of the in-crowd were selected for exposition. The Impressionists had attempted to bring a new order to things and even had their own salons as independents, but they were becoming as selective as the others, he said. He extolled the virtues of some artists like *Père* Pissarro and Gustave Caillebotte who tried to help out those in need, but he himself was able to paint and live thanks only to the generosity of his brother, Théo, not the Impressionists. Take Monet, for instance, he was becoming like all the others, fat, gloomy and filled with disdain for painters like Vincent and Signac. Monsieur Gauguin did not like him, not a single bit, Vincent said. *L'atelier du Midi* would become a beacon for young artists who work hard to achieve success. He would see to it that monastic discipline would reign and artists would be able to live in a real community. Artists need discipline in order to better manage their lives and paint creatively and freely, he said. Madame Ginoux asked him, was this possible given the nature of artists. He replied that if he did it himself, others would be able to follow him as a model. After all, he had worked very hard, sometimes beyond exhaustion, to prove to himself and others that work is a big part of a man's dignity, and art is the channel of that work.

My father asked him how he would finance this workshop and he answered, "If we work as a community, we can economize, buy supplies in greater quantities and take turns at cooking. This way we will save and we will get prosperous once our paintings sell."

"This sounds to me like a commune, Vincent," my father said.

"Not a political one but an artistic one."

"How are you going to attract other artists to this venture?" asked Monsieur Ginoux.

"Well, I will start with a great artist, Paul Gauguin, and as our reputation grows, we will assuredly begin to attract others, Bernard and Signac, for instance. Why, we might even attract some Americans such as this painter who lived in Fontvieille and came to see me, Mister Macnight. It will take time but it an be done. I only hope the community of Arles will be accepting of us as a creative group. It will become a hallmark for this city, you know. Other towns will envy Arles. In the future, people will speak of Arles as a center for artistic exploration and wonder."

My father said that Vincent was very happy entertaining questions about his plans without having someone always ignoring him or laughing at him. I just wondered if the others in town would feel like these three friends did. That's what I wrote in my new notebook. Yes, I have a new one. The old one was full. I put it in a safe place.

The Trinquetaille Bridge is a huge bridge that connects Arles with Trinquetaille on the opposite bank of the Rhône river. Vincent wanted to paint this scene because he liked the angle and the construction of the bridge with the stairs leading up to it. He painted other views of this bridge but this is the one I saw that day. In this one, we don't see the river. We see the people climbing the stairs, in particular, a woman dressed in dark blue at the bottom. That's Madame Valselle from la rue des Épingles. She greeted us and told me that I was a nice boy for having taken off my cap and saluted her. She made good *barigoule*, that's with artichokes, and *bourride*, the fish soup that I liked.

The bottom stairs are wide, very wide, while the others, going up, are narrower. There are twenty-six steps on the narrow ones. I counted them. To the left, we can see the arch under which people can walk. It's a different painting, different from those that Vincent painted previously because the perspective is geometric, Vincent said. It's about lines, angles and rectangles and other things. I hadn't studied geometry then and I knew little about lines and angles. It's a painting that offers the view of looking up and not straight ahead, as in a field or in a garden. There are no vivid colors except the red on the tree trunk to the left. The sky is not blue but a pasty color pink. The street's cobblestone are done in a mixture of blue, gray and pink. The bridge and the stairs, as well as the walls, are blue-gray with some lighter shade of color on the wall. The whole thing looks massive since that's what it is, a massive construction of cement. I'm sure this painting was a real challenge to Vincent, and I told him so afterward. He simply nodded.

"You're so *perspicace*," he said, "You notice things other people don't."

I then helped him with his easel, and carried his stool for him. He was going home.

14

Two Lives, Two Friends

Finally! Monsieur Gauguin had arrived at Vincent's house.

"*Enfin*," Vincent said.

He had been waiting for his friend a very long time.

"Mark the calendar, Camille," he told me, "October 20, 1888 will go down as a great day in my life. It marks the start of *l'atelier du Midi. Enfin!*" he said all proud of himself and with fire in his eyes.

I loved his eyes. They were of a deep blue with sparks of green and sometimes some gold flint, I swear. They changed with whatever mood he seemed to be in. Some remarked that he was a moody person, but they didn't know him as I did, not really know him. Sure, he was a moody person because he had so many things on his mind. So many things running through it since he was always creating something or other in his ever-busy mind. Always ready to paint or to draw. That was besides his concerns about money and his health. There was a lot going on in that mind of his. He wasn't abrasive as some people thought. He simply didn't want people around him who had no consideration for him as a human being and for his art that he loved with a passion. Some say he wasn't sociable, but they warded him off by their feelings of superiority and conformity. Deep down, he liked people. He truly did, but not people who wanted him to be what they thought he should be. They seemed to want to replace the person he was with someone else that he wasn't. For sure, he didn't meet people's expectations either in life or in the expression of his art. But, that was his destiny to shake up the world and make them see things differently. You either followed his path to the stars or wound up in the fields with the plucked wheat. And how he loved children. He would have been so happy with a family, but it wasn't to be. I could have screamed at certain people like Jeanne Calment who said terrible things about Vincent simply because she didn't like the way he dressed or the way he sometimes brushed her off.

"He's dirty, badly dressed and just plain disagreeable," she said. "Besides, he's not an artist. My mother says that he paints with thick blobs of paint and doesn't know how to draw, that's what my mother and aunt Crestino say."

"Wash your mouth, Jeanne Calment," I told her. "He's a real artist and he too knows how to draw, great drawings. You haven't seen any of his drawings and neither has your mother. As for your aunt Crestino, she's just a busybody, a blabbermouth who never has a good word for anybody. That's what my mother says, Jeanne Calment."

She got angry with me and replied with her hands on her hips with her cheeks all red, "You, Camille Roulin, you're nothing but a *voyou* yourself running around with that artist, the tramp. You're both off the beam."

I could have replied something really nasty then and there but I refrained from doing so since it wasn't worth the effort. Not with people like her who don't understand anyway. People don't understand that Vincent is different and that he doesn't play by their rules. Their rules hurt and they divide. I learned much later that Vincent was hurt so many times in his life that he refrained from trying to be close to anybody except my family and me. He suffered from being alone and rejected and especially from losing people that were so close to him. It happened so many times, he told me, like Kee Vos and Sien, two loves of his life back in the Netherlands. He found it so hard when his brother got married. That was another separation of sorts, a loss of intimacy that he had always cherished. Of course, he gained a sister-in-law and then a nephew but things were different after that since he considered his relationship with Monsieur Théo a burden and an intrusion in his wedded life.

The following day I got to meet Paul Gauguin. He was nice. He had a slight accent in his voice. That's because he was a Breton, I suppose. He had deep dark eyes that pierced into yours, if you let him. He told me that he had come to Arles to be with his friend, Vincent, and that Théo Van Gogh had helped him organize his trip. He came because he needed a new challenge in his life as an artist and Vincent was going to help him meet this challenge.

"Nice country this place. Plenty of bright sunshine," he told me with somewhat of a tinge of disdain in his voice that I could not fathom.

There was something about him that I sensed was different, not different like Vincent was, but different in a way that was aloof and conceited. I found him cold. He was distant and laughed at my cap. He thought that it was too big for my head. I blushed. When he heard me call Vincent by his first name, he told me to call him Monsieur Gauguin, which I did without hesitation but with a mock deference, almost. I didn't like him from the start and he didn't like me being there. I was just a kid intruding in his life. He didn't need kids around him. He had five back home, he told me. They were living with their mother in Copenhagen. Why were they living in Denmark? I wondered, but I didn't want to ask him for fear of getting an answer like "mind your business, you're just a kid." Besides, I didn't want to hurt Vincent since he was so glad to have an artist living with him now. He had prepared the house for him, washed the dishes, cleaned the floor, wiped the dust, emptied the waste and hung up several paintings on the walls, just for him. He respected Monsieur Gauguin highly as an artist, he told me. He also respected him as a fine cook. Vincent truly glowed with pride and anticipation at the arrival of Paul Gauguin. They were going to paint together, inspire one another, although he considered Monsieur Gauguin a better artist than he, live together in harmony and, best of all, form a community of artists that would rival the group of Impressionists back there in Paris. Exceptional light and brilliant colors would be their hallmark, he said. And their style of producing paintings would one day be recognized as superior to all others because people would buy their paintings and they would talk about *l'atelier du Midi* as *un phare dans l'étape ascendante de la peinture*, a beacon for the next stage of painting, he said with assurance and hope.

Vincent had very high hopes for his proposed community. I was glad for him and wished him much success. It was high time that he achieved success in his life, high time after what he had gone through. Then, he would most probably not have to worry so much about finances and where the next franc would come from and, yes, not have to depend so much on his brother. Indeed, he thought that with the arrival of Monsieur Gauguin things would change for the better and that finally his ideas for art and painting would be accepted and promulgated through the art of Paul Gauguin. Monsieur Gauguin would become his champion and his salvation in the pursuit of art and inspiration, he thought. All would finally come together like a giant *toile* that a weaver makes with all the threads he has on his loom, a giant cloth or canvas made up of many threads. Strong threads, threads of vivid colors. Vincent was the weaver of dreams.

I had sensed that I could not accompany both Vincent and Monsieur Gauguin on their trips outside the studio because I had become an intruder, at least that's the way I felt. Besides, Vincent did not invite me along as he had done so many times before. That was alright, I understood, even though it hurt me to think that they were out there enjoying the sun, tremendous views of fields, the quiet shade of the public garden and the fun of capturing the vivid colors and the light that rendered them so brilliant. Fortunately, Vincent did come by the house to visit with my father and mother and tell us about his excursions. Sometimes, he would bring some of his paintings. I felt that was his way of not totally excluding me from his adventures of painting. He would even talk about Monsieur Gauguin and his work that interested my father tremendously. My father was always interested in other people's talents and the results of those talents. Besides, Vincent enjoyed my mother's soup and joyfully accepted any invitation that my father offered, as long as he told my mother beforehand. My mother was starting to get used to my father's invitations to Vincent. My father really liked him. I guess he didn't get to like Monsieur Gauguin because he never invited him over for soup. Monsieur preferred to go to the restaurant and *rue des ricolettes*.

Two weeks went by and I hardly saw Vincent or his friend Monsieur Gauguin. I went to school, I read a lot and I did my chores. I played with my friends in the streets and watched the men play *pétanque*. I also played with my baby sister since she was already three months old and could sit and be entertained. She drooled an awful lot and I kept wiping her chins. She had more than one because she was so fat. She was one big ball of baby flesh and she smiled and laughed a lot. I kept coming back to my notebook, from time to time, and realized that I hadn't written in it for an entire week. Nothing about painting for over two weeks. I went to my dresser drawer and took out the three small drawings that Vincent had given me. I chose the one he had given me for my birthday, the Tarascon diligence that I so wanted him to do for me. I started looking at it carefully. It was beautiful and it was made just for me. The lines were sharp and crisp and made the diligence jump out at me. All at once, I was brought back to the reading of Tartarin and carried away to Africa. I imagined that Vincent and I were in that old creaky carriage rolling down the bumpy roads to catch the boat for the wilds of Africa. What a wonderful dream that was. Oh, yes, a daydream that brought me back to my friend's side. My good friend, the artist. Then, I started getting lonely without him wishing he would let me visit him.

Suddenly, one day, he came to the house and asked me to go with him to the Alyscamps. Would I? It was Wednesday afternoon and I was free. As I've said before, les Alyscamps are the ancient Roman ruins of Arles. When you walk in, there's a very long lane lined with trees and, in the fall, all the leaves are a bright yellow. The trees stand up straight and tall like soldiers in a line formation on either side. People go there to walk and enjoy the peace and quiet of the old cemetery. The sarcophagi are vestiges of old Roman tombs made of stone, explained Vincent. They're very old. Arles is an old Roman city and that's why we have the Forum, the Coliseum and the Alyscamps, our very own Champs Élysées.

Vincent painted **Les Alyscamps** with a predominance of yellow with tinges of red, being November and all. He eventually painted two others but from a different perspective, not the alley. The main color is red in those two. In the one he was painting, we can see the long lane of poplar trees with tight short limbs and leaves that reach for the sky. They look to me like long lemon lollipops. The sky is a November sky with a very dark blue patch at the very top and clouds that rise up to the patch of grayish-blue. The color of the ground matches the leaves in the trees except there is more red here. There are gray colored tombs on either side of the alley where people stroll leisurely. It's a simple enough view and the perspective gives it depth. Monsieur Gauguin also painted the Alyscamps but from a different vantage point. His painting looks at the trees from the right hand side only. The pale white polygonal tower of the Chapel of Saint Honorat can be seen in the background. The leaves seem to be a mass of reddish-yellow color with an evergreen in the foreground. Nice contrast. There's a lot of green in the painting with trees and shrubs. Three women appear to be standing still in the center. All three are dressed in Arlesian black with two having white scarves. There are also two paths. The one on the left is stone-gray while the one on the right is covered with orange-colored leaves. What catches your eye is the intense red patch on the right and the white patch on the left. They look something like huge rocks but they're not. They were probably painted there because Monsieur Gauguin wanted the sharp contrast of colors or perhaps they stand as symbols of something. Vincent said that Monsieur Gauguin was into symbols. Vincent is the one who showed me the painting, not Monsieur Gauguin. The sky is a brighter blue than the sky in Vincent's painting. It has a long ribbon of yellowish-white in it stretching upwards, while the blue is whitish in appearance on account of the clouds, I'm sure. There are no tombs in the painting. Later, when I did see Monsieur

Gauguin, I told him that I liked his painting <u>Les Alyscamps</u>. He told me that color for him was a way of transforming the actual physical landscape into some meaningful symbol and that he always saw things that way. He looks at something in nature and it becomes transformed as such in his mind like a moth that is transformed in its cocoon. I told him that this sounded very interesting and that perhaps some day he would teach me more about symbols.

"You see in my search for learning I keep notes in my notebook. Later, I want to write a book about all of what I've written down, I want to be a writer," I explained to him.

He smiled at me for the first time and said that this was a very good idea and that he would be pleased to be included in my book.

"I need exposure," he said.

Both Vincent and Monsieur Gauguin would work very hard during the day and then go to the café for drinks and relaxation. Monsieur Gauguin liked absinthe. I could not drink that. It was a very strong drink, my father said. He also said that, although Monsieur Gauguin could take the absinthe, it was more difficult for Vincent since he did not tolerate it as well. Monsieur Gauguin was a strong man with tight muscles and, I suppose, a strong stomach. Vincent had a very weak stomach. I knew that. He often had stomach cramps and, at times, he couldn't eat much of anything, especially spices. He wasn't made with the strong fiber of the tough Provençal type. Vincent's constitution was more delicate, his health more vulnerable. I was hoping that the two men would not make it a habit of drinking too much. It would certainly not be a good thing for Vincent, my mother said. Of course, everyone knew about their nightly excursions since this was a tight neighborhood where everyone knew everyone else's whereabouts and goings on.

Vincent then told me that he and Monsieur Gauguin had a different approach to painting. He liked the outdoor painting while his friend liked the indoor for better contemplation, since he preferred to work with his imagination. That's what he told Vincent he should do, more painting from the mind and his imagination rather than wander outside and look for things to paint. Because Vincent respected his friend's advice in art, he decided to do just that. Paint indoors for a while. That's when he started painting **Memory of the Garden at Etten (Women of Arles)**. Vincent told me that this was a painting from memory and that he was trying to depict things in a somewhat symbolic way, the Gauguin way. He also tried to incorporate the Arles experience with his memory of Etten. I asked him what was the difference between Impressionist painting and painting with symbols.

"Oh," he replied, "some people, especially critics, like to call it Impressionism and Symbolism. Two classifications of art as movements. It's just putting a tag on different ways of painting. I never liked branding my art as something others call or see as a movement. Impressionist painters were called that because an art critic who did not like Monet's painting entitled, *Impression,* called them "those Impressionists" as a derogatory term, and it stuck. I'm not an Impressionist. I'm not a Symbolist. I'm me. Impressionists like to paint the outdoors and the fleeting light of the north. They do it with colors that appeal to them while capturing nature. However, they each have their own style like Monet, Renoir, Père Pissarro and there's even a woman, a Mary Cassatt, *une Américaine.* Within the group, one can count Gustave Caillebotte that I like very much and Frédéric Bazille. They wanted me to join them but I refused. I didn't like Monet's attitude. He was a bit too superior-minded for me. He liked to tell people what to do. He has some very nice paintings but I prefer the bolder, more vivid colors. He told me I had no style. My style is..." and I chimed in because he had repeated it to me so many times, 'exaggerate the essential and purposely leave the obvious things vague,' I said and we both laughed.

"Some people want some nice photograph-looking type of painting or what I call cute and fluffy scenes to put on the wall of their living room. I don't paint for living rooms. As for symbolism, that's a bit more complicated to explain. Symbols are things that represent something else like a heart for love or the color black for death. Some symbols like the two I've just mentioned are overused. They become clichés.(I jotted down this word). The more interesting ones are those you can recognize as symbols like a butterfly and water, but the most complicated ones are too hidden and just not accessible to all except the painter or author. So, I stay away from deep-hidden symbols and look to significance."

"What's significance?" I asked.

"Significance is meaning with suggestiveness. I don't hide my meaning, I just paint it the way I see it. If I see a landscape with trees and flowers, I paint it the way the light opens them up to me and I create the landscape on my canvas."

"Just like the Harvest at La Crau with Montmajour in the background," I said.

"Yes, like that. And I draw significance from the sunflowers because, to me, they look like stained windows in a church. I don't impose this view. I only suggest it to those who would like to know what I think and how I see things. Some artist might see sunflowers as a symbol but I see them as possibilities of significance. One meaning that my eye can see and my mind can interpret as significance. To signify is to mean something or be pointed in a direction that lends itself to an image like a stained glass window in the case of sunflowers. But, that's my significance, my interpretation. I don't lock it into one thing and one thing only. I don't force my interpretation on somebody else."

"I see. But don't all artists create things in their paintings for others to see a meaning behind them?"

"Yes, in a way, but the artist should only suggest, not impose, as I said. If a person looking at my painting, any painting, asks 'What does it mean' then I would answer, 'Nothing.' If the person cannot find a meaning of his own, then I can't help him anymore since I've already suggested a meaning either in color or form. Do you get it, Camille?"

"I think so. If I don't get it then I don't deserve an explanation. Right?"

"Right. But it doesn't mean I can't explain certain features to you or even the reason for using certain colors or some background information concerning the scenery or the person whose portrait I'm painting. That's not talking symbols or even significance. You see, to me all art is poetry in its representation of light, color and form because I like to see things from the perspective of the magical suggestiveness of words. The poet suggests. He does not impose. I need to repeat that to myself and to others like you."

I was putting all of that in my notebook. I was learning again and so happy to do so. He explained things to me so well, Vincent. He had patience with me because I wanted to learn and he knew I appreciated his art and knowledge. Then, he started telling me about the significance of the painting about the garden in Etten.

"Does Monsieur Gauguin suggest?" I asked Vincent.

"Gauguin suggests but he goes further by implicating the viewer with symbolism because he loves the imaginary while at the same time dwelling on the intellectual play of the mind at work. For some people, that gets to be complicated as far as recognizing the significance of a work of art."

"I see," I said. "Then you chose to use symbols that are recognizable but prefer the reality of natural representations. Is that right?"

"Exactly, Camille. You're learning fast. I try to use symbols as Gauguin wants me to but sometimes I falter and end up casting the painting aside."

"Do you save the canvas?"

"I never waste canvases. You know that."

"Yes, I do," I replied.

"Now let's talk about my painting. It was done as a dream or a vision as Gauguin had recommended. There's a visionary mood here," he said. " If one is looking for spatial sense, there is none. There's no horizon, as you can see. There are contour lines in almost everything. I wrote to my sister about this painting: 'I do not know if you can understand that it is possible to express poetry by means of a good arrangement of colors and nothing more, just as one can express consolation by means of music. In addition, the bizarre, contrived and repetitive lines that twist through the whole picture are not meant to represent the garden as it normally looks, but to render it as we might see it in a dream, in its true character, yet at the same time stranger than reality.' "

He continued to say, "I recalled from memory the content of the painting while giving it a shape and colors to express my dream through my imagination. Does that make sense?"

"Yes, of course. It makes sense to me," I said without lying.

"Then, I told her that I was dreaming of her and our mother walking in the vicarage garden that I knew so well. And, I added: 'Assuming that the women out walking were you and Mother, even if there were not the slightest, most everyday and unimportant of resemblances, the deliberate choice of the color, the dark violet set off by the lemon-yellow dahlias would convey Mother's personality to me.' There's another twist to the painting. I don't know if you've noticed it but there are dots all over the clothes the women are wearing and tiny lines in the bushes behind them as well as the orange path on the right side. That's the effect of pointillism. That's another style that my good friend, Paul Signac, adopted. He's a disciple of Seurat. You may meet him some day since I've invited him to come and join me in Arles. I do hope that you can meet him, he's such a great artist and so skillful with his brush applying thousands of points or dots. They're all done so that the colored points complement one another and form one big color scheme. Remember how I told you about complementary colors?"

"Yes, I do," I said.

"Here, I've produced images from deep within me that otherwise would have been supplied by nature itself. However, these images are drawn from my past and not contrived nor modified by thought. It's all significance. Gauguin accuses me often of being too realistic and not dealing with symbols and the imagination enough. That's not my perception, not my style. Too often my work deals with the all too common folks, even the seamier side of life, Gauguin tells me. He chides me for my down-to-earth artistic mentality. But, that's me, I can't change who I am. He likes to couch his works in some imaginative or ideal framework. I like to paint on the spot; he doesn't. I like to paint outdoor and capture the light at a specific time of day or moonlight and starlight at nighttime. He likes to paint indoor even when he gets his inspiration outdoor in nature. I don't know if we will be able to remain together as a team anticipating others to join us and form a community of artists. I really think that he will go away some day, perhaps even sooner than expected, since we don't seem to connect as artists. I've tried, Oh, God, I'm still trying. What I like, he doesn't like, what I reject, he accepts, what I want, he doesn't want. What can I do? I tell you, Camille, I sometimes feel like *une cruche cassée*," a broken earthen vessel.

"No you're not broken, perhaps *un peu fêlée*, a bit cracked, but not broken."

"Yes, cracked like a madman, a *fou-rou*, a red-headed fool, they call me."

"No, no, no, that's not what I meant."

"I know what you meant. If the vessel is just cracked, can I repair it? is the big question. Can I mend it with time and consolation?"

I didn't know what to say at that very moment.

Monsieur Gauguin also painted his version of Vincent's painting of the Garden in Etten. It is called, <u>Old Women of Arles</u>. He painted some *Arlésiennes* walking against the chilling mistral in the public garden across from the yellow house. His colors are bold and range from red to orange, yellow and blue. What is fascinating are the bright yellow trunks of trees and the vivid red of the small fence in the foreground. The colors are really bold and striking, almost wild, I would say. He opted for an almost religious quality with the two women in the foreground holding on to their black shawls. The one leading the procession has the features of Madame Ginoux, bold and strong.

"It's primitive as an approach," he said. "I'm a primitive and Vincent is a romantic. He reads the Bible and I read 'The Odyssey.'"

I had heard of this book and I had told myself that I would like to read it someday. It's about the wild adventures of some Greek hero away from home after a long battle and roaming the seas for ten years. My teacher explained a little bit of the story to me after she had mentioned it in class.

The day after I met with Vincent to look at his recent painting, Sara came to visit him. Yes, Sara the gypsy, Mireille's mother. He had not seen her for a very long time. She appeared out of the blue, totally unexpected, he told me. She wanted desperately to talk to him, so he listened. She told him that the clans had stolen her daughter and had taken her somewhere and she could not locate her. She had been trying desperately to find her but they always managed to hide her so that she could not locate her. She wanted her back. No one would talk. They were all in this together, all very secretive and seeking their revenge on her, she said. He told her that Mirnanoun had come to pay him a visit and warned him about helping her find the child. She answered that she knew about the visit and she wanted to reassure Vincent that no harm would come to him if he would only try to help her find Mireille. He told her that she had lied to him about the *gadjé* and her true lover, Kevja, Mirnanoun's brother. She countered that this wasn't the whole story and that Mirnanoun had twisted things around. Then, he asked her if Mireille was Kevja's child. She hesitated and then said, no. Vincent pleaded with her to tell the truth or else he wasn't even going to try and help her. She then made all kinds of excuses to hide the fact that she had a passionate love affair with Kevja.

"Is Mireille his child?" he pleaded with her. "If you don't tell me the truth how do I know what you're telling me now is true," he told her.

Finally, she had to admit that Mireille was Kevja's child.

"But, I didn't lie about what I'm telling you now," she insisted.

"Do you know that they've changed her name?" he told her.

She replied that, yes, she knew.

He asked her what he could do to help her. She asked for some money since she was at wit's end trying to survive and, at the same time, find her daughter. No one, absolutely no one wanted to help her now that the clans had decided to completely exclude her from any and all gypsy activity and help. Why, even the *gadjés* were warned not to give her any aid whatsoever. Even the fishermen stayed away from her. No more food from any of them. She was doomed to die, she told him. He told her that he was sorry but he hardly had enough to survive himself and that he had to totally depend on his brother to get the money he needed. She then asked him to plead with his brother to get more money for her. He told her no, he would not, could not do that. She then insisted, but he refused.

"Why can't you get money by selling your paintings?" she asked.

He told her that he only wished he could, but that his paintings were not selling in Paris. He tried very hard to paint enough of them to offer a vast selection of paintings, but, try as he may, they would not sell. Her told her that his brother kept them for him and he put a lot of effort into selling them, but the results were poor. She said that if he didn't help her, she would do something desperate like jumping off a bridge. He replied that she had told him before that she was a survivor and that she would never do anything like that. That's when Monsieur Gauguin walked in and overheard what she was saying and he threw her out. Vincent was caught by surprise and didn't utter a single word. He was so embarrassed, he told me. Sara left crying. He truly felt sorry for her but he was helpless and, furthermore, he didn't want to get more deeply involved with this affair of passion, suicide, clan revenge and kidnapping.

"For once, I didn't let my heart control me and make me do things that I might regret later, but I truly like Sara, she's a woman of passion and destiny," he told me with a very sad eye.

I told my mother and father about this encounter and all my mother could say was, "*Pauvre enfant perdu, pauvre lui,*" poor lost child. "*Pourquoi se mêler avec des gitans?*" why get involved with gypsies.

My father didn't say anything. He just looked at me and shook his head. I could see that he felt sorry for Vincent. I was sorry for him and for Mireille. Sara too. What a mess, I told myself. I just wondered where they had taken Mireille and if she would ever see her mother again.

It was getting to be late November and the cold weather was settling in. I hardly saw Monsieur Gauguin outdoors and only saw Vincent once or twice passing by. He was going to the grocery store to buy some provisions, he said, and then he was going straight home. He loved the warm weather even the hot weather but didn't care for the cold. Especially when the mistral came. With the mistral howling like a monstrous force on all of us, shepherds sheltered themselves from it and tried to protect their flocks as best they could, mothers bundled up their children and farmers retreated to their *mas*. Town dwellers stayed sheltered in their homes. That wind goes right through you and almost paralyzes you, so powerful it can be. When it was really bad, I stayed home and read. I was now reading *Un coeur simple* by this author who had died not too long ago, according to my teacher. The author's name was Gustave Flaubert. It's a short story and I was almost in the middle of it. I was going to make it the subject of our next composition. My teacher allowed me to use this story instead of another one less challenging, she said, since I was a good reader and had already read several books outside of the assigned readings. She added that Flaubert was considered to be a master writer whose prose was a hallmark in French letters. He was a realist and he chose his words very carefully, *le mot juste*, she said, to render the exact meaning of his thought in describing situations and events, even objects.

"You can certainly learn from him as a writer," she told me.

She knew that I wanted to be one someday and she never mocked me for it. I was glad that she was helping me learn the art of writing. I liked school much more now that I had a new teacher who was interested in writing.

"Writing, like painting, is an art that must be mastered," she told me one day, "and that takes discipline and time, Camille."

She knew that I had a close relationship with Vincent and that he was also my teacher. She wasn't jealous of him and one of the few Arlesians who recognized the worth of Vincent's art. I introduced her to Vincent one day and from then on she always asked me how Monsieur Vincent was doing.

"Fine," I would say, "he's now painting a portrait or, I would say, he's preparing to paint Madame Firmonin's flower garden."

It was nice to be the intermediary between my teacher at school and my teacher outside of school. I told my father about this and he said that one never has enough teachers and that I was lucky indeed to have Vincent as my special teacher. I was indeed.

When one talks of a teacher, one must also talk about what he teaches and that, for Vincent, was his paintings. The next painting that I saw him do was, **The Sower**. It's about the sun as much as the sower from what I can see. A great big yellow ball of a sun. Vincent came back to his motifs, the outdoor world with the sun and the common man. However, in this painting, Vincent was attempting to meld his style with that of his friend, he said. Since Monsieur Gauguin had told him that art is an abstraction and that 'you should derive the abstraction from Nature as you dream, and think more about your own creative work and what comes of it than about reality,' Vincent tried to incorporate this notion into his "Sower" painting. It shows the sower in a dim light and not in the fullness of the rays of the huge sun. It casts him into a kind of dreamlike stance against a sky that is lemon-yellow with a bright yellow vibrating sun as background. To me, the sower looks as some kind of a phantom with hardly any visible facial features. The ground on which he is sowing is on one side purplish and on the other greenish with some red and white. And there, one can see the little short lines of the brush strokes. In the foreground, we see the trunk of a large tree that's bare except for some twigs jutting out and a few branches with burnt-orange leaves. It's a November tree. But, what strikes me is the fact that this tree overpowers the entire work. The vantage point of the artist is expressed quite differently from other paintings he has done before of fields and gardens. It sets a tone of dormancy and that's what Vincent wanted to do in adding a touch of the dream to his reality. He told me that he was really trying very hard to imitate his master teacher that he found in Monsieur Gauguin.

In his need to be reintegrated into his realistic self as an artist, I believe that he turned, once again, to portrait painting. Now that I can look from the vantage point of maturity and stepping back from it all and thinking about it more intently, I realize that Vincent was truly struggling with his identity as an artist of physical nature and not as an artist of abstract natural forces and physicality. He attempted to placate his friend's demands on him but it wasn't working. The more he tried, the more he drifted away from his true self as a painter of reality. Even though that tore him apart, he could not help but return to his vibrant self in Arles where he had found the fullness of his talent. Unfortunately, Monsieur Gauguin did not think that way and he considered Arles to be 'the dirtiest spot in all of the Midi where the people and the scenery are petty and small.' That's what he told a friend of his. Besides, Monsieur Gauguin kept talking about returning to Martinique and *les pays chauds,* the warm climate.

Monsieur Gauguin was a very tidy person, a rational, cerebral person while Vincent was not tidy, he was messy, and tended to be more a person of the heart. Monsieur Gauguin told Monsieur Théo that it was the general untidiness of the yellow house that struck him. He added that 'Between two such beings as he and I, the one a perfect volcano, the other boiling inwardly too, a sort of struggle was preparing. In the first place, everywhere and in everything I found a disorder that shocked me. His color-box could never contain all those tubes, crowded together and never closed.' Upon his arrival, he found that Vincent was 'floundering', he said, and that 'with all his yellows and violets, all this work with complementariness—a disorderly work on his part—he only achieved soft, incomplete and monotonous harmonies.' That's when Monsieur Gauguin set out to straighten Vincent and his artwork. He undertook the task of explaining things to Vincent and Vincent listened to him attentively because he wanted to learn how to improve his skill at painting and color motifs. Vincent was very malleable and an easy learner, but he didn't realize then that he was going *à rebours,* against the grain, of his natural skills as an artist. It's a wonder, to me, that the two ever came together as co-founders of the *atelier du Midi.* But, of course, this had been Vincent's idea in the first place. I don't think that Monsieur Gauguin had sincerely adopted this notion. Monsieur Gauguin was an artist with a strong will and a determined frame of mind that spurred him to have everything fit according to his pattern and scheme of things when it came to painting. He didn't allow Vincent to pursue his own way of seeing things. He trivialized his paintings and demonized his way of thinking. How could the two even live together? was my question. Of course, back then, I simply accepted everything that Vincent told me about Monsieur Gauguin and how much of an influence he had on him. Yes, an influence that would wrench them apart. I wrote in my notebook that sometimes Monsieur Gauguin was mean to Vincent. He would talk loud to him and drag him to *la maison de tolérance,* where the women of the night were and drink absinthe late into the night. People talked about them, even Vincent's good friend Madame Ginoux.

Madame Ginoux was a friendly woman and she and her husband, Joseph-Michel, were good friends of my father. Madame Ginoux became a friend of Vincent and he shared his love of books with her. He introduced her to Charles Dickens of England where he had spent some time and the American, Harriet Beecher Stowe, who wrote "Uncle Tom's Cabin." Apparently both authors had touched her feminine sensibilities. Knowing that I loved reading and wanted to become a writer someday, she gave me a couple of books from her library collection, one was "Indiana" by George Sand and a translation of Dickens' "Great Expectations." I admired the woman and the way she appreciated Vincent and his work. Not too many women wanted to sit for Vincent. She was one of the very few along with my mother. She had, at times, sat for him in the yellow house. When Monsieur Gauguin, who flattered Madame Ginoux into having a portrait session with him, convinced Vincent to join him while he was making a charcoal drawing of her, Vincent became Monsieur Gauguin's pawn. He followed the master's every inclination, it seems.

Madame Ginoux was very sensitive to flattery and was a bit vain. My mother used to say that she was *fière comme un paon*, proud like a peacock, showing off his fan feathers. She loved to pose in front of people not just for artists but for people who admired her and her *toilette*, her dress and bearing. She was a true *Arlésienne*, a woman of Arles to the core according to some and especially to Monsieur Gauguin and Vincent. Her husband delighted in the compliments given to his wife. The Café de la Gare indeed profited from it.

In **L'Arlésienne: Madame Ginoux with Gloves and Umbrella,** Madame Ginoux is wearing her regional black dress with a white scarf or *gazo* at the neckline and the Arlesian traditional headdress known here as a *capello* with its wide trailing black ribbon. Vincent painted her fine chiseled features, her straight nose, luxuriant black hair and eyes gazing into the void as if reminiscing of past vagaries, perhaps, and with a faint smile on her lips. Vincent usually liked to paint his sitters looking directly at him but this time he chose to do otherwise. She is leaning on her left elbow as she rests her head on her left hand while her red umbrella and brown gloves lie on the table next to her. The yellow background, as yellow as the sunflowers, contrasts with her dark figure and intensifies the impression of strength of character. She was indeed a strong woman, a woman of Arles, a woman who knew what she wanted and got it, said my father. While Vincent was painting her portrait, Monsieur Gauguin was standing behind Vincent watching him paint.

He quite jokingly said to Madame Ginoux, "*Madame Ginoux, Madame Ginoux, votre portrait sera placé au Musée du Louvre, à Paris,*" your portrait will hang in the Louvre some day.

I could see the smile on her lips until Vincent told her not to move. Little did she know that those were indeed prophetic words. *Ah, oui, L'Arlésienne !* Later on, Vincent would do another portrait of Madame Ginoux substituting the umbrella and gloves with books to give the sitter an air of intellectual pride. And, still later at Saint-Rémy, he would do four portraits of her based on the charcoal drawing by Monsieur Gauguin with whom he was still corresponding, thus revealing the deep influence of his friend and master on him.

Monsieur Gauguin's painting of Madame Ginoux is far different from Vincent's version. Café at Arles (Madame Ginoux) shows Madame Ginoux sitting at a table in the foreground of the same Café de la Nuit that Vincent had painted. The billiard table is right behind her. There's a black and white cat near the front leg of the billiard table. On the café table sits a half empty glass of absinthe with a soda siphon nearby and two sugar cubes in a small plate. Madame's features are much bolder, more manly than those as seen in Vincent's painting. She has a large face. The left side of her face rests on her closed left hand with the elbow leaning on the table, much like Vincent's painting. Although she is wearing the traditional Arlesian black dress with the white scarf, the ribbons of her headdress are not shown. She is wearing an amusing smile and she is looking somewhat sideways, not directly at the artist. In the background, we can see my father, yes, my father, sitting at a table with three women of the night. He sometimes went there to have a drink or two, at times accompanied by my mother. They went there to meet people and chat about the latest events or the latest gossip in town. A lot of people went there. There wasn't much to do in Arles at night. There's a man slumped over another table while a Zouave is staring vacantly into space. The wall is painted fiery red contrasting with the somber colors of the patrons. A trail of smoke wafts across the room. I don't know if Monsieur Gauguin painted this scene from memory or not but I doubt that he did it with the people there as he shows them. He liked to reconstruct things in his own mind, he often said. I told Vincent that I preferred his portrait of Madame Ginoux to that of his friend. He answered that each artist has his own style and ways of seeing things.

"Monsieur Gauguin is a master artist and I don't pretend to be superior to him," he told me.

There was a lull in the activities in the yellow house as Vincent and Monsieur Gauguin engaged in discussions about the practice of art and art theory, especially about portraits. Sometimes the discussions were heated, *électriques,* and I refrained from going to their house simply because I didn't want to intrude in their discussions that, I thought, at times, turned into arguments. If I happened to go by the yellow house, I could hear them arguing.

My mother knew that I wanted to go there and seeing me moping around the house, she told me, "Why don't you go to see your friend Monsieur Vincent?"

"I don't want to go today," I replied. "Maybe tomorrow."

"What difference does one day do? Today, tomorrow, it's all the same."

"But, *maman,* it does make a difference to me."

"Do as you wish, *mon garçon.*"

She sensed that there was something going on in the yellow house with Vincent and Monsieur Gauguin.

"Il s'arrache le coeur avec la peinture," she told my father about Vincent. She thought, and she was right of course, that poor Vincent was tearing his heart out over his paintings.

My father said nothing. He kept quiet, but he knew. He knew that Vincent was struggling with his art and with his lack of success with it. He knew and he encouraged him to continue in spite of the difficulties. He knew that success comes hard and that hard work and discipline are required for any measure of success. He knew that Vincent wanted so desperately to form a community of artists in the south. He knew. He also knew the tension that existed between Vincent and his artist friend, Monsieur Gauguin. And, in his heart, he wished all the success in the world for Vincent, his dear friend and mine. Oh, how I wished that success would come to Vincent and that he would enjoy it and not have to struggle with money and the lack of acceptance by others, as well as the separations and rejections that had splintered his life so far, especially that. As I sit here today, June 1907, thinking back about Vincent's short life and his art, how sad, so very sad that success was so elusive for him in his lifetime and how he never managed to have his dreams come out the way he wanted them to. He sure was a dreamer, a spinner of elusive dreams. I really think he was too far ahead of his time. And, to think now the world is clamoring for his art. How ironic and sad.

15

Close Ties and Separations

As November was slipping away into December, the last few days of November saw Vincent painting a self-portrait. It's a good one, as far as I'm concerned, since it captures the real Vincent, the Vincent that I knew. It shows him in a serious mood, he was serious most of the time, and he had to be in a "yellow" mood that day since he painted himself wearing a bright yellow jacket with a green background to bring a nice contrast to the painting. His dark reddish hair turning to shades of deep blond is well combed. His features look chiseled what with his high-cheek bones, his strong nose and lightly bearded chin. What attracts your attention are the eyes, those deep blue piercing eyes under tufts of bright blond eyebrows. It's an intense look that he has, a very intense one. It seems to go right through you as viewer. It's the look of a man who fiercely looks at himself and the world and says, "I see what makes you tick, Vincent Van Gogh. I can see you with all your strengths and weaknesses. And, I can paint all of it, if I want to." He signed it and dedicated it on the lower right side, to a friend of his and Monsieur Gauguin, Charles Laval, " A l'ami Laval." I asked him who this Laval was and he told me that he was Paul Gauguin's traveling companion to Martinique the year before. Both of them had then settled in Pont-Aven in Brittany. Vincent had asked for self-portraits of Laval, Monsieur Gauguin and Émile Bernard as a deal to trade self-portraits. He was so impressed by Laval's rendition that he wrote to his brother Théo saying: "The portrait is very powerful, very distinguished and precisely one of the paintings that you talk about: that one has in one's possession before others have recognized the talent." Vincent recognized true talent when he saw it, I'm sure.

Vincent once showed me some other self-portraits and I loved the one that he did in 1886 in Paris. **Self-portrait, Paris 1886**. It's the same serious gaze but not with the blueness that's in this one. I like it because it shows a certain *noblesse* about the artist, a strength of character that lies beneath his vulnerability and tenderness. It reflects the image of the boy of thirteen back in Holland in that revealing photo that he showed me. Some people say that he was a poor student, a young man riddled with all kinds of weaknesses, and an adult with serious mental problems, but you need to scratch the surface to find the genuine creative artist that he was. I think these self-portraits reveal that. His behavior should not mar the perception of his talent. His skill as an artist far compensated for his lack of civility that some people claim he demonstrated. I know he was a very complex man and that he rubbed people the wrong way, but I take him on his talent and merit. Of course, I may be prejudiced. I suppose I was prejudiced from the start and I still am today because I realize how time has proven him right, as an artist. What remains of his life outside his vast artistic contribution is but chaff to the wheat, I say.

Now comes the time for me to tell you about my two portraits by Vincent. He was on a roll with portraits, I suppose, and he decided to do the entire Roulin household, including me. I was overjoyed and overcome with warm appreciation. My dear friend, my teacher of captured light and colors of the outdoors, master of people's portraits, incomparable draftsman and, above all, the painter of stars was going to do my portrait. My father was proud and my mother said, "Now you be on your best behavior. We don't want him to think that we're not civilized. You and Armand must accept this task with *fierté et honneur*," with pride and honor, she said.

I thought she was a bit exaggerating things. After all, Vincent was my friend and he already knew the family quite well. Besides, we were doing him a favor by sitting for him since very few people wanted to. I realized later that she was both proud of this venture and, at the same time, hesitant if not somewhat apprehensive of Monsieur Vincent. That's how she still referred to him, Monsieur, and she tried to correct me every time I said Vincent.

"La politesse n'est pas perdue sur les étrangiés," she would say, politeness is never lost on strangers.

My father would smile with that expressive smile of his and tell her that, after all, Vincent was no stranger to our house.

"Men don't understand these things," she would say, then walk away.

I loved my mother but she could be sometimes hard to fathom at times.

The first portrait Vincent did of me was with my school uniform, *mon costume écolier*, that I never liked but had to wear. It looked more like a smock and I had a cap that went with it. I actually liked the cap.

It looked a bit like my father's "Postes" cap. I wasn't sitting. I was standing next to a straight-back chair with my right arm on the top of it. I was gazing really at nothing, somewhat daydreaming, I suppose, and my mouth was wide open. I noticed that after I saw the painting. It's somewhat of a silly pose, come to think of it, because I look *fada*. I look stupid. My mother told me afterwards, "Why didn't you close your mouth?"

"I don't know '*man,*" I replied.

But, I really liked the cap with the gold braid. Just like a postman or an officer of the garrison. The colors are mostly blue since I'm wearing a blue outfit with a deep blue cap, but the contrast comes with the two colors of the wall behind me. Vincent made that up because those were not the true colors. The top is red and the bottom is orange. It makes a nice contrast, I must admit. As for my features, they're not exactly what I thought they ought to be, but I guess that's what Vincent saw and painted. My nose is peaked and my eyes look huge. I suppose that Vincent wanted to emphasize my large blue eyes.

"They look like big water drops in the sockets of your eyes," he would tell me. That's it for **The Schoolboy (Camille Roulin).**

The other portrait, I really like. I mean the second version with the blue cap. It's a different type of cap. Almost too big for my head, but I like it. The painting is simply called, **Camille Roulin,** but I call it, "The Boy with the Blue Cap." It's a big flat *crêpe* type of a cap laying there on my small head. It really draws your attention. I think it becomes the focus of the work, not that the face isn't central. It's of a bright blue color with short white lines highlighting the composition of the blue colors. What with the green jacket and the red button at the top (Vincent's signature), there's a perfect contrast made with the sunflower yellow of the background. If you look closely at the very top of the portrait, right above my cap, he painted some kind of halo effect and that proves to me that Vincent really and truly loved me. He did that with people he held in esteem like Monsieur Boch and those he loved. I feel blessed by an artist who was my hero. As for my features, my nose looks better, looks more natural (I have a big nose), my chin is pointed (makes me look delicate as a young boy) and my lips, firm and red. But, it's my eyes that I like. I'm gazing straight ahead but a bit downwards as if I'm in a trance or something, but it's an intelligent gaze, my precocious gaze, I call it. The blue eyes with the intense gaze of a boy of talent. The budding writer. Yes. Both my mother and my father really liked this portrait and my mother thanked Vincent over and over again when she saw it.

"*Ah, mon petit garçon bleu,*" she cried, "*mon petit Camille chéri.*"

"Oh, come on '*man,*" I said, "I'm not all that small nor am I blue, just my eyes and my cap."

"Some day, this will hang in some museum for all to see," my father said, "then you'll become renown, perhaps before you become a famous writer."

We all laughed together. Even today when I recall the experience of posing for Vincent and the result of "The Boy with the Blue Cap", it gives me goose bumps. I'm sure Vincent was proud of this work as he was for so many others. They were all *ses petits enfants*, his little children. He had fathered them all. If he didn't have children of his own, he could very well claim his works as his children. *Il les avait tous enfantés*, he had given birth to all of them.

Next came Armand, Armand Joseph Désiré Roulin. That's his full name. He was sixteen and I thought somewhat too blasé about portraits and having to sit for Vincent, but he did it, twice. My mother wanted him to be on his best behavior and not move as Vincent had told him. She also wanted to make sure that he wore his finest. For the first one, he wore his black jacket and his black felt hat with a broad brim. He had on a white shirt with a bow at his neck. His cheeks are ruddy and his lips seem to be pouting. I don't know why. His eyes are looking downward and they appear to be sad as if he's about to cry or something. Perhaps depressed? I don't think he had his heart into it that day. I know my brother, when he didn't like something, he showed it. He has a thin blond mustache but dark hair that shows below his hat. Vincent painted the background a somber green perhaps to reveal the melancholy of the sitter. I don't know. My brother never mentioned this painting afterwards. Never did.

However, the second portrait is very different, in tone, mood and colors. It's called, **Portrait of Armand Roulin**. In this one, Armand is wearing a citron-yellow jacket, it's not sunflower-yellow but it's yellow, with a black vest and a white shirt. He has on his black hat, slightly tilted, that sits just right on his head. It makes him look debonair. The entire portrait looks debonair, I think. This time, the soft green background contrasts well with the yellow jacket. It helps to lighten the tone of the entire portrait. Armand is not smiling but his red lips are firm, full and natural-looking. They even look sensuous. Vincent painted that well. Armand still has his pencil-thin blond mustache but this time the portrait, being full-face and his gazing straight ahead, makes him look rather handsome. Of course, the bold look with his strong chin and jawbone lend him an air of distinction, I think. He doesn't have my eyes. He has brown eyes, soft brown eyes that are gazing just a little to the left but at the same time gazing with a frank and sincere look. When I look at that gaze, I see a certain tenderness but I would never tell him that. He's a fully grown man now, a peace officer in Tunisia and has put on a lot of weight.

There's yet another portrait of Armand. It's the one with what Monsieur Gauguin would call primitive colors. I suppose Vincent was still very much under the influence of his friend and wanted to show him respect for his color rendition and style. It's, **Young Man with a Cap**. Some people will not recognize Armand in this one but it was he. Vincent has him with a cap similar to mine but without braid. It's a dark blue cap with a light blue visor. His black hair juts out from underneath his cap, *dépeignés*, my mother would say. Vincent painted it in mid-December. This time, Armand has on a bright green jacket, white shirt and red neck scarf. His facial expression is serious and intent and his dark gaze shows that. Both his nose and his lips are full and, I think, a bit exaggerated. He only has a shadow of a mustache in this one. His complexion is bronzed and he looks like a gypsy to me. The background is true Vincent, bright sunflower yellow. Armand liked this portrait. I didn't much care for it.

Next came the first portrait of my mother. Oh, she was hesitant about sitting for Vincent. She was somewhat shy and at the same time anxious to get it over with. She did it to please my father and, I think, to please Vincent because he kept saying how hard it was to find anyone to sit for him. She always had a certain sympathetic feeling for Vincent although reserved and hidden. She was, after all, a mother and a mother acts according to her instincts. I believe that she always felt that Vincent had a rough life and constantly struggled with himself and with the world. He was born under an unlucky star.

"*Son étoile n'a pas toujours été brillante,*" she said about Vincent, his star was not always shining.

I guess she too believed in stars.

I think the emphasis on the part of Vincent for the first portrait of my mother was her youth. After all, she was ten years younger than my father. At thirty-seven years of age, she was still in her prime, my mother. She doesn't appear to be quite the same person she is the *Berceuse* pose. That's my opinion. In this one, she's wearing a green dress, *un peu décolletée*, a bit low-cut, and she wears her blond hair pulled back. She has a faint or a forced smile and her features are youthful looking. Her eyes are gazing a little bit askance and not directly at the artist. She is wearing the earrings she liked, the ones with the deep purple stones. My father had given her those for her birthday. Vincent painted her with fair complexion and full bosom. She was a woman *bien plantée*, well developed, as my father would say of people who were strong and stocky. In the background, which is painted a mustard-yellow, there's a window through which one can see pots with bulbs sitting there like giant dollops of chantilly. Vincent put that there probably in a symbolic way because my mother was always tending to her potted plants and herbs. She was a woman who tended life be it human or plant life. Also, she symbolized, for Vincent, the maternal quality that he so revered. Behind the pots is a drawn path in reference to la Place Lamartine. I think this symbol, although Vincent did not like to use symbols as Monsieur Gauguin did, may convey the notion of vigor, emergence and possibly birth-giving as a path to mothering. A path to life. That's what I think. Vincent liked my mother, he liked my father a lot, and he liked us, the children. We had become his family of Arles, his Japanese land of light and color. Later on, he would reveal the life-giving maternal side of my mother by painting her with the cradle cord.

Of course, one must not forget the baby. Marcelle was going on five months when Vincent painted her big, round and wide-awake face. My mother had dressed her up in the little white dress and hat that would have been her baptismal outfit had she been baptized. In **The Baby Marcelle Roulin,** you can see her fat jowls, her pudgy forearms and hands and her heart-shaped mouth. Her complexion is that of a young child, light and creamy. But, it's her eyes that hold your attention, big, round, almost bulging eyes that are staring straight out. She was not smiling when Vincent did this portrait. He's showing the serious side of young Marcelle. This is not Marcelle who later would always have a gentle smile on her face. Vincent painted the background a light green and it contrasts well with the creamy complexion and the white of the outfit.

Monsieur Gauguin also captured my mother's features in a portrait painted by him a short while after Vincent painted his. It is called simply, <u>Madame Roulin</u>. At first glance, I thought that it wasn't my mother that he had painted. She looks so stiff with her stylized features since they do not reveal the warmth and gentleness that she usually displayed. She is staring straight out as if in a trance. Her reddish-blond hair is pulled back tight revealing her wide bold forehead. She isn't smiling, just placid-like. She has her hands and arms dropping from the armrests of her chair into her lap. She's wearing a dark green top, plain with no ornament. We can see a door with windows on the left. The lower part of the wall is white while the top part shows a bright yellow path with green grass and a patch of reddish something next to the tree trunk. If there is symbolism here, I don't get it. A yellow path leading to where? Is it part of a garden? Is this all part of the stylized bold color effect? It's a Gauguin painting and I have reservations about it. Of course, I'm prejudiced, as I've said before.

Monsieur Gauguin is a very interesting man. He's an artist of fine quality, if you like his work. He has very strong ideas about art and he loves abstraction. He's not an idealist and certainly not a romantic, as he stated before. He classified himself in the artistic realm of primitivism. He loved bold, fierce and energetic colors and lines. He had the wildness of the flora and the fauna in his brush. I firmly believe that Monsieur Gauguin sought the primitive instincts in his paintings in order to be faithful to his own imaginings and thought processes. Stepping back as I do today, it becomes clearer to me that what Monsieur Gauguin was trying to convince Vincent of was his own forcefully held principles of order and deliberation of the mind captured on canvas with the deliberate, powerful and symbolic rawness of colors.

I am told that he once wrote to Monsieur Schuffenecker telling him: "Clearly the road to symbolism is filled with perils...at bottom it is something which is in my nature, and a person must always follow his temperament. I am well aware that I be understood *less and less*. But what does it matter if I move away from the others...You know that when you come right down to it, I'm always right about art."

Well, that's Monsieur Gauguin for you, always right, always cock sure about himself. After all, he wrote with chalk on one of the inner walls of the yellow house, "*Je suis sain d'Esprit, Je suis l'Esprit Saint.*" I am sound of mind, I am the Holy Ghost. A play on words, *un calembour*, quite possibly to ridicule Vincent's episodic spells. All in jest. Right? He thought he was the Holy Spirit of Light and inspiration while living a life of a non-believer. He laughed at Vincent's faith in Christ and the Bible. He rejected the monastic outlook that Vincent proposed for the yellow house as the *atelier du Midi*. What Monsieur Gauguin did not want was to become a *bonze* with Buddhist convictions that Vincent so earnestly espoused. Monsieur Gauguin was considered by many to be too self-indulgent and hedonistic to lead a monastic life. What he wanted was a sane, efficient and orderly atmosphere in which to paint. He didn't always find it with Vincent, I must admit. Vincent's monastic outlook and Monsieur Gauguin's vision of the spirit were far apart. One sought the spiritual discipline of austerity while the other pursued the road to exuberance and rationality. Ironically, it was Vincent who proclaimed natural realism. Monsieur Gauguin favored primitive symbolism. The two never could reconcile their differences either in art or personality. They died with their wounds unhealed. As for my mother's portrait by Monsieur Gauguin, I find that it captures the primitive effect well, but I never quite understood primitivism and, therefore, I tend not to feel too close to her portrait.

The one portrait that I do like of Monsieur Gauguin is his self-portrait, <u>Self-Portrait: "Les Misérables."</u> He signed it that way, "Les Misérables" A l'ami Vincent. This is the true Monsieur Gauguin, in my estimation. His head is slightly tilted to the left while his angular-shaped face with a hooked nose reveals the features of a Breton man. His bulbous blue eyes appear under his half-closed eyelids like the gaze of cat ready to pounce on its prey. He does have the air of a *fauve*, I think. He wrote to Monsieur Schuffenecker that he looked like a bandit and that he classified himself as a distrusted Impressionist. He wrote, "I've done a portrait of myself for Vincent...It is, I believe, one of my best pieces of work...A brigand's head, at first glance, a Jean Valjean [*Les Misérables*] who also personifies a discredited Impressionist painter."

With his short-cropped hair, his thick neck and his sturdy shoulders he looks more like a boxer than a brigand. As a matter of fact, I am told that he loved boxing and he even tried this sport from time to time as well as fencing. The long, thick, brown mustache over his sensuous lips with the bearded chin add to this look. The shawl-like green jacket with the slate-blue shirt are complemented by the greenish glow on the right side of his face. The background has a burnt orange effect while large white flowers and smaller blue ones with red buds and green leaves dot the surface. I'm sure that these posies have a symbol behind them but I fail to grasp the meaning. Perhaps the joy of youthful enterprise or even new beginnings such as springtime. In the upper right hand corner, he painted the profile of his and Vincent's friend, the bearded Émile Bernard. Both he and Bernard were asked to exchange self-portraits with Vincent. As for the inscription, *"Les Misérables,"* it may refer to the state of the poor and out-of-favor young painters in which he and others of the circle of friends found themselves. This self-portrait of Monsieur Gauguin makes a bold statement. Vincent really liked this work and I do also. It reveals the high artistic talent that Monsieur Gauguin possessed.

As for the portrait of Vincent painting sunflowers that Monsieur Gauguin painted so well, it's a superb work. It was Vincent's favorite subject matter, the sunflowers, of course, and Monsieur Gauguin caught the right tone, the right moment in time and the right concentration on the part of Vincent painting sunflowers that makes this work genuine. Monsieur Gauguin related how he hit upon the idea of painting Vincent's portrait while he was painting the still life subject he was so fond of-----sunflowers.

"I did it for Vincent and for me," he said. "I needed to do this portrait to remind me of Vincent, not only painting sunflowers as a naturalistic expression, but also as a symbolic one."

When the picture was finished, Vincent told the artist, "It's me all right, but me gone mad!"

I think that Vincent was beginning, at that point in his life, to feel the sting of depression stemming from his deep fear of losing someone he cared for again. He sensed that Monsieur Gauguin was going to leave Arles soon. The two of them had broached the subject before but now the matter appeared to be closed. The friend was leaving him and the dream of a southern community of artists was leaving with him. Things were too electric lately for matters to be resolved easily. Matters of ideas and convictions on art, of personal feelings and of diametrically opposite temperaments. In any case, Monsieur Gauguin's <u>Van Gogh Painting Sunflowers</u> has the quality of stylized Impressionism and I don't know how to say this any better. The theme of someone painting at his easel had been done several times by some Impressionists. <u>Monet at his easel in his garden at Argenteuil</u> by Renoir, for instance. Vincent the artist with his easel and the sunflowers in a Majolica jar are realistic while the rest of the painting is more stylized. The four sunflowers are huge and range in tones of yellow, brown and reddish-orange just the way Vincent liked to paint them. You can see his delicate right hand with brush while he's looking intently at the sunflowers. He's wearing a brown jacket and not his usual straw hat. His red beard shows well while his light brown hair recedes from his high forehead. We can't see his eyes and they seem to be squinting. His face is serious as he usually is while painting. There is that bright yellow path behind him that appear again like the one in my mother's portrait. The path, the green grass and the dark tree trunk form the background. Symbolic of what? The slate blue floor or ground makes a nice transition from the colors of the sitter painting the sunflowers and the background colors. Vincent never painted a portrait of his friend Monsieur Gauguin while they were living together. I wonder why? Perhaps his friend did not want him to or maybe he did not feel as if he could do justice to his friend whom he considered his master artist. I like this portrait of Vincent because it shows him doing what he most liked to do, painting. Not only painting sunflowers but painting in general. He was obsessed by it. It became his mistress who had cast her spell on him and would never let go. Through his art, painting as well as drawing, he could reach the stars and they called to him from their infinity. Through the attraction of flowers and their multitude of colors he was able to reach the rapture of natural beauty. Through the bright light of Provence, he was able to capture his own bright light.

December. *Le temps des fêtes, Noël et le Jour de l'An.* Yes, Christmas and New Year. Time for *les santons*, those lovely little clay saints that are handmade here in Aubagne and other places in the Midi. My mother had a small collection of them. They were stamped, *Thérèse Neveu.* I usually helped her set them up in the living room under the big lamp where the light shined on them at night. My father didn't care for them but he said, at least, they were the product of *la Provence* and displayed the artistry of our own craftsmen. And then, I could look forward to my uncle Marius's gift once more. He never faltered, never forgot me. Perhaps, he would get me some toy but I much preferred books and maybe an atlas. I was becoming more and more interested in world travel with the possibility that some day I might go to Africa.

It was about this time that my father announced that he had taken a post in Marseille, a promotion for him. He was going to be in the *service des itinérants,* and I don't know exactly what that entailed. He announced it during a meal while Vincent was there. We were eating hot *pistou* soup, Vincent's favorite. All of a sudden, Vincent dropped his spoon on the floor. He tried to reach for it and he spilt some soup on the tablecloth. He was all apologetic while my mother was offering him another spoon and mopping up the spill. He seemed to be frozen in his speech. His eyes had become watery. My father asked him what was wrong and he answered that, once again, he had to face a departure. A departure that would hit him hard, he admitted. Losing a friend is painful, he said. My father reassured him that he wasn't losing a friend and that he would keep the friendship intact. He would even return home, once in a while. He had to, he said, to be with his family.

"But what if the position becomes permanent, then won't you and your family have to move to Marseille?" he asked.

My father simply muttered, "Yes."

My mother did not say anything since she knew about the conditions of my father's work. I just sat there dumbfounded at seeing Vincent that way and anticipating leaving him in the near future.

"Do we have to go?" I asked my father.

My mother answered in her usual soft-spoken manner that a family has to follow the breadwinner, *le gagne-pain*. Would it be soon? I asked him. He replied that it would be sometimes the following month. I would have to go to a new school just when I was starting to like the teacher and, besides, I had just gotten a 17 on my composition on Flaubert's tale of Félicité and her parrot, Loulou. I had written about the bonds between them that made her see Loulou as more than a pet parrot. *Une note de 17*! "Think about it," I said to my astounded parents. I had never gotten that kind of a mark before.

"Next time try for a 19," my mother said.

"*Maman*, when you get a 14 or a 15, that's a very good grade with the average being 13. A 17 is super good. Over the top."

"Well, try harder," she said.

My father was very proud of me and I could see that he had lost his low impression of my intellectual talents. Vincent congratulated me and so did Monsieur Gauguin. I think that Monsieur Gauguin was reappraising his consideration of me and my talent for writing. I later learned that he was not at all strong in writing. It was a good thing that he had turned to painting.

The latest and most eye-catching news in the local **FORUM RÉPUBLICAIN** under *Chronique locale* was to be found in a small column on the next to last page. It talked about a gypsy woman who had hanged herself on the outskirts of Arles, and no one had claimed her body. She left no name or address behind except for a very small sketch of herself, a drawing signed Vincent. People began to wonder what relationship she had with the local artist. The article read: **It was reported Friday night that a woman, probably a gypsy, was found dead, hung with a noose around her neck with a rope that was tied to a limb of a tree in a vacant field. The woman, in her thirties, had black hair and held in the clasp of her hand a medal of St. Sara tied to her wrist with a red thread. Police found a small drawing of the woman signed by a Vincent in her pocket. They are investigating this death and have, so far, ruled out foul play. The body was moved to the potter's field for burial.** My God! Although the article was practically hidden inside the paper, people read it and soon began to suspect something suspicious about the *étrangié*. What had he done now and what kind of relationship did he have with a gypsy, of all things. Vincent did not enjoy a very good reputation with the locals to start with, and now, with this piece of news, his reputation suffered even more. Vincent had not read about it and knew nothing about Sara's death until Madame Ginoux rushed over to tell him about the news story that she had read that Sunday. Of course, she had many questions that she would have liked to ask Vincent but, out of respect for the artist's talents and the good relationship she and her husband enjoyed with Vincent, she refrained from doing so. I knew it had to be Sara. Vincent knew for sure. Who else could it be?

My father went over to talk to Vincent and he found him crushed by the news. He remembered her coming to see him at the yellow house and begging him to help her and that he had so wanted to do so, but could not give her any money that she had asked for, and had then left in tears. That he remembered. However, he never thought, although desperate, that she would take her life. Unless, someone had lynched her. No, that couldn't be, he said. But, one never knows about the vengeful ways of the clans, he stated. Taking her own life? No. She was not that type of a person. She had a very strong will to live. Unless, she had become so desperate for money and so depressed about the loss of her daughter that she didn't want to live anymore. Desperation does strange things to people. Vincent did admit to my father that he had a brief love encounter with her outside of Saintes-Maries-de-la-Mer one day, but that had long been erased from his memory. However, her visit to Arles had brought it back to him, he said. Vincent felt the deep pangs of remorse and stayed by himself in his room for several days without eating or talking to anyone. Monsieur Gauguin thought that he was being exceptionally moody. After all, you don't get that upset over a woman, he told my father. My father did not know what to do about this tragic matter. I thought about Sara a long time, Sara and her long lost daughter, Mireille. What a tragedy, I told myself. What a loss. What a severe blow to Vincent who must accept another separation. What is worse, the very worse blow, is that Vincent received a letter from Sara a few days after her death telling him that she was pregnant with child and that the child was his. That she could not give birth to a *gadjé*, the child of a person with no money, not much of a reputation and no bright promise for any kind of a future. A child *gadjé* whose father was under a gypsy curse and whose mother was an eternal wanderer. Poor child would be forever cursed with having no real family. In the letter, she was pleading with him to please meet with her to resolve her problem. Apparently, she had waited quite some time for an answer, an answer she never got. The letter got lost in the mail and Vincent only received it a month after it was mailed. The one child he never had, the one family he never could have, now utterly lost. He told me later that this had hurt him more than losing his friend Sien, the woman in the Hague he had loved and wanted to marry. He had had so much tearing apart in his life, his family, Kee, Sien, Mauve, Boch, the Netherlands, Le Borinage, and even his Christian ministry, they were all episodes of separation and loss. How much more could he take, I wondered. How much more. There has to be a breaking point, I told myself.

Vincent told me after his isolation that he had contemplated his plight and remembered the curse that Mirnanoun had placed on him. Was it coming to fruition, he wondered. Although he didn't believe in curses or hexes, he still wondered about their power to exert a certain influence on people's lives. He was having recurrent headaches, buzzing in his ears, dizzy spells and suffered from a malaise in general. Monsieur Gauguin tried to help him but nothing seemed to work. Except the therapy of his art, of course. But, how was it possible to impinge on someone's fate? Could someone's destiny be linked to some magical curse? How? Couldn't someone's free will and determination reverse such a blight on his life? Vincent knew that fatality, *la fatalité des choses,* was intimately and mysteriously linked to the mind set of the gypsies, but how could that affect non-gypsies like him? If one didn't believe in it, how could that have any influence on that person? How could it? All of these questions and more lingered on Vincent's mind. That's what he tried to explain to himself, my father and to me. If Vincent didn't have the answers, I certainly had less than none. I was totally confused with all of this gypsy sorcery. I was going to try to read up on it but not then, I told myself. There were more important things to think about like cheering up Vincent.

16

Volcanoes and Empty Chairs

*M*onsieur Gauguin had branded Vincent a volcano, although he realized that he himself was seething and the tension between the two artist friends had become very electric and, at times, fiery. Sparks flew, words flowed like hot lava. They more and more disagreed about things such as the care of finances, art theories and untidiness on the part of Vincent, although he tried so hard to be clean and tidy. *(Schoon, schoon,* cleanliness and beauty, his mother had drummed into him when he was young). When things fester and seethe inside for too long, then they explode. I must say that Vincent had become more sensitive to things that seemed to rub him the wrong way like some of the remarks made by Monsieur Gauguin about his style of painting and his choice of colors. He tried to conform to Monsieur Gauguin's rules and ideas on painting but he just could not do it, he told me. He could not accept, any longer, not being himself as an artist. Besides, Monsieur got on his nerves and Vincent got on Monsieur's nerves. I could tell. So, I stayed away from the yellow house more and more. I read my new book, "Les Misérables" by Victor Hugo. My, that was a huge one! Madame Ginoux had lent it to me. Then I went to the local library to look at the collection of small scale boats. Boats brought you somewhere besides going fishing.

My father asked me to do some errands for him and that's when I met Jeanne Calment with her friend Loulou Froidebout. Imagine that, a name just like that of Félicité's parrot, I told her.

"Who's Félicité and what parrot?" she replied.

"If you haven't read the book then you would not know what I'm talking about," I said.

"What book?"

" *Les Trois contes* and one of the three tales is, *Un coeur simple,*" I told her.

"You and your books," she said.

"Ah, forget it," I replied.

"Yes, you and your books and that artist friend," replied Jeanne.

"What do you mean?" I asked.

"Well, you're always in a daze about books and that *fou-rou* is not any better with his *bagatelle* on his back always looking for something to paint, I suppose," Jeanne said with disdain in her voice.

"Those aren't nothings he's got on his back, those are the tools of his trade," I told her.

"Anyways, he's got another friend now and he doesn't need you," she taunted.

"What do you know about painting? Nothing. A big fat nothing," I answered her.

"You don't know anything either, Camille Roulin. Just because you hang around him doesn't mean you know anything about art," she replied in her caustic way.

"I learned a lot from Monsieur Vincent and I've got it all written down in my notebook."

"What notebook?" she asked.

"The one that's ever faithful to me and I carry it with me all the time in case I need to write something down."

"Show it to me," she said.

"No, because you'd laugh at it and I don't want you to see it anyway."

She put her two hands on her hips and said in a loud voice for people to hear,

"Camille Roulin, *tu es un écrivain manqué. Tu n'arriveras à rien dans ta vie*," you're nothing but a failed writer, you'll never amount to anything.

Some people were turning around to look at us. I told Jeanne Calment that she knew nothing about writing, just like she knew nothing about art.

"Besides," I told her, "I'll have you know that I got a 17 on my last composition. Fry that on you hot stove of a temper," I said.

"That's because the teacher takes you as her pet. You don't ever deserve a 17. Take that you big *tête de chou*," cabbage head, she shouted.

Now people were really looking at us. I started getting red in the face. Loulou dragged her friend away from the street into the nearest shop.

I told a little boy who was then staring at me, "What are you looking at? Haven't you ever seen a boy who got a 17?" I said with a crack in my voice.

I went home.

When I arrived home, my father asked me for the purchases I was supposed to have made for him. My hands were empty. I had forgotten to do his errands, so upset I was by Jeanne Calment's remarks about me and my 17.

"I'm sorry, papa," I said and dashed out to get what he wanted.

I didn't see the look in his eyes but I'm sure it was a surprised one. That afternoon, I sat down and wrote a long letter to Vincent.

Dear Vincent,   *December 6, 1888*

It seems it's getting harder and harder to be with you and talk to you. I miss you and our walks together. I miss learning from you all the things that please me and those things that give me inspiration that I write down *in my notebook. I don't know how to tell you all the things that I want to tell you but I'm going to try. First of all, I'm sorry that you lost your good friend, Sara. She was a nice woman and I liked her a lot. I'm sorry that I can't be with you in time of your need to talk and share your feelings. I know that I'm probably too young for you to fully express your needs, but I would certainly try, if given the chance. You see, I may be young but as you've said, I'm "precocious." I understand better than most children my age and more than grown-ups think I do. You have to give young people a chance. Second, I don't quite under-stand the hard times you and Monsieur Gauguin are having but I'm sure things will get resolved. I do know that Monsieur Théo has worked very hard to get you two together and it's worth your while to try harder and patch things up with Monsieur Gauguin. I'm sorry but I didn't want to intrude in your relationship but I care about you and I don't want you to think I'm a busybody. I'm not. Third, I want to thank you for supporting me in my school work by giving me ideas on Félicité and Loulou. That's why I did so well on my composition, I'm sure. Fourth, If ever I get to be a writer and get published someday, I want you to know that I will dedicate my very first book to you. Fifth, I think I would like to travel and see the world, someday, when I'm grown up and I would like you to accompany me. It's on me, I will pay for it. I know that artists don't make much money. However, I do hope that someday you'll be able to sell some of your paintings to make money so that you can live a better life than now. All this skimping and saving just to buy some bread and coffee is not the way to live. I also hope that*

Monsieur Théo will come to stay with you. You so love your brother and he's so close to you. I'm not close to Armand. You know that. He's a good brother but I'm not close to him or rather he's not close to me. I hope that when baby Marcelle grows up, we'll be close as brother and sister. You know, as close as you and your sister Wilhelmina are. Last, I want you to know that my mother likes you very much even though she doesn't tell you too often. I don't think she's ever told you about her feelings for you. She keeps them hidden. She's a bit shy, my mother, not like my father. I know she calls you " mon enfant perdu" but she doesn't really think you're lost. I think she means that you're a bit un-certain about things and especially with people here in Arles. I realize that people here don't treat you right. They don't respect you for what you are. They don't know you and they don't bother to find out. Some of the kids throw stuff at you when you're passing by, I know. They're a bunch of ignorant and foolish boys and "têtes de chou." Someday they'll regret it, so don't take it bad. As or me, I would never do that. I would throw flowers at you, not vegetable stocks. Sunflowers, that's it, sunflowers, just to make you smile. At last, I'm finishing, thank you for making me look at the stars at nighttime. I now can see them as you do. They're the sparkle of the Creator, as you've said. Infinity! And most of all, thank you for being my friend.

Sincerely
Your good friend, CAMILLE

P.S. I forgot. I bought you a gift for "les étrennes."

I put the letter in his mailbox since I didn't have a stamp. I didn't get a letter back but he gave me a small drawing of my notebook that I cherish to this very day. At the bottom where he signed it, he wrote *"Le carnet de l'écrivain,"* my notebook, and he calls me a writer. He then attached a short note to the drawing, " *Merci de tes bons mots. Ton ami toujours,* " thank you for your kind words. Your friend always. I know he kept my letter because his brother Théo sent it to me after Vincent's death. I'm looking at it this very moment. It's something that's dear to me since it reminds me of the time I was growing up with Vincent.

There wasn't much happening in December at the yellow house, except that Vincent had decided to paint two empty chairs. He said later that he expected Monsieur Gauguin to leave one of these days and he wanted to paint some symbolic work that his friend Gauguin had so often advocated and even pushed him to do. But, it was going to be his way, he said. Monsieur Gauguin was putting final touches on his portrait of Vincent painting sunflowers. And, he must have been busy with cooking or with his letters to friends up north or even to Monsieur Théo. I know he wrote to him, from time to time. Monsieur Gauguin did not like the cold weather and especially the mistral, he told Monsieur Théo. No one liked the mistral, that's for sure.

As for the two chairs, one is called, **Paul Gauguin's Armchair**, and the other, **Vincent's Chair with his Pipe**. I wasn't there when he painted the chairs. When I saw the paintings, I recognized the chairs and knew the symbols behind what he painted. It wasn't hard, two empty chairs, two friends apart. The colors also added to the symbols, and Vincent explained how to me.

"You see, symbols must not be too hard to decipher," he said, "or else they become what some people call, esoteric, which means only understood by a very few."

E-s-o-t-e-r-i-c, a new word. "I'll put it in my notebook," I muttered.

Vincent's chair is a straight-back chair, yellowish natural wood with a woven rush seat. It's a rustic chair and has Vincent's pipe and tobacco pouch on the seat. The chair has a yellow greenish look illuminated by daylight. It stands on a red tile floor that contrasts with the flat green door on the right. The wall is a combination of blue and light green with yellow highlights. The brush stroke effect makes it look like stucco. The wooden box in the back has what looks like some giant bulbs. That's where he signed his name, probably because he wanted the symbolic effect of a possibility of springtime and growth. The overall effect is that of isolation and emptiness. He will no longer sit with his friend for a *tête à tête*. His friend's chair will also be empty.

Monsieur Gauguin's chair is a different kind of chair. It has armrests with curved legs, a more sophisticated chair, symbolic of what Vincent thought of his friend. The rush seat is predominantly green with yellow stripes. The color of the wood is a reddish-brown with some green highlights on the legs. It stands on a flowery floor perhaps painted to look like a carpet. The wall is a bright green with swirls of a darker color. It matches well the green tone of the painting. To the left, a gaslight, emitting a halo of bright light, juts from the wall. This light complements the lit candle on the chair seat, symbol of the presence of Monsieur Gauguin when he was there. The light of thoughts and new ideas. Two books, modern novels, as Vincent put it, one partially on top of the other, sit on the chair seat next to the candle. The total effect of this chair with an empty presence is one of eloquent desolation. Vincent had the talent of painting simple objects like chairs and shoes and make them look elegant in their forms and color. Elegant like a simple flower or a moth, or even a clump of dirt in the light of the sun. Yes, there is beauty in a clump of dirt. He did say once that beauty lies not only in the flowers but in mud and the withering grass. These two paintings, I would say, are elegant by their forms and colors, desolate by their symbolism. Empty chairs. Empty hearth.

17

Joy and Madness

Most of the leaves had fallen.The sky was often gray and the weather, in general, was not too good. I was doing well in school and waiting patiently like the other students for Christmas vacation. I was excited about going to visit my uncle, Marius, and his wife, Marioto, in Marseille. It wasn't too far away. A short visit. I had to get used to it, for I would live there someday. I liked visiting them. My aunt was a good cook and my uncle, well, he was just a nice fellow. Everybody liked him. He owned a restaurant called, "La Cigalo Canto," the cicada sings in our Provençal language, and he and my aunt spoiled me. They had no children of their own. I was their favorite nephew, they told me, but I wasn't supposed to tell anyone. How lucky I was to have such good relatives. I wished I could have visited my grandparents in Lambesc, the Pellicots, but I never had the chance to and besides, my grandparents died when I was very young. Grandparents are very important in a child's life. I wonder if Vincent knew his grandparents. I thought of asking him but I never got around to it. I know that his father's mother lived with them when he was very young but he did not have a good relationship with her, at least his mother didn't.

Calendau's grandparents, on his mother's, side lived with them. He loved his grandparents. They were very kind to him and his sisters. He had four sisters. It was a big family, nine people living together. He said there was a lot of *féminin* in his house, a lot of females, but that's alright, he said, he got to be spoiled by them. His sister, Magalouno, was a rare beauty. Boys ran after her and she liked it but didn't say so. She reminded me of Madame Ginoux a bit. Very lively person.

This is what I wrote in my notebook on Monday evening,

Sunday, December 2-------I was so excited about going to the big show yesterday that I didn't have time to write my adventure in my notebook yesterday. I still can't believe it! Vincent, Monsieur Gauguin and I went to the GRAND MENAGERIE OF THE INDIES on Boulevard de Lices, on the other side of Arles. At first, my mother hesitated allowing me to go with the two artist friends but my father convinced her that it was a chance of a lifetime for a young boy to go to a Ménagerie since wild animal shows do not come to our part of the world too often, he told her.

"But what about the danger that exists there?" she asked. "All those wild animals on the loose."

"Augustine, (my father only called my mother that when he was very serious about things) Augustine, don't worry so much. After all, do you think they let the animals loose in the crowd? Heavens, no," he said. "They have special guards to take care of them and cages for the animals."

"How do you know, Joseph?"(she, too, called my father by his first name when she meant business).

"Because I know," he replied.

"Truly? Well exactly how do you know?"

"I've been to one of these ménageries before," he said with pride in his voice.

"When? Tell me."

"I went to one in Avignon when I was growing up in Lambesc."

"How old were you then?"

"I was about Camille's age."

"And your parents let you go?"

"They came with me."

"Oh," she said somewhat intrigued. "I guess it's alright for Camille to go then," and turning to me she said, "Be careful, be very careful and stay with Monsieur Vincent and his friend."

I answered, "Monsieur Gauguin, *maman*, Monsieur Gauguin."

"Yes, Monsieur Gauguin, the man from Brittany. But, be careful, I tell you and don't do things that will shame us in public. You know what I mean, don't you?"

I answered her very politely and reassuringly, "Yes, *maman,* I always do what you say, don't I? Am I a *polisson*?" Am I ill-mannered?

She looked at me with a smile that expressed both her contentment and admiration.

So, we went to the big show. There were lions, tigers, leopards, panthers, snakes, elephants and other animals all in cages. So many of them. They must have all come from Africa, I told Vincent, but he told me that some of them came from India. Monsieur Gauguin started to draw many of them on a large pad. Not the entire animal but the heads of lions and panthers. I was wishing that he would draw an elephant, my favorite wild animal. Tartarin's animal. Vincent watched me and I could see there was delight in his eyes. He told me that he was having more fun watching me than watching the animals. When it was time to leave, I told both of them I was hoping we could have stayed longer but I knew we had to leave sometime. It was then that Monsieur Gauguin gave me one of his drawings. The head of an elephant. I put it in my drawer with the other drawings. I loved drawings, especially from my artist friends. I suppose Monsieur Gauguin and I became friends then and there at the GRAND MENAGERIE. He was a primitive and I was a primitive at heart.

I did not see Vincent for over a week. He finally came out of his house like a turtle out of his shell, I would say, and he came to pay us a visit. He looked thin and gaunt. His face had the pallor of a ghost and his eyes did not have the glint to which I was accustomed. He spoke with few words and my father tried very hard to reassure him that he was his friend, the entire family was his friend. He thanked my father and told my mother that he had come to get some family warmth that she always provided him.

"How about staying for soup?" asked my father as he looked at my mother.

"*Nous avons toujours de la soupe dans le chaudron,*" the pot is always full of soup, she said.

He accepted with a faint smile as he handed me a booklet. It was Charles Dickens's "Christmas Stories" in translation. I took it from his hands and thanked him over and over again. Thumbing through it, I could see that there were several drawings illustrating parts of the stories. I was anxious to start reading the stories that very night. My father told Vincent that he shouldn't be spending his money on me. Vincent replied that it had cost only a few centimes and that he was only too glad to get me something that I would enjoy.

"Nothing puts glee in the heart like a Christmas story by Dickens," he said.

My father replied by asking him, "Is that the Englishman who writes about the poor and the social conditions in England?"

"Why , yes," answered Vincent.

"I've heard about him. Being a republican and mindful of the conditions of poor people everywhere, I'm interested in a writer like that."

"Well, he writes not only about poverty in England but he writes novels in which the characters come alive and who stir us to compassion. He writes about real conditions and real people. He is definitely a good social observer. I like Dickens."

"You were once in England, weren't you?"

"Oh, yes. I was first in Ramsgate teaching young boys the basics, then in Isleworth where I preached my first sermon in Mister Jones's church. I even went to Whitechapel, the remote section of London where the poorest of the poor live. Dickens mentions it in one of his books. I loved being in England and preaching the word of the Lord but I was living on nothing. I was poorly paid and I was getting thin, and just worn out, so I decided to go back home to Etten. I so wanted to become a preacher and a shepherd of the people, the poor people, but the theological school in Amsterdam refused me. I was told I was a poor candidate and had too weak an intelligence to succeed in theology. It's then that I went to Le Borinage," said Vincent with a hint of nostalgia and regret.

I was thinking all the while about how school sometimes hurts you rather than help you.

"Then you speak English," my father told him.

"Yes, I do," he replied.

"I wish I did because it widens your perspective on people everywhere."

"Why would you want to learn English?" asked my mother.

"Because, I'd like to learn it, that's all."

Turning toward Vincent, she said in a somewhat strained voice, "I don't why he wants to learn a language he will never use around here, and besides English is a hard language to learn with all its thuh sounds."

My father said nothing. I just glanced at my booklet. My mother left to go in the kitchen to prepare the soup.

Then my father turned to Vincent and said, "By the way, did you hear about the meeting of the Félibrige with Mistral last week? It was in **Le Forum Républicain**. I read about it. The *capolièr,* Joseph Roumanille, presided over it. He's very well known, he and Frédéric Mistral. They're trying to promote our culture here down south. *La culture occitane,* especially our dialect, *la langue d'oc.* I don't know much about all of that. That's like reviving the past and I don't much care about a past that was given to the whims of the bourgeoisie."

"Yes, I know about the movement and its work. I was hoping that Monsieur Mistral would invite me to one of the meetings but I never got an invitation. Perhaps, they think I'm too much of an *étrangié* to blend in. I would like so much to be part of this culture. It's so rich and the language so melodious. I guess I don't fit in, or else they don't want me on account of my reputation around here. You know, *un voyou et un fou-rou*. I know what people say behind my back. I only wish I could tell them, I'm not a lunatic, I'm not."

He looked at my mother while avoiding my eyes. She had just come out of the kitchen.

My mother told him in a calm and kindly voice, "You're not a lunatic and we don't consider you that way."

"Now, now, *mon ami*," my father said, "we certainly don't think you're a stranger and we've told you that before. You are assuredly not that crazy redheaded man that some people say, no, you're our friend and Arles should be proud of having you here."

After a lull in the conversation, my mother invited Vincent to please come and join us for the evening meal. He was rather quiet during the meal. He said hardly anything but he did glance, once in a while, at my baby sister, Marcelle, who was sitting in her high chair next to my mother eating her little bowl of soup. The baby smiled at him and we could see the beginnings of a smile on his face. Vincent left around eight and proceeded to tell me that he had not forgotten me and that he was a bit under the weather.

"That's alright," I said, "I'll see you next time."

Madame Ginoux and Madame Gaspardin were busy getting ready for the *réveillon*, our Christmas eve celebration. They were neighbors and worked together to prepare a big *réveillon* for many in their neighborhood. They enjoyed having a lot of people around them. We were invited but my mother told Madame Ginoux that she preferred having *le réveillon en famille,* at home. Christmas celebrations start early with us in Provence. They begin on December fourth, *la fête de la Sainte Barbe* and end at Candlemas on February second. The locals begin by sowing their *lou blad de Calendo*, the Christmas wheat. When it starts sprouting, they place it above their fireplace. People use it for decoration on their Christmas table. Families perform the *Cacho-Fio*, a traditional ceremony during which a Christmas log is blessed with some wine and taken around the house three times before putting it in the fireplace to burn. At the table, there are all kinds of food such as, *salade de chèvre chaud, saucissons, daube provençale, calissons d'Aix et berlingots.* I love *berlingots,* those hard candies from Carpentras. Of course, we mustn't forget the wines, Châteauneuf-du-pape, if you can afford it, the Gigondas, a splendid red wine and the wines of Cassis, the elegant flower-scented white wine, or the velvety reds. We only had these wines at Christmastime at our house. Oh, how I love Christmas and its celebrations, *à la provençale*, of course.

We also have the Provençal costumes. We can't forget that. Vincent always delighted in seeing our women dressed in their traditional festive costumes. Of course, he hadn't seen them all because he wasn't here for all our festivities. These costumes vary according to the taste or personality of each woman. The traditional Arlesian costume consists of a long colorful skirt with a black *ego*, an under-blouse with tight sleeves. On top, there is a white pleated shirt covered with a shawl, sometimes made of white lace. There are many headdresses, all worn on top of a bun. They can be *à la cravate*, it's knotted like rabbit's ears, *à ruban*, with a lace-trimmed velvet ribbon, or *en papillon*, butterfly wings of lace. My mother had one and my father called her *mon papillon*. She didn't wear it too often, only at Christmastime. I must say that our women are very elegant in their costumes and rival those of other provinces. Vincent would have liked to paint them but so many of them recoiled from having their pictures painted by him. I don't know why. They would be famous today.

I had in my possession for a long time a lock of hair that I got from a girl that I knew very well in Arles. She was a girl that I liked very much. Vincent used to tease me about her. Her name was Soulanjo. She was a pretty girl with jet black hair and dark silvery eyes like a midnight star. She was a shy girl who avoided the company of boys. She had just one friend, Esterello. Soulanjo came from the other side of town. I asked her once to pose for Vincent but she refused saying that her mother wouldn't like it. She had the prettiest face with a complexion of the pink color of fresh morning dawn. I thought she was pretty. Some of the boys used to laugh at me for liking her because she limped a bit with her left leg, but I liked her anyway. Who cares if she limped, I told them.

"She's a broken doll," they would say.

Not broken but a bit *fêlée*, I would answer them. But that was alright. Vincent told me that beauty is not always found in perfection and I believed him. Besides, he wasn't going to paint her leg, just her face. Too bad she didn't want to sit for Vincent. Today, I would have the memory of her lovely face in a beautiful portrait by my friend Vincent. Too bad. Oh, I threw the lock away when I found out she was going to marry Sandre Tenaille, a young mountain climber from Le Luberon.

I wrote in my notebook that today was December twenty-four. Christmas eve. The weather was cool with heavy dark clouds in the sky. Really ominous clouds. It looked like rain. That's what I wrote. What I did not write is that something was brewing inside Vincent. His volcano was soon to erupt. The only thing I could say about the events that took place after the night of the twenty-fourth came directly either from Monsieur Gauguin or from other people who witnessed them. So, I've reconstructed those events in my mind from my sketchy notes in order to make them more understandable to readers. It was all very difficult to do since I wasn't there and I had to rely on others to give me the facts.

It was a most anguishing time in my young life and I still feel the effects of it today. These events especially touched my father, I should say, hurt, since he knew Vincent well and held him in high esteem as a man and an artist. My mother, well, she kept everything in her heart. It frightened her even to think about those terrible things that happened that late December. After all, my family was close to Vincent and we didn't expect those things to happen to him. I must say that Vincent was at the end of his rope and the rope was fast splitting. I'd say that the volcano inside Vincent erupted and the seething cauldron that was Monsieur Gauguin boiled over. Two friends, two very different personalities, two people at odds with one another and two artists who could not be together without hurting each other. That's my view on the things that happened that fateful end of December, 1888. What a way to end the year, I thought then. What an awful way. Did Mirnanoun's curse have anything to do with it? I wondered then and I wonder now. Here's what I wrote in my journal notebook then.

December 24. While the entire town was having its *réveillon*, Vincent and Monsieur Gauguin, after a hard day's work, went to have a drink at the café where they usually went. Well, they had more than one drink, absinthe on top of it. All of a sudden, Vincent throws his empty glass at his friend for no reason. Monsieur Gauguin gets up, picks him up around the waist and takes him home where he puts him to bed. He then and there decides to leave Arles as soon as possible.

December 25. It's Christmas day. While Vincent is sleeping, Monsieur Gauguin goes out for a walk, crosses la Place Victor Hugo when he hears familiar footsteps behind him. He turns around and sees Vincent with a razor in his hand approaching him. Vincent lowers his head and turns around and goes back home. At least, that's what Monsieur Gauguin said about the encounter on la Place Victor Hugo. That is so strange of Vincent. He never acted that way before, at least not that I know of. That night, Monsieur Gauguin sleeps in a nearby hotel not wanting to sleep again in the yellow house. While he's gone, Vincent cuts off his left ear lobe. There's a great loss of blood. Apparently, he had cut an artery. He washes himself and puts a bandage on his wound. He then puts on his Basque beret and goes to the rue Bout-d'Arles where he finds Rachel to give her his well-cleaned ear lobe in an envelope.

"Here's a souvenir for you," he tells her and leaves.

Once at home, he closes the shutters, puts a light on the window sill and goes to bed and sleeps. In the meantime, Rachel opens the envelope and at the sight of the piece of flesh, faints. Her *patronne*, Madame Virginie, calls the police. She shows them the lobe.

December 26. The morning following the event, the police call on Vincent. They see that everything in the house is covered with blood. There are wet towels with patches of blood on the floor here and there. They find Vincent in bed all curled up in a ball seemingly inanimate. It's around 7:30. Monsieur Gauguin comes back to find the police there. They start asking him questions. Outside, there's a noisy crowd just when the *Commissaire Central,* Monsieur Joseph d'Ordano, arrives. They tell Monsieur Gauguin that they found Vincent dead in his bed.

"Let's go upstairs," he tells them.

Monsieur Gauguin touches ever so lightly Vincent and he finds that his body is warm and he's not dead. He tells the police to talk to Vincent for fear that if he himself talked to him it might be fatal. The *commissaire* calls for a doctor. Vincent speaks to Monsieur Gauguin and tells him not to alert his brother since he doesn't want to worry him for nothing. He then asks for his pipe and tobacco. He's then taken to the hospital in Arles. That's how the story unfurled, we were told.

At first, we didn't know too much about the incident except my mother worried when she heard the tumult in front of the yellow house. I wanted to rush out and go see what was happening but she told me not to go while people were milling around and yelling. So, she told my father to go and investigate what was happening. As my father was stepping out of the house, Madame Ginoux came running. She told my mother what had happened, at least what she knew about it and what people were saying. As soon as I heard about the accident, I thought it was an accident, I became really worried about Vincent. I wanted to get all the news about his condition, Was he hurt badly? Was he alright? What happened? Where was Monsieur Gauguin? Why was the police involved? Where were they taking Vincent? and all those things kept running in my head. Madame Ginoux said that, as far as she knew, Vincent was alright and a doctor was taking care of him. No mention of the ear lobe and Rachel of *la maison de tolérance*.

We found out about the ear and the splattering of blood from my father who was able to go inside the house to see what had happened. It was terrible, he said. Further details were seen in our local newspaper that Sunday, **LE FORUM RÉPUBLICAIN : -----Last Sunday, at 11: 12 at night, a man named Vincent Vangogh, painter, native of Holland, presented himself at the maison de tolérance number 1, asked for Rachel, and gave her....his ear telling her: "Keep this object preciously." Then he disappeared. Informed of this fact that could have only been that of a poor crazed person, the police went to this individual's house the following morning and found him sleeping in his bed, giving hardly any sign of life. This poor wretch was admitted to the hospital urgently.**

This is what we read with sadness in our hearts. Why? was everyone's question.

Having been informed by Monsieur Gauguin in a telegram, Vincent's brother, Monsieur Théo, arrived in Arles and quickly went to the hospital where he met with a Doctor Félix Rey. This one informs Monsieur Théo that Vincent is thrashing about and has had a very bad spell of delirium and that he's in a pretty bad state. He stamps his feet, shouts and is quite carried away by hallucinations of both eye and ear. Sometimes, he sings, the doctor says. The physician infers epilepsy as the cause. As for his ear, it has already begun to heal with a scar being formed. Fortunately, no infection, states the doctor. Théo is relieved to hear this news although he is very concerned about his brother's mental health. Doctor Rey would have liked to suture the lobe back but the *commissaire* brought it to him too late.

"Gangrene, you know," said the doctor.

He then placed the lobe in a container with alcohol. Young Doctor Rey reassures Théo that his brother's present crisis is temporary and that Vincent will recover. He tells Monsieur Théo that he can go back to his business affairs that await him in Paris.

Before leaving, Monsieur Théo came to our house to talk with my father about the situation at hand. I was so glad to finally meet Vincent's brother whom he so loved and with whom he corresponded so frequently. My father sat down with him while my mother listened attentively sitting in her stuffed chair. I was sitting on the floor next to my mother listening intently and with an eager heart to get more news about my good friend. I didn't have my notebook with me but I registered everything in my head exactly as I heard it. Monsieur Théo told my father everything that he knew, everything Doctor Rey had told him about Vincent and what his own feelings were. Monsieur Théo coughed a lot, he looked tired and his face was pale. He also told my father that he had to go back, not just for business purposes, but that he was getting engaged to his girlfriend back in Holland. My mother smiled hearing this. He told my father that Vincent was placed in an isolation cell for his own protection but that the doctor would see that he was taken out as soon as he saw progress. The doctor was very nice and very compassionate, he said. He also said that he knew how much of a very good friend my father was to Vincent and he thanked him for that. He also thanked my mother and even thanked me for being his *companion d'aventures*. God! I thought, he knows about me. He told me that Vincent had mentioned me to him in one of his letters. I was so pleased that my heart started to cry along with my eyes.

My mother gave me her handkerchief and my father patted me on the back saying, "Now, now, we mustn't let this news shatter us. We must help Vincent, not grieve him."

Knowing that my father would look in on Vincent, Monsieur Théo left for Paris the very next day. My father assured him that he would keep him posted.

On the following Wednesday, after my father had gone to see Vincent at the hospital, he wrote a letter to Monsieur Théo, and this is what he said: " *I am sorry to say, I think he is lost. Not only is his mind affected, but he is very weak and down-hearted. He recognized me but did not show any pleasure at seeing me and did not inquire about any member of my family or anyone he knows. When I left him, I told him I would come back to see him; he replied we would meet again in heaven, and from his manner, I realized he was praying.*"

Two days later, he wrote another letter to Monsieur Théo after my mother had gone to see Vincent the previous day. This is what he wrote: "*He hid his face when he saw her coming. When she spoke to him, he replied well enough, and talked to her about our little girl and asked if she was still as pretty as ever. Today, Friday, I went there but could not see him. The house doctor and the attendant told me that after my wife left, he had a terrible attack; he passed a very bad night and they had to put him in an isolated room, he has taken no food and completely refused to talk. That is the exact state of your brother at present.*"

I did not get to see those letters myself, but, later on, my mother told me about them and that my father had kept a *brouillon,* a draft, of the letters sending the neat copies to Monsieur Théo.

My father then hired this cleaning lady to help him clean up and fix the yellow house. They both worked at it for the better part of the day until it was done. Meanwhile, Vincent was still in his cell turning and turning in his lonely isolation not knowing what to do alone and apart from his painting, books and the world. I asked my father if I could go see Vincent.

"Not now," said my father. "It's not a good time. Let's wait until the doctor gives us permission."

On December 29, Vincent was released from his cell and placed in the ward at the insistence of Doctor Rey. Vincent was happy to see other patients convalescing there. It was a long room with two rows of beds on either side partitioned with white curtains. Some patients warmed themselves around the stove in the center of the room. Vincent ate well and regained his strength, according to the doctor. The following night, Pastor Salles accompanied Doctor Rey and they visited with Vincent. Pastor Salles was a local Protestant minister who took an interest in Vincent. The doctor urged Vincent to write to his brother but he refused angrily. The doctor did not give up and talked tenderly to Vincent who finally relented and wrote to Monsieur Théo about his improved condition. Two days later, January 1st, Vincent was allowed to go out for a brief outing. My father insisted on taking him out for a walk. After all, it's New Year's Day, a time for celebration, argued my father. That's the latest news about Vincent, the hospital and his doctor. That's what I wrote in my notebook.

The walk ended up with a visit at the Roulin home. I was anxiously waiting for Vincent's arrival since I had been biting my nails over his situation. We were all happy to see him again and we didn't ask questions about his situation because we feared embarrassing him. He told us that's he was fine, a bit confused, and did not remember much of anything that went on in the last several days. Thank God! I muttered under my breath. I gave him the gift that I had bought some time ago and he asked me why was I giving him a gift. I told him that it was *les étrennes du Jour de l'An* and that every child and even some grown-ups get some at New Year's.

"Open it," I said.

"But I have nothing for you," he replied.

"It doesn't matter," I said. "It's my gift to you and I didn't expect one from you."

He opened it and saw that it was a brush, a paintbrush. I had gotten it at Calment's shop where Vincent goes for his supplies.

"It's a nice one," he said. "I will cherish it."

"Please, don't just cherish it, use it," and he started laughing.

It was good to hear him laugh. We sang and we ate all the while he was with us. Then, my father told him that they had to return to the hospital since he had promised Doctor Rey that he would have Vincent back an hour later. Vincent got up and very quietly went with my father. The next day, Vincent was allowed to go to his yellow house and look at his paintings. He was most delighted at seeing his painting of the yellow house again. He dreamed of picking up work again, especially when the orchards would be in bloom once more. He told my father that, at last, he could start again *"son petit chemin,"* his little road. He returned to the hospital and later met with Doctor Rey in his office. Vincent recognized the extent of the situation and he was sorry for it. The doctor reassured him that in a few days he would be able to leave the hospital for good. That's pretty much what I've learned about these few last days after the incident, and reconstructed it for the reader.

On January 7, Vincent left the hospital and went home. He was so very happy. I could see it so plainly in his face, in his eyes and in his voice. He was so grateful to my father that he invited him for dinner at the restaurant Vanésias. Grateful for all the help he had given him.

"Only a real friend would do that," he told my father.

For the very first time, I saw my father speechless. Two days later, January 9, Vincent learned that his brother had gotten engaged to a Johanna Bonger in Amsterdam. He was overjoyed. He was glad that his brother had finally found a woman who could make him happy. However, he also got some bad news. The manager of the property where the yellow house stood informed him that he had signed a lease for the yellow house with the owner of a tobacco shop.

"The damn sleazy manager, this Monsieur Bernard Soulé," said my father. "He took advantage of Vincent in his absence to break the lease. He doesn't care. He's the big boss and manager of the four-story hotel behind the yellow house. Heartless man."

What was Vincent going to do? I asked myself.

18

Still Life Paintings and Stillness

V incent had until Easter to prepare for his departure from the yellow house. Vincent was angry, angry because it was he who had the house rehabilitated since no one had lived in it for quite some time. It had been simply filthy and a sore spot in the neighborhood. He had the outside of the house painted as well as the inside, and he had cleaned up the entire inside of the house himself. His mother would have been proud. What he did was to make the house livable and the manager was now kicking him out. Why, he even had the gas installed at his own expense. He was angry indeed. Worse, he knew that the date my father would be leaving was getting closer and closer. What was he going to do? Where would he live? Where would he paint? Moreover, he was broke after paying all of his debts. He had no more money to buy food. He had to borrow some. It was January 10 of '89 and he had to make due until he received money from his brother at the end of the month. The only thing he could do to relieve the pressure of little food and no money was to fast and hope things would get better, he told me. I offered him my piggy bank and the one franc and a few centimes I had left over after I had bought his brush, but he said no.

"I'm not about to break a child's piggy bank for the price of coffee and bread," he said.

I asked my mother if we could spare some food and she gave me some bread and some pâté flavored with juniper that she had made.

"Take the rest of this coffee too," she said.

I only wished then that I could have had more money to give Vincent. I was a poor child from a poor family. My father didn't make much as a low end civil servant. We weren't poor as many who are dirt poor in our town, like the Marchouts and the Clouterands, but we had to economize to make ends meet and we had to go without certain things such as new shoes and brand new pencils that I practically wore out writing in my notebook. I asked around if I could do errands for people. Some said yes, but it did not pay since they thought I was being kind to them. Others paid me with *calissons* or *berlingots*. That's not what I wanted. I wanted to help Vincent out with money. One day, this old woman asked me to paint the shutters in front of her house. They were weather-beaten. I chose a sunny day to do it on a Wednesday afternoon. It took me two hours. First, I had to clean them up. What a job! The color was yellow, just like sunflowers. The lady paid me thirty-five centimes. Not much for two and one half hours work, but I took it. The following week, Monsieur Calment asked me to deliver some fabric to a client of his and I earned twenty centimes more. That same week, I helped Monsieur Ginoux clean the floor in his restaurant and he paid me forty-five centimes. Now, I had a entire franc's worth at my disposal. It wasn't much but I had earned it. Every centime. I put all of my centimes in an envelope, sealed it and put it in Vincent's mailbox. He would not have liked it if I had given it to him personally. It was an anonymous gift. That's what I wrote on the envelope, "From an anonymous donor." I was so glad I could help. I was trying to repay him for all of the art lessons he had given me by allowing me to walk in his shoes, so to speak.

What Vincent found to ease his troubles was painting. Yes, he started painting again. He started assembling objects from his poor existence for a still life: a drawing board, his pipe and his tobacco pouch, a box of matches, some sealing wax, an envelope of one of Monsieur Théo's letters, an empty bottle of wine, a water jug, a book, a candle that he had already used for the Gauguin chair painting, a burned out matchstick, an annual, *l'Annuaire de la Santé de Raspail,* and four onions, probably because, according to Raspail, onions have a certain therapeutic quality to them.

"Now, the arrangement needs not be too orderly," Vincent said to me. "It needs some spontaneity and naturalness," and he set out to make his own arrangement for the still life.

First, he took the two onions and a white plate and set that about the middle of the wooden table, then he placed one to the left of the plate and another smaller one on the annual. In front of the plate, he put his pipe and tobacco pouch but he took out the tobacco and placed it on the pouch. Next, he put the matchstick on top of the envelope in the right hand corner. The envelope faces opposite the viewer. Then, the matchbox with the rectangular red sealing wax to the far right corner of the table. A little bit to the left, the lit candle in a green candle holder, right on the edge of the table. Directly behind the table, about the middle, stands a green jug with spout filled with wine. In front of the table, facing the jug, stands an empty wine bottle. That's the arrangement he chose to make. They're all ordinary things but given the Vincent touch, they look somewhat extraordinary. The wall behind the table is painted blue with speckles of yellow and red. The table is a simple wooden one with a large yellow drawing board on top. All the objects are on this drawing board, perhaps symbolic of the artist's drawing tool on which he sets his work. The jug reflects the light on top with yellow touches. The candle is lit. There is life in this still life. The candle holder is of a dark blue with golden edges. The overall ambience of this work is one of structured naturalness, I would say. It's done by the artist who understands the layout of objects in a still life without too much arrangement that might make the painting overdone and overly structured. This **Still Life: Drawing Board, Pipe, Onions and Sealing-Wax** is a lively work. I think it reveals some kind of return to life and activity on the artist's part. Vincent was pleased with it and he put it up on the wall in the kitchen.

Vincent did other still life paintings such as, bloaters on a piece of yellow paper, oranges, lemons and blue gloves and others with crabs. I told you he chose common ordinary things for his paintings. The one painting that is revealing to me is the **Crab on Its Back**. What a good symbol of the artist, Vincent, on his back struggling to turn things around and especially himself, so that he doesn't remain on his back useless and helpless. No doubt he looked at himself in the mirror and thought, who am I? Am I this shell of a man with part of his ear cut off and wondering what's going to happen to me? Or, am I the other Vincent, the pipe smoker who smokes his pipe in all serenity and wants to be calm and collected? Will he always be the unsure man who feels like a hunted animal and who looks over his shoulder to see if the other self, the mad self, is not coming out? Will he remain on his back helpless like the crab? The crab painting is a fine work. Vincent painted it with an artistic realism that shows his mastery of drawing and painting. The colors of the crab are real. The shell definition is real. The perspective is real. It's yet another work where he shows us his capacity to use common everyday life things and turn them into art.

Vincent painted two self-portraits with the bandaged ear. He's smoking in one of them. He used the mirror to help him out. He didn't want to do it from his imagination. He wanted what was real, he told me. I never talked about the incident with his ear but he knew I was dying to find out more details. Kids are full of questions, aren't they? Well, one day, he told me one reason why he had done it.

"It's only one of the reasons, but I only remember one that is clear to me. The others, well, they're in limbo" he said.(Limbo, another word for my notebook).

I responded, "You don't have to tell me if you don't want."

"I want to because you have questions and perhaps doubts in your mind like a lot of people do. I don't owe the others any explanations. I've already told your father. He was very understanding. When you grow up, perhaps you'll understand too. It's hard to understand the motives and actions of a man like myself. I did it in a frenzy that caught up with me and my sanity, pushing me to violence. My head was buzzing and my ears kept ringing. It felt terrible. There was anger building up inside me and I could not stop it. I had to direct it to myself and not another. I didn't want to harm anyone, especially Paul. I was so frustrated and so full of crazy thoughts and volcanic feelings that I thought I would blow up. Without knowing it, I took my razor and looked at my face in the mirror. Coldly and rationally, I slashed part of my ear. There, I had done it. I had severed part of my body so that I was sacrificing part of myself to regain, or should I say, maintain, my sanity. You see, that was a sane act I did. A rational act that most people do not understand. Had I wanted to mutilate myself, I would have cut off the entire ear. Some will say that it was an insane act but I say it was perfectly sane. I had to regain my wits before my bubbling volcano erupted.

The blood started oozing out and that's when I fully realized what I had done. It was more serious than what I had expected. I'm sorry, I didn't want to tell you all the gory details. I don't fully know what made me do it, Camille. I can only recollect part of it, the sane part in all of this. *Je ne sais pas tous les détails de mon acte d'auto-violence.* I'm not a martyr. I'm certainly not masochistic. I don't want to harm myself. The doctor thinks it was epilepsy, but I'm not sure, the doctors are not sure, no one is sure. I wish it were a disease, this thing that haunts me, then they could probably find a cure for it. God! I don't want to go through that again. I'm afraid I made a fool of myself."

I didn't know what to say or what to do.

I simply told him, "I understand."

"Do you, Camille? Do you?"

"I think so," I replied.

I went home feeling sorry for Vincent and saying to myself, what a terrible thing not to have control of yourself in moments like these.

"I never want to be that way," I told myself, muttering in low tones.

My hands were cold and I felt like I was going to cry. I just felt frozen as if my body wouldn't move at all.

Vincent's self-portrait, **Self-Portrait with Bandaged Ear and Pipe**, is a view of self, vulnerable and yet in control. Serenity reigns with the man with the bandaged ear smoking quietly his pipe. As I've said, he used the mirror and partly his imagination to paint this one. In the other one, he looks haggard and somewhat unsure of himself. However, these paintings attest to his renewed strength and control over his art. In this particular one, Vincent's green eyes are the same eyes as before, piercing and intelligent eyes. His face is strong with red lips that are full and healthy. He's smoking his faithful pipe. He told me once that smoking his pipe made him feel at peace with himself. It was very relaxing for him. He's dressed warm with his green overcoat and his furry hat pulled down to his ears. He's wearing some kind of white scarf for, after all, it's winter. This scarf blends in well with the bandage as far as the painting goes. The lower half of the background is fiery red while the top part is reddish-orange with some yellow vertical brush strokes at the very top. Overall, the painting shows a man both confident in his abilities and possessing enough strength and determination to survive any ordeal. He may have had his moments but he was not a lunatic. He was not some kind of wild creature, *une bête fauve*. The colors of the background reveal, I think, the lively disposition he has toward his art. He was still full of fire and passion. He will not let himself sink into the lifeless colors of depression. The awful blues. He's still fighting insomnia, as he told his brother, Théo, but he's going to be fine. He's going to conquer this thing that's got him confused at times. If it's the curse, well then he's going to fight it that much more. Besides, he doesn't believe in it. Curses are for gypsies and those who allow themselves to get caught in its web. That's the way he feels and thinks, he said.

Every morning Vincent went to see the doctor (he wasn't a doctor yet, he was an intern) to have his bandage changed. The ear looks good, he tells him. It's healing fast. Good news. As promised, Vincent brought a canvas and his paints to do a portrait of Félix Rey that day. He liked the young man who was filled with kindness towards him. He made the doctor sit down and positioned him so that he was looking straight at him with his piercing dark brown eyes. He painted him full round face that he had, a long somewhat curling dark brown mustache with a pointed beard. His hair is in a brush, short, dark and straight up. His eyes may be piercing but they're kind looking. What is most striking are his very red lips, full and slightly pursed which makes him look like a dandy, somehow. His left ear is painted red, perhaps to remind the painter of his recent incident and the affiliation with the person who took care of him. Doctor Rey wears a blue jacket with large reddish-pink buttons. The background is very interesting. It's done with a green base, red dots all over, small black ovals and pinkish swirls like feathery scrolls. Very decorative as background. Vincent must have thought of *égayer la toile*, bring joy to the canvas, by doing this. It may very well be that he liked Félix Rey a lot and wanted to render him a warm artistic accolade. He signed it in bold letters, VINCENT ARLES 89.

It's a very good portrait of Doctor Rey, I thought. It's a vivid testimony to Vincent's skills as an artist always seeking ways of perfecting his craft with bolder colors and using his sense of imagination melded in his ever strong sense of naturalness. Vincent liked it. It had been done with the heart. However, Doctor Rey said he liked it but accepted it, we are told, with reserved satisfaction because, deep down, he did not really like the painting. The strong contrast of colors, these green reflections, the red on the forehead, the beard and the hair left him a bit dumbfounded. Madame Calfortin who knows Madame Rey, mère told Madame Ginoux when Félix brought the painting home and showed it to his parents, they thought that the artist had made fun of their son by painting such a thing. Why, they thought he must be mad doing such a ridiculous thing like that, so much so that they put it up in the attic. Later, they used it to fill a hole in their chicken coop. Imagine that! What kind of ungrateful snobs are these people, I thought. *Ignorants et ingrats!* Of course, Vincent never knew about all of this or else he would have been insulted. To think that people like that think they can appreciate art. But then, I may be too sensitive about Vincent's works of art.

In order to fully reestablish himself into his art, Vincent returned to his much-loved sunflowers. He painted three canvases with big sunflowers in the middle of January. Two with fourteen and one with twelve. Sunflowers are beneficial for him. Flower therapy. It was cold and everybody felt it, especially Vincent. His strength was not quite up to what it should have been, said Doctor Rey, and so he gave him some quinine tonic wine. Vincent made me taste it. It tasted bitter. His brother Théo told him to eat better. My father told him the same thing too. I didn't tell him anything.

Classes started up again and I was reading everything I could get my hands on, Hugo, Zola, Daudet, Maupassant, Dumas, Balzac, all these authors who succeeded in life as writers. I wanted to read "Uncle Tom's Cabin' by that American woman but I couldn't read English then. Perhaps later, I said. It's one of Vincent's favorite books. It's about slavery and the poor conditions of disadvantaged black people. I didn't know there was slavery in America. They used black people to do their hardest work like picking cotton and cleaning houses and doing the cooking. They came to get them in Africa. When I go to Africa, I'll not treat black people like slaves, I told myself. They're people like me except they're black. Vincent told me that there were many slaves that came from Africa and were treated unfairly by whites. Not just in America. Slaves working so terribly hard in order to survive. That's probably why people say "*travailler comme un nègre*, work like a Negro, I suppose. I didn't know of any of them in Arles, just gypsies. They worked hard too but so did the farmers, the shepherds and the common people of Provence. I've seen them. That's why I was determined to stay in school after I got over hating it. I wanted to become a writer and that took a certain determination to stay in school and learn what I had to learn in order to succeed. I couldn't give it up and I couldn't keep on hating school. Give up on my writing? Absolutely not. Perhaps, I realized then that I was growing up.

19

Lullabies and Petitions

 oday is January 17, a new year, and my mother is working hard
 preparing for my father's departure for Marseille in three days.
That's what I wrote in my notebook. Here's the rest of it. She's washing his clothes, ironing them and making sure that everything is clean
and ready to be packed. I think she keeps busy so as not to think too
much about his leaving us. Marseille is not that far but far enough that
my father won't be home every night. Sure, he'll be back once in a
while but that's not like working here in town. He won't be able to go
to the café for a drink and talk with the people there. My father likes to
talk. It relaxes him after a long day's work. Sometimes, he likes to play
pétanque with his old friends on Sunday afternoons but he can play
pétanque in Marseille too. I like having my father home with me. It
feels safe and secure. Besides, he teaches me things like how to tie a
three-corner knot or how to make paper boats with newspapers. Vincent is going to miss him for sure. He came over the other night and I
could see that he was a bit nervous and tried to talk to my father about
his leaving Arles, but his voice cracked now and then. He left after only
a half hour. I didn't get a chance to talk to him. He came to tell my
mother that he was going to do her portrait soon. She didn't say much. I
think she's afraid of being alone in his house while my father is away.
There's nothing to be afraid of, I told her. I don't see why she would be
afraid. My brother Armand hangs around the house a bit more these
days. It's not because my mother told him to. I think he's somewhat
edgy about my father leaving. I'm not nervous, just sorry that he's leaving. I know that we'll all join him sooner or later but still, I would
rather he stayed with us. It means more money, he told us, and I know
we could use more. My mother is tired of pinching the franc, she says.
As I sit here today gathering my thoughts, I can recollect these very
moments as if they happened just yesterday. What a wonder memory is.
  Blàsi and Milou came over the house to get me to play with them
but I told them, no, because I wanted to stay inside. It was cold out
there. I was doing my homework. They thought I was crazy. They
didn't like school and they breezed through their homework without

paying too much attention to what they were doing. Sometimes they would ask me about what we were reading in class since they hadn't done any of the assigned readings. They didn't read much and they fell behind fast. Sometimes, they would ask me to copy what I had written and I let them just because I didn't want them to be punished for not doing their assignment. To think about how I used to hate school and it was such a chore for me to finish my homework then. But, I learned to like school especially with our teacher, Madame Hugonet, who gave us more interesting assignments. She told me that if I worked hard she would see to it that I got to go a good school after I finished here. I wanted to get an education and learn about all those things that interested me like geography, history and novels. I didn't like math, especially advanced math that I knew I would have to take later on. No, I didn't like math at all. My father said that math would help me later on in life. Help me with what? I asked him. He said that math taught you all kinds of things like calculating the width of houses, the measurement of kilometers and kilograms as well as the formulas for getting things to work. I didn't think I wanted to go beyond much more than kilograms and kilometers. Let the others figure out the widths of houses, I told myself.

My father left January 20th. Vincent was here with us when he left. We had a small party for him. My father embraced us all and held the baby in his arms for a long time. Then, he took her and made her laugh while bouncing her on his knees. He sang to her. He didn't look sad at all. I shook hands with him and then he grabbed me by the shoulders and gave me a big hug. I didn't want to cry because I was too old to cry and, besides, I was a boy. I tried to hold back my tears but they just kept coming and filling up my eyes. I have big eyes so there's a lot of water that gets into them when I feel the way I felt when my father left. Vincent told me that it was alright to cry. He wished he could have cried when he left home but he didn't. My father held Vincent's hand for a long time talking to him until Vincent couldn't talk anymore. Vincent had only a small bandage on his ear.

After that Armand shook my father's hand and my mother said her goodbyes. She was good about it. No tears, no words of warning about what my father should do or not do. Just *aurevoir*. We all went to the train station with him and saw him off. Monsieur and Madame Ginoux were there as well as Madame Calfortin and Madame Génélard, our neighbor. They all wished my father well and Madame Ginoux gave my father a bottle of wine. Madame Génélard told my father that she was going to look after my mother while he was gone. I wished that I could have taken the train with him.

"C'est un brave homme," he's a good man, Vincent told my mother.

She lowered her head because I think she would have cried then and there. We went home and my mother made us some *soupe au pistou* just as she used to before my father left. Vincent stayed with us a long time that evening. I think he was lonely.

Berceuse, or *bressarello* in our language, is a word that means the one who rocks a cradle, or it's the name of a song that one sings to put a child to sleep. *Berceau* is the name of a cradle. *Bercer* means to rock. So, you see, several words can be made with the same stem. Vincent was in the process of painting a portrait of my mother called, **La Berceuse**. He told me that the title came from a book written by a Dutch writer named, Van Eeden that meant "lullaby or a woman rocking a cradle." My mother was nervous when Vincent showed up to bring her over to his place to paint her picture because she was alone with me and my baby sister. My father was away, of course. She had Madame Génélard watch over Marcelle while she was gone. It was early evening. She cooperated with Vincent and sat down in a chair but I could see she was nervous. Vincent told her to relax, that he wasn't going to bite her. She smiled faintly. She did trust Vincent as an artist but she was cautious about being alone with a man, a stranger, although he wasn't really a stranger to us. Besides, I was there with her.

Vincent would paint several versions of the same painting, "La Berceuse." He loved doing it because he thought my mother was a good mother and a pleasant woman who took good care of her family. She was the hub and the heart of the family, he said. Mothers were fortunate since they were givers of birth, the ones who gave life to a child like an artist who gives birth to a painting, but this was human life, a baby with new life, he said. Vincent so loved children. He would have been a good father, I know. But, I said that before.

I think that I mentioned that my mother was younger than my father. She showed her lively spirit and her energy by working hard in the house and taking care of all of us. She had a youthful face. Vincent reveals the maternal quality in her and shows her sitting with a cord in her hands. She used to rock my sister, Marcelle, in the crib with that. My mother told me that she had rocked me in that same crib when I was a baby. Armand too. You see, it's been in my family for years. My mother was a big woman but she moved with grace and agility. She wasn't fat, just generous in her bodily appearance. I'm being nice here but it's true. She was a common person from a very common family in Lambesc, just like my father. We were common folks and that's why Vincent liked us, I guess. He didn't go for snooty people.

Vincent painted my mother with her hair pulled back into large braids. The color of her hair is orangey-blond, just like he painted it. He described this portrait to his brother later on that he had painted her "dressed in light and dark greens. The orange of her braided hair rises from yellow to citron and her skin is chrome yellow." Colors to express the lullaby and the one who rocks the cradle. Soothing colors, vivid colors, lively colors. The background is an imaginary one with flowers just like the one he did of Félix Rey. This time, they're huge white flowers with yellow centers and touches of red on a bright green background. The same black ovals with red dots appear on that background almost like peacock feathers, I would say. But the thing that impressed me the most is her face, her young and maternal face, even though she is casting her glance downward out of shyness, perhaps. My mother's face. It's a serene face with the gentle smile of her full red lips. Her nose and her eyes are like mine. I get them from her. Her demeanor is truly *accueillant*, welcoming, I would say. Her hands are resting in her lap with the cord loosely entwined around her fingers. They're gentle, giving hands, hands that have known much work and scrubbing. My mother was always the dignified *Arlésienne* and that's what Vincent captured in this portrait. Dignity and motherly care with kindness for her young child. I like it. I always liked that painting. I think it was one of Vincent's best and one that he liked very much, as much as his sunflower paintings.

As a matter of fact, he told his brother, Théo, later on: "If you place *La Berceuse* in the middle flanked by two canvases of sunflowers, it will make a sort of triptych...The yellows and oranges will appear even brighter next to the yellows on each side...I intend for this to be a sort of decoration that might be placed at the end of a ship's cabin."

He envisioned this painting as an icon of maternity. In one of his conversations with Monsieur Gauguin, he conceived the notion of painting this picture so that sailors would feel the sea was rocking them as a mother gently rocks her child. Good idea, I thought. He was clever that Vincent, very clever. I don't think that my mother's picture ever got on a ship but, later on, when the painting got to be known, some sailors may have pinned copies of it to their hammocks.

With my father and Monsieur Gauguin gone, Vincent had no more adult companions or friends except Doctor Rey and maybe some people he knew at the Café de la Gare. One day, Doctor Rey counseled him to go see a show or some entertainment to give him something to do and have some fun. He needed cheering up. Vincent chose to go to a performance of *La Pastorale* at *Les Folies-Arlésiennes*. I've never been there. My mother and my father went and they enjoyed it. It's not like *Les Folies Bergères de Paris*, my father said, but it was good. I'm glad that Vincent went and enjoyed himself. He was, by then, completely recovered, he said, and could plan to turn his life around now that Monsieur Gauguin had gone. He was still thinking of his *atelier du Midi* and the possibility that his friend Paul Signac might join him in Arles. Possibly Monsieur Bernard too. That would have pleased him tremendously. I wondered if the studio he planned remained a distinct possibility as far as implementation and reality. We who were his friends tried not to dash his hopes. Only lift them up a bit.

Vincent still felt the over-excitement and nervousness that he felt before and thought of refraining from too much activity, but activity was the sole therapy for him. Creative activity. He worked some more on his triptych with my mother's portrait and the sunflower drawings as a sketch to concretize this plan. Vincent still worried about his mental state whether or not it would change at any moment's notice. However, he was constantly reminded of the Provençal saying, *"Dans ce bon pays tarasconnais tout le monde est un peu toqué,"* in this land of Tarascon, everyone is a bit touched. So, he moved on.

Vincent felt his weakness and tension returning but he tried to overcome them by daily walks, as Doctor Rey had suggested to him. He felt tired most of the time. He felt a bit desperate at times. He told me that he had to pull himself together for if he did not, he would lose control again. I tried to encourage him and keep his mind off his illness by reading to him from the books that I had. I read parts of Maupassant's, "Pierre et Jean." It had just come out the previous January. It was about two brothers, one a doctor and the other a lawyer who go fishing in Le Havre at the beginning of the story. Then, the whole story unfolds. Vincent had already read it but wanted to hear it again. Myself, I had just started the story. We talked about it and he explained to me some of the situations in the book such as, Jean's inheritance and Pierre's suspicions about his brother's birthright. It's seemed very interesting but a bit complicated for me.

Father got home two weeks after he left Arles. He was here with us for one day only, but we were glad he was home. I stayed home with him until he decided to go and pay Vincent a visit while my mother was making lunch. We didn't stay long but Vincent was glad to see my father again. He told him that he was going to see the doctor again and that he had gone to see his friend, Rachel, and told her about his hallucinations. Those terrible hallucinations. Chills and fever sometimes accompanied them, he told my father.

"Please continue to see Doctor Rey," said my father. "He's going to control those things that seem to take a hold of you."

We said goodbye and Vincent wished my father well on his return trip to Marseille the following afternoon. When we got home, my mother was putting lunch on the table. It was Saturday afternoon and I helped my father fix the kitchen faucet since it was dripping. I handed him the tools. My father was pretty good with tools. My mother and father talked over some business that they had and I went to my room. Father left early the following afternoon. He told us that he would be back in a week or two.

It was February and the promise of a new spring was in the air. We were able to get out more often and feel the warmth of the sun when the sun was out. Poor Vincent, he started to get frustrated and discouraged and he got his feverish spells again. He even thought that someone was trying to poison him, he told Madame Ginoux. He became dispirited and confused at times, he told her. He thought he was facing madness again. He got angry easily, he told her. Madame Ginoux tried to encourage him and told him that assuredly no one in Arles was trying to poison him. I stayed out of his way since there was nothing I could do. I only wish then that I could have. My mother told Madame Ginoux that the best thing for Vincent was to go back in the hospital for treatment. Doctor Rey admitted Vincent the following day. By mid-February, his brother got worried about him since he had not heard from him, but the Doctor reassured him that Vincent was coming along just fine.

Vincent was allowed to return home after four or five days. However, he took his meals and slept at the hospital. On coming home, one day, he found his studio in shambles. During his absence, there was a flood and the waters had ruined some of his works. I helped him clean up the mess. The neighbor, Madame Génélard, came in to wash the walls. On February 21, the exact day he first came to Arles, Vincent took up painting again.

"It's an anniversary of sorts," he said. "I came here thinking I could paint in the bright sun and enjoy the warmth of Provence and I did. I found my creative niche here. However, I didn't expect these incidents of madness in my life. I desperately want to continue painting and I want to stay here in Arles," he told my father on his return trip.

Vincent followed the advice of Doctor Rey. He went out more and took long walks in the public park and in the neighborhood, although it was quite windy at times. What was depressing, if not discouraging, was the fact that a group of kids started to throw rocks and cabbage stalks at him yelling, "Au fou!" Crazy, crazy.

Even the grown-ups said those insults under their breath when they saw Vincent pass by in his old overcoat, his fur hat and the bandage over his left ear. They all knew about the scandal in town. The fact that he went to see Rachel, the prostitute, and gave her his cut ear lobe. Everyone knew it because every one had read it in the paper. A scandalous fool, he was, they said. Who would work in the heat of the sun with an overcoat on, a big fuzzy hat and a scarf? Who but a damn fool, they said. So, the children pursued him and even went to his yellow house to try and climb the walls and peer through the windows. One day, a small crowd gathered in front of his house and shouted insults at him.

"Go home, you good for nothing. Go away. We don't want you here anymore. You're a menace to the town and a damn lunatic," they shouted.

Vincent opened his shutters and started shouting himself. He told the crowd to get away from there and leave him alone. That he wasn't a lunatic. They were. He even added some swear words to his shouts. Some pretty nasty ones too. I just stood at the far edge of the street not wanting to get mixed up in this mad scramble. I was deeply troubled and deeply sad at seeing my fellow Arlesians behave that way. I knew some of the kids and some of the grown-ups, and I started to hate them for what they were doing to Vincent. He deserved better than that, I thought. I felt helpless and angry, not knowing what to do. I went back home and told my mother about the incident. She told me not to get involved with Vincent's troubles. That it was a sad thing, indeed, but I should not mingle with the crowd because I might infuriate them more since they knew that I was a close friend of Vincent. The entire neighborhood knew and even some people who lived outside the neighborhood, like Madame Damasou who lived way out across the Trinquetaille bridge.

"They're but angry people losing their calm and even their heads. Besides, he's old enough to take care of himself," she said.

This was not the worst of it. There was a petition with thirty signatures or more demanding that the mayor put away the lunatic, Vincent Van Gogh. That's how the petition designated him, a lunatic. Of course, my mother did not sign it. Neither did Madame Ginoux nor Madame Génélard nor Madame Flourènço. But, there were enough signatures to warrant the mayor to put Vincent in prison. He was not allowed to write, he could not smoke, he could not paint. Shut up in a small cubicle without fresh air. Meanwhile, the police closed his house and put seals on the doors. They were offended by some of the paintings they saw inside the house, they said. They thought it was an insult to the neighborhood. What did they know about art? Vincent was under lock and key with guards at the door of his cell. Wasn't someone overreacting here? Could anyone think of a greater sense of insecurity on the part of these townspeople and their police force, not to mention the mayor, Monsieur Tardieu? Doctor Rey was sick and no one could reach him at the hospital.

"What can we do?" asked Madame Ginoux and Monsieur Calment.

Yes, Monsieur Calment was taking Vincent's side. After all, he was a good customer of his. Along with some other friends, they went to see the mayor and demanded that Vincent be released from jail on the premise that he was not a thief nor a criminal. He wasn't. The mayor was sorry, he told them, but he had to enforce law and order.

"Do you think that's law and order when a group of people interfere in someone's private matters, a citizen's rights to privacy?" they said.

"But, Messieurs, dames, I have the responsibility of controlling the behavior of deranged people under my jurisdiction. Besides, Monsieur Van Gogh is not a citizen of Arles."

"He is too," replied Madame Ginoux red in the face. "He's been with us for over a year and that makes him a citizen. He is a French citizen, I'll have you know and every French citizen has the right to live wherever he wants in France. Is Arles not a part of France?"

Monsieur le maire backtracked and, after a few days, he had the prisoner released, probably because the local elections were due the following month. Madame Ginoux recounted everything to my mother and did not leave a single word out. I just said, "Wow! How good a friend she is that Madame Ginoux." Of course, Monsieur Ginoux was there too but he's more like a sheep than a lion. Besides, it was found out that Monsieur Ginoux was one of the complainers who had signed the petition. What a strange man, I thought.

Upon leaving his cell, Vincent told himself that he wanted out of that quarter into a new place away from such people. Maybe a return to the northern country. He told my mother that he had had enough of it and that he was definitely moving. Pastor Salles offered him to try and find a place where he would be free of these people. Nice man this Pastor Salles. Later, Vincent told Madame Ginoux that he had written to his brother telling him about the officials and their behavior. He wrote: *"L'administration est comment dirais-je, jésuite, ils sont très très fins, très savants, très puissants, même impressionistes, ils savent prendre des renseignements d'une subtilité inouïe,"* the officials are, how would I say, Jesuitic, very, very shrewd, very knowledgeable, very powerful, even impressionistic, they know how to get information with an incredible subtlety.

He wasn't afraid of them, he told her, but he feared their tactics. She told him never mind the people, his friends would take his side. It's later that he discovered that it wasn't his neighbors who had signed the petition but others, even some from far away.

Vincent wanted to have his house reopened but they would not do it, so he was spending his days at the hospital. I went to see him there. We walked in the garden and we talked about his upcoming paintings. He did not want to give up his art just for the sake of a few people who were upset by some aspects of his behavior. Why didn't people leave him alone, he kept saying over and over again. I told him that the teacher reprimanded the kids who had thrown rocks at him the day following the incident.

Vincent was very happy when I saw him since he got news from his brother that the artist friend, Paul Signac, was on his way to Cassis-sur-Mer and he was going to stop in Arles to see him. He was overjoyed. He showed me the letter. Monsieur Signac arrived three days later. He was surprised to see a man who was as sane as anyone, he said. Doctor Rey allowed Monsieur Signac to take Vincent out. Vincent wanted to bring his friend over to the yellow house, but they would not authorize the reopening of the house. Finally, they relented and the house was reopened. Vincent told me that Monsieur Signac was delighted and even surprised to see all of the paintings Vincent had done. What colors! What intensity of light! That's what Monsieur Signac said beholding all the paintings there: "Le Café de Nuit," "Les Saintes-Maries," "Les Alyscamps," "La Berceuse" and over there "La Nuit Étoilée."

"What creativity!" he exclaimed.

Vincent and his friend spent all day discussing art, literature and some social questions, he told me. He was so, so happy to finally have someone with him who understood him and stimulated him. This get-together with a friend, an artist, did so much good for Vincent's mental state. He talked about getting back to painting.

"After all," he told me, "I lost so much precious time being torn apart by my illness and those ugly people. I could have produced so many works then."

In the meantime, March had practically flown by. Vincent was still living at the hospital but feeling better. He went home to get his painting materials and some books, "Uncle Tom's Cabin" and "Christmas Stories" by Dickens and others. He wanted to read and paint. A few days later marked the beginning of April and the weather was now very mild. The orchards were in full bloom. Vincent was continuing to recuperate but after a week or two, he realized that he was going to miss the time of the blossoming. But no, he did have enough time to capture some of the last blossoms of spring in the orchards he so loved to paint if he pulled himself together. April, what a marvelous month in Provence. What a time to go outdoors to paint and follow my teacher in art, I thought. I kept wishing to recapture the many adventures that Vincent and I enjoyed while he sought sites and objects to paint. Doctor Rey and Pastor Salles tried to convince Vincent to shut down the studio completely even though he had dreamed of such a workshop for a very long time, the yellow house and *l'atelier du Midi*.

When my father arrived in town, he went to the hospital and he and Doctor Rey and Pastor Salles were in agreement that Vincent had no choice but to give up the studio and move out. Besides, he had only a couple of days to vacate the house. He decided to do it. He would get another apartment, he said, and Doctor Rey helped him find one, a two-room apartment belonging to his mother. That would be his studio from now on, he said. He felt that he was a complete failure with the other studio. Bankrupt too. How could he ever pay back the huge debt he owed his brother, he wondered. He told my father that he might never be able to repay all the money he received from Monsieur Théo. At one time he had thought that by selling his paintings he would be able to make a substantial profit from the sales and his brother would get his money back. However, that was not the case since his paintings did not sell. Too bold a way of painting, overdone and far too digressive from the established theories of art, they said. That was the Paris crowd. Gauguin had sold one of his for 500 francs. Why couldn't he do the same? he wondered. Nothing seemed to work in his favor. So, he decided to live within the enclosure of his monastic way of life and struggle to survive in his own way. Vincent said to my mother, after my father had left, "Your husband gave me some sound advice. To take care of myself and never worry about my art since it will not only survive but flourish one day soon. So, I trust him and his *bons mots,* his kind words. He reminds me of Camille Pissarro, my artist friend in Pontoise. He's such a good-hearted person. Everybody likes him in the circle of Impressionists. He's kind to everyone. He was so kind to me. Among all of the artists I knew in Paris, he was the very best, both as a person and a friend."

"A kind old man with a beard much like your father although your father is not as old," he told me.

"His name is Camille?" I said with some amazement in my voice.

"Yes, Camille, just like your name. You enjoy the same first name as my dear friend, Père Pissarro. It's a good name, a name that rings true and bright."

"Is he a good artist?" I asked.

"Yes, Camille, a very good artist of the outdoors and of common people, peasants and common things such as, ploughed fields, grazing cows and apple picking. To me he was another Millet. Same touch with nature, same earthy tones, same attraction to the ever-changing pattern of light and shadow. You should see his haystack that he painted. A huge golden cone against the white puffy clouds in a blue sky. And his red roofs, what a painting!"

"I'd like to meet him someday. Another Camille." I sighed.

One work that he wanted to accomplish was the ward in the hospital where he was. He thought that this would be a therapeutic venture for him and it was. When I went to visit him at the hospital one afternoon after class, he was finishing his painting, **Ward in the Hospital in Arles**. He was just adding some light touches to the wooden floor in the picture. We see five men sitting on chairs clustered around the stove warming themselves. One is reading his paper while the others are smoking. The stove pipe connects the stove to the ceiling like a long upside down "L." Two men are seen standing on the right next to a small table with a jug on top. Another man is walking, away from the others. On the left, there are two nuns with long white aprons carrying what looks like pails of water to wash beds or something. On either side, there is a row of beds enclosed with long white hanging curtains. All of the curtains are closed except for the three we see where there will be activity with the washing down that the nuns are about to do since they are coming towards that way. What with the long rectangular ceiling with its huge beams and the long wooden floor painted in perspective, the room looks very long and vast. At the very end, there's a black cross hanging on top of the door. It's a Catholic hospital, l'Hôtel Dieu. The atmosphere is one of calm and cleanliness. No patient seen here is suffering. There may be some but they're sheltered in the curtained cubicles. The colors are natural and restrained. They go from an earthy tone to a soft white and greenish effect. There's a wooden enclosure with large windows where light is emanating in the middle of the left wall. It just seems to hang there as a beacon or something. Perhaps, it's a watch tower of sorts. Vincent told me that it was indeed a small room where the nuns could watch over the patients, especially at night. It was always filled with light and he wanted to show a lighted effect in the dimmed ward. With his painting of the hospital ward where he had stayed, his work revealed to me that it had not been an unpleasant experience for him, just a place where he had to be during his illness. A place where he had met kind people such as Doctor Rey. A place filled with common people in common ordinary circumstances since illness was a common thing among humans. He wasn't a lunatic, he was an ordinary person with an uncommon malady, he said.

His next painting was outdoors where he preferred to be, out in the orchards. Vincent and I walked outside of Arles center and went to this orchard owned by Monsieur Chalouton. Vincent had been there before. This time, he chose a different perspective, that of a grand view of Arles in the background, the orchard in bloom in the center and the gnarled poplar trunks in the foreground. There's a blue-purplish feeling about this painting. Perhaps, it hints at the state of mind Vincent was in when he did this, but I can swear that he was in a very happy frame of mind that day. He was singing a kind of lullaby in Dutch and I couldn't understand a word of it but the melody was sweet. Probably, the painting touches upon the condition that the artist was in before he painted it and it evokes somehow the pain and struggle he went through, not only when he went to the hospital but especially when he was labeled a "public menace." In any event, he had put all of this behind him and he now felt joyous and enthusiastic as an artist.

Arles in the background has a lovely blue-violet tint to it. Peaceful and calm. There are some red roofs out there but the yellow structure with a red roof, far in front of the silhouette of the town, makes a nice contrast to the quiet colors behind it. This is the town where, not too long ago, Vincent had seen *de la hargne et des huées*, as he called it, spite and outcry. But now, in the quiet and still moments of the orchard, he could relax and just paint to his heart's content. Maybe, just maybe, he was unintentionally putting symbolism into it with colors and placement of forms and objects such as the poplar trees. Are the trunks barriers to an open view of things? Are they some form of bars as we see in prison cells? Is the gnarled presence a symbol of old and tortured feelings on the part of the artist and on the part of some people who could not stand his presence? Is the orchard in bloom symbolic of a new spring and renewed life? Has Vincent's own convention of spatial continuity been broken here? I leave that to those who like to ponder symbolic meanings. I do think, though, that Monsieur Gauguin's influence remained with Vincent throughout the rest of his career as an artist, and that new ways of seeing things and expressing things were constants with him, but it did not change his style and his light and color concept. At least, I don't think so, as I reflect on it some twenty years later. The grace and beauty of nature is here in this painting. The total effect of the colors becomes a harmony of complementarities to the entire scheme of light and color. The blues, the violets, the purples, the greens with the whites, all lend themselves to the lullaby of soft harmony. Even the harsher purple of the tree trunks is in tune with the softer violet hues of the background. One thing that brightens up, *égayer la toile*, are the yellow-orange sprouting branches that give the trunks some life and the promise of springtime. But, even without the symbolism, it remains a bright spot on the canvas itself, I think. Vincent's **Orchard in Blossom with View of Arles** is a testimony to the artist's revived energy both physical and artistic that signals, once again, his vitality as a creative artist who delights in naturalness and the vibrant sun of Provence.

My father returned home for two whole days toward the end of April. He took advantage of the weekend. While he was here with us,

Vincent asked to paint his portrait. This would be the third time he would paint my father. He liked him because he sat still and was a good sitter who was always willing to pose for Vincent, unlike so many other people. As a matter of fact, he sat for Vincent three times while he was here. He didn't mind. He knew he was pleasing his good friend who needed friendship and consolation. I was glad to see both of them in company of each other while I watched. All three pictures are very similar to the first ones with the exception of the flowery background. I guess Vincent liked what he did with my mother's portrait and he decided to do the same with my father's. One has very similar flowers and green background with ovals, red dots and swirls, while one of the other two has a lighter green background with white daisies, poppies and blue flowers. The other has swirls and flowers. All three have my father in full uniform with his cap and the letters "POSTES" in the front. They're all done with the bust only, not full length. It's also the same frontal view with pretty much the same expression on my father's face, serene and content.

Vincent told my father, after he was finished with his paintings, that he was seriously considering going to an asylum for a while. He thought that it would do him good and that he was still afraid of falling back into his hallucinations with the buzzing in his head and ears. Worse, a relapse of inner fear and tension with the constant trepidation of violence and madness. That's what he was afraid of. He didn't want to lose his sanity and do harm to himself and to others. He admitted that he had not been feeling too well these past few weeks. But first, he wanted to discuss the *atelier* concept with my father. Should he shut it out of his mind permanently. Should he keep his options opened. After all, he had cleaned the yellow house up and put in a lot of effort and money to spruce it up, gas and all. That had cost him a pretty sou. All that was lost now. He admitted that he didn't have the heart to do start all over again. Then, he said that his brother had gotten married and he didn't want to be a burden on both Monsieur Théo and his wife, Johanna. What with new health problems stemming from old ones, he didn't think he could prevail anymore on his brother.

"It seems to me that it would be wise to commit myself somewhere where I could get the care I need without bothering others. I want my brother and his wife to live in peace without the constant worry of having me sick and off the rocker," he told my father.

"*Cher ami*," said my father in a low and reassuring voice, "you mustn't think of yourself as a menace. You're not mad. You're sick but not mad. That incident will not occur again."

"How do we know, though. Are you sure? Are you absolutely sure?"

"I am sure as much as I can be, knowing you and your potential to be well again. You have spiritual depth, Vincent. You can heal yourself, I know. You can find strength in your creative powers. Are you not sure of those anymore?"

Vincent looked at him and replied, "Thank God I have not lost them. But, I worry that they might be diminished by the constant aggravation of my mental state which is always in a flux, it seems."

"Then, perhaps a stay in an asylum for a while would do you good. It would relieve your pain of constant worry. What do you have to lose? Ask your brother if he thinks it's a good move. I know you don't want to bother him, now that he's married, but he'll find out about your situation soon enough, don't you think?"

"I don't know. I just don't know."

"Why don't you mention it to Pastor Salles then?"

"I think I might. He's a pretty stable and wise person, just like you."

My father seemed to blush.

"No, I'm not a wise person, just a common ordinary man who likes to give advice when it's needed. I'm only offering what little wisdom I have, that's all."

"Yes, you are wise indeed, very Socratic," replied Vincent.

When I was alone with Vincent, I asked him what Socratic meant. A new word for my notebook, I thought. He told me that it was a word after the great Greek philosopher, Socrates. That Socrates did not write a single word. All of his ideas and thoughts were in the form of dialogues he had with people around him. He never preached, he never told people what to do. He only helped them find the truth. So, Socratic means wise and a lover of truth.

"How did we get to know about him and his ideas if he never wrote a word?" I asked him.

"Good question," Vincent replied. "Although he never wrote down anything, his disciple, Plato, is the one who wrote about him and all of his ideas. You see, that's how we know about Socrates and why we teach his philosophy."

"What's philosophy?" I pursued.

"We don't have time for me to teach you about philosophy. Besides, I know very little about it. You'll learn philosophy when you're at the university later."

"I don't know if I'll ever get there. I have a mediocre mind, you know, and my grades are not that strong," I told him.

"Don't start with that again. You are intelligent and you can make it through the university some day. It's not like taking theology at a seminary, you know."

"But will I succeed? Will I be able to take courses that deal with abstractions and ideas?"

"That's precisely what philosophy is all about. When you get to that stage, you will have the capacity to deal with all of this. Your mind will have matured by then. If you can deal with words and ideas now, you can deal with philosophy later. Trust me."

As we walked back home, I told myself, well, my father is a philosopher, hey? Socratic? I rushed to my room and wrote "Socratic" in my notebook thinking that later I would write the definition down.

This time, my father told my mother that he was looking for a place in Marseille for us to live in. My mother told him that she wanted to look at it before he made a decision and he consented.

"Can I go too?" I asked.

My mother said, "We'll see."

We had our Sunday evening soup with Vincent early since my father was leaving on the 18:16 train. My father also told my mother that he was writing to Vincent's brother just to reassure him of Vincent's well-being and state of good physical health as well as his state of mind. He wanted to tell him that if there was anything he could do to help out, he would try to do everything in his power to do it. My father was a good person, a very good person. He would never abandon anybody, especially Vincent. After all, he was like family. That afternoon, father told Vincent that he had decided to stay permanently in Marseille and that the family would eventually follow him there. Vincent did not say a word.

Vincent's artistic vision began to change. I don't mean that he didn't see the same things or paint the same things. No. But, he saw and painted them in a more direct or closer way, like focusing on things more intently. I don't know how to put it really, but his paintings sought to bring reality closer to his eyes and to his consciousness. I

mean, he still painted the familiar and the common but in a very focused way like the two butterflies he painted. **Two White Butterflies** is
a very good example of focused painting. I was with him out in the
field when he spotted those butterflies. He stopped what he was painting and switched canvas.

"Butterflies wait for no one," he said, "not even painters."

This painting is an intense close-up of two small butterflies in a
patch of tall grass. It's like putting on a magnifying glass to paint.
There's no wide view nor scenery. He used to like going out there in an
open field and just paint everything. I don't mean everything in sight
because he did seek some focus, but it was a vast view, a view that ex-
panded to sky and skyline, mountains and hills, background of cities
and towns and vast as the artistic eye would allow. But now, it was
simply two butterflies in the grass up close. Not much color either. Just
the pale white of the butterflies and the greens of the grass. There is
some yellow and some black, just brushed in here and there. However,
the greens are well blended. It looks like tall grass growing wild and
flourishing. Any symbols in that? I don't know. All I know is that Vincent liked the two butterflies hovering there, playing and stealing his
attention. One thing for sure, Vincent, the artist, stopped in motion two
white butterflies that day. He painted them.

The yellow flowers painting is another one with a very focused and
close-up view. **A Field of Yellow Flowers** is a one-dimensional kind of
work. Everything, practically everything is yellow, flowers and grasses
with the exception of some black strokes here and there. There are a
few patches of sand color under the clumps of grass but overall the
work is yellow. That's what Vincent wanted and that's what he got. He
also painted, **Clumps of Grass**. It's yet another close-up work of one
color, green with black lines and some blue ones but very faint. What
can I say, it's grass from up close. Clumps of grass, very common and
very banal from people's viewpoint. At one point, I asked Vincent if
the "Clumps of Grass" was a still life. He told me it wasn't because it
was a natural setting, not a "dead" one. That's why in French we say,
nature morte. I found that out when I was learning English. Why don't
they say "dead nature," I wonder. I must say, however, that both paintings are not my favorites but who am I to tell Vincent what to paint. I
must admit though that the paintings are fresh and bright and will certainly figure in Vincent's vast collection of works as being different. I
prefer the vast landscapes, the wide and open space and the bright vivid

palette of colors that Vincent is so very good at painting. He must be sifting things out, I wrote in my notebook.

Well, things were moving here in Arles. What with the *atelier* closing for good and the "house of light" turned over to an unknown tenant, Vincent was now established in his new apartment. I saw it. It was small but comfortable. Madame Rey was nice but somewhat aloof since she realized that this was the artist who painted her son in a pose that still remained, for her, unacceptable, according to her standards. It's funny how some people react to such things. I'm sure she loved her son but it seems to me he was grown-up now and please, let him make his own choices and live his own life, please. She seemed to control his every move. She told him to do this, not to do that and so on. My mother was not like that with me or my brother. I would have gone nuts. I knew I was still very young then and needed supervision but not constant scrutiny. Doctor Rey was a professional. He was a kind, intelligent and responsible man. But, he was simply under his parents' thumb, I thought. Well, today as I recall all of this, I realize that, in France, mothers are domineering and children, even though they've grown up, daughters and sons, yes, sons too, stay close to their families and live with them even when they have reached full maturity. Only marriage separates them from home. I mean living there. That was my society for a very long time and still is today in 1911. Mothers and sons. What a cultural enigma. Will it ever change, I wonder.

Vincent's love for gardens can be seen in his painting, **The Courtyard of the Hospital at Arles**. I think it's a marvel of perspective. I know because Vincent taught me about perspective and how it works. He not only paints very well but draws marvelously well with a talented hand, but I've said that before. He learned perspective and taught himself by doing it over and over again. I know most artists know perspective and use it in their works, but with Vincent, it's a supreme art so well does he do it. He had seen the courtyard several times and its garden while he was at the hospital. He had liked the geometric design of it and, of course, the flowers and the shrubs. It was truly a respite from internment for him, being out in the garden like that. He didn't like to be "enclosed," as he put it. He liked the wide open spaces of the outdoors where one can breathe and wander at will.

The courtyard was all in bloom being late April. Vincent had already done a drawing of the courtyard in pencil, reed pen and brown ink on paper, but now he was doing it the full-blown way, all in color

on canvas. It was a beautiful and sunny day with just enough shade
hovering under the galleries. Vincent and I were spectators, it seems, to
a vast array of flowers, shrubs and trees.

He described it as such, "This is an antique garden in front of the
galleries with a pond in the middle and eight designed beds of forget-
me-nots, Christmas roses, anemones, Ranunculus, wallflowers, daisies
and so on. (He knew his flowers pretty well.) You can see that under
the gallery there are orange trees and oleander. Except for three heavy
black tree trunks that seem to move like serpents, see over there, and
four large bunches of dark shrubs in the foreground. It is a picture quite
full of flowers and spring green."

It was indeed a beautiful scene to paint. I sat there in gentle
amazement and watched him paint in the silence of the whispers of
colors.

The drawing is done from a different perspective than the painting.
The painting focuses on the galleries on the right, two levels, with
arches at the bottom and the yellow trim on white. A small wall separates that side with a tool shed in front of it. Then, there's another
gallery to the left but we only see part of it. There are people at both top
levels while at the bottom, the one on the right, there's a lone man
walking, probably a laborer. There is also a wide path that separates the
right gallery with the garden, and close to the tool shed, a nun in her
white apron, is frozen in time, walking. Vincent placed the tall large
tree trunk immediately to the forefront on the left and the other two
trunks are placed, one toward the right and the other slightly in the
middle toward the left gallery making a kind of triangle. I was taking
notes rapidly while Vincent was painting. In the front, stands four dark
green box shrubs and to the far right stands a rather tall bush with elongated palm-like leaves. The orange trees and the oleander are in big red
pots inside the right gallery.

Now, in the round pond, right in the middle of the courtyard, floats
some water lilies. All around the pond there are eight well-measured
little gardens with small paths separating them. That forms the large
outer circle. Vincent had a great time painting all of the brightly colored flowers, I'm sure. There's a lot of white, some red and some dark
color, probably deep purple, and a touch of orange. There are also
flowers that border all four sides of the inner pond gardens. In all, the
atmosphere is one of country delight and amazing geometric design.
The gardener must be a very versatile and artistic person always work-

ing to make this courtyard geometrically correct and bright with color and fresh with the fragrance of blooms. I liked what Vincent painted and I liked the courtyard garden. I could have stayed there all day but we had to go.

Since Pastor Salles had already talked to Vincent about a specific house where he could take refuge from his malady, some kind of asylum where he would be with people like him who suffer from psychological illnesses, and where he could go outdoor and paint, Vincent thought about it very seriously. As long as it's affordable, of course. It would have to be approved by Théo. This was the *Maison de Santé de Saint-Paul-de-Mausole* in Saint-Rémy-de-Provence, some twenty-four kilometers north of Arles. So, on April 29, holding a letter from Monsieur Théo in his pocket, Pastor Salles went to negotiate with the director of the asylum, Doctor Théophile Peyron, for Vincent's admittance there. To the great dismay of Vincent, the director was going to charge twenty-five francs per month more than Vincent had anticipated, and that he would not be allowed to paint outdoors. When Vincent told my father on his next visit home that he would be restricted more than he had thought and that the expenses would exceed his expectations, my father told him to try and negotiate some more with this Doctor Peyron. Vincent was losing hope of ever finding a suitable place where he could paint and have peace while being taken care of. He told my father that since his requests had been rejected, he was going to sign up for the Foreign Legion, at least, there he would be able to get out of Arles and its hold on him. My father told him that was a five-year commitment and to think about it seriously. In the end, he figured that he didn't really want to go far away and suffer the hardships of the Legion nor the loneliness of being away from friends. He would ultimately have to submit to whatever conditions Saint-Rémy would impose on him. What else could he do?

"Probably I would be better off if I did not exist at all, better off for my friends and my brother," he told my father sadly.

My father answered him, "Please don't say that, Vincent, don't ever say that. We all want you to live and prosper in your art and in your life. Your brother, who loves you more than anyone, needs you to live. Remember that and don't think of not existing. Not existing through violence, especially. That would be a serious injustice to yourself and to all of us who love you. Please don't get discouraged. They will help you and save you and your mind at the asylum. There's no doubt in my mind that you will be able to negotiate your painting outdoor with the director, once he sees your work. He'll see what kind of a genius you are. As for the expenses, talk to your brother, he may surprise you. He's always supported you, you know that."

"I know, I know," said Vincent. "You know deep down, I'm a very simple man with simple tastes. All I need is a glass of wine, some cheese, bread and a good pipe, that's all I really need to be happy. Not much, is it? And, of course, freedom to paint."

Vincent trusted my father's opinion and the fact that he was always good natured like a peasant is. That he always seemed happy and well grounded was a great comfort to Vincent. He told that to his brother in his next letter. He also told him that my father was like a father to him even though he wasn't old enough. He thought that my father was sincerely and tenderly worried about him and made him feel like he was saying to him, we don't know what will happen tomorrow but whatever the outcome, think of me.

And that made Vincent feel good, "Coming from a man who is neither sad nor bitter, nor perfect nor perfectly happy nor irreproachably just. However, he's a good man, a wise man, a man of feeling and a man of such tender belief in me," he told his brother, Théo.

My father also talked to Vincent about life and that, as one grows older, life is not considerably more pleasant. Yes, he talked to Vincent on a very personal level and Vincent believed him and trusted him. He was like an anchor in his volatile and pain-driven life. He didn't like being a martyr but fate had allotted him much mental suffering and pain and he tried to accept it without too much recoil from life itself.

"*Faut endurer, mon vieux*," my father told him, one must endure.

"I suppose I don't have a right to complain after what I've seen of other poor bastards," Vincent told my father.

Good news, Monsieur Théo wrote to Vincent and told him the price at Saint-Rémy was acceptable to him. Vincent had to go if it meant maintaining his health and sanity, he told him. He was going to wait until Pastor Salles was ready to take him, he told us. Yes, he was going to wait but not stand idle. He was going to paint. I told him that I didn't want to see him go but if he had to, then I would understand.

"Camille," he told me, "o*n ne fait pas tout ce que l'on veut dans la vie,*" one doesn't do everything he wants in life. "One must choose to live and create *malgré*, in spite of reversals and pitfalls."

I was getting to know that. In the meantime, Vincent painted. He painted peach trees in La Crau, a rosebush in bloom, red chestnuts, butterflies, pollard willows and an iris. He sure didn't stand idle. He kept busy and that was very good for him and for me. I hated to see him idle thinking and worrying about his sickness. That wasn't good.

My mother invited him, once in a while, to supper. She knew that it pleased him and me, especially. She also knew that Vincent was not going to be with us for quite some time. That we would be gone too. She cared about *son enfant perdu*, she really did. Vincent loved coming over and play with Marcelle. She was now crawling and babbling. She was nine months old and my mother told us that she would be walking soon. She was a precocious child, she said.

La Crau with Peach Trees in Blossom is a different type of painting for Vincent. It's so different, I thought. Different from the rest. It's all dapples of color instead of longer brush strokes. It's a sort of pointillism, Vincent told me.

"Remember what I told you about it with Seurat and Signac? They're dots of paint, some tiny some larger, but when well placed on the canvas, they appear as one big well-blended harmonious whole. It's all about complementary colors. Remember?"

"Yes, yes, I do now," I replied.

"Pointillism is a rather new movement and some have tried and succeeded while others have failed. I'm just a novice at it. Sometimes, one has to try new things, new techniques," he said. "Pointillism is not easy but when well done, its very pleasing to the eye. It's a challenge, alright. Consider working very close to the canvas and determining what color dots to put and where while remembering the complementary colors all the time. Not easy. What you wind up with is a dappled effect. Pissarro did a few of his paintings in a pointillist style but they didn't come out too well. People didn't like them. They did not reflect the true artist that he was, I'm sure."

It was a very beautiful late April day, cloudy but bright. We set out early in the morning. It was Sunday. When we got to the spot Vincent wanted, we set ourselves down and he prepared to paint the vista of the peach orchard in front of him. La Crau has such gorgeous vast open spaces. One can breathe there, as Vincent says. Not only breathe but create in and with nature. Vincent wanted to paint orchards before the blossoms fell to the ground, after all April was fast ending with May approaching in a day or so. I sat there contemplating the sky with the clouds high above us. Would it rain? We didn't think so. That's why we were here. The fresh smell of the grass and the delicate odor of the peach blossoms intermingled so as to put us in a delicious trance of odors combined with the transparency of light. I knew what Vincent was feeling at that very moment when he first applied paint to the canvas. Delicious harmony. I took out my notebook and started writing. *This is the day nature has made for us so that my friend can paint and I can write about it. This is the day I have decided to be totally dedicated to what my talents will allow me to be. Nothing else. This is the day I want to be, just be. I have learned many things from my friend the artist and I have stored them in my memory, thanks to you, good friend notebook. Thanks to nature for giving us this day full of the glory of light and color, full of words at my disposal, full of..........*I fell asleep in the warmth of the sun. When I woke up, I could see that Vincent had finished a good portion of the sky on his canvas. It was dappled, alright! Bits of blue and green with the white rendering the cloud formation. It was very intriguing to watch it up close, then further away. Vincent was right, it did come together. But how was he able to paint and make sense of it from up close?

The mountains in the background are a deep blue with the top of one, to the far right, painted with some white for the snow, I would say. Then comes the five houses with red roofs that he painted. All somewhat at a distance from each other. They're between the mountains and the orchard in the painting. Then, the main focus, the peach orchard all in bloom. Like powdered sugar or fresh fallen snow. There's a man crouching to pat his dog and right next to him stands a small tree with orange flowers to his right. I wonder what kind of flower it is. I'm not going to ask Vincent, I told myself, for fear of interrupting his concentration. Behind the man, there's a large blue cart with wheels and behind that is a pool of water. It must be part of the marshes. We can tell on the right of the orchard the blossoms have already begun to fall for we see pools of white petals on the ground. The ground under the peach trees is itself dappled with rich colors, blue, orange, green and some black. There's a center path. That's yellow. There's another one on the right and that's painted a dark orange with the white for the fallen blossoms. In front, there's a long fence painted primarily white, blue and orange. In front of that, there's some kind of a orangey ditch and green grasses with black tips on either side. Then finally, in the very up close foreground, there's the dapple of orange, blue and some white representing the open soil. It's a very exhilarating painting, I'd say. Exhilarating because it's spring and spring means new life and a new beginning. It can be seen also as a renewal for all of us, a renewal of constant new life that replaces the old. And, that's what I'm thinking of as I write about the painting of the peach orchard of La Crau. New life, new art style, new beginnings for Vincent, that's what I thought about back in Arles on that April day.

We walked back home late that afternoon. Vincent looked like a porcupine with all his art pack on his back and things sticking out here and there.

He had often told me that, "I look like a porcupine but I don't care since I'm the artist wanderer on the road and the road is free."

I asked Vincent to have late supper with us at home but he declined. I wondered why. He told me that he had something important to think about and that he was going to eat only some bread and cheese with some wine. And his pipe after eating, of course. I left him feeling a bit uneasy myself since I didn't know if he would be alright. He told me later that he was thinking about moving to the asylum and that it worried him somewhat since it would cost his brother a lot of money. That was besides the canvases and paints he had to pay for.

"Oh, I wish I could sell my paintings," he said. "I wish I could pay for things myself, what with poor Théo and a wife now. I don't want to bother you with my problems, Camille, but your father is away and I don't know where to turn to."

"That's alright, Vincent. I may not be able to help you too much but I'll listen," I told him.

"That's enough, Camille, just being here with me makes me feel wanted and heard. I need companionship, Camille, I need companions, especially when things get tough and I find myself so alone and isolated, and that's what I'm going to be at Saint-Rémy, isolated."

"Don't worry, my friend, I'll go visit you," I replied.

The next painting Vincent made was, **Rosebush in Blossom**. A simple rosebush filled with white roses. What is more simple yet more luxurious than roses. That's what Vincent wanted to paint. It's another close-up of a single subject painted in the brilliance of sunlight with simple colors and an artistic touch that is Vincent's. Roses are roses, I know, but when taken up close they become the focus of texture and fragrance. Everyone has seen, touched and smelled a rose before, I'm sure. What delicacy of touch and fragrance. How can an artist bring that to his canvas, I asked myself. When you glance at Vincent's painting you can practically smell the roses, so luscious are they. That's when all your senses come to play, even the ears, because you can hear the buzzing of bees around the roses even though they're not actually there. You can taste the rose petals because they're soft to the touch and taste when you put them in your mouth. Taste and touch. Of course, the sense of smell is brought in since its one of the essential senses in approaching roses. How can the painting bring you all of these sensations? Why? Because it's evocative. That was another word Vincent taught me. E-v-o-c-a-t-i-v-e, tending to call forth and bring into play something of the mind or senses.

The rosebush that he painted is a very large one. The roses are really white and pink not just plain white. It's a tall bush almost a climber. It's up close, very close so that you can almost touch it. In the background, we see other flowers, smaller and some just as tall. There are tall daisies and tall grasses to vary the scene. Closer to the bush, you have some larger leaves of yet another plant with some large yellow blossoms but the focus is the rosebush, as I've said. It's another of Vincent's attempt to bring him closer to his subject matter and derive from it the full sensual feeling of capturing beauty at hand. This is not a symbolic work, it's a fully realistic painting. It becomes symbolic if you try to impose symbolism on it like the rose as the symbol of love. That's too facile a representation and it's not the essence of the painting. Roses in a bush, that's all.

Finally, there's the single iris painting, **The Iris**. Another very simple work but a very expressive one, I think. Vincent loved irises. Witness the large patch of irises that he painted later at Saint-Rémy. Irises are tall flowers and masterfully made of curled-down large petals with bearded stripes running down in the center. Their color, or should I say colors, because they're made up of variegated colors, is not simply one uniform color. Take for instance, the purple or deep blue one that Vincent painted. If you look up close, you will find that there are many hues involved. They're delicately wrought as blossoms. Up close, one can see the fine coloration and the texture of the flower. Of course, from afar, they look uniform in color. Vincent's iris is of a deep purple-blue color. It rises on a tall stem all by itself since there's only one iris in the bed. The others are either wilted or have been cut. There's nothing less beautiful than a wilted and shrunken iris, I think. All shriveled up like a dead leaf. The large clump of sword-like bottom leaves open up like long green hands. The background is grass with some small yellow flowers interspersed here and there, so that you have a mixture of green and yellow. It's an appealing work, one that seems to taunt your glance into thinking that this lone and solitary flower standing there is representative of the artist himself since he's about to go away and be isolated once more. A solitary man but a valiant one like the sole iris that stands tall and is persistent in its flowering stage. A valiant blossom that was Vincent while living in Arles. And so, it is with a certain sense of nostalgia and accomplishment that I conclude Vincent Van Gogh's stay in Arles.

Arles-la-Japonaise, Arles, hantise de lumière et de couleurs, haunted by light and colors, *Arles, l'arlésienne séduisante,* temptress. A R L E S.

That's what I wrote in my notebook as a last entry for Arles, my city.

20

Asylum and Beyond

$\mathcal{C}$he word asylum has two fundamental meanings, one, the institutional facility for the care of the mentally sick and the other, a refuge, a sanctuary. I like the word asylum in regards to Vincent since both meanings can be applied in his case. He sought refuge from his haunting hallucinations, and sanctuary for his art and for himself(that's why he wanted so badly to establish his studio). He felt like a man pursued if not haunted by his own thoughts and feelings. As an institution, Saint-Rémy, where he sought help for his malady, was a place where he expected care and solace. Vincent was an alcoholic. He drank much too much, compounded by absinthe. That, he admitted to my father. He needed help that he never got. That's besides the other problems he had with his physical health as well as mental health. My father tried to explain it to me the best he could that Vincent was a sick man both in mind and body. Not that he was insane, no. He was a sick man. He needed plenty of help and that's why he committed himself at Saint-Rémy. It made sense to me. I so wanted him to get the help he needed, so that he would be able to be himself again and paint in the gloriously light-filled surroundings of Arles.

On May 8th, a Wednesday, I remember too well, Pastor Salles was ready to accompany Vincent to Saint-Rémy. It was a cloudy day. I was hoping that the sun would shine with its full brilliance for Vincent, but it didn't. Only a strained light came down from the sky and powdered the city of Arles with dots of light here and there. Vincent came to wish my mother farewell. My mouth and throat seemed paralyzed. I didn't know what to say or how to say it. I managed to plead with my mother to please allow me to escort Vincent to the train station.

"But, you're going to be late for school," and then, after a pause she said, "yes." That's all she said.

At the train station, there was Pastor Salles, Madame Ginoux and Madame Calfortin. No one else. The platform was bare. Vincent and Pastor Salles were taking the 8:17 train. I noted carefully in my notebook later on, that at 8:12 we saw the train at a distance. I could see the time on the large clock on the platform. I looked at Vincent and Vincent looked at me with sad eyes. I had tears inside me and they wouldn't come out. They weren't supposed to since I was holding them back and practically choking on them. I so wanted to show Vincent a happy face. Just for him. I tried hard to avoid his gaze. Then, we heard the roaring of the train followed by the whistle. Vincent extended his hand to me in a warm gesture, a hand I had seen many times with a brush, painting for hours on end. A sacred hand for me. I hesitated. I wanted much more. He knew it. Then I leapt towards him and hugged him the best I could. He felt stiff, at first, but then he hugged me fully and with restrained gratitude, I know because I felt it. Pastor Salles told him they had to leave. They boarded the train. Madame Ginoux and Madame Calfortin waved goodbye to them as I stood there very still. I had a big lump in my throat, I remember so well. It just would not go away. The train picked up speed and went away carrying my good friend, the artist, the creator of so many paintings and drawings. I, the witness to most of them, could only stand on the platform and wave goodbye. Little Camille, the companion adventurer to a man who loved stars and flowers. I looked up at the sky and the clouds were thinning. Light was making its fuller entry into the day of Vincent's departure for Saint-Rémy. Then, Madame Ginoux told me that I should be on my way to school. For me, it felt like a day that Daudet described in his story, "La Dernière classe." Like the pupil in the story, I would be late for class. My last lesson for learning from Vincent had gone by. The master was gone. I hurried to class. I was so glad that I did not have to deal with the rule governing the past participles that day. No lesson on the French language by my teacher today. Just a *dictée*. Good, I loved writing. But, no lesson either from Vincent on art, and no new words from him. However, I did learn a new one, a place called Saint-Rémy-de-Provence and the word *asile,* asylum. In class, in front of me, stood the blackboard, clean with no writing on it. I wanted to get up and write in big bold letters, not what Monsieur Hamel, the teacher in the story had written, VIVE LA FRANCE ! but VIVE VINCENT ! I simply stared at the board until Madame Hugonet called my name.

Vincent had told me that I could visit him sometimes with my father and I was anxious for my father to come home. He came home the following weekend but it was too soon to go to Saint-Rémy, he told me.

"Let Vincent settle in and then we'll see," he said.

I went to my room, closed the door and read. I didn't eat lunch. I wasn't hungry. My mother came in my room to convince me about eating with them, but I told her I wasn't hungry. Really. My father reassured me that next time we would definitely go and see Vincent. That afternoon I ate some cheese and bread. I was getting hungry. Would Vincent be alright there? Would he not be allowed to paint anymore? Would he be locked up for good? Would he lose his mind and forget me in time? Would I never get to see him anymore? Are they hiding things from me? What about my writing, would I lose the taste for it? I sure didn't feel like writing at that moment. What about my notebook, would I abandon it someday? All these questions and more trotted in my mind like a wild horse.

Pastor Salles told us that when they got to the asylum the director, Doctor Peyron, greeted them and took the certificate from Doctor Urpar that Vincent handed him, certifying his case. Pastor Salles told us that Vincent declared to the director that his mother's sister and other members of the family had had epilepsy. They would take that into consideration, he was told. The director then assured Pastor Salles that they would take very good care of Vincent and show him all the kindness possible. Then, they showed Vincent to his room. It had bars on the window. The door was made of metal and had a large lock. Pastor Salles stayed with Vincent until it was time to catch the train back to Arles. One thing, yes, Pastor Salles was told that the asylum had been, at one time, a cloister named, Saint-Paul-de-Mausole. It had been converted into a rest home, then a mental hospital. It was not the most joyful place but it suited Vincent's needs. Pastor Salles kept reassuring us that Vincent would definitely get well with time. That's what they had told him at the asylum. He even told that to Monsieur Théo in a letter. Monsieur Théo believed him.

Days went by and I was looking forward to summer vacation once again. It was June and the sun was bright and the weather very warm. Flowers everywhere made people happy to be alive and full of anticipation for the festivals and celebrations that summer brings. I was anxious. I was awaiting my father's next visit. He didn't get home before I finished school that month. I was exhausted just waiting, and I told him so.

"*Bien, mon petit Camille, il faut attendre pour tout dans la vie, tu sais,*" we have to wait for everything in life, he told me.

"I know, I know, but why wait so long?" I told him.

My father was home for two days and so he took advantage of that period of time to go to Saint-Rémy. We boarded the train early in the morning and headed north in the direction of Baux, which is on the same line as Saint-Rémy. We got there and hurried to get to the asylum. We wanted to see Vincent and how he was managing there. The director greeted us and called in Mère Épiphane, the mother superior of the asylum. She looked so solemn and being dressed all in black, I thought she was a jailer. She told us that only my father could visit Vincent in his room and that I would have to wait until he came down to talk to him in the private garden outside. So, I sat on the bench there in the hall and waited for them. It took several minutes, if not close to a half an hour, before they came down. When I saw Vincent, I yelled his name and immediately another nun came half running to tell me that it was "Silence ! Inside the asylum."

My father took me by the hand and led me outside. Vincent followed.

Once outside, we sat on the ridge of the pool. The little garden was filled with red flowers.

"Well, how have you been, Vincent?" I asked him.

"Fine, just fine," he answered. "How have you been, Camille?" he asked calmly.

"I've been anxious to see you," I said.

"Well, look at me. Don't you think I look fine?"

"Yes, but how is the painting coming along?" I ventured to ask.

"I just told your father that the director has granted my request to go outside and paint as long as I have a guardian with me. Isn't that great? I don't mind the guardian since he doesn't bother me at all. I even have spectators as I did in Arles. Patients mill around me when I paint and just watch, like you did, Camille. You know that I'm not committed here, I came here of my own free will. So, I have the freedom to do things on my own and that gives me great pleasure in not being restrained."

"How about the food and the place itself?" I asked.

"The food, well, is *comme-ci, comme-ça*. Sometimes it's tasteless and it smells moldy, but I manage. I'm not fussy, you know. The place in general is not too bad. I stay in my room and then go outside to paint when I want. That is my great solace."

Then, he turned to my father and said, "You know, Joseph, they give me a bath in a big tub twice a week for my therapy as a mental case, that's my treatment, very rudimentary."

"Do you get something out of it?" asked my father.

"It's soothing and I don't mind it. You know me, Joseph, I'm not hard to take care of."

"But how is it living here, Vincent?" inquired my father.

"Well, I'll tell you. It's not always very quiet on account of some the patients that are here. There are some very sick people. People who have severe mental problems, I'm sure. I hear howling most of the time, furious and painful to the ear and mind, but I call it *ma ménagerie*, my zoo, and tolerate it the best I can. After all, there are some here worst than me. I can't complain. Do you know what I cannot understand about these people here? It's their complete idleness. That gets to me. How can one remain idle all day long? Just doing absolutely nothing."

I listened and I cringed a bit inside of me.

"Listen," said my father, "can I bring you something the next time I come to see you, something you need?"

"No, just bring me your presence and your good cheer, that's all I want."

"How about paints and other stuff?" I added.

"No, Théo sends me what I need and they give it to me here."

"What about books?" I asked.

"Well, you can bring me Zola's "Germinal" when you come. I'd like to read it again. It reminds me so much of Le Borinage. I've just asked Théo to send me an edition of Shakespeare. I'd like to read *Richard II, Henry IV* and *Henry V*. You don't know Shakespeare, do you, Camille?"

"No, I don't, not yet."

"Well, someday you must read him. It's a must if you're going to be a writer."

My father looked at me with a somewhat inquisitive look.

Then, Vincent started to show us some of his paintings that he had done here at Saint-Rémy. There was one with large tree trunks covered with ivy, another one with irises, that one was a real nice one, another with a large moth called a death's-head moth, another with a huge lilac tree, another with a field of spring wheat and still another with a field of poppies, and finally one with cypress trees, and on and on. It all seemed to be a tremendous outpouring of creativity on his part. He said that he loved painting cypresses, especially when the wind was in them and they swayed back and forth. It was like the hand of infinity moving them, he said. I listened very intently when he started talking about his paintings. I felt I was back with him out in the fields watching him paint.

"I'm now in the process of conceiving a big canvas on which I will paint the stars at night. I see them from my cell window at night and they are glorious," he said.

"Just like the starry night at the café?" I asked him.

"No, much better, Camille. The stars here seem much brighter only because there are no other lights to dim their brilliance. There's movement in them, yes, I see movement like they're swishing about in the dark of night. I tell you, I'm going to paint what I see and what's in my head. I'm not crazy," he stated emphatically with fire in his blue-greenish eyes.

That's the Vincent that I know, that's the Vincent I admire so, I thought to myself.

"No, you are certainly not mad, Vincent," replied my father. "You are in your full capacity as an artist. You see things other people do not see because you're an artist. An artist of genius. I've said that before."

"And geniuses are crazy sometimes," said Vincent.

"No at all," said my father, "it's a wise and good craziness."

"You, Joseph, are the one who is wise, like Socrates and I've said it before." They both started laughing. It was good to hear that laughter.

The reader may be wondering why I'm bothering with Saint-Rémy when this work deals essentially with Arles. "The Boy with the Blue Cap----Van Gogh in Arles," is the title after all. Well, Vincent did go back to Arles while he was interned at Saint-Rémy and so there is continuity there. He even spent several days in Arles while in the care of the asylum. And, Vincent returned to Arles once he was released from Saint-Rémy. That's why I'm including Saint-Rémy. Vincent spent many days, more than days, months, almost a full year at this asylum, oftentimes painting. Besides, some of Vincent's best paintings were done at Saint-Rémy, like "Starry Night," "Irises" and "The Watch." Furthermore, my father and I came to visit Vincent at Saint-Rémy on several occasions. Another segment of the continuity with Arles. That's why.

The conception of "starry night" became an obsession with Vincent. It preoccupied him incessantly. The image of the heavens and the infinite tormented him, he said. Just like the "Night Café", he was intrigued, no captivated, by the stars and the mystique of nighttime.

"I'm going to capture the stars in the heavens at night when they're at their finest point of revealing to me the awe of infinity," he told us.

There goes infinity again. Will he ever get it out of his system? I thought out loud.

"What did you say, Camille?"

"Oh, nothing, it's really nothing. I was just thinking out loud."

He had mentioned the painting about the stars to my father and I when we had last seen him in Arles. I remembered. We left Saint-Rémy relieved that Vincent was well and in full control of his capacities for painting.

It was now early July, the month had just started, and I could not wait for my father to take me to Saint-Rémy again. However, I didn't have to wait for my father. Vincent came himself to Arles on the 6th. What a surprise. He had gotten permission to leave Saint-Rémy and spend the day in Arles to retrieve some of his paintings that he had left behind to dry. Imagine, Vincent home again.

Vincent could not get together with Pastor Salles and Doctor Rey since the pastor was on vacation and Doctor Rey was away. He had come down to Arles accompanied by his guardian, Monsieur Trabuc. Monsieur Trabuc cast an interesting figure, said Vincent. He had the face of an old Spanish nobleman. A veritable type of the Midi, he said. Charles-Elzéard Trabuc was sixty years old and was the chief attendant at the asylum. He was also a local farmer and Vincent, quite often, spoke to his wife, Jeanne, when he happened to be behind their house painting olive trees. She once told him that she didn't think he was ill. That he appeared to her to be perfectly sane. That had pleased him immensely.

Since Vincent was not able to spend the day with either the pastor or the doctor, he went to Madame Ginoux's house and spent time there. I happened to be there since I was helping her fold towels for the café. She was happy to see him and so was I. We had a long chat about his paintings and Madame Ginoux and Monsieur Ginoux talked about the café and their clients, many of which Vincent knew. Madame Ginoux served us refreshments. Monsieur Trabuc only took a glass of cassis. I had *un petit gâteau* and some kind of lemon drink. Vincent told us that he had gotten a letter from his sister-in-law, Jo, telling him that she was expecting a child. Both Monsieur Théo and Vincent were very happy about the news.

"If it's a boy, Théo and Jo want to name him after me, Vincent. They also want me to be godfather to the child. I told them not right now, not until I get out of the asylum. I'm going to be an uncle, Camille."

I told him that I was excited for him and that he did have family now and it was growing. He said that this news, not only delighted him, but gave him back his sense of belonging and being wanted. Vincent went back to the apartment and got some paintings that he wanted and then he and Monsieur Trabuc left on the 18:13 train for Saint-Rémy. I went to the train station to see them off.

Before leaving, Vincent told me, "Here's a little present for your birthday which is coming up soon," and he handed me a scroll of some type.

I thanked him and as he got ready to board, he said, "Oh, by the way, I finished my painting."

I said, "Which one?" and he pointed to the scroll in my hand and got on the train.

I stayed there on the platform gladdened by Vincent's presence here that day but somewhat sad that he had to go back to that place. I took the scroll and unrolled it. It was a drawing. A beautiful drawing of what he had been wanting to paint for a very long time, "Starry Night," except under his signature he had written "INFINITY 89." There was a note attached to it, "When you come and see me, I'll show you the painting." I went back home and placed the drawing in my chest with the others. I now had a collection of drawings, five by Vincent and one by Monsieur Gauguin. To this day, I have them all and every time I think of the stars and infinity, I look at Vincent's drawing that he gave me that day on the platform. It's very special to me.

My father announced to us that the entire family was moving to Marseille in September. I felt like I was going to be torn away from my city of Arles. Not that I didn't want to go to Marseille and be with my father, but I would never again be able to join Vincent in his painting adventures, as I called them. I doubted that I would go too often to Saint-Rémy to visit Vincent either. My father did tell me that he had written to Vincent and that he was coming along fine and thought that he could move back to Arles in a few months time. He's coming back to Arles and I'm moving away, I thought to myself. What about my notebook and my notes? Actually, I was now on my third notebook and, from that day on, I decided that since I wasn't going to be near Vincent and witness his work, I was going to turn my notebook into a journal.

July 10, 1889-----Today is my twelfth birthday. We had a small party at home outside. Madame Ginoux brought a *tarte aux abricots*. I love apricots. Vincent was not here, of course. My mother thinks that he will get better and might come to Marseille later to visit all of us. I was very glad that my birthday did turn out well after all.

We hadn't heard from Vincent for weeks. I wondered what had happened to him. My father was anxious about him too. It was the eve of la Bastille and my father had come home the night before. We were going to Saint-Rémy that day to see what was happening at the asylum. Did Vincent have a relapse? Was he alright? Why didn't they tell us if he was sick again? I'm sure my father had the same questions. This sickness of his sure kept us in suspense. His brother must have felt the same way. Madame Ginoux always said the same thing, about Vincent, it takes time. I wondered how long? Would he be like that the rest of his life?

We took the train and got there by mid-morning. The director told us that Vincent was well and that he had been very busy painting. That relieved both of us. My father asked to see Vincent. He came down and greeted us with the same good humor as before.

"We haven't heard from you or about you in several weeks," said my father.

"Oh, I've been busy and I didn't want to bother you too often. You see, I feel an attack coming on and I don't want anybody around when it hits me. I never know when it's going to happen. So, it's better if I don't see anybody, that way I embarrass no one."

"It's not a matter of embarrassment, Vincent. We're friends. Does it happen often?" asked my father.

"Not too often now, but I never know, I never know. It's best to be on guard. You see, I can feel an attack coming when I get tense and my hand is cold and my fist is clenched. Then, I feel like I'm going to hurl things and everything seems twisted and bent. I start seeing double. My ears start to buzz and my head feels very heavy. I want to scream. When my legs let go, then I know that I'm having an attack. So you see, I'm getting used to warning signs and I know that it's going to happen soon. I don't feel that way now, but I expect to get one any day now. I feel it in my very bones and deep down in my guts. Well, let's not get all upset over this. You're here and I want to enjoy your company. Camille, let's go take a look at my paintings and my 'Starry Night.' "

"Where are they?" I asked.

"Upstairs."

"But, Mère Épiphane doesn't want me to go up to your room," I said.

"I'm going to talk to her and we'll see," he said.

The three of us went upstairs and Vincent went to see the Mother Superior.

"Children are not permitted inside the patients' rooms," she insisted. "I've told you that before. I've even told the boy and his father," she said.

"Mais, Mère, Camille n'est pas un enfant," he's not a child, he told her with deep respect in his voice.

"Quel âge as-tu, mon garçon?" she asked me. How old are you?

"Douze ans, Mère." I said with feint maturity. Twelve.

"Je suppose que je pourrais te laisser y aller juste pour aujourd'hui si tu es bien sage." If you're really nice I guess I could let you go just for today, she told me condescendingly.

My eyes were pleading with her. Finally, she said, yes, and I was allowed to go to Vincent's room. The room was small and full of Vincent's paintings. There was only one window in his room, one with bars on it. I could see a garden and a large field outside almost as far as the eye could see. Vincent told me that it was from there that he could see the stars at night and painted his **Starry Night** from that vantage point. He could not go outside to paint, not at nighttime. He had to imagine things but that was alright since he had learned from Monsieur Gauguin how to apply his imagination to his art.

"Voilà !" he said and presented us with his painting of the whirling stars.

"Wow !" I said. "So, this is the famous painting you've been thinking about for months."

"Yes. This is my infinity painting and you know what I mean by that, don't you?"

My father did not say a word. I would explain it to him later. It was a masterful work of art. It was simply mind blowing. My father stared at it as if in an ignorant daze. The painting was nothing like Vincent had painted before. Sure, he had done "Night Café" and I was there, and he had done "Starry Night over the Rhône" too, but this, Oh, my!

The lines undulate and rise up to the skies almost like serpents. It's nighttime but it's not really dark. The stars have been transformed into giant swirls of light with movement within their very core. One can see constellations in a vertiginous movement of whirlwinds as if the mistral had taken shape in the stars. Even the moon's crescent is caught up in this whirling movement. I can see it on the right. It's a mystifying moon. Vincent told us that the church spire and the town painted here is not what he could see outside his window, as a matter of fact, it wasn't there at all. They are there out of some moment of memory.

"It's the combination of my imagination and memory at work here. When I express my imagination in symbolic colors and abstract lines as seen here, then I can give nature a mystical outlook. That's where infinity comes in, you see. The entire harmonious movement that you see here is not only visually artistic but visually spiritual. Spiritual with the recognition that I sense there's something beyond the stars, something mystical and other-worldly, but I cannot explain it in words, only in my art. When I think of Genesis in the Bible, I think of the Creator creating the movement of the constellations. Everything in Creation has movement, otherwise it would have been creatively static. Look at my painting and tell me that it's static. It's not. It's because it resonates with the Creator's touch. I too create, Camille. I create to imitate movement in life and nature."

I looked at him and he looked deeply into my eyes as if he was boring into my very soul.

"You don't know the American poet, Walt Whitman, but he would know what I mean. He's written words that resonate with me. He's a true poet. A poet of transcendance. You should learn from him, Camille. He's got words and ideas that will blow your mind, especially when he speaks about heaven and the Creator. Under that great starlit vault of heaven a something exists that one can only call the Great Creator of movement with eternity in its place above the world. That's what he infers in some of his poems. I can truly relate to him, this Whitman. You need to read his 'Prayer of Columbus' in which he talks about 'Heavens whispering to me' and 'Hemispheres rounded and tied, the unknown to the known.' That's what he has Columbus say when he's old and looking back at his troubles and doubts on his distant voyages. Columbus, *c'est moi*, it's me. I may have my moments of madness, that's my sickness. But, I'm not mad. Am I mad, Joseph?"

Before my father could answer him, he continued, "My madness is being creative with the talents I have. That's my madness, for you see I'm lucid. I know what I am doing and what I believe in. People do not always understand this."

My father responded to him by saying, "You're not mad, my friend, but you do have long moments when your sickness takes over you and you become incapacitated. You can't do what your troubled mind won't allow you to do. That's the problem. It's the sickness, that terrible sickness, that takes over and you have to be on your guard and let others help you. That's why you're here."

"I know, Joseph, I know," replied Vincent. "My painting, do you like it? Infinity exists, Camille, but not in a concrete, palpable way. It's in the stars. This painting is by far the epitome of what I mean by significance."

My father kept looking at the painting and nodding his head.

"Being here at Saint-Rémy has allowed me to contemplate, not only the stars, but nature and the cosmos and I can now that much more identify with them." And raising his voice he said, "I need to paint the stars!" and it resounded in and through the hallway.

At that point, Mère Épiphane came into the room and asked *"Qu'est-ce qu'il se passe?"* what's happening here?

"Rien, ma Mère, nous contemplons ma peinture, 'La Nuit Étoilée'," we're simply looking at my painting, he responded.

"Et bien, faites-le plus calmement," do it more calmly, she said, then left.

There was a long moment of silence before my father said in a low voice, "How does she like your paintings, Vincent?"

"Oh, she doesn't like them very much. I overheard Mère Épiphane telling one of the sisters, one day, that my paintings resembled *'des pompons de peinture ou des pâtés d'hirondelles.'* Can you imagine that? Pompons of paint or swallows' blots. She doesn't like the thickness of the colors, I suppose. But, that's me and the way I paint. However, she was going to ask me to paint something for their recreation room but the other nuns were opposed to it. So, I never did get her to ask me to paint one for her. Strange lady but kind."

I was still very much overwhelmed by "Starry Night" and somewhat confused by Vincent's explanations since they were too deep for me. I took notes anyway while he was talking. I even asked him to spell W-h-i-t-m-a-n for me since it was in English. It's much later on, when I had grown to a maturity when understanding gets into its proper focus, that I was able to grasp Vincent's words and meaning about the painting. Although, I'm still struggling with infinity.

July 31, 1889------My baby sister Marcelle's first birthday today. She started walking yesterday. Calendau's grandmother died the day before yesterday. I told him I was sorry.

August 10, 1889----Have not heard from Vincent. My mother says that I need to get out more instead of reading in my room. I know. It's terribly warm outdoors.

August 24, 1889-----My father came home today. Tomorrow is Sunday and we're all going on a picnic at Fontvieille. Good. I want to see the windmill. My father got a letter from Vincent and he's doing better. Apparently, he's been very sick. I wish I could go see him. I wonder if he's painting.

Weeks and weeks went by and we got no word from Vincent nor about his condition since his last letter to my father. We didn't get to see Pastor Salles either until we were ready to move to Marseille. It was early September and I had already said goodbye to my friends, Blàsi, Anfos, Milou and Calendou. I even said goodbye to Jeanne Calment when I was at her father's store. She was nice to me and did not ask about Vincent. All the neighbors came to wish us well. Madame and Monsieur Ginoux, Madame Calfortin, Madame Flourènço, Madame Génélard and her husband, Madame Tavan and Madame Gaspardin with her son, Ervé, all came to our house to bring us gifts of farewell. Doctor Rey was away in Paris.

When Pastor Salles finally came to our house the afternoon before we left, he told us that he had seen Vincent and that he had had a very bad spell. He was just getting over it. Vincent shouted all kinds of things, the director told him, and he had a high fever. He had to be locked up in his room. He wanted desperately to paint and kept saying that he needed to be out there painting in utter freedom, to see other people, other sights that, after all, he wasn't a prisoner. He had committed himself to the asylum, not the other way round, he kept insisting. Then, he fell into depression and his reason became impaired. "Over here, it's dead, *c'est mort*" Vincent shouted until they calmed him down. That's what the director reported to Pastor Salles.

"So you see, my friends, he's not ready to see anyone soon."

I went to my room and felt bad in my stomach and refused to have supper that night. My mother tried to make me eat but I said I could not eat anything at all. She left me alone after that.

My father wanted to postpone our departure for Marseille but my mother told him that we were all prepared and our trunks were ready and everything was waiting for us. Besides, we already had our train tickets. He relented and told my mother that he would be back in Arles to check on things and then go see Vincent at Saint-Rémy.

"What things?" my mother asked.

"Things," he said.

"Can I come with you?" I asked.

He simply said, "We'll see."

My mother just looked at him and began to pack a lunch for the train ride. The ride wasn't too long but I kept hoping all along that it would be much longer because I didn't want to arrive in a place I didn't know. Why move when we we're happy in Arles? Why not stay a while longer? Where were we going to stay? Who were going to be our friends now that we lost the ones we had in Arles? Was Marseille a friendly city?

Marseille was a much bigger city than Arles. Huge with a lot more people. It had many districts with the Vieux Port where all streets end. You could hear the cries of fishmongers, smell the sea air, and there stood, on top of the hill, Notre-Dame-de-la-Garde with its tall belfry and its huge gilded statue of the Virgin. There was also the old Panier district. Then, the restaurants, cafés, bars, and many more establishments. One could easily get lost in Marseille. It was not like Arles at all.

"*C'est comme des fourmis,*" it's like ants marching, said my mother after she had seen Marseille for the first time.

My father tried to reassure all of us that we would eventually get used to the city. Armand thought that the move was a fantastic one.

"We can move around here and do things. Not like Arles where you feel confined. And, the lovely Marseillaises, how many of them," said Armand.

I found Marseille strange and not too friendly. However, it was a new adventure and I would try to adapt. At least, my father would be home every night. Later, my father and my mother would talk about retiring in Lambesc when the two of them grew old, back to where we grew up, said my parents.

Pastor Salles wrote to my father that he had gone to see Vincent and that he was getting out of his torpor and hallucinations. But, he was in a bad humor that day he saw him on account he could not see why he should have to ask a bunch of doctors' permission to paint. That was *imbécile*, he said. But, he has found some serenity in his daily life here at Saint-Rémy, the director told Pastor Salles. He was painting again from morning 'til night. In spite of his frailty and pale color, he was eating much better and feeling energetic. Pastor Salles thought that Vincent would enjoy a visit from my father if he found it possible. My father told my mother that he was going to Saint-Rémy to settle things with Vincent.

"What things?" she asked.

"I want to know how he's really doing, if he's really well or not. I don't want to hear about him second hand. I owe it to him. I'm leaving next Sunday and I'm taking Camille with me."

My mother did not say a word. She didn't ask about "things." I felt so terribly happy inside that I asked my mother to prepare a good lunch for us and Vincent when we did go to Saint-Rémy and settle things.

We left Marseille on the 7:24 train and got to Saint-Rémy in an hour and fifty-two minutes. The train stopped twice only to admit other passengers. My father and I talked, then I read. My mother had packed a good size lunch and we thought we would have a picnic with Vincent. It was still mild outdoors and early October was a comfortable time of the year in Provence. When we got there, we greeted Vincent warmly and obtained permission from both the director and Mère Épiphane to have a picnic in the garden. Mère Épiphane was even very cordial with us that day. She no longer seemed like a jailer to me. We sat outdoors and Vincent seemed serene and happy, certainly happy to see us again. He told us that he loved this time of year at Saint-Rémy when the colors of autumn are just splendid.

He had just written to his brother how much he enjoyed nature in autumn: "The green skies contrasting with the yellow, orange and green vegetation as well as the terrains of all kinds of violet colors, the burnt grass where the rainfall has given a renewed if not final vigor to certain plants that start once again to produce tiny violet, pink, blue, yellow flowers stir my imagination," he wrote.

He didn't like winter at all and dreaded the oncoming of the cold weather and all of the misery it brings, but he avoided the subject and stuck to the balmy quality of autumn in Provence. We had a great time there on the grass eating our lunch. Vincent enjoyed the food that, he said, was far superior to the food at the asylum.

"*Comme des bouchées d'étoiles*, he said, like a mouthful of stars.

Vincent invited us to his room to look at some of his paintings. My father knew that this would please me very much. I took out my notebook and waited for Vincent to show us his work. He was so proud to have someone with whom he could talk about his art, although my father and I were not great connoisseurs. At least, we were receptive to Vincent's efforts in painting whatever he wanted to paint and have the consolation that someone was listening to him, really listening. First he showed us **Wheat Field with Cypresses** that he had just done. Then he displayed for us an entire series of peasant workers: the pinner, the reaper, the thresher, the sheaf-binder, the sheep shearer and the reaper with sickle. He even had a painting of a woman with a baby in her arms that, he said, represented the seaman' s wife waiting by the fire. He was back to imitating Millet again. "Wheat Field with Cypresses" reveals how much Vincent was into his new surroundings. Cypresses became one of his favorite trees what with their pointed height swaying in the wind.

In this painting, we see two dark green cypresses on the right. There are some rocks and a few bushes of a different green. The part of the wheat field that we see is yellow and swaying in the breeze. For the background, he painted the blue of the mountains, but what draws your attention is the sky. The green sky with its white and blue clouds. They're big and puffy clouds seemingly rolling with the movement of the light of the sun. There's stillness in this work but a stillness that's not only serene but also agitated by the rolling clouds. The color effect overall is calm due to the pervasiveness of the soft blue and green colors. Did Vincent find a renewed calm with this work? I think so. He needed it. He had learned to suffer without complaint, he told us.

In **Wheat Field Behind Saint-Paul Hospital with a Reaper,** Vincent returns to the warm colors of the yellow and the fiery red. The whole canvas seems to shimmer with heat. The stone wall with the house behind it and the other small house on the hill are absorbed by the intensity of the other colors so pale are they. Even the sky with its bright yellow sun blends into this composition of yellows and red. The reaper is only a small part of the scene but an important one since Vincent recognized the role of the reaper as final cutter and gatherer, I'm sure. Vincent wanted to show us more of his works but my father insisted that he rest since he was showing signs of weakness. He looked tired. Besides, we had to leave for Marseille shortly. We said our good-byes. Vincent invited us back. Winter is a long season, he said, and he so desired to see it pass by fast. My father promised him that we would return probably before the holidays. "Make it sooner," said Vincent.

We learned later that Vincent had permission to return to Arles in early November. He wanted to go there to visit Pastor Salles and some of his other friends. He spent two full days in Arles, we were told by Madame Ginoux. While there, he found out that there were trains that went from Arles to Paris for only twenty-five francs and he suddenly had the strong desire to be on board on one of those trains. But, he didn't go. Not yet, he said. He went back to Saint-Rémy and threw himself into his work voraciously, said the director.

Well, we did not go back to Saint-Rémy before the holidays. I'm sure Vincent was very disappointed but he did not say so in his letter to my father at Christmastime. I mailed him a card that I had drawn myself and enclosed it in a small gift that I considered to be a gift for New Year's. I knew that maybe he would not get it before then. It was a pair of woolen socks that Madame Calfortin had knitted for him. She wanted me to send them to him. She knew that the asylum had to be cold in winter and these socks would keep him warm.

Winter that year was cold, extremely cold and windy what with the mistral blowing cold winds that ripped right through you. We felt it in Marseille, so Vincent must have felt the winds in Saint-Rémy. Madame Ginoux and Madame Calfortin wore extra layers of woolen clothing that winter, they told my mother in a letter Madame Ginoux had sent her. I went to school every day not cutting any classes and I was beginning to like our teacher, Monsieur Latourelle, since he assigned us a lot of reading and explained the lessons well. I enjoyed the books he assigned to us, Flaubert's "*Trois Contes*" (I had already read *Un coeur simple*, as you know), Balzac's "*Eugénie Grandet*," Sand's "*La Petite Fadette*," Fromentin's "*Dominique*" and a new writer that teachers did not usually assign because he was controversial, Rimbaud's "*Une Saison en enfer.*" Our teacher told us that he chose Rimbaud because he was very good with words as a poet and if our parents objected to our reading his poem, then he would excuse the ones whose parents objected to the reading. Mine did not. Besides, they trusted the teacher and they trusted me in all of my reading selections. I did not read trash, they knew that. Not for a young man wishing to become a writer.

The holidays went by and we enjoyed our first Christmas and New Year's in Marseille. Some of our relatives came to be with us for the Christmas dinner. My uncle, Marius, and my aunt, Marioto, my uncle,

Roumié, and my aunt, Berenguiero, came as well as my cousins from Pélissane. I got some books from my uncle, Marius, this time. No toys. He said that I was getting too old for child's toys. He did give me, however, a globe of the world knowing my interest in travel. I was very pleased with my gifts. My parents gave me some clothes that I needed. I had been told that they were not going to spend money on something I didn't need since they had to be careful with their money. I knew that. They did buy my baby sister a small doll, one you can bend its arms and legs. My brother, Armand, got a pipe that he had been wanting. My mother got a box of white linen handkerchiefs from aunt, Marioto. As for my father, well, he was simply happy to have all of us with him at holiday time.

"I don't need things," he said, "just good company and a glass of wine."

That was my father.

We were marking Candlemas on our calendar when my father said that it was time to go and visit Vincent at the asylum.

"Don't you think February is too cold a month to go to Saint-Rémy?" my mother asked.

"I don't think so," answered my father. "Not in Provence. February is usually nice. Besides, we'll dress warmly."

I realized that the "we" included me. I had so very much thought about Vincent during the holidays, how alone he must have felt having no one, no family to be with him. I only wished he had his brother with him now and then.

"Why don't you come with us?" asked my father to my mother.

"Who's going to take care of Marcelle?" she replied.

"You can ask someone in the neighborhood," he said.

"A stranger? I don't want to entrust my child to a stranger."

"But, you know some of the people already."

"I don't know them well enough," she insisted. "*Allez-y vous deux,*" go you two, she told us with a swish of the hand.

So we went.

We took the train and we got to the asylum by mid-morning since the train wasn't full and it did not make any stops. My father talked to the director, Doctor Peyron, and he told him that he had been concerned about Vincent since he had not heard from him at all, not even a letter.

"Well, Monsieur Roulin," he said, "I have to tell you that Monsieur Van Gogh has had a bad time of it these last two months. It's been cold

and he doesn't tolerate the cold too well. But, he's well now. Why, he'
even painting outdoors nowadays. He loves the white frost and the fo;
on the land, he said. He's been painting the olive trees, the cypresse
and the mountains. So you see, he's been quite busy."

My father asked to see Vincent. The director asked one of Mèr«
Épiphane's assistants to lead us to Vincent's room. No questions wer«
asked about my age. We climbed the stairs and saw that Vincent's doo«
was ajar and he was touching up one of his paintings. He was surprise«
to see us. He begged us to sit down and we talked. He looked cold. H«
was wearing a blanket around his shoulders. I could see that he wa
also wearing his woolen socks. I was glad.

"I get cold but I insist on going outdoors to paint. *Je ne veux pas m«
renfermer dans lo cabano, comme vous le dites ici en Provence,*"
don't want to shut myself in a *cabano* as you say here in Provence, h«
said.

"How are you, Vincent? How are you, really?" asked my fathe«
with a slight tremor in his voice.

"I feel fine," he replied. "I take it as it comes. Sometimes, it come:
hard and fast and I just feel like I'm in a whirlwind, and other times 1
don't remember a thing. But, I always know that my work as an artist is
there to save me. It is my salvation, you know."

My father looked at him and shaking his head he told Vincent,
"You must not push this thing too far, this malady that drives you. I tell
you Vincent, you don't know what it will do to you. This monster inside. Don't push yourself. You must rest and get yourself together or
else you'll fall apart. Do they take good care of you here?"

"Don't worry so about me, Joseph. I know that I worry you as I worry
my brother, but I will overcome this *bête*, this thing in my head. I must."

I sat there with my eyes glued on Vincent. I didn't want to interrupt
him.

"By the way, I'm an uncle. Théo wrote to me last week that Jo had
had her baby. Vincent-Willem will be his name. I wish they had chosen
another name for such a tiny innocent child. He doesn't need my bag-
gage. My mother wanted them to name him Theodorus after my
father."

He invited us to share his hot broth with him but my father refused.
"Come then, take a look at my latest," as he pointed to his paintings.

This one is a take on Millet's style and peasant subject. **Evening:
The Watch** is a tender moment in the lives of a young couple. As a

subject for a painting, it's touching. The seated couple is watching their child sleeping while the wife is sewing and the husband is doing some basket weaving. The light comes from a gaslight hanging from the ceiling. It's like one of Vincent's stars with a vibrating halo around it. It gives the entire work a soft shimmering effect. Light comes from the hearth also and that's what throws the dark red light on the man's back while the woman is bathed in the brighter light of the gaslight. I know there's probably some kind of symbolism here but, as Vincent told me before, don't impose symbols when they're not there. I just take it as I see it, two peasants resting and watching a sleeping child. It's certainly a testimony to the affection Vincent had for children and for the tender moments of parenting.

The colors with the light thrown from above and sideways are what fascinated me. The bluish-green shadows on the floor and on the woman's left side contrast well with the reddish shadows. The child in bed is surrounded by a halo of white light perhaps representing innocence. Perhaps. Oh, I could not help notice the black and white cat sitting on the front stones of the hearth. Quietude, serenity and tender light abide here on the watch.

My father looked and looked at this painting and finally told Vincent, "This is one of your finest work dealing with peasants. It's real, it's what poor people do. It's young family life. There's a certain reverence that glows here. It holds you like a vision of soft light in a home where contentment lives. I really like it."

"That's what I wanted to capture, Joseph."

The second painting Vincent showed us was, **The First Step**. It's another take on Millet and it's another couple with a child. This time it's a little girl who's taking her first step in her father's garden as he is on one knee extending his arms to her. The mother is holding her with her two hands on the back of the child guiding her very first steps. We can almost see the little girl advancing ever slowly one step at a time, sometimes faltering, sometimes half-running as very young children do as they take their first steps. The first step is precious to parents. It was to mine when Marcelle learned how to walk. The dark bronzed complexion of both parents reminds one that these are peasants who spend much of their time out in the sun. The father has been planting seedlings in his garden and he has left the spade fall to the ground when he perceived his young child. What glee to both of them to experience the joy of walking on the part of their child. The little girl is wearing a

white bonnet and a white-pinkish dress while the mother wears a long
blue dress. This matches the blue work clothes that the husband has on.
Of course, he's wearing the much-needed straw hat on account of the
bright sun. There's a wheelbarrow behind him telling us he's been hard
at work gardening. The serenity of the scene is enhanced by the white
mas that has a flowering fruit tree on the right side of it casting light
blue shade on the cottage. The yellow-flowering bushes on the side of
the fence make for added brightness of color. The blue of the sky is
barely visible and the light is filtered through the clouds. However, the
garden is in full view and bathes in that special light of morning. The
yellow, white and green of the garden add to the springtime quality of
the painting. It's a vibrant work while maintaining it's soft elegance of
a quiet moment of the day rendered precious because a little child is
taking her first step. A moment of tender infinity, as Vincent would
say. I remember Vincent telling me that he could see infinity in a
child's eyes when he gazed into them. I'm sure he did.

The third painting Vincent showed us was, **Noon: Rest from
Work**. This was another in a series of imitation of Millet. It's a painting like the other two taken from memory and his imagination. I think
that Monsieur Gauguin would have been proud of Vincent with these
paintings, although Monsieur Gauguin didn't like Millet too much,
Millet and his romanticized impressionist dreams, he called his paintings. This painting reminds me of a day out in the countryside or in a
field of hay when the sun shines brighter and the sky is bluer than ever.
The heat is so intense that a laborer just has to take a rest. The colors in
this work are intense. The blue of the sky, the yellows of the hay, even
the shade is intense. The haystack and the cut hay against the deep blue
sky glow with yellow light. The other haystack at the very forefront of
the work sits in complete brownish shade. That's where our attention is
drawn. At the foot of the haystack lie two people, a man and a woman,
sleeping. But, is the man sleeping? He has a cat's face with a cat's eye
that's open. It's truly the features of a cat because I just don't see a
man's face here. I looked at Vincent and he looked at me and smiled. I
wasn't going to press the issue. Alright, a sleeping cat in the hay with
one eye open. Cats, like humans, sleep during the day. Is this something of a symbol? Is it a teasing on the part of the artist? *Un jeu de
symboles*?

The woman is sleeping next to the man. She's sleeping with her
arms under her head. She's wearing a bright white bonnet that women

wear around those parts. Her long dress is blue just like the peasants wear. As for the man, he's stretched out on his back with his shoes off. His short-brimmed straw hat hides the top of his head. He wears a blue worker's outfit. There, lying on his right side, are two sickles, tools of the peasants. A green-colored wagon with tall wooden racks, along with a pair of oxen and a man standing next to them can be seen at a certain distance. There is calm reigning here and a letting go. A lazy afternoon after a long morning stretch of hay cutting deserves a siesta. This is just a reprieve, a brief rest from all the work to be done by peasants. A cycle of seasons, a cycle or work. Still, what intrigued me was the cat's face on the man. I was going to ask Vincent about this someday. I never did.

Before we left, my father told Vincent that Madame Ginoux wasn't feeling well and that she had to stay in bed.

"I know," said Vincent. "She wrote to me. She said that she had wanted to send me a container of olives for Christmas but that she hadn't been well enough to do so. She sent me the olives for Candlemas and I wrote her a long letter sympathizing with her and her illness. I know what illness is. By the way, I plan to go to Arles around the 20th of the month to visit the Ginouxs and return their container. I promised them I'd go and spend some time with them."

"Well, we might see you there if I can get some time from my busy work schedule," said my father.

"How's your work? Do you like it?" asked Vincent.

"Oh, it's a job and I'm getting used to it. It pays more than *brigadier- chargeur* and that's what counts," answered my father.

I gave my hand to Vincent and he squeezed it with a strong handshake. I knew that things had not changed between us.

We got home and my mother announced that the baby had cut her first tooth. My father put a franc in her piggy bank and I placed two centimes in the slot. My parents were getting worried about the baby cutting her teeth since they thought that it was late, later than other children. My sister was now nineteen months old.

"That's why the baby has been fussy lately," my mother said to my father, "she was teething."

The next day, I went to the market and got twine. I wanted to mail Vincent a package, a book that I knew he would like. It was Dickens's "Little Dorrit" that I had bought at *le marché aux puces*, the flea market, right around the corner where we lived. I knew he would like it since it was a Dickens book. I didn't know what the book was all about except the clerk told me it had to do with prison life. I thought Vincent would like it since he identified with Dickens's books, his characters and their situations in life.

February 16, 1890------My father received two paintings from Vincent today. What a surprise! One is, **The Garden at Saint-Paul Hospital,** and we can see the bench where we sat when we had our picnic. It looks like daybreak or early evening with trees and red grasses. It's really nice. The other is, **Olive Picking,** with two women picking from an olive tree. One is on a ladder and the other is on the ground. I told my father that I wanted the "Garden" on the wall in my room. They put the other one in their bedroom with the other four paintings by Vincent.

March 2, 1890-----------My father got word from Madame Ginoux that Vincent had been in Arles but had one of his spells while over there. It was so bad that they had to get two men from Saint-Rémy to come and get him. It was probably one of his worst spells ever. This one is going to be a long one, a very long one, insisted Madame Ginoux. I'm worried about him.

April 1, 1890----------Today is "Poisson d'avril." We had fun at school trying to put paper fishes on the backs of others. The teacher caught my new friend, Arnaud. He had to write *Je ne pécherai plus*, I will no longer sin, on the blackboard forty times. Arnaud tried to correct the teacher saying that it wasn't *un accent aigu* but *un accent circonflexe,* not "é" but "ê. *Je ne pêcherai plus."* I will no longer go fishing. The teacher replied that what he had told Arnaud to write, stays.

May 2, 1890----------Still no word from Vincent.

Pastor Salles has written to my father saying that Vincent wanted desperately to go back up north. He had enough of the company of madmen, the cloister and those good nuns. He wanted to flee from the absurd religious hallucinations that he had been having lately. He wanted out. Besides, his brother had encouraged him to return up north. He had found a doctor in Auvers-sur-Oise, a Doctor Paul-Ferdinand

Gachet, who could take care of him. He lives in Paris but practices three days a week in Auvers, he told Vincent.

"He'll be able to watch over you and take good care of you. Besides, he's an enthusiastic amateur of painting," he wrote.

Père Pissarro could not take care of Vincent in Pontoise, so Monsieur Théo suggested Auvers and Doctor Gachet. There, he could rent rooms from Doctor Gachet and live at his house. Besides, Auvers was not too far from Paris. Vincent did not want to live in Paris with his brother and his family, Jo and the young Vincent-Willem. It would have been too much, he said. He did not want in any way ruining the daily lives of the people he loved. He was going to be fine in Auvers, he told his brother, just fine.

In the meantime, Vincent had been painting irises and roses and other flowers. It was springtime. He told the director that he wanted to finish these paintings before he left. His trunk was already packed. His brother wanted Vincent to have a guardian to accompany him all the way to Paris, at least as far as la Gare de Lyon, but Vincent had categorically refused. His only concession was to have someone accompany him as far as Tarascon where he was going to take the train for Paris. Then, he would spend two or three days in Paris with his brother, sister-in-law and nephew and then leave for Auvers. Those were his plans. That's what Pastor Salles reported to my father. My father asked himself when precisely would Vincent leave Saint-Rémy. I wondered too. Would I ever see Vincent again, I asked myself. Ever again?

After Vincent left Saint-Rémy on May 16, Pastor Salles returned to the asylum just to get the last report on Vincent from Doctor Peyron. He wanted to know about the stability and physical status of the patient. Doctor Peyron showed him what he had written as his final entry in the records documenting the release. It read as follows: **The patient, though calm most of the time, had several attacks during his stay in this institution, lasting two weeks to one month. During these attacks the patient was subject to frightful terrors and tried several times to poison himself, either by swallowing the paints that he used for his work or by drinking kerosene, which he managed to steal from the attendant while the latter refilled the lamps. His last fit broke out after a trip that he undertook to Arles, and lasted about two months. Between his attacks the patient was perfectly quiet and devoted himself fervently to his painting. Today he is re-**

questing his release in order to live in the North of France, hoping that its climate will be favorable. Under the heading "Observation," the doctor had entered simply : "CURED."

He then asked the doctor if he had told Vincent about the observation and he simply replied, "No."

Pastor Salles then asked Doctor Peyron if he could get a copy of the last entry and he was told that he could have one if he himself copied it, which he did. Pastor Salles wanted to send a copy to Monsieur Théo and let him know officially what the records showed since Monsieur Théo could not come down himself and get it. Vincent had been at Saint-Rémy fifty-three weeks. This is what Pastor Salles told my father. My father was shocked upon hearing the details of the last entry that Vincent had taken kerosene and tried eating his own paints. Poison himself! He didn't try to hide the facts from me knowing that, sooner or later, they would come out. I was just flattened by the news. I never thought that Vincent was so sick. To try and poison himself? Can you imagine? If he was that sick and that desperate, why did they let him leave the asylum? my father asked my mother.

My mother just said, " Things like that sometimes never get healed. *Mon pauvre enfant perdu,*" she sighed.

We did get some news from Madame Ginoux who had seen Vincent briefly in Arles before Vincent left for Tarascon. They had a short conversation and Vincent had shown her a holy picture of the Good Shepherd that Mère Épiphane had given him right before leaving.

Mère Épiphane had told him, "*Vous êtes tout comme la brebis perdue. Je prierai pour vous,*" you're like the lost sheep and I'll pray for you.

Vincent had put it in his pocket and intended to give it away to someone. He didn't know who. Madame Ginoux had no suggestions as for the disposition of the holy picture. She thought it was generous of the nun but a bit too Catholic. She too was *une républicaine.* Then, Vincent left to go to Tarascon to take the train for Paris. Madame Ginoux walked slowly back home and from then on resolved, ever so much more, to keep in touch with Vincent whenever possible, she told my father.

I never did get to see Vincent again. Eventually, I did get to see his painting of the almond tree branches in bloom that he painted for his nephew and godson, Vincent-Willem, **Blossoming Almond Tree**. It's a very simple but rich painting, rich in color and style. The top of an almond tree in bloom against a clear blue sky. Part of the magnificent orchards in bloom that Vincent loved about Provence. I told myself, he gave his nephew part of Provence and part of his love of nature. That was his gift. Several months after Vincent left Saint-Rémy, I also got to see his painting, **Old Man with His Head in His Hands,** that he had left behind until such time they would ship it to him along with some other paintings of his. I am told that it was painted after the lithograph "At Eternity's Gate." What an incredible painting ! We can't see the old man's face, of course, since he has it hidden in his two hands. We get a feeling of desperation here through a lonely and desperate feeling of solitude. Is the old man weeping? Is he overcome by some sad news or an inner feeling of helplessness as Vincent did at times. This time, Vincent did not just paint an empty chair but a chair with a man seemingly covered with misery sitting on it. It's a simple wooden chair without armrests. The old man is wearing a slate blue shirt and trousers much like the outfit the working peasants wear. The wall behind him is white and the floor is an ordinary wooden floor. There is a fire in the fireplace but the whole atmosphere of the place is one of barrenness and melancholy. Is he contemplating eternity as the lithograph from which this painting is taken seems to suggest? This is a work of remembrance or one of the creative imagination borrowing from another work of art. Either way, it suggests something about Vincent's life and work, I think. It opens a window on the personality of the artist who always identified with the poor, the peasants, the ones who have to struggle to live. Be it back in Drente, Nuenen and the Hague with the peasants, or in Isleworth with the sadly underprivileged, or in Whitecastle with the very poorest people, or even Le Borinage with the miners who worked like slaves, he always identified with those who had the least and whose existence was filled with loneliness and misery. Is there something out there like an infinity or an eternity for the poor? Or, is there but the void? A sharp and meaningless end to all suffering? This old man is the prefiguration of old age, if not senility, as seen by the artist in the future years of his own life. Will there be an end to solitude and loneliness, he might ask. Or, will it all have been irretrievably useless so that sadness will just keep on for the rest of his life? The only thing that Vincent had in life, and he knew it, was his art, art as his salvation from the loneliness of being and his driving force towards creativity.

June 22, 1890----------Dear journal, it's summer vacation and I don't really know what I'm going to do this summer. My father has plans for me; my mother has plans for me. It seems everybody has plans for me even my friend, Arnaud. I'd like to go and visit Vincent in Auvers but my father won't let me go all by myself. I'd like to ask Madame Ginoux to accompany me but I dare not do that. I wonder if Armand would accompany me? I don't think so. I guess I'll just have to stay in Marseille and do my chores. Good chance I have my reading or else I'd be lonely. I don't write too much in my notebook any more, just my journal entries. I'm on my third notebook, I'll have you know. I wonder if anyone will ever read me when I'm done taking notes, all the notes I've taken in the last two years? Will I ever become a writer? I hope so.

July 10, 1890--------Today is my thirteenth birthday. I got a letter from Vincent yesterday. It's the first time I get a letter in the mail. First time. The envelope was marked AUVERS-SUR-OISE. Inside, I found a short letter and a picture of some saint, I think. It's a man with a sheep on his shoulders. The letter reads:

"Dear Camille, Happy Birthday. I haven't forgotten you. I'm here in Auvers. I was living at the auberge Saint-Aubin but they wanted 6 francs per day, so I moved across the way to a very small room on top of a café owned by a couple named, Ravoux. I like it here. I can go out whenever I please and paint all I want. I just finished a portrait of Adeline Ravoux, the couple's daughter. You'd like it. It's all in blue. My blue girl. I also love the village with its rustic scenery. Last month, I painted the **Portrait of Doctor Gachet**. He's the doctor who takes care of me. He's a rather odd fellow but a likeable one. Would you believe, he has a dozen cats, five dogs, a goat, two peacocks and a turtle. Quite the *ménagerie*. I painted him with two novels on the table where his right elbow is. They're "*Germinie Lacerteux*" and "*Manette Salomon*" by the Goncourt brothers. When you get a chance, you should read these novels. They're both very good writers these brothers. I'm going to Paris on the 6th to visit my brother, Théo, and I'll be back shortly. I have enclosed a holy picture that Mère Épiphane gave me before I left Saint-Rémy. It's the Good Shepherd. I thought you might like to have it. Show it to your mother, she'll understand. As you know, I don't like holy pictures and pictures of the past. I want to live and create in the present, not the past. You understand, don't you? Besides, I know that I am and ever will be *la brebis égarée,* the lost sheep. I don't need a holy picture to remind me of it. The only shepherd that I admire and venerate is the peasant shepherd like Patience Escalier. Give your mother and father my very best regards.

Very sincerely, VINCENT "

Now that I have his address, I plan to write to him and tell him about my plans to become a writer now that I'm positive about it and things are moving in that direction. My teacher, Monsieur Latourelle, said that he was going to help me find a mentor. That's a person like Vincent was for me in Arles. Vincent was the first one to guide me with my dream of becoming a writer and how to appreciate nature. It's a gift. It truly is. I mean, mentoring.

July 21, 1890--------It's very hot today. I don't feel like doing anything. I reread Vincent's letter and I'm so glad he's getting to do what he likes best, painting. I do hope he'll sell some of his paintings and live a better life. He deserves it. I think he'll do well in Auvers. He's made new friends and he can visit his brother more often. His nephew too. Or, they can visit him. That will do him good. I think I'll write to him tomorrow.

August 5, 1890----------Sad news, sad sad news. I can't write about it today.......

August 6, 1890---------It's now evening. Sad. *Absolument triste. La nouvelle nous a porté un coup terrible,* we were just devastated. We just learned that Vincent has died. He died on July 29. We got a small announcement from Théo Van Gogh. It was all edged in black:

Monsieur Th. Van Gogh and all his Family have the great sorrow of sharing with you the loss they have just had in the person of VINCENT WILLEM van GOGH Artist painter deceased at 37 years old, July 29, 1890 in Auvers-sur-Oise.

Paris, 8, cité Pigalle-----Leyde, Heerengracht (Holland).

I took it in my hands and started to cry. Great big sobs. I couldn't help myself. Then my father wept silently and so did my mother. We didn't know what to say to one another. My father looked at me and my mother looked at him. He just stood there as if paralyzed. His face had turned pale. I went to my room and stayed there for a long time. I looked at the picture of the Good Shepherd that I used as a bookmark and stared at it until I thought of the stars. I went outside and looked at them shimmering there in the dark night. I remembered Vincent with paintbrush in hand painting little halos around the stars. I remembered as I will always remember him. How can I ever forget?

August 11, 1890-------Today was a day of tranquility in our house-hold. Everybody went about in a kind of slow movement and with few words. We were not angry with one another. No, we were still stunned and *figés*, frozen, as we say. It's been like that for almost a week. Even the baby has been quiet. Why, even Armand doesn't say much. He never did anyway. But, today is a day of mourning. Madame Ginoux came over last night and we all sat at the table reminiscing. She was visiting her sister in Marseille. She said that no one would have thought that Vincent could have done such a thing and my father asked her, "What thing?"

"Well," she said, "about Vincent shooting himself."

"Monsieur Théo did not tell us that," replied my father.

"Well, Vincent certainly did. My friend from Pontoise sent me the newspaper clipping of August 7 in which it says about Vincent shoot-ing himself in the chest. It says it in black and white, here read it," and she passed the article to my father to read.

She left visibly shaken and her hands still trembling. She left with-out her usual goodbyes. I think she was going to be sick.

August 13, 1890--------We only found out today that the funeral was held on July 30th. Madame Ginoux must have forgotten to tell us. My father said that he would have liked to go but it was too late to do what we should have done. Anyway, my parents sent their condolences to Monsieur Théo and his family. It was a nice card with black scrolls on it. I signed it too.

August 24, 1890--------When I think about it, I can't for the life of me think of a single reason why Vincent would shoot himself. I can't. I just can't. Maybe he was at the end of his rope. Maybe he didn't want to be sick anymore. Maybe he couldn't paint anymore. That would have done it to him. Maybe, just maybe....Oh, Vincent, I don't know why you did it but if you were here with me today I would tell you many things I never told you and wanted to tell you for a long time ever since Saint-Rémy. I thought you were like a bird in a cage over there. I wanted to tell you then that by painting "Starry Night" you let go of everything that weighed you down and so you flew, soared towards your infinity of swirling light and color. You were able to get out of the cage for that splendid moment of creativity. You became the stars and the moon. But, of course, you're already up there now. I mean in the infinity of the stars. That's one of the things I wanted to tell you then.

August 26, 1890-----------Dear journal, I can't write anymore. Not now anyway. I'm not abandoning you. I'm just putting you away with my treasures. My drawings. I feel my heart is in there and I don't want it to be separated from what I consider to be my perfect dream of creativity as explored under Vincent's tutelage. That's a new word I learned in class today, tutelage. It means care and protection. I like it. Well, I suppose I could come back to you now and then, just to write my new words. I think I will.

Well, there you have it. I did my very best to take all of my notes and make a story out of it. A story about Vincent and his life in Arles. It's especially about his paintings and some drawings. That's what I wanted to emphasize, his creative output in Arles and at Saint-Rémy. His stupendous creative output. How many paintings and drawings? I don't really know. All I know is that it's in the hundreds. I don't know if I've succeeded but I trust my efforts will not have been in vain. It took me six years to write this account. Off and on during my travels with my job. I then tried to find a publisher but to no avail. All I know is that Vincent came to Arles to paint. He did leave behind him a lasting impression, good for some, not too good for others. I have to say that Vincent did leave a lasting impression on me. Why, he changed the path of my life !

As a mature person now in 1912, when I look back at Vincent's life in Arles and I have to include Saint-Rémy, I fully realize that the artist that was Vincent had an enormous talent, bigger than I had imagined when I was ten through thirteen living in Arles and witnessing Vincent's tremendous output of works of art. How could one man produce so much in such a short span of time while living in Provence? It's beyond any wild imagining, I think. Vincent not only belonged to us in Provence and to the north countries of Holland, Belgium, England and France but he also belongs now to every person that has learned to appreciate his career as an artist. He truly painted his heart out with the bold, vivid and forward strokes of a vibrant brush that was destined to amaze anyone who enjoys color and light. Some called him mad, others sick with some kind of undetectable and unrecognizable disease, and still others simply ignored his talent. But, I'm convinced that the world will someday recognize that he was a genius like no other genius in the art world. Oh, Vincent, the world was never meant for someone as brazenly creative as you. You surpassed us all. You snatched fire from the gods.

Auteur, CAMILLE ROULIN, le 12 avril 1912

Epilogue

My name is Marcelle Roulin. I'm Camille Roulin's sister. My brother confided this manuscript he had all these years to me. The title is, "The Boy With the Blue Cap------Van Gogh in Arles." He gave it to me shortly before he died on June 4, 1922. He died of war wounds. He was only 45 years old. My brother went to school after *l'école élémentaire* to learn how to write but all they were teaching him was grammar, some stylistics and *la concordance des temps*, sequence of tenses, with an emphasis on *analyse de texte* that's very demanding. An atrocious analysis of words in a text. I know, I hated it myself. Well, he got tired of this and joined a shipping company. What he had wanted to learn was creative writing but they did not have that in their curriculum. So, he went out to sea traveling in the service of the maritime mail in *La Compagnie des Messageries Maritimes,* a shipping company in France. He always wanted to travel. Yes, he did get to go to Africa, to his great delight. He used to tell me that he was going to *le pays de Tartarin de Tarascon.* Somehow, he found time to write this manuscript.

I had never read it before three years ago. I found it to be fascinating. I never really knew Vincent Van Gogh but I remember my family having several of his paintings on the walls in our house. My brother used to talk to me about him on some occasions when he would take out his notebooks and read some passages to me. At first, I thought it was boring but then, as Camille explained what he had written down and the meaning behind it, I realized that my brother had truly captured the essence of this man and his artistic work. All of Monsieur Van Gogh's works ended up to be a huge collection of paintings and drawings, as far as I can determine today. My father, my mother and my brother, Camille, knew Monsieur Vincent very well. My father used to speak of him often and how he had been his friend when he lived in Arles and at Saint-Rémy. I was only a baby when he used to come over the house in Arles. I was barely two when he died. So, I never knew him personally. Camille was the one who was close to him because, according to his notes and our chats, he spent quite some time with Monsieur Vincent.

I never thought my brother could write so well and make a book out of his many notes. He must have worked very hard at it. For years, he worked and reworked this manuscript, he told me. He wanted so much to become a good writer and have someone else read and enjoy what he had written. He knew that he could never be like Flaubert, Hugo or Daudet, he told me, but he wanted to be recognized by the people in Provence, at least. He wanted not so much to be recognized as much as he wanted Monsieur Van Gogh to be recognized for his artistic worth and all the paintings he had done in Arles. That's what he really wanted. He tried repeatedly to get a publisher for his manuscript but they all rejected it saying that no one would want to publish an eleven-year old boy's account of Van Gogh and his life in Arles, even if it had been written by a mature person that was now Camille Roulin. Camille knew that he could not get his manuscript published before he died because he realized he did not have much time. He was quite sick at the end. That's why he begged me to take the manuscript and bring it to some publisher somewhere. But where? I asked. I did not know a thing about manuscripts and publication. Monsieur Joseph Roumanille's son, a *félibre* himself, helped me. He had contacts, he said. You see Monsieur Roumanille, fils was a very good friend of Madame Ginoux's cousin in Fontvieille. Her name was Madame Mathieu. She had her portrait painted by Monsieur Van Gogh when she was quite young. She often talked about him to me and how she had her portrait done by Monsieur Vincent. She's related to me on my aunt Simonou's side. Madame Mathieu is the one who introduced me to the young Monsieur Roumanille who led me to his publisher in Avignon. That's how I made the contact with a publisher who was, at least, willing to read the manuscript. So, there you have it. The story behind the manuscript of the published account written by my brother Camille. I want to give him full credit since I am but the instrument. It took quite a few years before it was finally published but I think it's worth it. Camille would have been very proud of it. I hope the readers enjoy it as much as I did.

Before I forget, there was a sealed envelope with a letter inside attached to the manuscript, and the envelope was dated August 23, 1913. Camille told me before he died that I was to open the note only after his death. It was a secret, he said. So, I opened it in 1922, the same year he gave me the manuscript. I was eager to see what was inside the envelope. Here's what it contained. I know that it was a secret to Camille but I thought I would share it with you since my brother is dead now. I don't need to maintain secrecy for the sake of secrecy. I feel it will shed light on the story and death of Monsieur Vincent.

It was on a yellowed piece of paper when I opened it. My brother had no doubt written it almost four years after Monsieur Vincent's death and had kept it all those years with his notebooks. The notebooks were in a small chest locked up for years. He had given me the key. Then, before his death he attached the note to the manuscript before confiding it to me. Here's what was written : *August 19, 1913 Today, I am writing down something that has been with me for twenty-two years. It was part of my special notes. It did not figure in my story about Vincent. It's a secret from a gypsy woman named Mirnanoun. She didn't tell me not to divulge the secret but I kept it for many years without telling anyone. She knew Vincent because she's the one who had put a curse on him in Saintes-Maries-de-la-Mer. Vincent never believed her and her sorcery. I remember, she had come to visit him in Arles to warn him and tell him about Sara. She meant business. Although Vincent did not believe in her power to put curses on people or, for that matter, in all so-called hexes and curses, he was wary of her and the strong possibility that her gypsy influence as a sorceress was real. Well, I saw her in Arles three years after Vincent's death. I was sitting on a bench in the public park when she approached me and told me that she recognized me as Vincent's friend by my blond hair and my big blue eyes. I was there for the day visiting Madame Ginoux. Mirnanoun started telling me how sorry she was about Vincent's death and proceeded to tell me that she had a secret to share with me. The secret was that she was the one who shot Vincent, not Vincent himself. "I shot Vincent," she said with a crack in her voice. "I managed to find out where he was and I went to Auvers-sur-Oise," she told me. "I found out through the gypsy underground. We do have one, you know." Then she paused and said, "I killed him." "But he did not die right away," I said. But what motive? "Madness. Moments and fits of madness. Especially when the sun is at its very peak of heat and glare and there's madness in the air. Yes, madness," she said with a resigned expression on her face. "The curse backfired," she told me. "No one knows the truth except you now. I had to tell someone before I fall fully into my own madness. I'm not a bad woman. **Je suis une bonne gitane**." I'm a good gypsy. Then, she added, "I had to get away from there as soon as I could. The black crows were shrieking and hovering over me. The crows of madness and death. I dropped the pistol on the* *ground and ran as fast as I could. I just had to get away." I did no know what to say to her. I was so struck by her declaration. She le, and I've never seen her again. I left Arles keeping her secret in m heart and relieved that Vincent had not killed himself but was the vic tim of someone else's madness. It did not rid me of the pain of knowin, that Vincent was dead and that he would no longer paint, but I was re lieved.*

Then to make matters more complicated, I met this other gypsy i, the Panier district of Marseille a while later, a man who called himsel, Matagot. He held me by the arm and practically frightened me t death, so deep and fiery were his eyes. I was afraid of the possibility o the evil eye. He was a gypsy after all. He told me that he had recog nized me and that he had been looking for me for some time. He said that he had been Kevja's best friend and to forget what Mirnanoun had told me about Vincent's death. She did not shoot him, he told me. "It', her madness. She invented that story just to show her control over Monsieur Van Gogh," he said. "She became delirious and had to be restrained by her clan, once she returned to Saintes-Maries. Yes, she did go to Auvers-sur-Oise but only after Van Gogh's death." The clan was the one who had sent Matagot to Marseille so as not to antagonize people against the gypsies. He apologized for disturbing me and left without telling me his real name or where he came from. I was thor oughly confused and did not know what to make of all this. Was this al, a ruse? Did Vincent shoot himself or not? We may never really know. And that's the secret, the mysterious secret that I have kept for years.

Signed : CAMILLE ROULIN

What a tragedy this madness of the Midi is. We of Provence live with the curse of being vulnerable to any kind of *folie* since we are vi- brant but sensitive people, sensitive to the sun, the mistral and the cycle of life in the Midi. That's why the people of Provence invented the term *fada*. Driven crazy by the heat of the sun and the ever-present gusts of the mistral as well as the constant shrill sounds of the cicadas in full force. Also, I have to think that gypsies have their own *folie* and that not all gypsies are bad. However, some do experience their own tragedy as the rest of the *Provençaux*. I trust that time will heal the death of Vincent Van Gogh and that his story, as told by my brother, Camille, will be instrumental in the healing process. I think it's a great story with Camille talking to us about so many of Monsieur Vincent's paintings and describing them to us who know so very little about them. They're so full of life, color and light of the Midi that I can see why Monsieur Vincent came to Arles to paint. He was in his creative glory in Arles, I believe.

When my father retired in 1896, he and my mother went to live in Lambesc. I will always remember that they had six of Vincent Van Gogh's paintings in their bedroom. They were all signed, VINCENT. They cherished them. However, my father did sell some of them to an art dealer named Vollard who had offered him a large enough sum of money. At least, that's what my father told Madame Ginoux. You see, my father always lived on modest means all of his life and he sold the paintings to improve his financial situation on retirement. My mother had not objected to the selling of the paintings. By the way, Camille did leave me his five drawings Monsieur Vincent had given him. He was so fond of them. He also had one from Monsieur Gauguin. I never knew this man from the north. I believe he died in the South Pacific some-where.

I don't know if people will read Camille's story or not but I know he put in a lot of work for many years. I would say some twenty years besides all of the note taking. I know that he really and passionately put his whole heart into it. As I've said, he so desired to become a writer. He wanted people to read his books since he contemplated writing several. One of them on the sunflowers and another about the sea. He never did get to write those. I'm sure people will realize how much effort and genuine interest he put into it when they read this story. It may even be translated so that people outside of France will be able to enjoy it. In English, Dutch, Italian and maybe German, who knows? Well, I've done my best to bring to the reader a story about a young boy and an artist whose paths crossed in Arles and who became good friends. I know my brother would be very proud of his book. I am. In the end, even though Monsieur Vincent met with a tragic death and my brother was left feeling horrible about it, Camille came to the realization that he and Monsieur Vincent were not losers but two people who were blessed by the stars. I think so. You see, my brother was a dreamer and I believe his dream came true.

MARCELLE ROULIN, le 15 octobre 1926

"*L'art, c'est un combat------dans l'art, il faut y mettre sa peau.*" Art is a combat---in art you have to sacrifice your own hide. Vincent Van Gogh to his brother, Théo (180N]